MY SOUL TO GIVE

A DEMON'S LOVE BOOK #1

M. A. FRÉCHETTE

Her soul for revenge—an easy choice.
But is the price too high?

COPYRIGHT

DEDICATION

This is for you, Samantha. For all the times you waited for something because I was so absorbed in writing, and you didn't want to bother me. You've always been so understanding, and I wouldn't have been able to write this book if it wasn't for your patience. Thank you for being the best daughter.

1

SOMETHING IN THE AIR

Celina smiled as the chickadee inched toward her seat on the pine patio chair. Its tiny claws poked and scratched along her skin, its beak pecking away at the seeds in her hand. She stifled a laugh as its feathers tickled the side of her thumb.

A raucous cawing in the distance startled her, and the small bird flew away. It didn't go far with all the feeders she had in her massive backyard, but her shoulders slumped at the loss of contact. "Bye, little friend."

A black shape swooped from a tree, and Celina jumped as it collided with the plastic bird bath at the far end of her yard, toppling it over. She got to her feet and walked toward it, twisting her hands together.

Please don't be dead.

Shaking her head, she bent down and lifted the heavy decoration, frowning at the crow lying on the grass. It spun back on its legs, and she gasped. "You're alive?"

Flapping noises from the forest's edge caught her attention, and her eyes widened at the two dozen crows perched on trees bordering her yard. The one that had knocked down the birdbath flew back with its kind, and Celina shrugged as she turned toward her deck.

"Might as well get more seeds," she muttered as she climbed the steps.

A high-pitched chirp sent goosebumps crawling up her skin, and she spun just as the crows dived at the chickadee she'd been feeding a few minutes ago. Their calls echoed around, black claws ripping away at the bird until she dashed down the deck, waving her arms.

"Stop!"

She crouched and tears blurred her vision as she stared at the dead creature, its wing folded at a strange angle, blood staining its little feathers. Clearing her throat, she straightened and took a deep breath.

Circle of life. Sooner or later, everything dies.

After refilling the water and adding more seeds to the feeders, she sat on the steps, focusing ahead. Her mind flashed back to when her parents' cottage once stood where her house now did, a perfect place to grow up. She used to play in the trees, run around, go on make-believe adventures…but it always felt like something watched her between the branches.

Her gaze moved to an empty spot in the yard. Without looking away, she felt on top of the glass table next to her, fingers fumbling for what she wanted. Grabbing a small piece of paper and a pen that lay next to the cordless phone, she glanced from the empty spot to the blank white sheet. Just lines at first, but eventually, she smiled at the little sketch of her backyard with a play structure, complete with a climbing wall, an upper clubhouse with a small lookout, and a slide now filling that gap.

The sun lowered, and the forest behind her house fell silent. A small chill ran through her as she stood, but she focused her mind on dinner preparations to push the unease away. She put her sketch on the glass table, and moved to the garden hose, making sure it was tightly shut before going inside. A crunching sound mixed with the squeaking of the outside faucet and she glanced back.

Nothing.

Her pulse quickened as the light faded, and she strode to the table. She frowned as she grabbed the phone, her sketch nowhere to be found. "Where—?"

Arms wrapped around her from behind and she screamed as the phone dropped from her hand, the battery flying out as it hit the wood. She spun, and something between a gasp and a laugh left her as she stared at her husband's hazel eyes.

"You scared me half to death." Her gaze went to the bouquet of white roses he held, and she forgot about her frantic heartbeat. "What's this? It isn't Friday…"

Thomas' lips curled into a smile. "Do I need it to be a certain day of the week for me to bring you gifts?" He handed them to her, his eyes more golden than usual in the setting sun.

"You're home early. Did something happen?"

"I wanted to see you," he breathed, drawing her closer to him. "And we didn't get the chance to celebrate your birthday last week properly."

Her cheeks warmed, and she grinned. "You mean we never left the bedroom."

"A good way to celebrate your twenty-fifth birthday," he said with a wink. "Well, as part two of your birthday celebration, I'm taking you out to dinner and a movie."

His words circled around her mind a few times before she could believe they were real.

"We're going out?" she whispered.

He nodded, but his expression became unreadable as he stared over her shoulder. She glanced back and shrugged at all the crows still perched in the trees. "Not sure what the hell is wrong with them today, but they're acting weird. Maybe there's something in the air."

Refusing to let anything dampen her spirits, she grabbed the phone and battery from the deck floor and squeezed them into her pockets to bring inside. "I'll just go put the phone back—"

She caught his gaze and stopped as he held out the sketch that she'd left on the glass table. Her stomach clenched as she focused on the piece of paper, averting her eyes from his.

"A place for you to play during the day?" His tone was light, but she braced herself.

Whenever they spoke of anything relating to children, his mood turned sour. It was no secret she wanted a baby; she'd dropped hints for a while before coming right out and asking him about it. But his answer had crushed her, and since that day, something like a wedge had slowly been pulling them apart.

They'd been a couple for nine years and married for five, so *why* wasn't he ready for kids?

"I was just doodling."

"I think you forgot something…" He went to the table and sketched something on the paper.

Assuming he'd erased her idea, her eyes widened at the swing set he'd added next to the climbing wall she drew. He walked past her and brushed a kiss on her head before going inside. She smiled ear to ear as she folded the paper and tucked it inside her back pocket.

A child. Had Thomas finally decided it was time? Did she dare hope after all those years?

"Must be something in the air," she whispered.

Once inside the house, she fiddled with the battery for a few minutes before slamming it back into the phone. "Phone's fixed," she called out.

It rang, and she yelped at how loud it was. She'd forgotten to lower it from when she was outside. Picking it up again, she answered quickly so another ring wouldn't blast through the house. "Hello?"

Silence. Breathing.

Thomas took the phone from her and brought it to his ear, his eyes narrowed at the telephone base. "Hello?" A voice murmured on the other side, and he glanced at her, his lips pressed together, before going into his office and closing the door.

He often got calls from clients, and when he was home, she almost always let him answer. She hoped he wouldn't change his mind about going out because of business.

A few minutes passed, and he walked into the kitchen, running his fingers through his light-brown hair. "Sorry about that."

"If you're busy tonight, it's fine—"

He cupped her face and kissed her. His free hand pressed on her lower back, drawing her against his body. The inside of her stomach fluttered as their lips parted, their breathing quickened by passion.

"We're going out no matter what," he said, placing a kiss on the tip of her nose.

She smiled, wishing time would freeze so they could stay like this forever. But the moment vanished when the phone rang again, and he clenched his jaw.

"Let's go."

Part of her wanted to ask about ignoring the call, but with the way he'd narrowed his eyes at the phone, she thought better of it.

Celina grinned in the darkness of the movie theater at the jump scare, wrapping her hands tighter around Thomas' arm. He leaned in, near her ear. "Enjoying yourself?"

She suppressed a giggle but gave a quick nod. He changed position, wrapping his arm around her shoulder, and she relaxed. Being herself around her husband was the best part about being married. She had Thomas. They had each other.

As the credits rolled, they ambled out of the dark room, and she stretched her arms over her head. "That was awesome."

"Nothing like a good maiming," he said with a chuckle.

She laughed, but her smile faded as her gaze rested on a couple standing not too far ahead. The woman had her hand over her swollen belly, and her partner beamed at her. An emptiness filled Celina from the inside, starting at her chest and expanding until it swallowed her heart.

Thomas squeezed her elbow and led her out of the cinema without commenting. The spring air was crisp, and without asking, he took his jacket off and wrapped it around her.

"Thanks," she said with a smile as they made their way to their car.

His hazel eyes stood out in the dim lighting. "Seeing that pregnant woman upset you." It wasn't a question.

She averted her gaze, but he stopped in his tracks, forcing her to stop too. With a sigh, she nodded. "Just a little."

"We'll talk about children again soon," he murmured, as though already deciding. "But not tonight."

She slipped her hand into her back pocket, sliding her finger over the piece of paper where they'd sketched a playground. "Promise?"

"Promise," he said.

A group of people stood near the vehicle parked next to theirs, and Celina slowed her pace. One man was leaning against Thomas' car, smoking a cigarette as he chatted with his friends.

Her husband cleared his throat as they approached. "Excuse us, but we need to get to our car."

A few of them looked up for a second but went back to their business.

Clenching her teeth, she strode to the passenger side and

stopped in front of the man. "Not sure how I'm supposed to get in with you leaning against the door."

He blew the smoke into her face and grinned when she didn't react. Holding her breath, she counted to ten inside her mind to keep from exploding on him.

I'd like to ram that cigarette right into your eyeball, asshole.

Thomas took her arm and pulled her back from them. "I've called parking security, so I'd leave if I were you."

"Yeah, whatever." The man straightened and put out his cigarette on Thomas' car door. "Must feel safe with a guy who calls for security pricks instead of dealing with his own fucking problems."

His friends laughed, and they strolled away, throwing jeers as they went.

Thomas rubbed his light-brown hair, still staring in the bastards' direction. "Sorry about that," he mumbled.

"Let's just go home."

A bitter smile twisted his mouth. "All right," he said, as though resigning himself to a horrible fate.

She frowned, wondering if it had something to do with the phone call before they'd left, but she said nothing as they got into the car.

PRICE OF REVENGE

The headlights cut through early spring fog that hung like a curtain drawn over the country road. Inside the car, the silence between Celina and Thomas hung just as heavy.

"Dinner and a movie was a great idea tonight. Thank you for bringing me out." She placed her hand on his leg and smiled.

He glanced sideways, his gaze locking on her. "I love when you smile like that. And I'm—"

He slammed on the brakes, flinging her into the seatbelt with a gasp. A noise like branches hit the car's roof as hundreds of crows dived at the vehicle, their black-feathered wings smashing against the windshield.

As quickly as they appeared, the birds flew off. Then, silence.

He grabbed her shoulder. "Are you okay?"

Celina nodded as her pulse slowed, and they both stepped out of the car.

Leaning forward, she checked the front bumper for blood or feathers, the headlights illuminating a small circle in the darkness. "We definitely hit some of them..."

His eyes glazed as he glanced back. "What?"

"Are you okay? You've been acting strange since we left the house."

He winked. "That's because I am strange."

"Really? Another group of crows acting insane, flying out of nowhere and crashing into us like something out of *Hitchcock*, and you're smiling and winking like it's a beautiful day in the neighborhood."

He wrapped his arms around her waist. "A murder."

She arched an eyebrow.

His smile widened. "It's what a group of crows is called—a murder of crows."

She opened her mouth to reply, but he kissed her.

Fine time to be romantic.

When he withdrew, his smile was gone, but the gentleness in his hazel eyes remained. "I'm fine."

They got back into the car and exchanged no words for the rest of the drive. Only the tires crunching over the stones as they pulled into the driveway broke the silence. She frowned at the sight of all the motion-detector lights flooding their property. "Probably just deer or coyotes. I told you it was a bad idea to install those things."

"Stay in the car." Thomas grabbed the keys from the ignition and stepped into the night.

He rounded the house and disappeared from sight. She kept silent, twisting her hands in her lap as she waited for him to return and tell her it was all right to go in.

She whipped her head toward movement in the dense woods edging their property. "Oh, stop being silly. It's just an animal," she mumbled.

A shadowy figure moved in the trees, and she averted her gaze.

Shut your eyes and look away, the shadow monster will not stay.

She glanced back. The shadow had vanished.

Unable to stand the silence in the car anymore, she stepped out. The damp, earthy smell reached her nostrils. The night air filled her ears with chirping crickets and the rustling leaves. "Thomas?" she called out, trying to control the irrational shaking in her voice.

No answer.

She marched to the front door, tired of waiting, but stopped when the lights went off and plunged her into darkness.

Her hand pressed against the side of the house as she crept around the back. She took one hesitant step, then another, on shaking legs.

One at a time.

Lights flickered through the kitchen window, and her gaze fell on the shattered glass of the patio door. Inside the kitchen, a man spoke in a quiet, hesitant tone, while a woman argued, her voice hinting at hysterics. Celina pressed herself against the paneled sidewall to listen, her pulse throbbing inside her throat.

"The letter said we'd get our son back if we kill you." The man's voice shook.

Black spots filled her vision as the word *kill* repeated inside her mind like a broken record. Her heartbeat raced with every passing second her husband was inside with whoever had broken into their house, as though time had sped up. She couldn't think fast enough to make sense of anything.

Should I go in? No…I should get help. Thomas took the car keys. What the fuck am I supposed to do?

Thomas' voice sounded higher pitched than usual. "I don't—"

Footsteps echoed from the living room, and the woman shouted, "We don't have a choice."

"Where's the wife? The letter said he's married."

Celina didn't wait to find out if they'd come looking for her.

She darted to one side of the house where the hedges hid her from sight and peeked into the living room window. Silence surrounded her like an unnatural force, and her chest tightened.

Tied to a chair in the middle of the living room, Thomas stared up at the intruders as sweat plastered his light-brown hair against his face. A man stood next to him, pointing a pistol at her husband's face.

She clamped her hands over her mouth, holding back a scream.

Thomas' eyes widened, and he struggled against his restraints. The cords of his neck stood out from the strain, and the wooden dining chair wobbled. "No! Please don't kill her. She has nothing to do with this!"

"Shut up!" The woman aimed her pistol at Thomas' temple.

The man put his hand on the woman's arm, and she lowered the weapon back to her side. "I'll… I'll do it."

A flash of light and Celina's eardrums ruptured into her skull. She choked down a cry at the sight of blood running down the side of Thomas' head and backed away from the horrific scene.

No…wake up. It's a nightmare…oh, God, I can't… Thomas!

She stared back at her reflection through the window, and then at the murderers who'd turned in her direction…

They'd heard her.

Celina dashed for the woods, ignoring the shouts and the gunshots as she wove around the trees, tripping and crashing, unable to find her bearings in the dark. Her side burned as she raced along the path. She pressed on the throbbing wound and warm liquid soaked through her shirt. She brought her hand up to her face. A metallic tang tingled her nose.

Blood.

They shot her.

She jumped at the sound of nearby shouting, her muscles tensing as her pulse throbbed faster.

Her foot caught roots and she tumbled, rolling, grasping at the dirt to stop the motion until she crashed into a ravine. She gasped from the pain but forced her mouth shut when footsteps above her sent a rainfall of dirt on top of her. A bright light flashed from above, darting overhead from where she hid.

"There's blood on the path, so I must have gotten her." The woman's words came on a gasp as she wheezed.

"If you shot her, she might die on her own out here," he said. "Besides, we only needed to kill the man to get Simon back."

The sound of cracking twigs faded away, and Celina let out a shuddering breath. A heaviness settled in her limbs as she lay on the ground, her chest aching with every beat. Her brain scrambled to catch up, but she clenched her jaw and pressed against her wound.

No. I need to go home. Help Thomas.

A lump formed in her throat, but she swallowed hard and got to her feet. Her muscles trembled, but she pushed forward. Tears streamed down her cheeks, and the pain in her chest worsened with every step she took.

She leaned against the black tree, her body cold and clammy. Even without a clear view of her surroundings, she knew where she was. The one place she'd avoided for so many years.

The first place she'd seen the dark silhouette.

Her shivers intensified and her teeth chattered. She had to get home. Call for help. Save Thomas.

With no service this far out of the city, they'd never bothered with cell phones. Heat surged through her body. Why couldn't Thomas have bothered to pay a little extra for outside service? She'd give him a piece of her mind when all this was over.

The image of him tied to a chair, motionless, flashed into her mind, and she shook her head. "No. No. No." Her mouth went dry, and she pressed her lips together to stop from throwing up.

Thomas was dead.

Let me die, too, then.

She squeezed her eyes tight, trying to breathe through the pain. This wasn't right. Wasn't fair. Everything hurt so much. And why?

Those bastards. They need to pay. I want them to feel this agony.

"You are dying, human," an amused male voice called down from the tree.

Her head snapped toward the branches above her. A pair of red eyes glowed, staring at her. She tried to run but collapsed with her first step.

Get a grip. Red eyes? Don't let your imagination kill you faster.

She clenched her teeth as she clawed her way to standing.

A figure materialized in front of her, and she backed against the tree. He stood a good head taller than her five-foot-five. His eyes still glowed a fiery red. "Do you surrender, then? Did they win?" He taunted her with the last, and she gripped at the tree trunk, digging her fingers into the bark.

Shut your eyes and look away, the shadow monster will not stay.

But when she opened her eyelids, he was still there. Her heartbeat grew louder in her ears as she gaped at the figure, her logic contradicting what her eyes saw.

"What will you do, human?"

Her gaze darted around, desperate for a path she could use to run back to her house, and away from…whatever this was. Suffering from delirium and visualizing childhood monsters wouldn't help her or Thomas.

Blood rolling down the side of his head.

Her knees quaked, threatening to take her down. She swallowed a few times, trying to keep the bile from rising too high. "Who are you?"

The figure raised his hand, and a light appeared and floated around the tree. "Just a demon. But I could be more if you would like."

She blinked quickly, his words weaving around in her mind like a spider wrapping a juicy prey in its web. Shuffling back, she winced as pain shot through her wound, tensing all the muscles in her body.

"What the hell does that mean?"

"You want revenge for the wrong that has been done to you, no?"

Her body tensed. "Revenge?"

"For your murdered husband," he said, putting pressure on every single word.

Each one was like a new bullet wound through her gut, constricting her lungs and making it impossible to breathe.

"I...want my husband." The words barely came out as her throat tightened.

He materialized again just inches in front of her, and she staggered back, gasping as she hit a tree trunk. Apart from the glowing red eyes, he looked human. His face was pale and his hair shined a deep black in the rays of moonlight peeking through the canopy of tree branches overhead. Her instincts screamed to run as fast as her legs would carry her to whatever safety she could find.

But running in a circle wouldn't help her; she'd be out of time before finding anything to keep him away.

Unnatural darkness clung to him, pressing on her soul. Deep down, she knew she couldn't escape him.

"As he is now, I cannot bring him back. But with my help, you can make sure he is avenged."

Her muscles quivered, but she narrowed her eyes at him,

fighting through the pain. "He's not..." The lump in her throat threatened to strangle her.

"He is not what, Celina?"

"I don't...believe in demons."

The light floated above them, revealing the malicious smile on his lips. "And yet, here I am, close enough to touch you...touching you." He rested his hand against her cheek, and a shiver tingled down her spine.

He felt real.

His sharp fingernail traced along her skin. "His killers should suffer for what they have done to your husband and to you, no?"

Fueled by his whispers of revenge, determination to survive powered through her. "I don't want to die." Even as she spoke the words, she examined the thought and came up with another.

Why would I stay alive if Thomas is... dead?

She stared down at the hand pressing over her wound, a sour taste building in her mouth as she focused on the blood. Her heart thudded, and her head spun.

He'd tell me not to give up...to live.

A sob escaped her, and uncontrollable tears streamed down her face. She squeezed her arms tighter around herself, desperate to increase her physical pain to numb the emotional one.

The demon gripped her chin, holding her face steady between his fingers. He leaned closer, her breath quickened, and he slid his tongue up her cheek. She shrieked and pounded her fists against his chest, trying to push him away, but a stabbing pain in her side forced her to cease the struggle.

He gripped her face tighter, forcing her to look at him. "Those are tears of anger. You want revenge, and I can help."

Her voice shook. "Why would you help me? What's in it for you?"

"Your life and your soul. But more importantly, you get to live long enough to seek vengeance against those who have wronged you."

She kept silent. With every word, blood ran between her fingers in spurts as though a dagger turned in the wound.

"You have two choices." He tilted his head and considered her with the fiery red eyes. "You can wait here, hoping help will arrive in time, or you can take my deal and live to get your revenge. All it will cost is your life and your soul."

She narrowed her eyes. "Oh, is that all?"

"Your time is running out."

He was right. She grew weaker with every heartbeat. Her body shivered, and her vision blurred. "Why not just take my life and soul now?"

"A demon cannot claim a good soul."

"So, after I kill those bastards, I won't be a good person anymore?"

I'll be dragged to Hell for sin while Thomas goes to Heaven. We'd never be together again.

"Your soul will belong to me."

She loosened the pressure on her wound, numbness flowing through her body. "I want to be with my husband."

"You would have to die a violent death with enough regret in your soul to go where he is now," he hissed, his tone impatient.

Her mind snapped, and her muscles stiffened. "What—?

"I suppose you could say he is in a limbo of sorts. You would not reach him, dying like this." His sly smile resembled a predator luring in his prey with empty promises.

But what if he's right? If Thomas is damned, why not join him in Hell to make sure those sons of bitches pay?

"I don't trust you."

He walked away but glanced over his shoulder. "I did not say you should."

Her vision darkened around the edges as though tunneling on the demon. A tingling sensation rushed through her body as her mind reeled with her situation. It wasn't fair. Nothing about any of this was fair.

Keeping pressure against her wound, she took a few shaky steps, reaching out toward him as her vision blurred. She grabbed his arm, and he turned.

"Deal," she whispered.

His smile widened as he stared at her. He grabbed her and threw her on the ground. She screamed as though a second shot had been fired into her body. The burning…the white-hot licks of pain. Her mind screamed to understand and process the shock as she choked and swallowed the bile searing the back of her throat.

He pushed her bloody shirt up and pressed his hand against her wound.

He's going to kill me. He'll rip the bullet out with his fingers… then torture me. He's real. Demons are real.

Her skin scorched, and her screams echoed through the forest. The smell of heated flesh turned her stomach. She kicked and her arms flailed in her desperation to get away from him, but nothing worked.

When the pain vanished, she opened her eyes. The demon loomed inches away from Celina's face, his hands on either side of her.

"Did you think making a deal with a demon would be painless?" He cocked his head as though confused by her stupidity.

Your stupid deal didn't mention pain, you condescending bastard.

"Get off of me!" She put her hands against his chest and pushed, but he didn't budge.

He stood and put out his hand, but she ignored him and struggled up on her own. She wanted to stay strong and independent, but when she staggered, he picked her up in his arms.

"I have healed your wound. However, you are still weak from loss of blood."

"Put me down right now!" She squirmed against his strong arms and the muscles clenching in his chest.

"You are a feisty one."

"Fuck off."

"Oh, such naughty language." He chuckled. "Consider it a rare compliment, dove." He placed her down at the foot of the tree.

Crouching in front of her, he smiled, his eyes the same evil glow as a moment earlier. He could end her life at any moment, and that grin left no doubt in her mind. The light floated down on the forest floor, shimmering off his pointed teeth.

She trembled. Monsters weren't supposed to be real.

"All you are missing is the cape and basket for your grandmother."

She gaped. "What?"

"I believe you are supposed to say, '*My, what big teeth you have!*'" he hinted with a grin.

Celina opened and closed her mouth, unsure of how to respond.

He surveyed her with an unnatural stillness. "What would you like to accomplish before I take your life?"

Asking for her husband's life lingered on the tip of her tongue, despite what the demon had said. Her mind fought against the agony in her heart, and all she wanted to do was beg the demon to take her life in exchange for Thomas'.

Thomas would be in as much pain as I am now. I'd never do that to him.

The gunshot sound echoed inside her ears, as though forever carved into her, and she curled her hands into fists.

We wouldn't be separated if it weren't for those murdering scum.

All her morals and values about the sanctity of life meant nothing as she thought of the two killers. Her voice caught as she cleared her throat. "They murdered my husband. I... you're right. I want them to die."

Thoughts of torture instruments from the Spanish Inquisition flashed through her mind. She still remembered learning about those horrible devices from her time at the Lumen Church when her mother used to force her to attend. She wanted to find the ones who'd taken her one true love away and hurt them so they could feel the same pain ripping through her heart.

"And will you kill all those involved? Or just the one who pulled the trigger?"

"Trigger...? How did you know they shot him?"

The words left a bad taste in her mouth, and she inhaled deeply through her nose.

He said nothing for a few moments. "We can sense things...little things, details."

"That's your explanation?" She didn't bother hiding her impatience.

"We can smell memories and see pieces inside our own minds." He leaned in, and his voice turned darker. "Be cautious with the way you address me; I can inflict more pain than you have ever imagined, and it would give me great pleasure to do so."

"And you listen to me, demon." She matched his tone. "If you hurt me, I'll get myself killed by someone else before my soul gets tainted, and you'll be left without a meal."

I'll take control of what's left of my life, you goddamned cocky bastard.

His face broke into a real smile as he laughed. "You will be most interesting to work with." He grabbed her by the neck, and though he didn't tighten his grip, the threat was clear.

"Oh, dove. Our time together will be sweet once your soul is truly mine."

Celina stared into his glowing, red eyes as his pupils retracted until they became vertical.

I made a deal with a demon.

A steep price to pay for her revenge.

3

AFTER THE NIGHTMARE

Sunlight fell across Celina's face, and her eyelids flickered against the brightness. The warmth of Thomas curled her lips into a smile, and she snuggled against him.

But it couldn't be Thomas. He was…

No. He couldn't be dead. It had just been a nightmare. She'd tell him about it, and he'd hold her, as he always did whenever she had bad dreams.

The wind rustled through the trees, and a crow cawed. It all came rushing back to her.

The demon. The deal. Thomas.

Her eyes popped open, and she focused on the surrounding trees. Celina's breath quickened, and her heart hammered against her chest. She withdrew from the body's warmth with a jolt, backing away so fast she staggered as she stood.

The demon sat against the black tree trunk. "Good morning."

She brought her hands to her head. "I thought I had a nightmare." Her voice shook. The lump in her throat made it difficult to breathe.

His eyes gleamed. "You are not wrong."

Celina ignored him, her shaking overwhelming her to the point that her muscles ached. She blinked back her tears, her chest tightening. "He can't...he can't be gone. This isn't real..." She glanced at him and swallowed hard. "You... you're real?

"Either that or my existence has been a lie for millennia."

She could see him clearly now, in the sunlight. He wore black clothes except for a vest as red as his eyes. His irises were red even when they didn't glow, and his jet-black hair fell past his shoulders, straight and shining. Her gaze lingered on his face for a moment longer than intended. She'd expected something more monstrous than the handsome features staring back at her. When their eyes met, she glanced away.

He chuckled. "A demon's charm."

She glared down at him. "You're not a demon. That's impossible."

"Then explain how your wound has healed." He stood and took careful steps toward Celina as though afraid to frighten her. It didn't matter how he approached; little webs of fear crept along her receptors at his nearness.

"Maybe I healed during the night and I'm just—" When he materialized in front of her, she covered her gasp with a trembling hand.

He caught her wrist in one hand and lifted the torn shirt over her abdomen with the other. "Explain this."

She studied her stomach. His long, black fingernails against her pale skin did not reassure her. A brand burnt into her flesh replaced the bullet hole. A pattern swirled over the puckered skin, but she couldn't make it out.

She filled her eyes with all of her hatred. "I never said you could brand me."

"It is my mark, part of the deal."

Yanking her shirt down, she covered herself. "Well, let's

get on with this deal then." She walked away, but her pace slowed, and she soon stopped.

"Not sure where to begin?" He gave a wry chuckle.

She rubbed her arms. "If I go home…his body…" Her chin quivered, and she pressed her lips together.

His hand squeezed her shoulder. When he leaned toward her ear, the hair on her neck stood on end.

"Humans are such pitiful creatures at times," he whispered, and then spun her around to face him. "Choosing revenge and pain instead of eternal, peaceful rest is the action of a determined mind. Do not show weakness now."

"Emotions aren't weaknesses, but I guess a demon couldn't understand." Her words fell like hard stones, and she folded her arms.

He let go of her, and she backed out of his reach. His touch alone drew all manner of dark thoughts to her mind—like wanting to cause unimaginable agony to the ones responsible for Thomas' murder. They'd pay with their lives, but she wouldn't sink to a demon's level and butcher people. She refused to give him the satisfaction of thinking his thirst for death rubbed off on her that quickly.

I won't play your games.

"Where should we begin then?" He ignored her last comment.

She glanced toward her house as she took a few deep breaths. He was right; her grief wouldn't be any help to her now. "I go to the house, call the police, and take it from there." She made a list for herself so her mind would stay occupied.

"Remember, you are suffering from blood loss. Walking too fast may cause you to faint, and though I can carry you around—"

"You will not carry me. Do you understand? You won't ever touch me again—"

"Or what?" His voice no longer held any amusement, and a shadow had fallen over his eyes.

He is the shadow.

"I won't threaten you since I don't know what demons are afraid of, but I'm telling you not to. That's all." She continued to walk.

"Me," he called out.

She stopped. His tone sounded factual, yet sad. When she turned around, he'd already caught up and then walked past her, keeping his expression hidden.

"What?"

"You said you were unsure what demons are afraid of." He waved his hand indifferently. "They are afraid of me."

Celina stood rooted to the spot. What did he mean? She didn't inquire further but would ask later; maybe after she dealt with the police.

She hadn't dealt with the police in nine years—since her parents died. Tears gathered behind her eyes again, but she blinked them away as she jogged to catch up with the demon.

"What's your name?"

"My name is in the Demos language. You would not understand it."

"Okay, well, what am I supposed to call you then?"

He gave her a sideways glance. "You may call me Mekaisto."

"And how did you know my name?"

"Because I went inside your head to find out."

She picked up her pace. "Stay the hell out of my head from now on, Mekaisto."

"I cannot promise you that."

Her jaw clenched so tight, her head throbbed. She took deep breaths, mentally hoping her headache transferred over to him when invading her privacy.

That'll teach him.

They reached her house. It looked different, empty. Her

mind flashed on a picture of Thomas, limp, tied to the chair, and her muscles tensed. She focused on the shattered glass scattered across the porch. It was as though someone had scooped her insides, leaving her hollow. Making the deal was the right choice, even if it meant her life and her soul.

I have a demon on my side this time, you sons of bitches.

"I'm going inside to call the police."

"And how will you explain your bloody clothes? Perhaps explain your wound stopped bleeding thanks to a demon brand? It is invisible to other humans, though I do not think that will be what concerns them if you tell them the truth."

She hated his sarcasm, and even more that he had a point. "I'll change before calling them and hide—"

"They are professionals, they will find the clothes. Change your clothes, and come back outside with them," he instructed.

Celina wasn't sure why she had to go outside again, but she didn't want to hear another sarcastic answer. She tiptoed inside, avoiding the shattered patio glass, her gaze shifting side to side with each step she took. Her husband's body was in the living room, but she shut her eyes and tried to ignore the smell of copper in the air.

Despite all her efforts, her vision blurred, and she muffled her sobs through her hands. Her muddy sneakers left a trail on the hardwood floor as she crept to her bedroom, barely seeing through her tears.

She picked up a shirt and sweater from the floor, and after she rummaged, grabbed a pair of pants from the chair in the corner of the room, and then put them on. Her gaze lingered on the clothes hamper where some of Thomas' clothes waited to be put away, her heart shattering a little more.

A white corner stuck out from her bloodied pants pocket, and she pulled out the playground sketch they'd drawn just a few hours ago. She couldn't stop the back of her throat from burning, her fingers tightening against the paper. After a few calming breaths, she slipped it into the back pocket of the jeans she wore and returned to Mekaisto with her bloody clothes.

She went down the steps of the deck to where he stood and thrust the clothes at him. "Here."

He took them and put them on the patio next to him. Without hesitation, he grabbed Celina and pushed her into the closest patch of damp earth. It hadn't hurt, but the surprise silenced her as she concentrated on fighting all the curse words begging to spill out. It wouldn't be in her best interest to let them escape.

"You will tell them most of the truth and only change the bare minimum of what happened last night. You ran into the forest, but you slipped and fell on the ground," his lips twitched, "many times. Your clothes must look like you are telling the truth."

"I don't suppose you could have thrown my change of clothes without me in them?" she said through gritted teeth. "And besides, I could've changed while waiting for the police."

He stared down at her. "It needs to look like you fell with them. Besides, this way seemed more entertaining," he grinned, "to me."

I hate him.

"I'll call them now." She got to her feet and fixed her gaze on the broken patio door. "You shouldn't be here."

Wings flapped next to her, brushing across her hair, and when she turned, Mekaisto had vanished along with her bloody clothes.

Celina stayed in the kitchen, as far away from the living room as possible. Part of her wanted to wrap her arms around Thomas' body so no one could take him away. But most of all, she wanted him to wake up, wanted him back. That couldn't happen, and the tightness in her chest continued to burn a hole inside her heart.

A police car and ambulance arrived. Two officers stepped into the kitchen, and she flinched as the glass crunched under their heavy boots. Both took their notepads out, and her attention shifted from one to the other.

She'd done nothing wrong but waiting until the next morning to report her husband's murder would need one hell of a good explanation. Between the lump in her throat and her nerves bunched at being questioned by officers, she was surprised she could utter a single word.

"Can you tell us what happened?" one officer asked. She glanced at his nametag: J. Blake. His light-brown hair had wisps of gray, his skin wrinkled around the corner of his eyes and mouth, but his eyes had a fire burning in them.

She told them the truth, as Mekaisto had instructed, but when she neared the part about seeing Thomas tied up, her voice cracked.

"Did you see their faces?"

"No…it happened so fast."

Yeah, lying to the police is a fantastic idea.

Celina wouldn't let them get to the murderers first. Mekaisto promised her vengeance.

"And what happened after that?"

"They…the man shot my husband." She brought her hand to her mouth, muffling a sob. A few breaths in and out, as the officers stayed silent, their pens hovering over their notepads until she continued. "I ran into the forest, and I guess I must've tripped and fallen because I only woke up this morning. I came back here and called 9-1-1."

"And the muddy footprints going to your bedroom?"

"That's where I called from since I didn't want to use the phone in the living room." She swallowed hard again.

The officers glanced at each other, and the nervousness

creeping through her heightened. She swallowed a more few times, her body trembling.

Shit—they can see straight through my lie. Maybe they'll think this is a normal reaction to what happened…

A paramedic stepped into the kitchen, carrying a large emergency bag. "I'd like to look at her if you're finished. I'll get the clothes and bag them for evidence." She didn't wait for the officers to respond before putting her bag down and rummaging inside it.

"We need to speak to the coroner," the second officer said. He had smooth skin, not a wrinkle of worry or a gray hair from stress. He pressed his lips together as though trying not to puke.

I don't think he's ever been around death before. Welcome to my world.

The paramedic surveyed Celina. "We should take you to the hospital, get you checked—"

"I'm fine."

"I'll run a few tests, at least, make sure you're healthy. All right?" She dug deeper into her emergency bag and let out a sigh as she shook her head. "I left the pressure cuff in the ambulance. I can do the check-up there instead, okay? But first, we can go to your bedroom so I can gather your clothes for evidence, and you can change."

Celina nodded as she trudged to her bedroom. After bagging her dirty clothes, the paramedic led her outside toward the ambulance. They passed next to the living room.

She wouldn't look. She couldn't.

Her eyes burned as she fought more tears.

A body bag lay on her living room floor, the love of her life reduced to nothing more than an empty corpse.

Her chest squeezed, and she pressed her hand against it. Part of her wanted to rip her own heart out to stop the pain. She called on the time he'd surprised her with an outing to a secluded lake with a picnic, trying to remember his smile. All her mind recalled was the terror in his face as the man raised his gun to his head one last time.

No. Remember his smile, his voice.

His limp body. Blood streaming down his face. She ran a hand over her face, trying to wipe away the horrifying memory.

The paramedic opened the back doors of the ambulance with a thunk, and Celina jerked.

When did we get outside…? Ugh, I'm losing my mind.

The woman sat her on the back of the ambulance and took her blood pressure. A man from the criminal investigation team rushed over to them and took out a swab kit. He reached toward Celina, but she flinched back.

The paramedic put her hand on Celina's arm and gave a sympathetic smile. "They need to swab the inside of your cheek for DNA and the palms of both your hands for gunpowder."

Celina nodded, hoping her consent would make her appear less suspicious.

Once the kit was packed up again, the man left without a single word, and Celina had just about had it. "Can I go now?"

"Your blood pressure is low, Mrs. Leviet. I would like to take you to the hospital and—"

"I don't want to go."

Celina stood and backed away. She hated hospitals. The sound of footsteps nearby caught her attention, and as she turned around, the paramedic reached for her. Mekaisto grabbed the paramedic's wrist.

Celina's eyes widened.

What the hell is he doing?

Thank God he didn't appear the same as he had a few hours ago. His jet-black hair now ended below his ears, and his eyes had changed to a rich maroon.

He released his hold on the paramedic and gave her an

apologetic smile. "I'm sorry for grabbing you like that, but Celina had a trying night, and I think going to the hospital won't do her any good if she doesn't want to go."

"And you are?" the paramedic asked while she rubbed her wrist.

"Ah, I'm sorry." He bowed but kept his eyes fixed on her. "I'm Kai, an old friend of Celina's."

The paramedic stared toward Celina, one eyebrow arched.

She cleared her throat, hoping her voice wouldn't shake. "I called him after calling the police. I was scared of being alone after everything." Celina glanced at Mekaisto. "Told him to come later, though."

Hope they buy this story.

"Well, since you won't be alone, I won't force you to the hospital." She turned toward Mekaisto. "But if she shows any signs of weakness, you bring her in straight away," she insisted, "no matter how much she refuses."

"Not to worry. I can be very persuasive." One corner of his mouth curled upward, and he slanted a glance at the paramedic—a truly devilish smile if Celina had ever seen one.

The other paramedics came out of the house with the gurney carrying the body bag, and she tensed.

"I'm sorry for your loss, Mrs. Leviet," the paramedic offered.

Celina nodded and bit her tongue to stop herself from crying. Getting shot had been less painful than this. Part of her wished the murdering bastards hadn't missed, killing her, and she gritted her teeth.

No. I'll watch them suffer. I'll make it slow and enjoy it. For you, Thomas.

"Yes, he was a good man," Mekaisto said, with a small nod.

She glanced up at him, and her fist curled to curb her violent impulse to beat him hard.

The police officers walked outside the house as the ambulance pulled out of the driveway. "Excuse me, Mrs. Leviet?" Officer Blake walked toward Celina as his partner returned to their car.

Please no more questions, I can't take this anymore.

"You're an acquaintance of Mrs. Leviet?" Blake flipped the pages of his notebook as he regarded the demon.

"I am."

He arched an eyebrow. "And what are you doing here?"

Celina told the same lie she had told the paramedic and, by the officer's frown, he didn't buy it. Still, Blake nodded but narrowed his eyes at Mekaisto before he glanced at Celina again. "You'll need to make other arrangements for accommodations in the meantime."

"I'll help her gather a few things and take her to a hotel until other arrangements can be made. I'll call as soon as we have the room number and hotel name," he added.

"You'll understand that as we investigate, it would be better for you not to leave town." His gaze rested on Mekaisto as he added, "Both of you." He handed Celina his card, then hurried to his police car and the vehicle pulled away.

Once she was sure they couldn't be overheard, she glared at him. "Don't you ever talk about my husband like you knew him," she ordered as her fists trembled.

He smirked and walked to the house.

This had been her dream house. She'd described it to Thomas long before they married, and he built it as a wedding present for her. When she stared at the white siding with dark-green framing, it tore open the emptiness inside her heart instead of bringing her the joy it once did.

One month after their wedding, Thomas had driven her out here, blindfolded, for a surprise. "Where have you brought me?" she'd asked as he'd taken her elbow in his hand and helped her out of the car.

Celina inhaled the fresh country air, the sun warming her face as she waved her hands around. Thomas came up behind her and wrapped his arms around her waist. "I thought it was time for you to see your wedding present."

Her hands darted to her blindfold, but he held them down, making her giggle. "I want to see."

He pulled at the knot behind her head, taking his time. She blinked a few times in the sudden glare of sunlight, and then brought her hands to her open mouth, her eyes widening.

The two-story house stood where her parents' cottage had once been. Her heart fluttered. The forest behind the house was as thick and green as it had been before they had to sell the property due to near bankruptcy. She thought of the dark silhouette from her childhood but pushed it out of her mind.

Childhood imagination, that's all.

"I hope it looks like you'd imagined." He watched her, still as a statue, waiting for her answer.

Celina turned to Thomas, her eyes wet and a smile on her lips. She threw her arms around his neck, laughing as he spun her around a few times. "It's perfect." She stared into his hazel eyes. "Thomas… Thank you so much for this, I—"

He kissed her, cutting her sentence short, but she didn't care. His hands caressed her back while her own hands traveled down his chest until she reached his belt. He withdrew a little and smiled. "Come into the house, I want to show you everything."

Even the inside looked as she'd described it to him. From the yellow kitchen with white frames and old-style countertops, to the tan walls of the living room with pine wood baseboards.

"How did you afford all this?"

He closed the front door behind them. "My company picked up new contracts. You won't have to work anymore, Celina. I'll take care of you."

When she reached to open one of the many doors in the hallway, his hand squeezed her shoulder. "This is the study—

for my work. I know it's selfish of me to ask, but would you mind if this stays a room just for me?"

He'd always been the type not to share everything, so she nodded. "Your man cave?"

"Exactly."

When they entered the master bedroom, Celina gaped. The large, queen-size bed even had her favorite dark-red bedspread, and he'd bought matching thick curtains for the window that took up most of one wall.

"I thought we agreed to no presents! I didn't get you anything."

Thomas closed the door, and once he reached the window, drew the curtains, plunging the room into darkness. They wrapped their arms around each other, and Celina's grip tightened on his back when he slid his hand under her skirt to reach her panties.

"*You* are my present, Celina." He'd slipped his fingers beneath the fabric and teased her.

She'd swayed against him. "I love you."

"I love you, too."

Their best days together had been when they moved in and fashioned the house as their own. Losing the love of her life buried all those happy memories. Her surroundings seemed to vanish, leaving her as she really was. Alone. He was her family, her friend, her everything. And now, she had nothing.

Why did he have to die?

Celina took a breath before going back into her house where she found Mekaisto in her bedroom, staring out the window.

Seeing him stand where Thomas had stood so often pissed her off. This was an intimate place, and he was already pushing her personal boundaries too far.

He glanced at her.

She slammed the door, not caring to have the criminal

investigation team overhead her. "You have no right to be in here. I just finished telling a bunch of strangers what happened last night, and you're in here like you own the place. What the hell is wrong with you?"

"It amuses me when humans hold my kind to their moral standards."

Son of a bitch.

She couldn't argue or fight, not after being so emotionally exhausted. Her jaw clenched at his confident action of showing up in front of everyone even if he looked more human now. He had put her on the spot; forced her to lie about who he was and why he was there so soon after her husband's murder.

"So, what the hell was all that back there?" she demanded but kept her voice low. "Old friend? Kai?"

Why am I instigating a demon? Nerves?

"It's easier to say than my full name."

"So, I can call you Kai?"

He studied her for a few seconds before turning back to the window. "We are old friends, no?"

"Cut the crap. We're not old friends. We're not even current friends."

He moved toward Celina, his eyes lightening to the red color she'd seen first. "You are playing a dangerous game with me, dove."

She flinched but held her ground as her heart raced. "Stop calling me that, I'm not—"

When he took her face in his hands and forced her to stare at him, her muscles stiffened. "I will call you whatever I please." His grip tightened a little. "Stop provoking me, or I will be forced to correct your behavior." He let her go, but she stayed rooted to the spot.

She tried to control her trembling. "Correct?"

"Yes. I am creative, and my methods are not pleasant." He added with a cruel smile, "Not for you."

While she stared at him, the horrible reality that nothing would stop him if he decided to hurt her crashed over Celina like being cornered by a wild animal. "I'll be right back. Just…bathroom." She darted from the room.

Once the door shut behind her, she locked it. Then she paced. The mistake of making a deal with a demon twisted a knot in her stomach. With her life slipping away, she had no other choice.

No. She still wanted the revenge Kai had offered. But at what price?

Her instincts screamed to escape, to get away from the demon.

Her head spun, and she was hit with a dizzy spell so strong that she gripped the sink to steady herself. She focused on the drain, breathing in and out.

What the hell was that about?

She slid her hand over where she'd been shot and frowned. Because she'd had to change her clothes so fast, she hadn't taken time to inspect the brand over her wound. She lifted the edge of her shirt and studied herself in the mirror. A wave of disbelief washed over as though the world around her melted away, leaving her numb as she examined the open-winged crow in the middle of a circle of thorns. She pushed her top back down, staggering away from the mirror. She gasped as though someone had plunged her head underwater, everything becoming too real.

Trying to calm herself, she closed her eyes tight against the drowning sensation. She pictured Thomas holding her and could almost feel him.

I'll stay strong for you.

She left the bathroom and headed to the kitchen. The criminal investigation team was outside, and some tension left her shoulders. A few dishes lay on the counter, so she put them away, her mind numbing. It was pointless since she wouldn't be living here anymore, but the act of doing something familiar let her mind relax for a few seconds.

I'm leaving this place. Thomas won't be with me anymore.

He'd been stressed after he'd got that phone call and she was too late to find out what had bothered him. She'd never be able to help him deal with whatever it was.

"What are you doing?" Kai asked.

She cleared her throat to make sure her voice wouldn't crack too much. "Putting my dishes away."

Kai's arms wrapped around her from behind and she squeezed the plate in her hand, holding her breath. Somehow, affection from him was worse than if he held a knife to her throat.

His hand rested on her chest. "Strange how love is all inside a human's mind, and yet your heart is the organ aching."

She tore herself away from him. "I wouldn't expect a demon to understand."

"What makes you think I—"

"Look, I don't want to talk about it with you. I've suffered enough." The plate in her hand shook, and her fingers cramped as she tried to hold it steady.

"No, you have not suffered enough. You'd have chosen to die if you knew what's coming."

"Don't talk as if you know how I feel, you fucking demon." Her tears cooled the heated flush of her rage, and she hurled the plate at him.

Kai lifted his hand and the crockery shattered into fine dust at his feet. His eyes locked onto hers, and without a word, he grabbed her wrist and dragged her outside.

"What are you doing? Where are you taking me?" Her voice rose higher as she tried tugging away from him.

He stopped near the edge of the woods and faced her, his glowing eyes silencing her questions. His hand rose and black smoke seeped from the ground, sticking to everything it touched. Kai pulled her against him and clicked his fingers.

The smoke seeped into the surface of all that it covered, and her eyes widened. The plants and flowers withered and died, everything turned ashen as though burned. He went back to the house and she followed, glancing back at the destroyed area of the forest. Though no words were exchanged, she knew he had shown her what he could do as a warning. He wouldn't just threaten her next time she attacked him.

Going back to the master bedroom, she grabbed a bag out of her closet to pack. Thomas' clothes hung in front of her, and a lump in her throat constricted her breathing. She swallowed hard, trying to make it go away. Grabbing hold of a sleeve, she waited for Thomas to come up behind her to get ready for work. But no one was in the house except for her, and the demon.

I won't let my emotions get in the way anymore. Kai will get that revenge.

"Once we get to the hotel," Kai spoke, making her jump and turn. He leaned against the doorframe of the bedroom. "You'll get some rest, and we'll start in the morning."

I'll never get used to him peeking inside my mind.

"Good."

"You'll have to write an obituary announcing your husband's death." His cruel smile drew an urge to attack him again, but she turned away.

"My husband didn't have a family apart from me. His parents were abusive, and he left the moment he turned sixteen. As for friends...he always had difficulty being social." She pushed aside the clothes she'd just hung yesterday, never to be worn again.

A light-blue shirt came into view. He'd worn it at a get-together she talked him into going to with her. He'd said something odd about her strange habit of keeping so many friends—or something like that—and flashed a winsome grin her way.

"So, your husband and I are not so different."

Her spine stiffened at the amusement in Kai's voice. "What?"

"I read your train of thought."

"You're nothing like him. Thomas was kind, considerate, and made me feel safe."

"Are you saying I'm cruel, merciless, and make you feel vulnerable?"

"Yes."

"I think you'd hurt my feelings," he leaned in closer, his smile widening, "if I had any."

"I rest my case."

Celina left by the back door, not wanting to go inside the living room. She could never go back in there, never. Once outside, she walked around the house toward her car. Kai stood next to the driver's door and held his hand out.

She arched an eyebrow. "What?"

"You are in no condition to drive, dove."

She glanced from his hand to his eyes but didn't argue and handed him the car keys. "Demons can drive?"

"Like humans, not all of us can."

She entered the passenger side and buckled her seatbelt. "Why do you call me *dove*?"

"Doves represent purity and innocence. And no matter how tainted your soul will get by the time you achieve your revenge, it will always be pure and innocent compared to mine."

4

———

CROW

elina's eyes widened as she walked into the penthouse Kai checked them into. The large room that served as both kitchen and living area was free of so much as a single speck of dust. She never understood how such shine could be natural. The king-size bed in the bedroom was swallowed by the massive amounts of open space. A large glass shower, tucked in a room of shining black and white marble, beckoned to her and she put her bag down on the floor.

There's only one room. One Bed. He wouldn't dare…

"I hope there's another bedroom somewhere in this huge, unaffordable place."

Kai lay on the dark-brown sofa, his legs dangling over the armrest, staring up at the ceiling. He'd reverted to looking as he had when she first met him and his long, jet-black hair splayed over the seat.

"No, just the one." His innocent tone contradicted the evidence in front of her, and her muscles stiffened. She wanted nothing more than to kick him. "And it is more than affordable for me. Do not concern yourself with that." The red irises were back, too.

"How can you...?" She eyed him. "You didn't threaten anyone, did you?"

Kai sat up straighter. "Me? Threaten someone? Why would you think that?" His eyes widened with indignation, but the corners of his mouth curled.

She crossed her arms. "I'm serious, Kai."

"I have legal human currency. That is all you need to know." He waved his hand dismissively.

"Fine, but what about the one-bedroom deal?"

"I thought sharing is considered a good trait among humans." His quip accompanied a mischievous gleam in his eye.

"Not a bed, no."

"Demons can sleep. However, we do not require it. Do not worry." He leaned back, this time sitting straight, and focusing on the ceiling again.

She glanced up. "What are you staring at?"

"We can see matter humans cannot. There is a whole other world. Care to see?"

"I thought you said only demons could see it."

Kai's lips curled and he held out his hand in invitation toward her. Unable to stifle her nervous blinking, she peered at it, her mind weighing the pros and cons. As much as this other world terrified her, she couldn't help wonder what could be discovered. She took his hand, and her pulse quickened as his smile widened. When he positioned her to sit on his lap, she squirmed in protest, but he grabbed her face and forced her to stare where he was watching.

"Do not scream," he purred into her ear, sending shivers through her body.

Her heart pounded, but she kept her eyes focused and nodded. Something hard and hot, like a burning needle, pressed into her upper arm, but as she continued to watch the ceiling, a fine mist swirled against the surface, growing thicker until she could see nothing else. As the smoke ebbed away, she swallowed back a scream.

A corpse-like creature crawled through a hole forming in the ceiling, clawing its way through, its mouth opened wide. She pushed herself against Kai, her fear pulsing through her throat and begging her to scream. She couldn't let it see her and cuddled closer to Kai, protecting herself with the strength in his arms. It disappeared from view, but sheer terror kept her eyes open wide.

She turned her head to the side and looked at him. "What…what the hell is that thing?"

"A creature from my realm. It feeds on human negativity, which is plentiful here." He smiled and brought his bloody fingernail to his mouth. "Especially in this room."

She ignored his sass and gaped from her arm to his face. A gash streamed a thin line of blood. "Did you cut me?"

"You never asked *how* I would show you what only demons can see," Kai teased.

She stood fast. "And what do you mean there's human negativity here?"

"Ah, my dove. I can feel the hatred and vengeance surging through you." He closed his eyes as though savoring the feeling.

She opened her mouth but snapped it closed. Did he have to speak in that syrupy, delicious tone?

What the fuck is wrong with me for even thinking that? I must be tired… overwhelmed.

He chuckled, his head still thrown back and his posture relaxed. Her mouth went dry, realizing he'd peeked inside her head again, and she marched to her bedroom. The slam of wood on wood did little to drown out the sound of her pounding heart.

Her mind refused to wrap around the idea of Kai as a demon. Monsters didn't exist. At least, she'd never met any up close and personal. And she wasn't altogether happy about meeting this one.

Sitting on the edge of the bed, she glanced around.

Where the hell is that corpse-thing now?

She wouldn't have had to deal with any of this if those bastards hadn't come into her life and taken everything from her.

Would Thomas have taken the deal with Kai if I'd been killed?

Her fingers curled into the mattress.

She'd been in a motel before, but never a hotel like this one. In her more rebellious days, after her parents died, she'd made a point of attending every party she could find. It was how she'd met Thomas. She'd strutted into the club, fake ID in hand, wearing a short skirt, tank top, and as many spikes as she could wrap around her wrists.

The bartender pointed to the side. "That guy's been staring at you for a while."

She glanced in the direction of his finger, and locked gazes with the most beautiful hazel irises she'd ever seen. Even in the darkness of the club, his eyes reminded her of a forest at sunset. He was the kind of guy who didn't have to try to look cool. From his black dress shirt, unbuttoned at the top, to the jeans held up by a belt accessorized with chains, he exuded a confidence that drew her in.

He stood in the center of a group of girls, some pretty, some mysterious, all beautiful in one way or other and all slimmer than Celina. This was a nightclub with its share of regulars, and a new face, especially one as hot as his, drew plenty of attention.

She smiled back at the bartender and shrugged. "Yeah, but he has a few to pick from, and I doubt he'll pick the girl on the chubby side."

"Nothing sexier than hourglass curves," a guy said from behind her, and she choked on her drink.

She spun around on the barstool, her gaze landing in the middle of a broad chest. The newcomer. "Er… thanks?"

Is he teasing me?

He smiled and held out his hand. "I'm Thomas."

She glanced down, her eyebrow arching. "A handshake? Really? Most people just make out when they introduce themselves."

"Is that an invitation?" He grinned. "I'd rather talk and get to know you first."

She stared down at her feet as the heat rose into her cheeks, gathering her courage. "Want to get out of here?"

Let's see if he's just another player…or if he's just playing a twisted game.

He smiled and nodded, taking her hand to help her off the barstool. "You haven't told me your name."

"Celina." Her voice came out on a breathless half-whisper as she leaned in to be heard over the music and caught a whiff of his cologne—woodsy and sweet.

They strolled outside, the hot summer air sticky against the sweat on her body.

"Do you have a place, or did you want me to take you somewhere?"

He's the same as the others. Just wants to screw with the chubby girl. Probably a dare.

Her heart squeezed at the way he looked at her—like she was the most important thing in the world.

Must be fake, but damn he's a good actor.

"You can take me wherever you want."

If I'm going to have sex for the first time, might as well be with the guy who isn't as much of an ass as the others.

They reached a motel with a crappy reputation. He glanced at her with a smile, and for a minute, butterflies fluttered inside her stomach. Thomas paid for a room, and once the door was locked, she lifted the hem of her cropped tank top, ready for whatever would come next.

He put his hand on her arm to stop her. "I thought we would talk."

She gaped at him, yanking her top back in place, her cheeks burning. "Oh... I thought...never mind." Her chest squeezed at the rejection. "It was stupid to think you'd want me." She tried sounding indifferent, but the hurt in her voice came through.

"I do...want you. But I want to get to know you first, Celina."

Unable to think of anything more than the sound of her name on his lips, she nodded. She'd done nothing past making out, but for a reason, she didn't understand—something more powerful than she'd ever felt—she wanted Thomas to be her first. Wanted him to hold her in his arms while his hands touched her, caressed her, showed her the meaning of passion.

Her blush deepened, and she glanced away.

"I'm sorry, I didn't mean—" Thomas' voice shook.

"I'm the one who should be sorry. I thought you were like every other guy in that club." Her gaze swept the room, avoiding his eyes. "And I thought...I mean, we're at a motel and...I..."

"Can I kiss you?"

She turned, her lips trembling as she opened her mouth in the smallest fraction of a measurement, imagining the feel of him against her. She nodded, her breath catching inside when he closed the distance between them. His lips sent a shiver across her body, and her pulse traveled straight south, his arousal pressing against her leg heightening the intensity of her feelings.

They withdrew, and he cupped her cheek with his palm. "Okay." His slight panting thrilled her. "Let's talk."

Celina giggled, and they spent the rest of the night lying next to each other in bed, chatting about themselves. He'd been sympathetic when she'd told him about her parents' deaths and being stuck with her religious aunt. Just someone to listen to her without wanting something in exchange had been such a nice feeling. Thomas had little to share, apart from being two years older than her and that he'd run away from home when he was sixteen. As the night progressed, he'd confided that his parents had been abusive and controlling all his life, so he'd left.

After that, they became one of those perfect couples who did everything together and shared all the same interests. Four years later, when she'd turned twenty, he'd sat her on his lap and handed her a small, ancient-looking box; an engagement ring. Everything had been so perfect.

And now…Thomas. Gone. And she'd made a deal with one of the devil's henchmen.

I miss you so much.

She bit the inside of her cheek to stop from crying, and once she got a hold of her emotions, her grip on the covers loosened. Closing her eyes, she collapsed back. The bed shifted, and her eyelids flew open.

Kai sat on the edge.

She screamed and scooted away. "How the hell did you get in here? I locked the door."

"You think locks and doors can stop me? I am from a realm you cannot even imagine. Do you need me to do that math for you?"

"I can do my own math," she grumbled. "Why are you in here?"

"I came to inform you I have called the officer named Blake to give him your new contact details. He says they will want you to come down to make an official statement soon." Pausing for a few seconds, he examined his pointed fingernails as he continued. "He also informed me that the lawyer responsible for your husband's will was looking to contact you, so I told Blake to forward your new phone number." He stared at her as though waiting for her reaction.

She concentrated on keeping her face a mask of disinterest. No weakness. He would enjoy it too much. "Fine, whatever."

"You should get your rest. A human can't take so many emotions all—"

"Don't talk like you know me." How many times would she have to tell him? She stood. "Now get out of my room."

He stood as well and glared with his vertical, thin pupils. He could be playful, but when he went full on demon-eyed, she shrunk back in honest fear. "You waste precious minutes of sleep while arguing with me. I said I would not sleep in your bed. I did not say I would stay out of the room, nor did I say I would not watch over you as you sleep."

"Creep."

"You expected different from me?"

Though he spoke with such lightheartedness, he held himself straight, his eyes a deep, blood-red.

Rather than argue, she dove under the covers, hoping sleep would come easy. It didn't. The memory of Thomas, tied to a chair, consumed her every thought. Without him, who was she? Lost and alone. As quickly as she wiped away a tear, another took its place.

"How did I fall asleep?" Instead of risking a look at Kai, she kept her focus on the ceiling. "Last night, I fell asleep without thinking of anything. Did you do that?"

"Burning a demon brand into human flesh takes a certain toll." He spoke with compassion she didn't expect.

She turned her head to stare at him and swallowed hard. "I don't want to be..."

"You would like to forget?" There was a softness in his tone, and she closed her eyes, let the sound wash over her, lull her into a fraction of trust.

A branding. She could take it twice if it shielded her from the images in her own mind. "Just to fall asleep."

"What happened once you reached the patio door?"

She sat up and narrowed her eyes. "I thought I told you not to look inside my mind anymore."

"How sweet of you to think you are in charge."

Celina put her head on the pillows and gave him one last icy stare before turning to the ceiling again. Was the corpse-like thing there, just invisible to her eyes?

"There was a man and a woman." She pulled in a stuttering breath. "The man said something about having to kill Thomas to get his son back or something like that. Then the son of a bitch shot him in the head! Thomas never hurt anyone. Ever."

"Then what will you do for your poor, sweet, murdered husband?" This time, something sinister in his tone drew her gaze to his cruel smile and glowing eyes that seemed to light the whole room. She inched away.

His darkness surrounded her, threatened to devour her. It cut her breath short. Her mind focused on the evil seeping through her surroundings as though feeding her the fuel for her rage. She gripped the blankets so tight, her fingers throbbed.

Thoughts of tying both the murderers down on chairs and making each other watch as she shot them in various places, haunted her waking moments. She wanted them to witness each other's pain as she'd done with Thomas.

Her voice wobbled on her first try, so she cleared her throat and began again. "I want revenge…against all of them. Anyone who was connected to Thomas' murder. I want to watch them suffer and hurt. I want them to pay." By the time she finished, she was almost shouting.

Kai smiled. "That is all I needed to hear…dove."

She averted her eyes, ashamed at her own words. He chuckled, and her pulse quickened. She needed to know how this all worked. Though she doubted he would give her much, she asked anyway. "Can you access any memory in my mind?"

"Only the ones you are thinking of. The others require much more work."

"Good to know."

"When you were ten years old, your parents brought you to their cottage on the land where your husband built your dream house, and you explored the forest in the property behind." His eyes gleamed as the corners of his mouth curled into a small smile. "You found a black tree down in a ravine. Everything was dead around it, so you assumed the tree was dead, too. When you broke one of its branches, however, you realized it still lived. You apologized to it, then took a bracelet you made for a friend who moved away the previous year and put it around the branch you broke."

Celina opened her mouth to speak, but no sound came from her mouth.

"You talked to it every day, sharing your dreams, your nightmares...but your family went broke and was forced to sell the property. You cried at the foot of the tree trunk, saying goodbye. From that point on, you had frequent nightmares of the tree melting under your feet as a crow with red eyes swooped down and carried you away."

"You said you could only read what I was thinking of at the moment." Seriously. How many lies did he have stored up?

"I did not search your memories," he said. "Those were mine."

"Yours? I don't—"

"Yes, you do. You have understood ever since you saw me sitting in the black tree right above you. Your human way of thinking just has not let you accept it, yet." He stood.

She sat up and scooted against the wall, drawing her legs to her chest. With the way he was speaking, her mind raced with worst-case scenarios of where he was going with this. Kai continued past the bed and stopped in front of the window. Dark mist swirled around him, blocking him from view. When it stopped, black feathers fell and disappeared into smoke once they touched the floor. A crow perched on the sill, his red eyes staring at her.

Celina inhaled a sharp breath. Her mouth went dry, halting her scream at the sight of the crow that had filled her nightmares for the last fifteen years.

This isn't real.

These kinds of things only happened in movies and the books she read. This wasn't reality. Then again, neither were demons or monsters humans couldn't see.

Celina's world crumbled around her. She'd survived twenty-five years in blissful ignorance, and now that the veil was lifted, she longed to put it back. It was too much. Had this bastard been stalking her since she was young, waiting for a moment, an opportunity, to strike?

Shit.

5

———————

HELPERS

The sun burned on the horizon, one final flicker of light before darkness would take over.

Kai soared over the city and flapped his wings until he focused onto the familiar woods where his tree stood. He glided down and transformed back into his demon form, his vision perfect despite the night. Every movement caught his sixth sense, though not out of worry.

Nothing threatened him.

His hand rested on the tree, and black smoke passed through his arm, darker than the night itself. He'd read Celina's mind when she'd thought he was a shadow, and he grinned at the idea.

How right she is.

He'd need help with his plans, and he knew exactly where to get it. His gaze moved toward Celina's house, and something inside him darkened. He'd frightened her, and something uncurled in his gut, reaching out clawed fingers to scratch at the base of what a demon wasn't supposed to have —emotions.

The trees shook when he cursed in his language, but he pushed the nameless feeling aside and concentrated. His call drew thousands of spiders to crawl around him—some from the ground, others from the forest canopy.

He extended a finger as a spider descended from a web. "Keep your eyes and ears open."

They scattered away at the command, and he turned to his tree again. He waved his hand, and glowing red butterflies appeared, lighting the woods in the color of delectable human blood. His messengers sunk into the bark and into his world.

His mind wandered to Celina again, and his hands curled into fists. The urges that pulsed through him whenever she came into his thoughts took all his power to suppress.

He glanced up at the murder of crows perched in the trees —the ones he'd sent out on Celina the night before—and ordered them to scatter to the locations he'd need to visit later. Their wings beat a dark percussion in the still forest as they obeyed his command.

My turn.

The crow form was the most constrictive, but necessary at times while in the human world. He flew over the city, seeking what he needed for the next part of his plan. Most of the stores were closed, but a few remained open late, and he made his way toward one.

In an alleyway between the buildings, he changed back into human form and dusted his black jacket as he stepped out onto the sidewalk. As soon as Celina woke, he'd start her on the path for revenge. He ran his fingers through his hair. It hadn't been the original plan, but he'd adjust it.

He smelled the girl at the counter before he even saw her. "Hello." She wore a red dress with black polka dots, matching the one he'd seen on a mannequin outside the store window.

Kai smiled and browsed inside the goth and punk store, picking out what he needed.

The girl walked up to him, a shy smile on her lips. "We're having a sale, so it's a buy one, get the other free."

He smirked, allowing his gaze to roam over her from head to toe. "How kind of you to inform me."

Her eyes narrowed, but a faint blush crept in her cheeks. He wasn't interested in her, but he never missed an opportunity to toy with humans; such sensitive creatures.

"Er...okay. Well, if you need anything, let me know."

"I most certainly will."

Her blush deepened, and she moved back toward the counter.

By the time he found everything he needed, the girl was talking on the phone, her tone of voice rising every so often. "Look, I don't care about that. No, you can't just..." She glanced up at Kai. "I'll call you back."

"I suggest you don't call her back."

"Excuse me?"

He let out a sigh. "I'll never understand why you take so much abuse but end up crying about it like it's not fair." He leaned over the counter, and the girl flinched back. "Don't call her back. It won't end well for you."

Her hand squeezed the phone. "Who the hell do you think you are?"

"The answer is somewhere in your question, but no matter." He grabbed the phone from her and shattered it with his bare hand.

Her eyes widened. "I...I don't want any trouble."

"Of course not." He sneered. "You can continue to support your abusive girlfriend's drug habit, or you can kill her and disappear. Either way, it'll end with you seeing me again."

She gaped at him. "Who—?"

Before he could reply, the bell rang as someone else entered the store.

"Amanda! You hung up on me, you dumb cow. What the fuck is your problem?" Scabs bled as the older teen rubbed the side of her arm, her left eye twitching as she walked toward her girlfriend.

A future murderer…how interesting.

"I told you I'd call you back." The girl trembled.

Kai tilted his head as he watched her, unsure if his presence alone affected her or whether her abusive girlfriend showing up caused her surge of emotion.

"You don't get to decide stuff, you stupid bitch."

Kai watched as the girlfriend reached Amanda and punched her in the face.

She gasped as the crunching sound vibrated across the room. Her hand went up to her nose, clutching it as blood poured out. "You…go back home."

Kai put the clothes on a nearby table and crossed his arms, waiting for the final blow he knew would come, but the image of Celina flashed through his mind.

I swear she will test my patience.

He took a few steps toward where Amanda lay on the floor and licked his lips at the sweet scent of her despair. It acted as a beacon for his kind—a drug they never got enough of. The look of terror in her eyes right before she lost consciousness satisfied him beyond words.

She's so close to the edge…I suppose that's enough, though.

Her girlfriend lifted her foot over Amanda's head, but Kai flicked his wrist, and she was thrown backward.

He approached the future murderer, a sneer on his face. "Such a pitiful human."

She glared for a few seconds before he licked his lips, the glow from his eyes reflecting off the mirrors. The girl scrambled to get away, but he chuckled at her pathetic attempt.

"No need to worry. It will be over soon enough." He breathed in the scent of impending death.

My favorite part.

She screamed when spiders crawled up her body, and as much as she tried to brush them away, they never stopped coming.

"My, my." He grabbed her chin and flicked one spider off. "There is quite an infestation in this store."

As soon as he let her go, they covered her face and entered her mouth as she screamed for help. Her body twitched as they ate her from the inside until nothing but her clothes and cell phone were left.

"Feast, my little ones."

He took the clothes he'd selected and walked out, the cheerful shop bell at odds with the scene inside as it rang above his head.

Kai sat on the bench next to the bus stop and let out a sigh of relief. It had been some time since he last killed, and the tension had worked its way into his muscles, stilling his usual freedoms. As the last grip of the ancient instinct ebbed away, he grinned and stretched, focusing his mind on the delicious death he'd witnessed.

This world is filled with monsters more terrible than demons. Humans are so amusing.

KNOW YOUR DEMONS

The setting sun filtered through the thin curtains hanging over the window. Celina stood, checking around in case Kai was hiding somewhere, but she was alone. She paused, stilling her every movement, waiting to hear the quiet sound of someone else breathing. Kai was a demon and could probably hide in plain sight. The unwelcome thought of the creature in the ceiling returned to her.

A crinkling sound caught her attention, and she reached into her back pocket, taking out the sketch of the playground. Tears filled her eyes, and she brought the paper against her chest, staring around as though Thomas would turn up.

Folding it, she slipped it back, wiping away at her cheeks.

Pain shot through her abdomen, and she gasped as she wrapped her arms around her waist. She curled into a ball, her body shivering with cold sweats as she took shallow breaths. Just as she opened her mouth to call out for help, the agony vanished, and she slumped to the floor, panting. Grinding her teeth, she stood, and her stomach rumbled.

I'm that *hungry? How long did I sleep?*

She went into the living room and spotted Kai on the sofa. His eyes were closed, and his breathing slow as if he was fast asleep. She tiptoed past his still form and dialed for room service.

"Steak, too."

At Kai's voice, her grip on the phone tightened, and her shoulders stiffened.

She glanced his way, but he hadn't opened his eyes. After she added his request to the order, she hung up. "I thought you were sleeping."

"I was, but I have fantastic hearing." He shifted into a sitting position, his body loose and casual, and faced her.

His red eyes stirred his revelation about her nightmares back to her mind, and she glared at him. "So, care to explain why you've been haunting my dreams and stalking me since I was a child?"

He shrugged, the merest lift of his shoulders. "We have plenty of time for that. You need only be patient, which I know can be difficult for humans. Now then, let us plot your revenge, shall we?"

The urge to debate filled her, to force him to answer her questions, but his glowing red eyes flashed brighter, changing her mind.

She'd ask later when he wasn't giving her the stare of death.

"Fine." She leaned against the counter in the kitchen area and crossed her arms.

"Your house is far from the city. You do not have neighbors for miles. No doubt the murderers had a car. Was there one anywhere near your house?"

"Not that I noticed, but they could've parked it down the road." A shiver coursed through her as Kai's question threw her back to that night. The smell of the cold air and damp earth filled the room, and she quashed bitter bile as it rose in her throat.

"Well, we will go out after we have eaten, and I will ask questions then."

"Ask questions? To who? About what?"

"A connection I have keeps check on everything morbid that happens in this area," he replied with a smile. "He may have information."

Their food arrived, but she was too concerned with Kai's plans to eat much. "I shouldn't have ordered this…" The scent alone made her stomach churn.

He pushed the plate closer to her, his eyes narrowing. "Eat to keep up your strength."

She gritted her teeth at being treated like a child but stayed quiet and forced some food down her throat. Everything that troubled her hardened her emotions, but it was for the best if it meant getting the revenge Kai promised.

Once they finished their meal, he opened the closet near the entrance of their hotel room. Hanging on the back of the door was a black, lacy dress. Panic flared through her as she took in the dress' length. It would barely cover her ass.

"That better be for you."

"I have my own clothes." He took it, running the fabric through his fingers, and narrowed his eyes. "We would stick out too much wearing what we have, and we do not want to do that where we are going."

"Where's that?"

"A goth club." He handed her the dress and his pupils dilated.

She opened her mouth to argue about the length again but closed it. Thomas would have told her she looked beautiful in anything. He reached into the bag hanging on one of the other hooks, and handed her black eyeliner, winking before reaching toward his own clothes.

She glared at him before stomping into the bathroom to change. The large mirror allowed her to see her entire body, and she twisted as she inspected every angle of the tight-fitting dress.

It's even more risqué than what I used to wear as a teen.

She moved closer and applied the eyeliner, laying it on thick. Her red locks fell on her shoulders, looking more vivid than usual as they contrasted against the black. She squinted at her reflection, her pale skin almost glowing in the brightness of the room.

A sigh escaped her as she wondered what Thomas would have said if he saw her in this style after so many years. She could almost hear him the night she'd worn a revealing dress before going out to a fancy restaurant.

He'd glided his fingers over her curves, his lips parted. "You look breathtaking."

Not wanting to reapply eyeliner if she cried, she clenched her jaw and left the bathroom.

She found Kai inside her bedroom and shrank away from him. Dressed all in black, he wore a long trench coat with belts along the sleeves, making him look intimidating. The demonic jet-black hair and red eyes matched perfectly with the whole style.

If people only knew it was all natural.

"A little short, no?" She glanced down at her dress, then to him.

Kai stepped in front of her and crouched, wrapping his long fingers around her bare legs and forcing a gasp from between her lips.

"I cannot see your undergarments; therefore, the answer to your question is no." He offered his words as a flat statement, and then he stepped back and smirked at her.

Her face warmed, and she glanced away, her hands clenched into tight fists at her sides to stop herself from hitting him. Kai took her elbow, but she yanked free.

"I don't need to be walked." She left the room without him.

Near the front door, she found a pair of knee-high boots and put them on. The skin at the back of her neck prickled as she felt Kai's gaze behind her, but she ignored him and walked out.

The May night air spread goose bumps over her bare arms and legs, brushing her skin as she walked next to Kai. She tugged on her dress, uncomfortable with the way a few people gawked at her. She felt naked compared to the jeans and hoodies she usually wore.

Kai stopped in front of a large building with flashing lights. The goth club, called The CrowBar, occupied a large section of the surrounding buildings. Music blasted through the double metal doors.

"Once we are inside, do not stray," he instructed in a steady tone before walking toward the door. The bouncer opened it for them despite the long line of people waiting to get inside the club.

Strobe lights and dry ice disoriented Celina. The dance floor was packed with people dancing close together. Every booth was occupied with people making out—some with more than two people and others more than just kissing.

She glanced at Kai, but something up ahead held his attention.

"What is it?" she shouted over the music.

"Stay right here." He spoke without looking at her and stalked away.

Not wanting to stay near the doorway, she treaded toward the bar. "Can I get you something?" the bartender asked.

She shook her head, giving a polite smile.

"Is Adam here tonight?" a girl next to Celina shouted to the bartender.

"In the back room, sweetie, but he's not seeing anyone. Discussing something about nasty business the other night. Break-in gone bad or something."

I lost my soulmate, and these people call that nasty business? Insensitive assholes.

She frowned at the bouncer blocking access to another section of the club. Odds were, they wouldn't let her waltz in.

Kai must be in the back room talking to this Adam guy. Is he going to make me wait here while he does everything?

Celina hastened back toward the door leading out. People still lined up to access the club, but she rushed along the outside wall of the building until she found what she sought —an alleyway. The buzz of the red neon light reading *Delivery* hummed in the darkness.

"Lost?" A stranger leaned against the building wall, the red neon light making him look eerie with his piercings and chains.

"Just looking for a friend, thanks." She repressed a grin at what Kai would say if he found out she'd referred to him as a friend.

"If he's in the back room, I can take you to him if you'd like."

"I'm fine, thanks." She stopped in front of the door before she turned toward the guy again at the sound of keys jingling.

"Door's locked." He straightened, strode to the door, and unlocked it. His dyed fire-red hair glowed brighter in the neon sign's effect. He stepped out of the way and gestured her to go in first.

"You're just gonna let me go in?"

He nodded.

She didn't ask further and stepped into the back of the club. The hallway to her left had a door at the end. The bar. Stairs descended to her right. The music was loud again, and she looked from left to right. Which way?

"If your friend is meeting with the owner, then they'll be down here." The guy started down the stairs.

She peeked down the long flight of steps, unable to see through the dark doorway at the end. A shiver of apprehension ran through her, and she ignored the twisting of her gut as she followed him down to Kai.

"Thanks for your help. Er, what's your name?" She hurried to catch up to him.

"Haku." He didn't look at her as he turned the third corner.

Her forehead moistened with sweat as downstairs turned out to be much more of a maze than she'd imagined. If she separated from Haku, she'd be lost down here.

"I'm Celina." The sound of the music faded as they moved farther down hallways.

"I'll be honest." He stopped and glanced over his shoulder with a grin. "I don't care to know my dinner's name."

Two nights before, she would have thought his remark was dark humor. But after everything she'd gone through with Kai, her muscles stiffened. She turned to run, but he grabbed her and dragged her down the corridor as a piercing scream worked free from her lungs and echoed from the walls.

Fuck!

He threw her into a smaller room and slammed the door behind him. Her gaze darted all around, her mouth dry despite swallowing several times. A woman leaned against the wall and stared at Celina with hunger in her eyes.

"Oh good, you found a stray," she said with a sneer. "You know how I love when you pick a female—my favorite."

"You love both males and females. I've seen the way you flirt." Haku grinned and glanced back to Celina. "Apparently she was looking for her friend, but I don't think that's true."

"It's true! And he'll come looking for me." Celina rubbed the goosebumps on her arms.

She refused to listen to the taunting voice inside her head, brushed aside the growing knowledge that Kai had been right.

I should have listened to him.

She grew cold as she pictured the possibilities. He might not save her, and she'd be left with Haku and his friend... or he could rescue her, and she'd face his anger. She shuddered. Neither one appealed.

"Well, we'll feast on him when he comes looking for you." The woman laughed. Her eyes glowed red, and her pointed teeth gleamed when she opened her mouth.

Haku approached Celina, his own eyes emitting a soft red glow. He pinned her against the wall, a sneer on his face just as his mouth hovered over her neck.

"You feed on demons, then?" Anything to distract them.

He drew away and studied her, his brow furrowing. "What?"

"I made a deal with one, and trust me, Kai won't be happy if you eat me."

"Kai?" The woman's voice trilled higher, and she moved closer. "Mekaisto?"

"That's him." The panic in the woman's voice stilled Celina's satisfaction for a moment. Fresh fear at the danger Kai presented trickled through her.

"Mekaisto doesn't make deals with humans." Haku glanced from Celina's face to her neck.

"There's one way to check." The woman grabbed his arm and shook him.

"I'm aware of how to check, Linda," He didn't take his gaze off Celina as he put his hand in front of her and passed it back and forth as if he held a metal detector.

His hand stopped, hovering over her gunshot wound. He'd found the brand left by the demon. He moved to lift her dress, but she kicked him hard in the leg and pushed him away. Linda grabbed her from behind and held Celina with ease as Haku grasped her dress and peeled it over her abdomen. She would have been a lot more pissed off except his eyes widened and he dropped the dress with a gasp.

"It's true then?" Linda whispered, letting Celina go.

"How could you make a deal with that monster?" Haku asked, observing Celina as he shrank back.

"He isn't just another demon, I take it?" she muttered. Her heart pounded harder at the terror Kai invoked in these demons. He'd mentioned demons feared him, and this was what he'd meant.

"Of course, he isn't," Linda murmured.

"So, what is he then?" The more terrified they became, the more Celina's curiosity burst.

"You made a deal with a demon you know nothing about?" Disbelief hardened his voice, and she flinched.

"Well, you don't keep online profiles, do you?"

"Did he tell you where he'll take you after he claims your life and soul?" Linda asked.

"I supposed it would be Hell."

"Hell? Mortals do love to invent their little idea of what horrible place awaits those who sin, but you haven't got the slightest idea." Haku gripped his hair as though wanting to rip it out. "Only the dark realm exists. A place where evil beings come from, a place without mercy run by a psychotic tyrant. Many, like us, leave that realm to get the fuck away from him." His footsteps echoed from the hollow walls as he paced the length of the room.

"Sounds like Hell to me," Celina said through gritted teeth.

Linda scoffed, but her gaze darted around the room. "Worse."

"Okay, so I'll be taken to a place run by a psychotic tyrant, but I—"

"Mekaisto *is* the psychotic tyrant."

"I believe I like that title," Kai announced from the corner of the room, where he leaned against the wall and studied his fingernails.

He looked up, his gaze coming to rest on Celina. She should have been terrified, but instead, calm washed over her. She trusted him not to break his deal by letting others have a taste of her. The two demons cowered at the opposite side of the room, staying silent.

He materialized in front of her.

"Did they hurt you? Do you wish for me to kill them?" Kai glared at the two demons, pinning them in place.

"They scared me, but by the way they're trembling, I'd say we're even."

He stared back at Celina, his eyes flashing and turning into angry slits. "I was clear about you staying where I left you."

"You don't get to order me around. Thomas was my husband, and I want to help." Her foot slid across the floor as she fought not to back away. She'd have to stand her ground so she wouldn't lose control of the situation.

He opened his mouth to say something, but the door opened, and he rolled his eyes as another demon entered. He was tall, and his hair curled above his ears. A business suit gave him an air of authority.

"Master," Haku and Linda spoke in a single, reverent tone as they bowed.

The newcomer glowered. "Terrorizing my children?"

"Not my fault, Adam, they were toying with my dove." Kai shrugged.

"Well, you've asked your questions and found your human." Adam's eyes glowed red. "I respectfully ask you to leave my club if your business is concluded."

"Repeat what you told me. Tell her, and then I will take my leave." Kai made his way to the two demons. They flattened themselves against the wall, their gazes on the floor as if to avoid staring at him.

"Tell me what?" Celina whipped her head toward Adam.

"A man by the name of Thomas Leviet came here inquiring about a religious group a little over two months ago. I told him I have no dealings with anything close to churches, but he wanted to know how to enter a certain section of an old church. I gave him a blueprint of the building in question. As for his murder, I have heard nothing about it. That's all."

Thomas came to this demon? Was that what had him worried the night they murdered him? Was that *why* he was killed?

No. It had to be a mistake.

Thomas would never have had any dealings with these…things.

"There must be a mistake. Why would Thomas come to you?" She glared at Kai and pointed an accusing finger at him, "Did you tell him to tell me this? Make me think my husband was a—"

"Are you accusing me of lying?" Kai matched her tone and expression. She doubted it was a fraction as petrifying on her face.

"Oh, because thinking a demon will lie is so farfetched." She crossed her arms and took another look around the room. The odds were against her, one human in a room with four demons. "Anyway, let's go."

She slipped around Adam, but he reached out to stop her, his fingernails digging into her flesh. Celina glanced over at Kai, whose jaw clenched and eyes narrowed, but he said nothing.

"Did you know Thomas Leviet? By the sound of it, you thought you did, but…"

He was hiding things from you, didn't want to talk about what was bothering him. The study he kept under lock and key…he had secrets.

"We're not talking about the same person."

"Brown hair, tall, strange mannerisms."

She yanked her arm out of his grasp. "You could be describing half the men in the city. Sorry if I don't take the word of a demon." Her mind focused on the demon's words as she jogged down the hallway, but she was forced to stop.

I don't know how to get back upstairs.

Adam couldn't have spoken of her husband. It was impossible. Then again, demons weren't supposed to exist, yet there she was with a few. Had Thomas been aware they existed? The phone call he'd received that evening; whoever called hadn't spoken to her on purpose.

Adam made his way onto her murder-suspect list.

"Celina?" Kai's voice resonated in the never-ending hallway.

She turned, and he approached her. "What?"

"I have no gain in lying to you. The—"

"I know!" She shouted the words but calmed herself before continuing. "Look, no matter what you tell me, I won't believe you. So don't bother trying to get me to trust you at all."

"That is a prejudiced mentality, no?"

"I don't care. You're taking my life and soul once we're finished with your plan, so it's hard to trust you."

"You made this deal by your own choosing." He took a step forward. "And the point of making the deal was that by being a demon, I can help you get revenge. If you will not trust me, then why did you agree to the deal?"

"You're the one who told me not to trust you when we first met."

"That was before we made the contract."

She didn't want to keep thinking of that night. What mattered was focusing on Kai's offer of avenging her husband.

But who did I make a deal with?

"So, you're the king of the other realm? The one we refer to as Hell?"

"Does that make a difference to you?"

She shrugged. "I suppose not." It was too late to second-guess her choices, but she'd make changes to their deal while she had his attention. "We have to make rules or something."

"Rules are made to be broken."

"I'm serious, Kai. I don't want to be left out of the loop. From now on, when you talk to…well, others on the subject of my husband, I want to be there."

"As you wish." He bowed a little, a smirk on his face.

"And another thing."

He sighed. "There would be more."

"Stop being so cryptic with me. You can't tell me that whole story about when I was ten years old and then turn into the crow from my nightmares with no further explanation." She crossed her arms, waiting for his answer.

His vertical pupils dilated. "I did not know you required further explanation."

"Well, I do."

"I was perched in the black tree when you broke the branch. I was there every time you came to talk to it. That is why I know the intimate details of your life. You shared yourself with me."

"And what about what those two demons said?"

"That depends on what they said."

"They told me you don't make deals with humans." She forced her voice to remain steady, her gaze to be constant. "But they wouldn't say why."

His glare burned hot as she spoke, but he said nothing. After a few moments of silence, she pressed on, even as his eyes threatened to ignite something.

"So? Is what they said true?

"Since those are answers that have nothing to do with our deal, I am not obligated to tell you."

"Fine, but if I'm not allowed personal questions, then neither are you."

"I do not ask personal questions. I go inside your head— so much more amusing."

She narrowed her eyes, her hands curling into fists as she followed him out of the maze-like basement.

"I'm going to bed. Tonight was too weird for my brain," she announced as soon as they entered the hotel room. Her head pounded and she blinked a few times, trying to get the black spots out of her vision.

"I find it strange Adam gave him a blueprint and let him get away." His eyes focused on a faraway spot in the distance.

She stopped in her tracks and spun. "What do you mean by *get away*?"

"People who do business with Adam know he is the creator of Sanguis demons."

"Sanguis demons?" She arched her eyebrows.

"A type of demon that feeds on blood and life energy. You met three tonight."

"Okay, but what do you mean, *get away*?" She took a step toward him, eyeing him as she repeated the question he'd sidestepped a moment earlier.

"When someone wants something from Adam, they know the prices for his services are steep."

"Steep? Like your prices?"

Kai stopped a few inches from Celina and bowed a little, so he was at eye-level with her. "As I said before, you made that deal of your own free-will."

"I'm not saying otherwise, just stating that taking my life and soul is a steep price."

"Is it?" he asked with a smirk that showed his pointed teeth. He put his hand on the back of her head and grabbed a fistful of hair.

She gasped a sharp intake of air.

"After you take revenge, there will be blood on your hands. Is it not fair to exchange what is most precious for the lives you take?"

"They started it by killing my husband." She spoke through gritted teeth, and her eyes welled with tears as his grip on her hair tightened and pain receptors fired all over her scalp.

"Perhaps your husband was the one who started it?" He released her, and she staggered.

"Never accuse him like that! You didn't know him, so you better shut your mouth."

He sighed a little and barely spared her a glance. "If your husband tried skipping out on his part of the deal, Adam may have hired people to kill him."

"Thomas wasn't—"

"The sooner you stop thinking your husband was a saint, the clearer your mind will be. Revenge takes clarity of thought."

When Celina flipped her impatient gaze at his face, he grinned.

"It will be faster."

She didn't buy his concern for her need to speed this. "You mean the faster you get my life and soul."

"Both." His answer, along with his deep chuckle, froze the air she breathed, tightening her chest.

Something bothered Thomas before they murdered him, and he'd been involved with demons. She hated to admit it, but there were things about him she didn't know. Why didn't she know? It chipped another piece of her already broken heart.

But more important was to discover what else her husband had hidden from her. More than likely, she'd find out the reason for his murder and the identities of the killers too.

Time to do some digging.

7

LIES AND DECEIT

The phone rang, and Celina kicked the tangled blankets off, almost missing the call.

"Hello?" Her voice cracked, still half-asleep.

"Good morning. May I speak to Celina Leviet?"

"This is she."

"I'm calling on behalf of Mr. Graull, the lawyer handling your husband's will."

Her chest tightened. She'd been so busy with demons, revenge, and Thomas' secrets, she forgot about the will. "Yes?"

"Mr. Graull wondered if it would be at all possible for you to come to his office this afternoon. I apologize for the last minute—"

"It's fine. Is one o'clock okay?"

"Yes. Thank you very much, Mrs. Leviet."

She trudged into the bathroom and entered the shower stall to wash away the smell of the nightclub. After what happened with Kai, she'd gone straight to bed without even taking off her clothes or makeup; eyeliner smeared under her eyes, giving her the hollow sockets of a skeleton. Her mind flashed back on the days when she'd embraced the goth life-style with this look.

Her knees wobbled, and she pressed her hands against the tiles, keeping herself upright.

Relax, or you'll pass out.

The hot water washed away her worries for a few minutes, at least. The idea her husband had contacted demons, knew about them, weighed on her mind. He'd hidden in another world while she, like the rest of humankind, had been oblivious to any existence outside her own. He'd never told her. How long had he kept this secret?

Celina snatched the towel off the glass door and wrapped the soft terry cloth around her.

"Humans take so long."

She spun to Kai and slipped on the wet floor. He caught her before she hit the cold hard tile, and his arms circled her waist as he pressed his body in closer than necessary.

"Stop sneaking up on me!" Heat spread over her chest, cheeks, and ears.

She retreated until she slammed into the bathroom countertop. Her gaze focused on her feet, desperate to concentrate on anything besides the fact he was much too close while she wore nothing but a towel.

Kai put his hands on either side of her and grinned. "You should be used to me by now."

"Getting used to a demon takes longer than a few days… much longer in your case." She tugged the towel higher.

He put his hand on her thigh then trailed higher, lifting the towel as he continued along the path. "I am certain you could get used to me."

Her cheeks burned. "Mekaisto, stop!"

Lust pulsed between her legs and moisture wet the tops of her thighs.

His fingers stilled, and he stared at her for a second before he backed away. "If you do not want to play, then what would you like to do?"

"Would you mind calling room service for some breakfast?" Her breath came in short, quick puffs.

Kai gave her a grin and left the bathroom.

What the hell was that?

Celina splashed cold water on her face, trying to regain her composure. She leaned over the sink, taking slow, deep breaths, her cheeks still burning.

I'm just confused. It won't happen again. I love Thomas. I won't betray him like that.

When she stepped out of the bathroom, Kai sat at the small kitchen table with a banquet spread over the top. "You did not specify what you wanted." He glanced at all the food with a cocky smile.

She couldn't help gasping at the sight of all the different breakfast items cluttered on the table as she sat in front of him. "I swear, if this all ends up on some rich guy's credit card and the police come looking for us..."

"I am neither a thief nor a beggar." His vertical pupils thinned, and he smiled. "I have enough assets to survive as a human for as long as I like, which has already been some time."

She stared at him. "Can I ask you a favor?"

He surveyed her, and she took his silence as a yes.

"Could you please stop sneaking up on me or coming into rooms without at least knocking first?"

"Why?"

"It's called personal space." She sighed. For claiming to be so well versed in the ways of humans, he had no clue as to simple human decency.

"Yes, and I take great pleasure in invading yours."

"I can tell," she replied. "Does that mean you won't grant me the favor?"

"It would not be good for you if I did."

"Why not?"

Kai leaned in across the table, and she pressed her back into her chair as his smile turned cold. "Revenge is a dangerous thing. There are times I will need to come into close contact with you to accomplish our deal."

"You weren't protecting me from anything in that bathroom." Her cheeks flushed at the memory.

He smirked. "When I take your life and your soul, I plan on invading all of your personal space. It would be better for you to get used to that now, so it will be less painful when your life ends."

"You plan on making me suffer?"

"It will be… painful for you, yes." He sat back down in his chair and grabbed a piece of toast. The way he said it sounded like there was a double meaning, and that he was playing with her head…again.

"Well, in that case," she paused for a moment, "please pass the bacon."

Celina blinked, unable to digest the number of zeroes in the amount she had to have heard wrong. "How much money?"

She sat in the lawyer's office next to a silent Kai, while he explained the situation. In his most human form, Kai wore a black suit, tailored to perfection to fit his body. It exaggerated his natural air of superiority, over-shadowing the lawyer in his own office. Celina wore a suitable mourning dress for the occasion, which he'd bought for her along with some other needed clothes.

"Four point five million dollars, Mrs. Leviet." Mr. Graull shifted in his seat. "Your husband put his inheritance money into a high-interest savings account."

"Inheritance? What inheritance?"

"He didn't tell you?" He looked surprised. "The dividends of his inheritance are the reason he never had to hold a job or work steadily."

"What do you mean, never held a job? He went to work every single day at the translating company *he* started." What kind of buffoon lawyer was this guy? Of course, Thomas worked. "He started his business when he was twenty-one. He never took a single day off during the week!"

Thomas would come home from work late and exhausted. But every Friday, he'd bring home a gift for her. Except for the day they murdered him…the day he wanted to celebrate her birthday by going out.

We should have stayed out all night. Stayed at a hotel. We'd still be together.

Deep down, she knew it was a lie. But at that moment, she hated herself for not suggesting a hotel.

"Mrs. Leviet." The lawyer's voice took her out of her spiraling guilt. "If your husband had started a company, there would be records. Papers on file with the province and the federal government. It would be a part of your inheritance, and we would have found it when we searched his assets." He eyed her with one cocked brow and his lips compressed into a tight line. "Do you have the address for his business?"

She pulled out one of Thomas' business cards from inside her purse, a heavy feeling weighing down on her. Her gaze focused on the lawyer's desk nameplate: James C. Graull.

The tap-tap of the keys as the lawyer's fingers glided over the keyboard in perfect time with her heart until it skipped a few beats. He turned his attention back to her, lines etched into the corner of his eyes.

"What?" Celina asked.

"I'm looking at records for this address, and only two companies rent there. The suite number you gave me doesn't even exist in that building. One is an environmental consulting company, and the other is an office of Statistics Canada." After a few more quick clicks of his mouse, he rotated the screen to show her the information.

Celina's world spiraled around her until the bottom fell out and she could do nothing but stare. After a few shallow breaths, she blinked her confusion away.

"I'm sorry, but I have to go." She stood and bolted for the door, not caring if Kai followed or not.

She had never gone into the suite where Thomas worked. Whenever she met him at work after she had shopped a little, he always had met her in the lobby.

The traffic zoomed past them on the busy street as she strode down the sidewalk.

Kai leaned in close to be heard over the noise. "You want to see for yourself?"

The amusement in his voice grated on her nerves. She glared at him over her shoulder. "Just don't, okay? For once, just shut up."

The more she learned about Thomas, the more she realized she hadn't known him at all. In the nine years since they'd met, he'd kept more secrets than she could count. Her stomach clenched as anger gripped her insides.

Dealing with demons. Inheriting money. And now a company that doesn't exist? What's fucking next?

Trying to outrun her own thoughts, she veered around other pedestrians who didn't have a demon following them like a shadow. The address circled in her mind, repeating itself like a mantra. Her gaze caught the golden numbers on the front of the building, and she stepped inside the familiar lobby.

Not bothering to wait for the elevator, she climbed the stairs to the second floor. Her footsteps echoed inside the quiet hallway as she glanced at the first unit number, passed the washrooms, then the last door.

No other doors. No Unit Three. No translating company.

Her neck prickled. The lawyer had no reason to lie, but she'd clung to the hope he'd been mistaken. She focused on the space between the two doors. Why had she never thought to visit him in his office as a surprise?

Of course, with their home being so far removed from the city, it had been easier to believe he'd gone to a job every day rather than her husband having been an epic liar.

The corners of Kai's lips curled. "Your husband kept secrets, dove."

Words couldn't come. Her heart squeezed inside her chest at another of Thomas' betrayals. Instead of taking Kai's bait and raging, she stalked past him and almost ran all the way back to the hotel.

She slammed the penthouse door behind her, her rage at the world unsatisfied by the crash of wood on metal as it closed under the sheer force of her fury. She'd sold her soul to a demon to get revenge for a common liar.

No, not common. An extraordinarily well-gifted liar.

To believe Thomas was anything else would cast her in the light of a simpleton, and that she was not. No. She hated Thomas. She'd been a fool to trust him so blindly. What was it her mother said? *Don't trust people. They will always disappoint you."*

Fine time for her to realize her mother was right.

She grabbed her purse and took out the sketch of the play structure and swing set they'd drawn. Holding it on each side with both hands, she gritted her teeth as her fingers jerked, but didn't tear it.

With a frustrated scream, she rammed it back in her purse and turned to the phone instead. She ordered a bottle of rye whiskey from room service, determined to have a moment of rest or to drown herself in the bottle trying.

Kai walked in as she broke the seal on the bottle.

He stood next to her. "What are you doing?"

"Oh, don't worry, crow boy. I'm not trying to kill myself." Her bitter laugh burned in her throat.

What happens if I don't want revenge anymore?

He snatched the bottle from her hand and poured it down the drain.

"What the hell are you doing?" She tried to grab it from him but stepped back when a crack fissured a small part of the wall in front of her.

Celina sighed. Her will to fight, along with the cool amber liquid, seeped down the drain. She threw herself on the sofa as a painful emptiness spread through her chest.

"Suicide will taint your soul, and while I'd be allowed to claim it, that's not how I want it." Kai's footsteps resonated through the room as he stepped in front of her and looked down with a scowl.

Not that he would care, but she needed to talk, get it all out. "I made that fucking deal with you for nothing."

"You had no choice. Only your motives have changed. And you'll get answers about your husband you never would have otherwise. It's not a bad deal when you consider you'd have died as an oblivious, trusting wife with visions of Thomas' murder clouding your white light of death."

She had no one, except a demon—a *demon*—to share her troubles with.

"Where did he go all these years? I mean, I've watched TV, seen the movies where the husband pretends to go off to work every day, but instead is running off to see his other family. I'm not stupid. Or maybe I am. Maybe I should have seen, realized he was keeping me locked up out there. And you know what else?"

She sat up and looked at Kai, whose eyes narrowed at her question.

"He hid the money he was just going to give me anyway. Does that even make sense? Why not just tell me? It's not like I could've spent it. He never let me go anywhere."

The words poured out of her. And without Thomas, she would never get any answers to the thousands of questions his death sprung upon her. She raked her fingers through her hair, wishing she could grab Thomas and shake the answers from him.

"It's—"

"And you. You made that deal knowing Thomas was a lying bastard. You knew! How could you not since you've been stalking me forever?"

Kai stayed silent as he sat next to her.

She clenched her jaw, her teeth gritting. "You're almost as big a piece of shit as Thomas." As soon as her fury took hold, it ebbed, and she leaned forward, her elbows on her knees. "Oh, God. I thought he loved me."

"It was a simple lie. It doesn't mean he—"

"Simple lie?" She shook her head. "It doesn't matter. A lie is a lie."

"People hide things all the time. It doesn't mean he didn't love you."

"And what the hell do you know about it? You talk about love like you understand the concept," she poked a finger into his chest, "but all you understand is hate and fear, rage and terror. You're a fucking demon. Stop trying to pretend like you're a friend."

Getting to her feet, she paced a few steps, her hands pressed against the sides of her head. She grabbed a glass ornament on the table beside her and hurled it against the wall. It smashed, and glass splintered across the floor. She glanced at Kai but focused her stare back on the shattered pieces to avoid looking at the danger lurking behind his eyes. Biting the inside of her cheek, she cursed herself for letting him see her outburst.

Way to lose your shit in front of him.

Celina shuffled forward to clean up the mess but stepped

on a shard of broken glass. She dropped to the floor and gasped at the shooting stab of pain in her foot.

Kai stood with a sigh and crouched in front of her. "Humans are so sensitive about such small matters." He took her foot in his hands and gently removed the sliver of glass.

"That hurts!"

"I imagine it does." A smile appeared on his lips.

She held her foot, wincing at the worsening sting. Blood stained her palm when she pulled her hand away. Kai took her hand in his, glancing between the blood smear and her eyes. Hunger burned behind his blackened irises as he brought her wrist up, closed his eyes, and licked the blood from her hand.

She struggled to pull away, but he tightened his grasp. When he opened his eyes, chills ran through her body. He'd reverted to his demonic appearance. His vertical pupils glowed red as he continued cleaning away the blood.

He took her foot into his lap, and the throbbing stopped.

"Why me, Kai?" She needed to hear him say it.

"You broke my tree and then tried to fix it." A sweet smile at odds with his appearance curved his lips. "It drew me to you. And now, I want to return the favor." His fingers trailed up the inside of her thigh, disappearing under her dress.

Tears welled up in her eyes. "Then why are you trying to break me?"

"Only to fix you, over and over again." Kai pulled her in and kissed her so gently tears streamed down her cheeks faster. She pushed him away, and he withdrew, gazing at her without blinking.

He scooped her into his arms and carried her to the bedroom. Celina faded in and out, emotions numbing her body. Once he put her on the bed, he stepped toward the door. "Sleep now."

"Kai," she called out. "Will you stay? Just until I fall asleep?"

Even after he forced a kiss on her, she couldn't face the night alone. The bed shifted as he lowered his body next to her. She concentrated on the glowing red of his eyes, trying to escape the turmoil in her own mind.

8

———

TIME

C elina had drifted to sleep, but Kai continued to stare at her. Her eyes flickered from time to time, as though dreaming of horrible things, and he grinned at the idea that it was one of the nightmares he had implanted in her mind when she was just a child.

Another pang of that nameless feeling swept over him, but he pushed it aside. He bent low, his black hair sweeping along her neck as he kissed her forehead. He shut his eyelids tight as she let out a small sigh, and his fingers glided over her body, instincts urging him forward.

His hand curled, his sharp fingernails digging into his flesh, and he withdrew quietly.

Something needed to be taken care of, but he'd only leave her while she slept.

The trip through the air took only a few minutes since the hospital was nearby. He landed on a windowsill, inspecting the surroundings. The parking lot lay bare of vehicles; many had left, and only a few remained on the night shift.

This is always much too easy.

Kai walked through the front doors in his human form so as not to attract attention and stepped into the elevator. The basement could only be accessed by key, but that didn't stop him; locks were never a problem. He pressed his finger against the keyhole and a spark illuminated the button with the letters 'B/SS.'

Down he went.

The doors opened at the end of the descent, and he sent his darkness ahead to fill the long corridor. He walked forward, his footsteps echoing while the cameras and lights burst, sparks of electricity flashing around him.

The coroner was on break, and no other humans were inside the morgue at this hour, except for the dead ones.

Adam.

The demon materialized next to him and bowed. "Yes?"

"Your children have been neglecting their duties." Kai grabbed a few files on the desk and shuffled through them. "Many of their contracts have come to an end, yet the victims still have their souls. They belong to us."

"Apologies, Mekaisto, but—"

Kai straightened and stared Adam down. "Are you going to make excuses for them? How pathetic."

Adam stiffened and glanced away. "I apologize on their behalf. I'll be sure they collect no later than tomorrow night."

"I have been informed that you no longer send Haku and Linda to Shiriki."

"They always come back so...maimed." He looked back up with pleading eyes. "It takes me weeks to heal them. They don't ever recover fully from his experiments."

Kai took a step forward, one of the medical forms still clutched in his hand. "He is my second in command. To disobey orders from him is unwise, Adam." He leaned forward. "Could it be that you are becoming attached to your children?" His lips curled into a sneer. "How sentimental of you. Though I suppose it would make sense. Having once been human has always been a Sanguis demon's biggest weakness."

"You seem sentimental for that human female." As soon as he finished his sentence, Adam's eyes widened, and he bowed low. "I...I apologize, Mekaisto, it wasn't my place to say."

Kai brought the death certificate up higher and stared at the name of Celina's murdered husband. A sigh escaped him. "You are not wrong."

Adam glanced up, sweat beading down his face. "I—"

"You have a new child, no? Denzel, I believe his name is?"

"Please, Mekaisto, if it's punishment you want to inflict, don't—"

"Silence." The room shook, and the Sanguis demon pressed his lips together. "Send Denzel to me during the next royal court."

"He's still young and doesn't understand the hierarchy of power. He spends his time fighting with Haku and Linda or running away from me."

"Then this will be my opportunity to...train him." Kai's smile turned cruel at the thought of breaking in a new demon; it had been far too long since he'd had that pleasure. "Now, get out of my sight. And be sure to let your child know what happens to those who keep me waiting."

Adam bowed and vanished as Kai returned his attention to the paper. A few notes here and there, a fake signature, and the body was ready to be released. He couldn't wait anymore. For the first time in his existence, time mattered, and he only had so long.

Everything had changed that day, and the clock ticked for him...and for Celina.

9

SUSPECTS

Once the morgue released Thomas' body, Celina contacted the crematorium. He'd always been emphatic over his wishes for cremation rather than burial. *"We all have to burn someday,"* he'd said with a grin, referring to her aunt's belief that all non-believers would burn in Hell.

She arranged the funeral as quickly as possible, unable to cope with any of it well. She'd go home to scatter the ashes on their property, but not too soon.

The service was open to friends and family, but the showing room was sparsely populated. The few people who came to pay their respects presented themselves as clients he'd met through business dealings.

I guess he'd been doing business somewhere or under the table.

Kai stood by her from the beginning, but she was more uncomfortable around him since the night he kissed her.

He leaned toward her ear. "Given any thoughts to your next step?"

She glanced toward him while his gaze flitted from one person to the next in the room. "Already planning whose soul you'll go after next?"

He leered at her, a vicious smile on his lips. "I plan on

enjoying you for an eternity. I will have no need of other souls beyond yours."

She sighed and turned away from him. "Charming."

Her back muscles tensed when her aunt came in among the new arrivals. Celina called her a day before the service, not wanting to argue with her. Aunt Marie loved pushing her beliefs onto other people and talking death with her would have left Celina angrier than a demon who missed out on his meal.

"Celina. Good to see you." Marie gave her a small nod but narrowed her eyes at Kai.

"Oh, this is an old friend. Kai." Celina's gut wrenched as she presented the demon destined to take everything she had left as an old friend. "Kai, this is my aunt on my mother's side, Marie."

"Pleasure." A smirk tilted his lips.

She fought the urge to nudge him, clamping her arms at her sides to hide the frivolous rebuke that didn't belong at a funeral.

He's dead. It's real now.

She reached into the side pocket of her purse where she'd stuffed their playground sketch. Rubbing the paper between her fingers, she let out a quiet exhale; she'd almost ripped it up out of anger. Something she would've regretted forever since part of her felt as though it still connected her to him.

"It's been some time since we've had a long chat."

Celina remained unfazed by Marie's dry tone and raised eyebrows. "I've been busy."

Kai gave a small smile. "If you'll excuse me?" He gave Celina's elbow a slight squeeze and moved away to the guest book.

"Well, since I never see you anymore, I thought I'd bring this today." Her aunt took a large envelope out of her purse and shoved it into Celina's hands.

Curious, she opened it. A familiar pendant and a strange

red stone fell into her palm. She lifted them, reading the identical tags; both showed the year her parents died.

Celina's mother had given the pendant to her when she was nine and had told her she had to wear it when leaving the house. The day her mother borrowed it to go out, Celina lost her pendant…and her parents.

I haven't even thought of it since that day. Has it been this long already?

Imagined memories flowed through her mind; what her life could've been like if they hadn't died. With a sigh, she focused on the items, pushing the past back where it belonged.

She didn't recognize the red stone. A darker red shape jutted from it. She peered closer and swiped her thumb over the smooth red surface. A button. She shook her head as all the urban myth warnings she'd ever heard returned to her at once. *Never press the red button.*

When she put them both into the envelope again, she noticed a folded piece of paper with an address in the downtown area and the word *located* scribbled in her mother's handwriting. She placed the envelope in her purse, determined to research further when she got the chance.

One investigation at a time.

"After the accident, I kept them since I became your guardian, and you weren't to have those until you turned eighteen. I've been packing old things in the last few months and found them. Seems like your husband's funeral was the only time I could give them to you."

"Thanks." Celina gritted her teeth to stop further words pouring forth. The kind that would sully Thomas' funeral.

It wasn't his fault my family was weird.

Kai made his way back toward them with an innocent smile, though she had a feeling he'd been listening in the whole time.

Marie acted as though no one had joined them. "It's a shame you didn't make proper service arrangements for your husband. I could have helped with that if it was a matter of knowing what to do, you know. I—"

"My husband was an atheist. It wouldn't be right to go against his wishes."

This is what I have left now that you're gone, Thomas: my aunt and a demon.

Marie raised her head higher, narrowing her eyes. "I wasn't too surprised to hear about *how* Thomas passed away."

"What's that supposed to mean?" Celina's chest ached as heat rose through her.

"Well, people who don't believe in God often lose their way, and evil finds—"

"How dare you speak about Thomas like that? He was a good man."

Grief and rage flowed through her heart until Celina was sure her whole being would break from the pain.

"I'm afraid not, dear. By not accepting the word of God, he chose the dark path."

"There is no God." Celina enjoyed the red shade her aunt's face took when her speech was interrupted. Just like old times.

"You'll be joining your husband in Hell, I see."

"There's no Hell either, Marie." Her hands clenched at her sides, and her stomach rolled as she battled her exasperation.

Kai chuckled. "He's not in the dark realm."

Celina's mouth dropped open, and she wanted to kick his ankle to shut him up.

"Ah, are you another one who doesn't believe in the truth of God, then?" Marie studied Kai from head to toe.

"God exists, but not in the way you might think. When you die, you rest. You feel the surrounding warmth, the peacefulness, and although you'll see none of your loved ones again, you know they're safe. Well, it's what I've been told by an old friend." He shrugged one shoulder.

"Are you mocking me, sir?" Her voice climbed higher, and her face became redder. She'd be the queen of the red light district if she became any more animated.

"No, I'm telling the truth."

Marie fidgeted with the cross around her neck. "You know, Thomas came to my church about two months ago, asking questions. He, too, mocked our faith."

"Wait. Thomas was at your church?" Celina leaned close, her heartbeat pulsing in her ears.

More secrets. This was becoming too much for her.

"As I said, mocking us. And if you plan on keeping this kind of company, your soul won't have the chance to be saved."

"While I appreciate your concern for me by insulting the man I loved," she gritted her teeth, "and who was murdered in front of me, you don't need to worry." Aiming for the darkest smile she could muster, she added, "I already sold my soul to the devil."

Her aunt's eyes widened, and she glanced at Kai. Without another word, she moved away, and Celina sighed.

"Interesting choice of words." Kai's voice tickled her ear as he pressed closer.

"Well, I didn't lie." She tried shrugging off the effects of his scent, but she could almost taste it. "Humans would consider the dark realm as Hell, and since you're the king, that makes you the equivalent to what we refer to as the devil."

Kai chuckled as though amused by her way of thinking.

A few more people came over to pay their respects while she continued to force a smile. She attempted to mingle with the few people who had bothered to come when she grew tired of standing in the same spot and looking like a sideshow for the pitying masses. A small snort forced itself from her.

Pitying masses…not with only six attendees.

She wandered to the entrance, hoping to catch some fresh air, when her friend, Namika, stepped in front of her.

"Hisashiburi," she said. *Long time, no see.*

Celina hugged her, memories of their youths flooding her mind as a dam broke. Tears ran down her cheeks as she tried recalling the last time they'd seen one another; too long.

Namika held her tight and sniffed loudly. "I'm so sorry for your loss."

She tried replying with thanks, but it came out as a muffled sob.

Her friend rubbed her back, and after a few minutes, they drew away to look at each other. Celina wiped underneath her eyes and smiled. "How long has it been?"

"About four years." She placed her hand on Celina's arm and squeezed a little. "The last time was at the get-together when you brought…" Namika paused. "Your husband." Her lips curled in the same pity smile on the lips of every other person in the room. Somehow, hers instilled Celina with warmth absent from the others.

She glanced toward the large window at the far end of the room, the sunlight bathing Thomas' urn in golden light.

Like his eyes.

"How did you know?"

Namika gestured to where Marie stood. "Your aunt told me."

"How have you been?" Celina changed the subject. Talking about Thomas only raised her pulse and plunged her into a well of despair.

"I came back from Japan a few months ago, visited family."

When they'd met, Namika had just moved to Canada.

Despite how timid she'd been at first, they became the best of friends.

"That must have been nice."

"I'm also doing my Master's degree in business."

A pang of jealousy ran through Celina, but she smiled. "So, you've been busy." She had wished to attend university after high school, but after meeting Thomas, so many things seemed to be in the way. "I'm happy for you, following your dreams like this."

"I suppose you'll be free to do what you want, now," she said quietly as she glanced toward the urn. "I mean…"

"What?"

"Well, I always thought—and I'm sorry for saying this, I really am—but I always thought we lost touch because of your husband. I mean, once you two got married and he sealed you away in that house in the middle of nowhere, it was almost like he was keeping you…well, prisoner or something." Namika bit her lower lip and fell silent.

Celina narrowed her eyes and was about to retort something nasty about Namika not knowing Thomas, but it would have been a harsh judgment to deliver when she learned something new each day herself.

Instead, she shook her head and smiled. "It was my dream house. He built it for me. I wasn't a prisoner there. I was happy."

"But every time I called, if he answered, you were too busy or just unavailable. And when you picked up, it always sounded like you wanted to meet, but then you'd call later to say it wasn't a good time. It was weird."

Celina wasn't sure what to say anymore. She'd wanted to go out at first since she was so sheltered in her dream house, but every time she tried, Thomas always said something that changed her mind.

Flustered by the memories, she glanced about for Kai, the only part of her life that kept her steady. A sudden feeling of heaviness expanded from within her core, and she was appalled by her own feelings. But the truth was Kai was the only one she had.

Is that so bad?

"I should go back."

"I'm sorry, I didn't—"

"It's fine," She smiled. "It was so good to see you. Thanks for coming."

But despite her sudden acceptance of her fate, a part of Celina sank; this would be the last time they'd speak.

At least I got to see her.

Celina returned to the main room with a heavy sigh. She shouldn't have left it in the first place. Her gaze returned to the urn, and she plunged her hand back into her purse, grasping their sketch and trying to hold on. As she moved to the small table covered with a white cloth, she took out the piece of paper and unfolded it with trembling hands. A playground they'd never build together for a child they would never have.

Her stomach knotted as she tried picturing what he or she could have looked like. Would their child have his light-brown hair or the red hair she'd inherited from her mother? She seemed to lose the ability to fill her lungs as she pictured Thomas' hazel eyes looking into their child's face. Her hands curled around the paper, but before she did more damage, she folded it and placed it back into her purse.

She spun, her gaze met with Kai's, and she uttered a soft curse. He'd probably searched her mind at some point and found out everything she'd been thinking.

"Everything all right?" His hand rested at the small of her back, applying gentle pressure.

She rolled her eyes. "Oh, yeah. It always is, isn't it?"

That's right, search inside my head. I hope you drown in your own curiosity.

He chuckled, and she pressed her lips together.

"Mrs. Leviet?"

She lifted her attention from Kai. "Yes?"

A man wearing a shiny suit and expensive-looking shoes smiled, and she pasted on one of her own as she'd done throughout the service. "I'm sorry for your loss. I worked with Thomas, and he often spoke of you with such fondness. I'm sorry we have to meet under these circumstances." He took her hands in his and squeezed.

"I'm sorry, but what's your name?" Celina pulled away and smiled. She'd gotten used to Kai's touches, but she wouldn't be tolerating it from any others.

"Oh, I'm sorry. I told you I worked with your husband but never introduced myself. My name is David Corval."

"Well, I hate to inform you, but my husband never had a real business. He lied." A sob caught in her throat, stealing her breath as she took out her frustration on this perfect stranger.

I'm pathetic... taking it out on someone who had nothing to do with this whole mess.

David's head snapped back, his reaction as fake as the smile she'd kept plastered on her face all day. "I don't know what to say. I'm sorry to hear that, and I am, of course, surprised."

"What kind of business dealings did you have with my husband?"

"Your husband worked as a translator. Or, well, I thought he did. The matter was delicate." His hard smile showed he wouldn't speak about it further.

"I understand." *More flies with honey.* "Would you mind me asking when the last time you saw my husband was? Or heard from him?"

"I believe I saw him about three weeks ago. He gave me what I asked for, the information I needed to have translated that is, and that was it."

"Well, thank you for coming today. I'm sure Thomas would appreciate it."

"Of course." He reverted to his original charming self. All traces of animosity faded. "If you ever need to talk or you're just lonely…" He took a booklet from his pocket and wrote something on it. "Don't be shy to call. It wouldn't be rare for a widowed woman to need comfort." He finished with a smile and handed her a card with a phone number scrawled on it.

After David moved on, Celina's hands shook as they curled into fists, crumpling his card into a small ball. "Who the hell flirts with the widow at a service?"

Kai remained silent, but the fury in his gaze as he stared at the man didn't escape her notice.

David spoke with Marie, but his smartphone rang, disturbing the quiet of the room. The businessman strutted away, talking rapidly.

"I'm gonna go talk to my aunt for a minute."

Her aunt stood alone, shoulders slumped and back hunched.

People moved toward the exit, and she grabbed her aunt's arm before Marie could do the same. She jerked free, glaring at Celina and brandishing the cross around her neck. The room was empty, save for Celina, Kai, and her aunt.

"If what you say is true, then you've got the devil in you, just as your mother had, and will join her in Hell." She took a few steps away.

"I wouldn't be so concerned where others end up. You, however, will make it there." Kai's eyes twinkled with mischief.

"Who—?"

"That's a small detail. Where did you get that cross, Marie?" He reached out and Marie jerked back, her eyes wide with horror.

Darkness emanated from him, and Celina backed away

until she bumped into the wall. He didn't look so pleasant now, even in human form.

"I—"

"Didn't that belong to Audrey?"

"Audrey?" Celina repeated.

"When your eldest sister was discovered to be homosexual, you disowned her. It brought shame on your family, a shame for which Audrey killed herself." He waved his hand, and the door slammed shut. The color drained from Marie's face, the cross in her hand shaking. "You were raised thinking if you believe in God and push your beliefs on people, you will go to what humans call heaven." An ominous chuckle bubbled in his throat.

Celina couldn't believe her ears. "Did my mother know about this?" She stared at her aunt as though seeing her for the first time.

"She had a tolerance of sin," Marie spat.

Why hadn't her mother ever told her Audrey's death hadn't been natural? The tenants of Yonah Church were anti-suicide; had that been why she'd hid the truth from her?

"Did you think you could get away with encouraging Audrey to commit suicide and not have your soul tainted from it?" Kai tilted his head to the side as he always did when something seemed to baffle him. "I'll be sending my most vile demons to collect you, Marie Anne Tayen."

Her aunt scurried from the room as if all the atheists of the world were on her heels.

"Are you insane?" Celina shouted at him.

"Perhaps. But as your aunt is well-known as a religious fanatic. I doubt telling people the devil threatened her will help her cause."

"Yes, fine, but what was the point?"

"To show you that if your aunt was tainted enough as a teenager to encourage her own sister to commit suicide, perhaps ordering a murder isn't so farfetched. Your husband came to see her at her church—something you mentioned as strange, considering he was an atheist. Meaning there was a connection between your aunt and him."

"Valid points." She glanced at the door her aunt walked out of as unease trickled through her.

What the hell were you hiding from me for so long? Was everything you told me a lie?

10

HINTS FROM THE PAST

C elina and Kai walked into the police station and were immediately assaulted by sound—the shouting at police officers, footsteps pacing against scarred tiles. Nothing had changed since the last time she'd been there, after her parents' deaths.

A desk sergeant directed Celina and Kai to a seating area to wait for an officer. Celina wrung her hands in her lap. She wanted to get this whole thing over with.

"I wonder if they have any suspects yet." She said it more to herself than to Kai and jumped at the sound of his voice.

"Have you given any thought to that?"

She straightened. "That?"

"How you'll get your revenge if the authorities find the murderers first?"

"Why the hell would I have to worry about that? Even if they're in prison, you'd be able to get to them. Locks and doors don't stop you." Her tone grew as deadly as she could manage.

With a cocky smile, he glanced down the hall, and she followed his gaze. The officer who'd been at her house, Blake, strode toward them.

"Mrs. Leviet, please follow me."

Celina and Kai stood.

"Just Mrs. Leviet." He pinned Kai back with a look.

"I'll be right back." She gave Kai a weak smile, hoping he'd stay and behave.

"This way." Blake waved her toward a door down the corridor and Celina trembled at the thought of doing this without Kai's strength pressing her forward. She wished he'd be there with her; he'd become an anchor of sorts.

At the thought, she shook her head. Needing him didn't mean anything. She was just used to having him around ever since her life fell apart.

Once inside the small office, Blake closed the door behind them and sat at his desk. She sat across from him, reading the posters about safety and laws.

"Your friend called us with your new contact information." Suspicion rang in his voice. "I asked to speak with you, but he said you were still sleeping."

"I've slept a lot the last few days. My emotions have me a little overwhelmed."

Can you blame me?

"Understandable." Though his tone said he didn't mean the sentiment.

"Have there been any developments in my husband's case? Any suspects?" She leaned forward.

Blake crossed his arms. "I'm afraid I can't discuss that with you, Mrs. Leviet."

Fury pumped through her blood, but instead of lashing out, she lowered her eyes and looked at the silver ring still circling her finger. "Of course. I'm sorry."

"Was anyone else at the house the day of the murder?"

"No." She clasped her hands together. "I thought I was here to write my statement, not be questioned again." She cringed at the thought of writing the experience of it all, but to be questioned again would kill her. Celina shuddered at the mental image of the body bag in her living room and pressed her lips together.

"We go over things when details don't match up." Officer Blake leafed through the pages of a big white binder marked with a case number on its spine.

"Don't match up?" Afraid he might hear her heart hammering against her chest, Celina took a shallow breath and steadied herself.

"Your friend, Kai, was there not long after we arrived. You stated you called him after you called 9-1-1, yes?"

"Yes." Her body shook. Had they found proof she lied when she gave her statement? She was planning a murder, so in the best interest of staying off their radar, she kept her face blank, her eyes clear and wide.

"We've checked your phone records, and after the 9-1-1 call, no other calls were made. You said you didn't have a cell phone."

Celina fidgeted in her seat. She'd thought of the lie on the spot when Kai appeared, and she hadn't done it well. If they arrested her, the plan for revenge would fail. Would Kai free her? Would she be forced to run from the law while trying to make her dream of avenging Thomas' death come true?

Remaining silent wouldn't help. "I don't understand how that could be. There must be a mistake."

"I'll be frank with you, Celina—may I call you Celina?" When she nodded, he continued. "I don't think you murdered your husband, but I know you're lying. You're hiding something."

Yeah, I'm alive because of a demon.

"Should I be talking to a lawyer?" Sick and tired of the whole thing, she simply wanted to get on with the plan, and with the police on her case, it would be a lot more difficult.

The phone on his desk rang, and he answered. Always uncomfortable when people spoke on the phone in front of her, as though eavesdropping on a private conversation, Celina looked away, pretending not to listen.

"What do you mean? Are you sure?" Blake's voice shook, and Celina straightened in her chair. "Yes. Thank you."

He hung up and stared at her, a faint red creeping up in his cheeks.

"That was my partner. I don't know what happened here, but we received a second report from the phone company, and…we were wrong. The call is on there."

Oh, Kai. What did you do?

"Technology isn't always foolproof. Mistakes happen. It's fine." She tried balancing between understanding and insult, so he'd know she hadn't appreciated being called a liar.

Even though I am. Thomas would be proud…

He nodded and pushed a lined sheet of paper in front of her. "Once you finish writing your statement, you're free to leave. Would you prefer being alone?"

She nodded as she grabbed the pen and wrote as Blake stood and left his office.

Celina returned to the waiting room and gave an almost imperceptible shake of her head at Kai's over-innocent smile. As soon as they stepped out of the police station, she whirled to face him. "How the hell did you do that?"

"There's little I can't manipulate."

"Okay, but how did you know what was going on?"

"A deal between a human and a demon is physical, dove. I can access your mind from a great distance." He surveyed her, a small smile curling his lips. "I could sense your discomfort and fear, and I acted."

"I thought we talked about you staying out of my head?" She huffed out a sigh. "You're lucky I needed you."

He took a step closer, his smile changing from sweet to malicious. "Do I get a reward?"

Celina rolled her eyes and continued walking to her car. "Now that this is done, what's next?" She was tired of waiting. Ever since going to see Adam, every detail she discovered added another layer of mystery to her husband's murder. She had more questions than answers.

"For now, I recommend you go to the hotel. I have business to attend to in my realm."

She drummed her fingers on the car door. "Now?"

"You can always go scatter your husband's ashes," he suggested and then vanished.

Celina cursed. Reaching inside her purse, she frowned when the envelope her aunt handed her at Thomas' service brushed against her fingers. She took it out and stared at the three lines of a script—an address.

But to where?

She popped open the door and climbed inside her car. The street name was well-known, so she turned the ignition key and drove off.

She pulled up in front of a seven-story high rise.

Hmm. Security guards at the door.

She'd come this far, and she wouldn't let them stop her. Not now. She had too many questions, not enough answers, and she wouldn't get any sitting out in the car whining over this one tiny obstacle.

Looking down at her purse, she debated whether to drag it inside with her, when a guard tapped on her window. "Can I help you?"

Celina stepped from the car, not sure what she expected to find here. As she grasped for an explanation, the guard pulled a wand from his back and swiped it in front of her. He turned, hurried back to his post, leaned down, and whispered something to the other man. Without a word, they each opened a door, and the one who'd checked her for weapons motioned her inside.

Baffled, she hesitated for a moment and then hurried past before one or both changed their minds.

The lobby had been decorated right out of the Victorian

Era. Light-red carpets highlighted the crimson tones in the mahogany furniture. The bright blue and red wallpaper clashed with the furnishings but seemed to pull together the look the decorator had gone for.

The doors whooshed shut behind her. Something about this place was unnatural, but she couldn't figure what had the hairs on her arm standing at attention. A grandfather clock ticked nearby. She imagined she heard whispers, but when she spun to look, the space was empty.

Her stomach churned as her vision spun, the whole room blurring as though trying to merge. She reached out to the side and grabbed hold of an armrest, steadying her breathing as her muscles weakened.

Footsteps echoed in the hall behind an archway, and a woman sauntered in. Her dark gray hair, tied in a tight bun, reminded Celina of an old school teacher she'd once had. She wore an old-fashioned dress, matching her to their surroundings. Her small eyes fixed on Celina.

"I'm sorry to bother you, but I'm here to see the person who lives in the room—" Celina bit off the end of the sentence as the old woman's eyes widened, but she nodded and raised a wrinkled hand to point to the flight of stairs.

By the time Celina reached the third floor, her heart pounded in her chest, the dim light sending eerie shadows along the walls.

The address had a small number sign with a seven next to it. Each floor had a single, numbered door at the end, so she stopped at the top floor.

The walls here, all crafted of dark wood, had paintings hooked at random intervals, while the carpets were the same light-red as downstairs. Constant whispers wafted up the stairwell.

After a few courage-gathering and calming breaths, she knocked on the door.

It swung open, and a pair of gray eyes gazed back at her.

The man had shoulder-length, light-blond hair, and appeared about the same age as Kai, though that meant little.

"Hello." Oh, why hadn't she thought this through? At least considered what to say when she arrived. "This might sound weird, but I—"

He opened the door wider. "You're here for information, no?"

She crossed her arms and stepped forward.

More red and blue wallpaper hurt her eyes, clashing with the same color, but differently patterned carpet covering the floor. He ambled over to ancient filing cabinets lining the walls, pushing spider webs out of his way while she waited near the door. Searching through the drawers, he appeared to be trying to find the right documents. From time to time, something within earshot creaked and shut again.

He returned with a thick notebook and opened it. "What information do you require?"

"Someone gave me a note with your address. They found it in my parents' car after they died in an accident. My mother's name was Elizabeth Tayen and—"

He snapped the notebook shut and his eyes bored into hers. He said something in a language she didn't understand, a language that shook her whole body.

This is all wrong.

"I'm sorry to have bothered you." Celina turned to leave but froze when he slammed his hand on the door, holding it shut.

Her heart leaped into her throat and she spun around, shrinking back. His pupils were vertical, and the irises had transformed from dull gray to reflective silver. His hair, pure white.

"How ironic that you would come on your own." He sniggered.

"You're a demon." Her voice cracked.

Why, oh why, hadn't she listened to the churning in her stomach? Why had she done this alone?

Kai might have scared her, but he'd saved her. This guy… creeped her out. Her body shook violently. This was no Sanguis demon.

"I am so happy. I have not had a toy like you to play with in so long. Females provide such sweet sounds." The demon grabbed her by the hair and yanked her forward.

Celina screamed, but that was all she could do.

11

SIN

The eyeballs embedded inside the cavern walls watched as their king walked alongside them, their gaze fixed on his every movement. Shadows slithered around the floor as Kai stepped inside his throne room, and those gathered inside bowed their heads.

"Where is Shiriki?" Kai's voice boomed across the room.

One of the Sanguis demons came strutting forward. "We haven't seen him in a few days, and he ordered us not to disturb him while he was doing his experiments."

Kai stopped in his tracks. "Was that my second in command's order?"

"He said if we bothered him, he'd add us to his test subjects." He swallowed loudly.

"And do you know what *I* will do to you if he is not here within thirty minutes?" The walls shook and cracked, causing more of the shadowy tentacles to twitch along the room.

The demon's eyes widened, and he ran out with no more excuses.

Kai sat on his throne, the metal covered in thick layers of various skins—mostly human.

He glared down at the whole room, a foul temper burning

through him. He had to hold court from time to time, but whenever he was in his realm, he lost the connection he had with Celina; he had no way of knowing what she was doing, if she was all right.

Complete silence…

One of his advisors, Maili, stepped forward and smiled. "Mekaisto. I would like to put forward my suggestion again, about—"

Kai raised his hand to silence her. "I know what your request is, and the answer remains the same." His gaze swept across some subjects in the room. "It would only be greed and the prospect of power that would will you into the position." He leaned forward in his chair and locked eyes with the Viscus demon. "And I will not have that."

She glared back but remained silent as she stepped back into the small crowd.

Adam appeared from the back of the room, shoving his way forward until he stopped in front of Kai. "I brought Denzel, as you requested, but I'm begging you—"

"Not now." Kai moved toward a side door and beckoned the Sanguis demon. "We have other matters to discuss."

Adam followed, hatred gleaming in his eyes, but he knew the hierarchy and didn't dare challenge his king. "Is this about the human you've made a deal with?"

"Was there anything else about Thomas Leviet that you remember?"

"Haku pulled the club's records after you left with the human girl, and I jotted a note down about him keeping information in a safe inside his house."

Kai's lips curled. "Oh?"

"The only reason that was important was that we asked where he would keep the information given to him, to make sure it couldn't be traced back to The CrowBar."

"Return to your club, Adam, and be assured," his smile turned cruel, "Denzel will be well looked after."

The Sanguis leader pressed his lips together but vanished without a word, and Kai walked back to his throne room, already going over in his mind what he'd be discussing with the new visitor he'd requested.

His eyes burst into bright red when he glared through the crowd. "Why is Shiriki still not here?"

The Sanguis demons in the hall, those not used to Kai's mood and tendency toward theatrics, gulped down their fear and stiffened their stances so he wouldn't see their trembling limbs.

The Sanguis demon who had been tasked with finding Shiriki lurched through the door, his staggering steps bringing him to within inches of where Kai sat. Blood oozed from fresh gashes gouged deep into his face and arms.

"Apologies, Mekaisto, but he said he's too busy and—"

"Bring him." Kai's stare could have frozen all of Hell. "Now."

He could not have…

"Oh, so threatening," a younger demon muttered.

Kai's gaze found the one who'd spoken, and his lips curled into a malicious smile as he beckoned the young demon forward. "You must be Denzel, Adam's newest child."

The newest demon came forward, his punk clothing adding to the look of rebellion already etched all over his expression. "I'm no one's child. That fucker saw to that when he kidnapped me five years ago."

The Viscus demons whispered among themselves, but Kai sensed they wouldn't hold back much longer if this new demon continued to speak with such insubordination. He'd be ripped to shreds in a matter of seconds.

"Someone informed me you spend your time fighting your elders and running away from your master."

Denzel crossed his arms over his chest. "So what?"

The muttering grew louder, and the young demon glanced

over his shoulders. He shrugged before turning lazy attention back to his king.

Kai stood, and the room fell silent again. "I like your spirit. But it seems too much humanity remains within you, and that will be a problem."

"I didn't ask to be made into a monster," he spat back.

"Then shall I undo the damage?" He stopped in front of Denzel and clicked his fingers.

"What do you—?" Denzel didn't finish his question before chains sprang from the floor and wrapped themselves around him, burning hot red. His skin melted against the metal as he whimpered.

"The thing is, demons cannot die unless they are killed by higher demons. And once you die, you cease to exist." Kai bent a little, so he'd be at eye-level with Denzel. "Do you wish to just disappear?"

The young demon struggled, but the more he did, the tighter the metal squeezed. He screamed as a loud crunch from his bones resonated through the room. "No!"

"Then you will need to be educated." Kai clicked his fingers, and the burning chains vanished.

He took a few steps forward and stared at the melted flesh as he licked his lips.

"Now…let me heal those for you."

12

DEMONS' NATURE

The rope dug into Celina's skin and strained her wrists with excruciating pain. Her arms stretched as she hung a few inches from the floor. The rough material creaked under her weight as she swayed, and her head throbbed at the back where the demon had hit her.

She glanced around, groping for her thoughts, trying to pull them to the fore as they swirled like soup in her head. *Think.* For fuck's sake, she had to think.

Artificial lights hanging from the ceiling illuminated the room in a clinical-like way, their occasional buzzing noise covering the sound of boiling water bubbling inside a large cauldron. The fire roaring underneath gave off an eerie red glow like the whole place was part laboratory, part dungeon.

Tables lined the walls, all of them holding body parts in various-sized jars. Most of the organs twitched as though still alive. A purple curtain hung in one corner of the room, and from the haunting rasping sounds, she didn't want to know what lay behind it.

Hell's laboratory and dungeon extraordinaire.

Human corpses hung from hooks in the ceiling, creating a stench so intense she couldn't understand why she hadn't thrown up yet. Six more live victims hung along the wall like Celina, and by the looks of their mangled scars, they'd been here a long while.

The door opened, and the white-haired demon ambled inside, pushing a tray full of sharp instruments. Celina's eyes widened and panic coursed through her, bringing a fresh wave of nausea with it. She wriggled her hands, ignoring the tight binding slicing into her flesh as she tried to free them.

"Please let me go." She choked back a sob, glancing at the collection of blades.

The demon gave her a broad smile. "You should be thankful to contribute to my experiments." His silver eyes shone like cold, hard steel.

"Experiments?" Her voice cracked.

She hoped she'd already been here long enough for Kai to worry about her.

The demon stepped closer to her and put his hand on her side, not taking his gaze off hers. She gasped at a sharp stabbing sensation and pressure under her ribs as he punctured her cold skin with his claw-like fingernails

"Yes, experiments to further the science of the soul." He backed away from her and crossed to the largest of the tables in the middle of the room. "Unfortunately, my subjects die before I find the answer I am seeking."

He licked his bloodied fingers as he jotted down notes. From time to time, a louder rasp came from behind the curtain, sending shivers down her spine.

"Who are you? Why are you keeping me here? I belong to another demon—"

"Yes, Mekaisto." He opened a jar containing a heart and gazed down into the green liquid as if mesmerized. "And, although we are not supposed to touch what is his," he looked up , "I feel I am an exception."

"Who are you?" she asked again.

He stared at her and moved to the small tray he rolled in

earlier, searching through the instruments until he picked up a knife with jagged teeth. The demon strolled up to her, and without ever losing the smile from his lips, leaned the weapon against her abdomen.

"Where would you like it?"

Her eyes widened, and she shook her head. "What? No—"

He plunged the knife into her arm, and she screamed, the agony forcing bile up her throat. Her breaths quickened through her whimpers. The wound throbbed, contracting in time with each beat of her heart, and the blood warmed her freezing skin as it streamed down her arm.

Since making the deal with Kai, she hadn't been afraid of dying because she was guaranteed safety, in a twisted way... until their deal ended, anyway. The idea of being tortured or even killed by another demon without ever achieving her revenge started a slow spiral of terror.

Kai will save me. He always does.

The demon returned to the table, passed a cotton swab over the bloodied knife, and placed it underneath a micro-scope. A smile widened to the point of showing all his pointed teeth, and he glanced at her.

She focused on him.

I need a plan.

He took the heart he'd been examining out of the jar and cut small incisions into it. The thing pulsed frantically under his hold on it, and her eyes widened as she held back a cry. He whispered a few words in another language again, the familiar cadence the same as when she'd been about to leave this hellish place.

"What...what's that language?"

He didn't look up from his work. "*Demos.* I can call dark-ness forth with it." Putting the pulsating organ back in a jar, he stared at her. "How old are you, Celina?"

He knows my name...

She shook her head, pressing her mouth into a tight line to

keep from answering him, but he glanced up, and a hopeful light gleamed in his eyes; he'd hurt her if she refused to answer. His cold stare dared her to remain silent.

She had no power, and that knowledge sat like a hard stone in her middle.

"Twenty-five."

He nodded, as though to himself. "Well, I hope you enjoy your stay with me, however long that is." He gave her a small bow. "However, as your visit was unexpected, I hope you will forgive me while I do not pay attention to you yet." His eyes gleamed. "I promise we will have fun soon if you stay obedient."

Oh sure, I'll just hang here.

Her hands were mercifully going numb.

Get him to talk.

She gathered her courage, but her voice shook. "What's your name, then?"

He gazed at her and cocked his head to the side as he studied her and then broke into another smile. Again, he approached her, but without stopping by the tray of torture instruments.

"Are you always this forward with demons?"

"Yes." She turned her head to the side. If she could just engage him long enough…

"My name is Shiriki."

"Please, let me go! I won't tell Kai."

He ignored her and walked to someone hanging on the other wall. The man kicked, a feeble twitch of his legs, and let out a harsh croak as though he'd lost his voice a long time ago.

Shiriki leaned in, glancing around at his body. "Do not over exert yourself, Stephan." He lifted his chin, and the man's eyes widened.

"Pl—" He coughed, unable to get words out.

The demon nodded with a satisfied smile on his lips as he

walked back to the tray of torture instruments. "I think they might be ready."

He took what looked like a strange spoon with sharp edges and strode back to his prisoner. The man's croaks became higher until he managed what sounded like a scream, his legs flailing.

Celina stopped breathing when Shiriki moved away, leaving the man mouthing muted sounds, the two gaping holes in his skull bleeding down his face.

At the sound of splashing, Celina turned her attention on the demon again. He stared at the eyeballs floating in the liquid, tracing the glass with his long fingernails. "Have you ever heard the expression *the eyes are the windows to the soul?*" He didn't wait for her reply before he continued, "They always seem to be filled with emptiness once removed, though." He muttered something about keeping them attached to the nervous system as he glided back toward the mutilated victim.

This time, Shiriki detached the man from the wall and dragged him to the table. Celina's stomach dropped when he threw his victim to the floor. The near-corpse clawed forward, his fingers scrabbling for purchase on the cold concrete. It only took seconds for the demon to grab a long, pointed instrument from the tray and stab it straight through the man's arm. The blade pierced the stone floor, anchoring the exhausted human as his gasps ripped the air.

Celina closed her eyes against the casual display of Shiriki's strength. All this time, Kai could have snapped her in half as easily as waving his hand.

"Oh, dear…I had planned on taking the nerve endings." He turned the man on his back, causing the victim's anchored arm to crunch at an odd angle. "No matter. I can always use a new human heart." He clapped his hands together with a wide smile.

She buried her head into her arm as the man's body

twitched and shivers rippled inside her, but she had no way to block the horrible sounds.

When they faded to occasional moans and whimpers, she dared a glance at him. His face paled, and blood dribbled from a hole the demon had ripped in his chest. Shiriki hummed a tune she recognized as *Ring Around the Rosie,* that smile still on his lips. The demon tugged inside the hole for a second before ripping out the man's heart and placing it inside a new jar.

"Why don't you kill them before chopping them up like that?" Her voice cracked as she stared down at what was left of a person who had died in complete agony.

Is Kai going to kill people like this for my revenge? No. I'll tell him I don't want that. But I want to make them suffer for ruining my life…

Shiriki stepped nearer to her and waved his hand. The ropes detached from around her wrists and she fell to the floor, shrieking as pain radiated from her wounds, flooding her body with that one sensation and blocking out all else. Even drawing breath hurt. She scrambled back and curled into a ball against the wall, her body shaking.

He crouched. "I do not kill them because they are less amusing without the screaming. It is music to my ears." Shiriki's face lit with ecstasy, and he returned to his table to grab a saw.

While he moved to a woman hanging among his victims, Celina inched farther from him, trying to reach the exit from this horrible room. The newest victim begged, and Celina glanced at the demon, her stomach churning and roiling when he placed the saw above the woman's knee.

"No! No!" Her begging went ignored as the demon drew his arm back, and the metal teeth grated through the fabric into the skin.

Blood spurted, soaking the material of her pants, and the shrieking rang through Celina's ears. Shiriki placed the severed leg on the table and grabbed a medium-sized metal plate, glowing yellow-red from a fire barehanded, the heat not affecting him. He placed it under the woman's stump. The smell of burnt flesh and the rasping screams accompanying it would haunt Celina's nightmares for the rest of her life, she was sure.

Another of the victims, a man, strained harder against the rope around his wrists, his voice muffled from the gag in his mouth. Shiriki grabbed his face and turned his head to the side so he'd look at the woman he'd just amputated. "You will be much braver than your wife, no?"

Once the man was freed, he bolted to the door, his bound hands swinging wildly side to side. An invisible force hit him in the back with such strength that he hit the floor with a crunching noise. He gasped through the gag, his fingers fumbling at the material as he pulled it out of his mouth. He let out a gulp when Shiriki grabbed the back of his neck and pulled him to his feet.

"This is the third time you have tried running away." He smirked. "Remind me, Victor, what I said I would do on your third attempt."

He shook his head. "No, please. Not that—"

His grip tightened. "Remind me."

"You…said you'd give…me a bath." He muttered the words, a shudder passing through his body.

Celina's stomach clenched.

Is he going to…?

It was worse than what she'd thought.

Shiriki lifted the man's hands above his own head and pulled them down behind him, the noise of his shoulders dislocating covered only by his wails. Once his hands were behind his back, Shiriki picked him up, and without a word, threw the man into the cauldron of boiling water.

Celina threw up between her hands and turned to the side, heaving as more vomit forced its way up her throat. The sounds were too much, her shaking so terrible she was sure every bone in her body would shatter.

Her breath caught in her throat when the demon materialized in front of her. She had trouble keeping eye contact with him for too long. His stare pierced her.

"Your turn."

She shuffled away, the cold floor sending a renewed shock through her body as her wounded arm pressed against the hard surface, but Shiriki grabbed her hair and pulled her up.

Distract him. Anything!

"How did you know my parents?" Her voice shook so much it was barely audible.

"That is a long story, and I would rather show you something, pet." He crooned the cold words.

She flailed her arms in a desperate attempt to hit him, but he yanked her toward the thick purple curtain. She pressed her feet against the floor, trying to stop him. But, just like with Kai, her feeble display of strength didn't help. He pulled the curtain back, still holding her arm tightly so she couldn't run off.

She froze at the scene in front of her, her stomach threatening another wave of vomit.

The body of a human hung from wires and hooks. The woman had bits sewn on, but the black stitches were large and uneven. Her chest, stomach, and one of her legs had gaping holes, revealing multiple beating hearts.

"I have been vivisecting humans for quite some time, trying to find out where the soul resides in the body. What it really is." His smile widened. "Many of my kind believe souls are useless because they belong to something weak. However, time and time again, a human's soul has proven to be powerful in its own right—almost like it is an entity." His hands squeezed, and she jumped. "If I can find out where it lives, what it can do…imagine the possibilities." He finished with a sigh.

She swallowed hard. "Does Kai know?"

"Mekaisto is the one who set me on this task."

The woman let out a keening sound as though she pleaded for mercy or maybe death.

Celina brought her trembling hands to her mouth. "She's…alive?"

"To some extent, you could call this being alive." Shiriki shrugged. "But I drilled into her vocal cords to stop her from screaming day and night. They were such beautiful screams. Alas, they drew the attention of dark creatures that wanted a taste." He pulled her toward him, so her back rested against his chest, holding her steady as he leaned toward her ear. "I do not allow others to taste what is mine." He licked the side of her face, and she yelped.

He released her and turned her to face him again, his eyes piercing hers as though daring her to run after what he'd done to his other victim.

Celina rubbed her arms and glanced just below the hanging body where a few torsos twitched, their chests wide open.

No hearts.

She stared back up at the beating hearts inside the maimed human, her stomach clenching. "You're fucking sick…" She'd barely whispered it, but the words needed to come out.

"I prefer to think of myself as a scientist of—"

She rounded on him and glared, forgetting her fear in a moment of pure disgust. "Your experiments are not fucking working, you twisted son of a bitch."

The demon leaned toward her, and she froze as he grabbed a strand of her hair. "That is why there is Plan B."

She took a few steps back. "Stay the fuck away from me!"

Shiriki appeared behind her, his hands on her shoulders squeezing hard. "Care to test if it would work on you?" He sniffed her hair, his warm breath causing her to tremble.

He kicked her in the leg, and she fell to the floor with a gasp. She screamed as he plunged a knife above her knee and sliced all the way down to her foot. Blinding sweat poured down her forehead, and tears streamed down her face. She glanced at her leg and almost passed out. Blood ran fast from the wound, the light of the fire revealing how wide the cut had been.

"I can end the pain," he said as he moved to his tray of instruments again. "All you have to do is cooperate."

"Kai, please... help me." The plea tore from her as a whimper. She stared up at Shiriki who came toward her with a large metal hook in his hand.

The walls turned black, and Celina's heart raced when Shiriki glanced all around the room. The only light flickered from the fire. Haunted screams hung in the damp air.

"What do you think you are doing, Shiriki?" Kai's voice echoed inside the room.

She couldn't see him, but a flicker of hope swelled inside her. He was there to rescue her. The pain would stop.

What the fuck is wrong with me? My savior is the king of demons.

"She came to me, Mekaisto," Shiriki said, but his voice was tense now.

"You thought that would change my laws?" Kai's tone was dark, sending chills through her.

"I believed that, under the circumstances, I could play with her."

"Celina," Kai called out. "I need you to obey me for once."

His tone held sinister amusement, and she wanted to scowl at him for it. She mentally ticked off all the times she hadn't done what he'd told her to. All right, so it was a pattern. But he could have saved his rebuke for a better time.

"Close your eyes and do not open them until I tell you to, no matter what you hear."

"Okay." She squeezed them shut.

Whispers, moans, and distant growls joined in with the other haunting ones. Her curiosity piqued, but she pressed her good hand across her eyes.

Don't look. Don't look. Don't look.

Rumbling sounds shook the room, and the floor beneath her burned through her clothes. Sweat tickled her skin, but she rocked back and forth in a slow motion to keep from moving her hand away from her eyes. Her toes curled as the heat rose, and screams pierced the air as though millions of people were being tortured all at once. The haunting sounds filled her mind with horrifying images.

Her body trembled, pained howls forcing her to the edge of madness.

"She is mine," Kai spoke, and she strained to hear him over the terrifying sounds. "You know not to touch what belongs to me."

"Just wanted…to get to know her…a little." Shiriki's breaths pushed out in rasps.

"Celina," Kai whispered next to her ear, making her jump. She kept pressing her hands against her eyes. "He hurt you, did he not?"

"Yes."

"And would you like me to hurt him for you?" he spoke quietly, darkness in his voice.

The wounds on her leg and arm throbbed, sending renewed pain across her whole body. What Shiriki had done to all those people surged her hatred forward.

"Yes."

"Just wait a little longer, and I will heal your wounds."

His presence left her side, and she was alone again.

She nodded even though he was already gone, keeping her eyes closed and covered. Though she tried hard not to imagine what Kai was doing, the sounds of choking, gagging, and bones cracking were hard not to distinguish.

The whole room seemed to rock around her, as though she

was floating on a liquid surface, and her heart slowed. "Kai…"

The screams faded. The noises grew distant and soon the weight of darkness lifted, leaving only the sounds of the renewed moaning from the other people hanging in the dungeon.

Kai's voice hissed as he spoke. "I will finish with you later, but in the meantime…"

Someone drew near to her again, and she knew it was Kai.

"You can open your eyes now."

She lifted her head and opened her eyes to find Shiriki gone. Her gaze focused on Kai, who had the same form as when she first made the deal with him. He said nothing as he crouched and inspected her wounds.

Her arm took less than a second to heal, but when his hand traveled to her leg, he hovered over it with a frown. Her vision blurred a little, and she groaned as the room spun again. She blinked several times, and when she focused again, he held her face in his hands.

"Celina, this will hurt, but I need you to keep yourself from fighting me." His voice was strained, and she clenched her jaw.

He's worried.

"What's…wrong?" He usually seemed to be able to heal any wound. Even her gunshot.

"The knife had chemical properties; it will take a little longer." He grasped the end of her pants and stared into her eyes. "Hold on."

With one movement, her pant leg tore from her ankle to her thigh, and she cried out. His hand pressed into her blood-soaked flesh, and although she tried her best, her hands still went to his, trying to push them away.

"Stop! Please, it hurts." She cried harder, but he continued to dig inside the gash.

She threw her head back with a shriek and then…no more pain.

"Celina?" His voice had turned dark again, but her eyes still met his as she panted.

"I…I'm okay. I can stand—"

She gasped when Kai lifted her into his arms and moved toward the door. "We are leaving," he announced.

"Wait! The others, we have—" she started, her voice cracking again because of all the screaming she had done.

"They belong to Shiriki."

"We can't leave them here." Despair flooded through her at thoughts of someone rescuing another person and abandoning her there, with the knowledge of what she would have had to endure.

He stared down at her, his pupils turning vertical. "I have no use for those humans, nor do I plan on seizing Shiriki's test subjects."

She squirmed out of his grasp and stumbled back toward Shiriki's tray, grabbing the sharpest knife she laid eyes on. Her wounds might have healed, but a phantom pain inside her leg still caused a shudder through her spine with every step. She reached toward a victim, intending to set them free. Or even slice their throats to release them from agony, her grip tightening around the weapon. Their eyes turned toward her, the barest glimmer of hope flaring after who knows how long they'd been tormented.

The flicker of an end in sight died as Kai gently took the knife from her hands and pulled her away. "No, dove. These are not yours to kill."

A sinking, horrible feeling knotted her stomach.

The only reason Kai rescued her was because he had a use for her, and he made the rules—hell, he was the fucking rules. Kai was a demon, not her friend.

Once they left the room and came to a flight of stairs going up, Celina frowned.

I guess he brought me into the basement after he knocked me out. How long was I unconscious?

Kai carried her all the way up, and as they reached the lobby, he stared down at her. "Try to take deep breaths."

Why didn't he materialize with me? Is it because I'm still feeling weak?

The old woman she'd seen when first entering the building approached them and bowed. Kai spoke to her in Demos, and Celina took deep breaths, as Kai had instructed.

After they left the building, Kai put Celina into the passenger seat of her car. She stayed silent, trying to control her overwhelming desire to hide in a corner and cry for eternity. Torture broke her mind, and her wounds still ached despite the physical evidence having vanished.

He drove to the hotel and opened a back door with a simple flick of his wrist, avoiding people seeing her bloodied state. Once in their room, he settled her on the sofa, watching her from under lowered brows, with eyes burning in fury.

"Why were you there?" He pronounced each word with such force she recoiled a little.

"My aunt gave me something that was found in my parents' car accident. Since you left and I couldn't continue on with our plan, I checked out the address. I didn't know a demon lived there. I mean, how could I?" All these mysteries were collapsing around her, and she wasn't sure which bothered her more.

Her husband's murder and his connection to this dark world she didn't know existed or her own parents' connection to a demon. *That* demon.

When Kai's hand reached toward her face, she flinched.

"Does your fear of me now repulse you?"

The thoughts of what happened still over-rode everything else. They worked their way through her, clinging to all else and leaving a sticky residue in their wake. She saw their images when she closed her eyes, heard those people through the silence. She'd never be free of the memories.

"That demon said you ordered those atrocious experiments. And what you did back there, leaving all those people there to suffer, made me realize something."

"Do tell."

"I have to remember what you are, remember your nature."

Putting his hand on the back of the sofa, Kai tightened his grip on the material. "You know a demon's nature, then?" He pulled himself forward, so they were face-to-face, his eyes flashing. "I would be more than delighted to show you my nature if you would care to have a better understanding." His voice darkened with what sounded like hatred.

She clenched her fingers into weak fists. He hadn't touched her, but the heat radiating from his anger burned against her skin, and her vision dimmed until only sparks of white light danced in front of her.

What was happening? Was he showing her his nature? No. She struggled to break free of the darkness and continued to fight.

"Let me go, Kai." Her whisper echoed in her mind.

When she opened her eyes, his face was inches from hers. Had he done this? Weakened her until her body surrendered and her mind fogged? She couldn't think, couldn't form the words to speak, until he stood and crossed the room, stopping in front of an open expanse of wall.

He spoke in the Demos language again, and Celina wanted to hide from the piercing tone. She didn't draw her gaze away as his sharp fingernail etched strange symbols into the wall. A bright, red light shone as he stepped away from the portal, revealing a squirming figure on the other side.

What is…?

She put her hands over her mouth and pressed her lips tight

to keep from retching when she recognized the white hair. The flesh on Shiriki's face had been torn or cut away, leaving nothing but the slimy muscles shining in its wake. He struggled against all the chains binding him. A fire roared beneath him, blistering his legs and peeling his skin, releasing a foul stench.

Strange whispers and garbled screams seeped into the room around the demon. Kai asked Shiriki something and crossed his arms. Shiriki answered, blood dribbling from his mouth to the fire in a hissing noise.

As the hole closed, Shiriki eyed Celina with an expression worse than murderous hatred or bitter resentment. It looked like fondness.

What the hell?

"I will finish the business I must attend to in my realm," Kai announced. "Stay here." He strode to the door but turned and gave her a burning glare. "If you do not obey, I will finish what Shiriki started. Understand?"

The door slammed behind him, and Celina immediately began to pace the room, unable to keep still. The pain of her torture rushed back in a flood of nightmare memory, and she struggled to breathe.

She took a shower to wash away the blood and sweat, searching to calm her thoughts, but it didn't work. Knowing it would be easier to give up than fight any longer, she slipped on a nightgown and threw herself in bed. She drew her knees in, unable to stop the tears rolling down her face.

She'd left those people in Shiriki's hellhole. Why couldn't she have fought harder for them? No one deserved that. No one.

He's imprisoned. What will happen to them?

Her existence had been normal, dull even, for so long. Until her entire life, everything she'd known, crashed down around her. She whimpered, drawing her knees even closer and threatening to cut her breath, but she didn't care.

It hurts. I don't want to think about any of it. I want to be with you again, Thomas.

Her emotions roiled and churned. After what happened, she couldn't seem to stop shaking. Not only from the physical pain and not just from knowing others suffered for his pleasure.

So much terror and pain. I can still smell the death-like decay, and yet… I feel drawn to it. Those whispers call to me—is that Kai's doing?

She'd always been afraid of the dark, but this was like nothing she ever imagined. When he'd told her to close her eyes and the darkness enveloped her, it dragged her down into the depths of pure evil.

A part of her wished she'd died at the foot of that black tree. Then she wouldn't have found out the man she loved lied to her for all those years, or about her parents' connection to a demon. She slid out of bed, and stared out the window, focused on the sky she thought she'd never glimpse again. The screams inside her head weren't fading; if anything, they'd become louder as time passed.

She focused back to the outside and watched as the sky turned from light to dark blue.

I won't let this break me. I still have to avenge Thomas. I need to find out everything.

As difficult as it was, she pushed down all the thoughts of Shiriki into the depths of her hatred and used it to fuel her determination to getting revenge. If those sons of bitches had never killed Thomas, she would never have had to witness those horrors.

She made a mental image of her suspects, her heart pounding against her chest as her hatred grew. So far, her suspects included Adam, her Aunt Marie, and David Corval. All were possible, but none likely. The idea of taking revenge on her aunt tightened her chest; Marie was the only family she had left. The other two would be easy enough. She'd even take a few leaves from the white-haired sociopath's book. Though how she would kill a demon, she didn't know. Deep down, she hoped that it would be David, wanting to see his smug face turn to despair.

What's wrong with me? Why do I want to inflict pain on someone without even knowing for sure he's involved? Does Kai have that kind of influence over me?

With a sigh, she laid in bed again. Just as her eyes drifted closed and her thoughts scattered, one last idea found a home. What if she never found the people responsible for Thomas' murder? If she could die with an untainted soul, it would save her from eternal torment.

Can I stall Kai, and just live with him like this a while longer?

13

UNWANTED AFFECTION

From the lowest dungeons, all the way up to the throne room, the dark realm burst with heat, melting some of the victims imprisoned inside. The inferno even affected the demons, though most remained silent as Kai's quiet seething tore at their immortal bodies, sheering chunks of their flesh away, burning them until their skin glowed with embers.

He drummed his fingers on the armrests of his throne, ignoring the shrieks of pain resonating through his domain. "Fetch my advisor."

Maili walked in and bowed, trying to fight the crushing pressure emanating from her king. "Yes, Mekaisto?"

"Send Denzel back to his master."

"You think he has suffered enough already? After the way—"

Before she could blink, a large gash opened on the side of her face as Kai loomed inches away from her. "Are you questioning me?" He forced his claw-like fingernails into the fresh wound and tugged at her skin as she screamed. "Question me again, Maili. I need to take my rage out on something."

He ripped a chunk of skin off, and she stumbled back with a shriek. Blood streamed between her fingers as she held her hand against the gaping hole in her cheek, her body trembling violently. Without waiting to be dismissed, she bolted from the room.

Kai paced from wall to wall, unable to leash the anger vibrating through him.

He had hurt his dove, destroyed her innocence by letting his darkness seep into her.

Something inside him twisted, and his rage darkened. Suppressing his instincts had always been difficult, but since he'd become pressed for time, his urges deepened. When he'd reached out to touch her, comfort Celina, and she flinched…

I could have extinguished her.

Attending to his subjects took longer than he intended, but his mood caused a cautiousness he hadn't been prepared to deal with. They all picked their words more carefully as they complained or requested favors of their king. Even after he completed his official duties for the day, he stalled, putting off his return to Celina as long as he could manage. His urgency to see her faltered, replaced instead by shame at what he'd done.

How would he face her?

Shame?

He scoffed at the idea.

Standing in front of the door to their hotel room, Kai sensed two other humans inside with Celina.

Friends.

He strolled through the door and the laughter he'd heard died.

"Having a little get-together? And you didn't think to invite me?" He kept his tone polite and amused, but by Celina's wide eyes, he knew she'd heard the fury in his voice.

She stood and gave him a small smile. "This is my friend

from high school, Namika." She gestured to the woman on her right. Namika blushed, and Celina continued, "And her friend, Yasuo." Celina avoided his burning gaze. "This is an old friend of mine, Kai."

"Are you staying here with Celina?" Yasuo's tone voiced the disapproval behind his words.

"No, I'm renting the room for her, so she doesn't have to go back to her house until she's ready." He smiled as he explained patiently.

I would love to rip his flesh right off his pitiful human face…

Namika stood and walked up to Kai. "You must be the reason Celina is coping so well with everything that's happened to her."

Celina gaped from her friend and back to him.

Kai's mood changed to amusement. "Anata wa shinsetsu desu," he said with a smile; *you are kind.* "Celina was there for me a few years ago. I'm only returning the favor." He glanced at Celina, his eyes gleaming.

"Well, we're sorry we've imposed for so long. We should be leaving." Namika turned to Yasuo who stood as well, and they headed to the door.

After they left, Kai grinned as a chill passed through Celina when he leaned in. His breath whooshed against her skin, and another shiver shook her body. "Did your friend bring you a play toy?" He aimed for an amused tone, but fury crashed over him in waves.

She shot him an icy stare. "She brought him so we could have a conversation that didn't revolve around my husband's murder."

Celina grabbed the coffee cups and carried them to the small sink in their room before returning to the sofa.

He concentrated on her and smiled as she wondered how many languages he spoke. "I speak every human language, colombe." His grin widened—*dove* in French.

"I'm sick of you being in my head."

"Why do you try to hide from me?" He took a few steps closer. "I know you as well as you do."

"That's not the point, and you know it." Her eyes flashed, and her anger bubbled through him.

"Are you angry with me?" Again, shame clutched at him.

"Am I...?" She glared, and her hands curled into fists. "You attacked my mind with your...your...*demon* darkness. And on top of everything, you're the one ordering that fucking monster to experiment on humans."

"That business does not concern you."

She flinched at his hard tone, and his anger vanished. He rolled his shoulders, relaxing as he aimed for a gentler approach. "I am sorry for hurting you." He'd never been so sincere.

Such a strange emotion.

Her eyes widened for a few seconds, but she turned away quickly. "It's...just don't do it again."

He turned the conversation to the previous subject since it didn't seem to affect her as much. "In the future, if you wish to play with someone, you can always ask—"

"Don't, Kai."

He sat down close to her, his human body affected by the radiance and dimensions of her beauty.

She crossed her arms. "If you want to go *play*," she air quoted his words, "with someone, feel free. A good-looking demon like you won't have any problems picking up a woman to fulfill all your...urges."

Kai's eyes narrowed and the darkness inside him spiked, but Celina didn't budge as she stared back at him, unblinking. "With so little challenge, it would hardly satisfy my urges."

She scooted farther away from him. "Isn't that what easy girls are born for?"

"While I could amuse myself with any woman of my choosing, there would only be sex involved, and the satisfaction would end quickly." He rested his arm on the back of the sofa and grinned. "Well, not quickly, but…"

She straightened herself to face him. "Again, I don't—"

"I am a demon, Celina. Above all else, demons love the hunt." He smirked when her eyes widened.

"So, you see having sex with someone as a hunt?"

He sighed and ran his fingers through his hair. "By your expression, I would say you still do not quite understand."

"It's *your* twisted logic."

Interesting…

"I take my time, stalk my prey first, count the number of breaths she takes, imagine her screams…"

She arched an eyebrow. "That's not at all creepy."

Kai ignored her. "I am a creature of infinite time; the world creeps by, yet an intimate moment is so fleeting, it feels as though it is gone in less than a second." He stopped, expecting an interruption again, but she stayed silent. "The pleasure is heightened by the danger, and in the throes of passion, I could lose my control and revert to the form least likely to be found pleasurable by my…partner."

He lost himself in the images in his mind, pinning down Celina's body, taking her in a way she could never recreate with a mere mortal.

"Hunting is simple. There is always one in the crowd that stands out but rarely is it the one searching for the one-night stand. No…" Kai locked his eyes with hers and saw goosebumps rise on her arms. "The one unsure of what society wants her to be, the one desperate to be loved and appreciated. She is the one I seek."

"So, social outcasts are your type?"

His eyes pierced her until he could see through her mind again, to all those curious little fantasies.

He smiled. "It's about finesse. I listen to her, and as she speaks more confidently, I brush a hand over her skin," his hand skimmed Celina's neck as he brushed her back, "just enough so she shivers with anticipation of what my lips would feel like in the same spot." He delved into her mind as his words worked against her disdain for him. "Then I caress her in a way she won't notice, but her subconscious will let her lean into, let her mind take over, and her body will beg for more."

"She'd notice if…" She followed his gaze to his hand on her knee.

"Are you certain?" He'd worked his own body into a sensual frenzy as he'd drawn her into his web.

She stared at him, her cheeks flushing. "I—"

"Eventually, I suggest a night filled with pleasure." He couldn't contain his smile as he moved closer. "I keep touching her in small ways, maintaining physical contact at all times." His hand inched up her side until he tucked a loose strand of hair behind her ear. She sucked in a breath, and he cupped her cheek.

He sat close to her, and her scent calmed and excited him at the same time.

"Kai?" Her voice wavered.

"Sex is fleeting." He took her chin and drew her close. "But intimacy is endless, a continuous moment of gentle touches," his hand dropped back to her knee, and then made its way up her thigh until she let out a small gasp, "personal boundaries broken, and pleasures that go beyond sex."

She sat as if frozen. "It's still a one-night stand."

"Mine last longer—and you reveal not only your body." His hand moved to the middle of her chest. "When you are intimate with a demon, you reveal your soul. You make yourself vulnerable and open."

"Considering you'll have my soul sometime soon, I'm not giving you a free sample." She drew away from him and stood suddenly. "I won't be your prey tonight."

Another surge of heat rushed through him, but he pushed

it down with a deep breath. "You would set me loose on another human?"

She glared at him. "I wasn't aware I had a choice about what you do outside of our deal. That would be on you, not me."

"You think you control what I do within our deal?"

She rubbed her arms when he stood. "Not when you say it like that."

"Celina…" He stopped in front of her and leaned into her personal space, drawing a lungful of a scent he would only ever associate with her.

He wrapped his arms around her, swallowing the shiver that shook her body. "What are you—?"

"Let's play. I can assure you, you will not regret a night in my arms."

I want you. Against all my instincts, I need you close.

"Let me go, Mekaisto." Celina pushed him as hard as she could, and he withdrew as disappointment withered his gaze.

You are trembling again, my dove… Is it because you are scared you will give in? How far can I push you until you bend?

"What if I say no?"

She glared at him, but Kai's smile widened. He could feel, even smell, the pulsing between her legs begging him to take her.

"Isn't it enough you're getting my life and my soul? Now you need my body, too?" She pushed against him again, but he only held tighter, unable to let her go. "Why are you doing this? I just lost my husband, found out things that break my heart. I can't sit and flirt with you."

"What I am offering you is the chance to forget."

"No!" Her hands clenched to fists as she shoved even harder against his chest. "No! You want to take everything I have left."

He grabbed her wrists, pushed her back on the sofa, and pinned her down, his body hovering over her. "What is your life without your body?" He tilted his head and flicked his tongue across his lips. "You never asked what selling your life and soul meant specifically. Allow me to enlighten you now." He moved until his face loomed only an inch from hers and her breath caught. He let go of her wrists, but his gaze pinned her to the spot.

"What?" Her voice ached just above a whisper.

"I own every inch of you…*body* and soul."

Her face flushed, and her lips trembled. "I never agreed to that!"

"You agreed to live. The details did not matter to you."

"I was dying! You told me I didn't have much time left, so it—"

His smile widened. "Even if you had all the time in the world, it would not have made a difference. Humans never read the fine print."

The scenarios racing inside her mind—what it meant for him to own all of her—bent a smile on his lips. Images of being tied to a bed as his tongue explored every part of her body, bending over so he penetrated her from behind, cries of passion. More exciting images came to his mind. He longed to push her beyond human limits, punish her to hear her beg. The fantasies were endless.

Tears welled in her eyes, and Kai's amusement ebbed.

She is mine…so, why am I hesitating?

He took her in his arms as he sat, holding her against him.

She struggled, but the lack of ferocity in her actions told him it was half-hearted. "Kai, stop."

"I will suppress my nature for you, and—"

"I want nothing from you, you fucking monster!" Tears dripped down her cheeks.

"Then—"

"Let me go!"

He held her even tighter and didn't stop her as she flailed at him.

"Hush, Celina, let me take care of you." His words calmed her, and she stared at him, all the fight flowing from her body.

He leaned in, and his lips grazed over hers. The connection, the touch surged through him, but her mind still fought her loyalty to Thomas.

She tore her lips away, and her hands gripped his arms. "Please, stop."

His body begged her to accept his touch, but his mind gave into her will, and he pulled back. "I will hold you until you fall asleep."

I will give you whatever you need.

14

EVIDENCE AND DEALS

Celina woke up, a scream dying in her throat as she dripped with sweat, visions of Shiriki's dungeon looming in her mind. The darkness in the room only intensified her panic, but as her vision adjusted, her heart slowed, and her mind focused on the feel of Kai's arms around her.

"You are safe. Calm down, dove." Kai's voice, even in a whisper, pushed her anxiety to the far corners of her mind.

She laughed and drew away. "You contradict your own cruelty. One minute, you remind me how badass you are, ready to take my soul and punish me for eternity. Then you hold me like a baby and coo such sweet words in my ear."

"I have hardly done anything cruel to you."

"I don't feel like arguing with you. From a human's perspective, I'm not safe anywhere near you. Now let's get this shit over with."

He chuckled at her sarcasm and drew her to his chest. "From a demon's perspective, I am much too caring to you. You have seen Shiriki's amusements, and mine are far more grueling for my subjects."

As the rain came down in sheets outside the window, Celina shuddered with an awareness of the strong muscles of his chest, the way his arms cradled her, and his hands caressed her outside her clothes. "Kai?"

"Yes?"

"Why did you tell me to close my eyes when you came to get me from Shiriki? What didn't you want me to see?" His hand rubbed small circles against her back, and she shuddered.

"The dark realm overloads the minds of living humans. Your subconscious would have suffered beyond repair. Even your brief exposure has tainted the time you have left on Earth."

"Tainted, how?" She pulled back and looked up at him.

"That is not the last nightmare you will have. And to see me in the demonic form I had to take to punish Shiriki would have overwhelmed you. I could not risk losing you to your own mind."

"Wait—demonic form? But I've seen you like that already."

"I have three demonic forms, two human ones, and one animal."

"So, I haven't seen all three?"

"You have seen two." He ran his fingers through her hair before resting his hand against her back. "When we made our deal, I was in my lowest demonic form. After the seal, however, when I had pointed teeth and vertical pupils…that is another."

"So, neither of those is your true form?"

"They are not. You will not see it until the day you make good on your end of our deal."

"Two human forms? I've seen one, yes?"

"Yes, and I will stick to that one until I return to my realm," he took her chin in his hand so he could lean in close, "and drag you along with me."

She frowned. "I swear, every time you show me the side of

you I want you to be, you purposefully remind me you're a demon."

He cocked his head to the side. "Is that why your feelings are drowning you in confusion?"

Celina pushed him away and used a pillow against her chest to instill distance between them. "I don't want to talk about that."

I won't betray Thomas just because he betrayed me with all his lies. Two wrongs don't make a right.

"As you wish." His voice lowered as though she'd disappointed him, but he let it drop.

"By the way." She clutched the pillow in her hands. "I know you only came to get me from Shiriki because of our deal, but still. Thank you."

Kai pried the pillow from her grasp and tossed it to the side. The details of his irises were vivid as he closed the gap between them. "I came to get you because my feelings, unlike yours, are not mixed."

"Yeah, okay, I get it. I'm the tasty soul at the end of a workday for you, nothing—"

In a move that stilled the words in her throat, Kai cupped her face in his hand and urged her toward him. His lips pressed over hers in a move both tender and frightening, intense and soft. Every thought she had told her to pull away, but as her doubts quickly burst into nothingness, she was left drowning in a pool of passion as his lips set her body on fire.

He withdrew, his lips still brushing against hers as he spoke. "Again, my feelings are not mixed. I am a being who knows what he wants and a king who gets it."

She kept her eyes closed. "Demons can't love. If you could, then you wouldn't claim my life and my soul once my revenge is over." She opened her eyes, seeking an answer to her feelings in his deeper, darker pupils.

He's comforted me when I've been scared, made me feel safe.

"Love is complicated. It is not something demons are supposed to feel."

"Well, as I said before," she withdrew as her chest grew tighter, "let's finish this, shall we?"

Kai sighed but told her about the safe Adam mentioned—the super-secret safe Thomas had. "A safe? What safe?"

How many more secrets did Thomas have?

"Perhaps you would care to search for it?"

His office. He'd kept everything in that damned room. The time had come for her to discover exactly what else Thomas had hidden from her. "Yes."

"I think we should go to your house then." He stood as he spoke.

She nodded and followed him out of the bedroom, grabbing a sweater on her way.

Finally back on track...but what else am I going to find out about Thomas?

While Kai drove, she considered what he'd said about her being damaged for the rest of her short life. "Am I really going to have nightmares forever? What about once you take my life and soul?"

Kai's eyes darted sideways, a cruel smile appearing on his lips. "Then you will live inside the nightmares."

Gravel crunched under the tires as they pulled into her driveway. Familiarity washed over her, and she closed her eyes.

By the time she found her key and entered, Kai was already inside.

"Why didn't you unlock the door for me?" she asked, narrowing her eyes.

The corners of his mouth curled. "You did not say the magic word."

She gritted her teeth. "Never mind. Stupid..."

Her footsteps faltered as she entered the living room, but

the chair, ropes, and blood she had left were gone, and her heart fluttered.

He didn't let me in because he cleaned everything before I'd see it.

It was as though nothing had ever happened. Her pulse sped and she glanced around, half-expecting to realize she'd been dreaming the whole time. Thomas would come up behind her and bring her back to bed, whispering words of comfort and telling her everything was all right.

Except it isn't. You're dead, and I have no one.

Kai leaned against the wall between the kitchen and living room, staring at her.

I'm not alone. My demon is here.

A gentle smile curled his lips. "Where is your husband's office?"

At her direction, Kai moved down the hallway and stopped in front of the only closed door. He rested his finger on the light wood, and Celina's eyes widened as creepy black veins slithered their way to the keyhole. With a loud click, the door unlocked, and he twisted the knob.

She crept in behind him. Before, out of respect for Thomas' privacy, she'd always remained outside. By entering, she felt as though she was disappointing him from beyond the grave. The room had floor-to-ceiling shelves lined with books, and the reclaimed wood floors and walls gave it a comfortable cottage feel. The only light came from the three large lamps in the corners of the room. An imposing oak desk cluttered with papers and more books stood over a maroon area rug in the middle of the room.

Kai searched the shelves, taking out books and flipping through them with interest. She moved to the desk, her gaze resting on a picture frame with a photo of her. Ignoring the soreness in her throat, and the dark mood at being lied to for so long, she rummaged through her husband's private papers.

"I don't think the safe would be in here. I mean, it's not that big of a room. There's no place to hide it."

His eyes flashed red as he surveyed their surroundings, and a smile curled his lips. He moved to the edge of the rug and crouched. Her heart hammered when he lifted the corner, revealing a small trap door.

"A good hiding place." He opened it to reveal the safe, a tumbler lock on the front.

"I hope you can break this thing open because I have no idea what the code is." She crossed her arms and stared down at it, wondering what new horror she'd discover about her husband.

"I am curious…" Kai muttered, more to himself as he spun the dial a few times.

It clicked, and the door popped open.

"How did you know the code?"

He shrugged. "I used your birthday." He opened the door, and the light caught the silver front of a shiny round disk.

She reached out a careful hand and lifted it from the dark depths of the safe and then spun it around, letting the rainbow colors bounced off the surface. Her heart raced faster as she read the words scrawled in Thomas' neat, curvy handwriting: Lumen Evidence.

Lumen members of the Yonah Church?

The one she'd attended as a child? That must be why Thomas had visited her aunt.

"Do you have the machine that plays these devices?" Kai asked.

She couldn't get any words out, so she nodded and moved to the living room with Kai following close. Celina had promised herself never to linger in this room, the memories still too painful to process, but she needed answers. Her body trembled as she crouched in front of the television and a blue light flashed when she turned on the console. As she inserted the disk, her heart roared in her ears, and she backed away when the recording started.

A grainy picture without sound appeared on the screen of a man wearing a hoodie, pointing a pistol at two people. A man and a woman sat on the floor inside what looked like an ordinary house. The woman burst out crying as the man mouthed something, his body shaking.

Celina's fingernails dug into her hands as she clenched her fists. She recognized the man. She would never, could never, forget the face of the man who'd pulled the trigger that changed her life forever.

The man with the hoodie pointed to the side, and the one who murdered Thomas nodded, tears streaming down his cheeks. He returned, holding a terrified boy who looked in his early teens, his hands bound behind him. The gunman forced him into a kneeling position and smacked the pistol against the back of the boy's head, making him fall forward.

His parents' mouths dropped opened, and tears streamed down their cheeks, but the man's shoulders slumped, and his arms hung at his sides, as though unmoved by their grief and fear. Celina didn't need sound to know the parents were begging for their son's life.

He moved away from the camera, and the parents cried over their son's unconscious body. He returned, dragging a boy who looked to be about six years old, his body limp.

The mother reached out to her boy, but the man hit her in the face with the handle of his pistol, and she fell back. He moved away from the camera again, and this time, it took longer for him to return. When he did, the boy wasn't with him anymore. He grabbed the eldest son and flipped him over his shoulder before, once again, vanishing from the camera. Time passed, the parents still sobbed, the mother's forehead bleeding from the gash the pistol inflicted. Then the camera turned off, and the video paused, announcing its end.

"The parents in the video…they were the ones who murdered Thomas. The ones who tried killing me."

"What is written on the disk?" He stood.

"Lumen evidence." She mumbled the words and then turned to the static buzzing across the television screen. "It's the name of the followers of the Yonah and Giona Churches. My mother used to speak badly of them after she stopped attending." She glanced at the television. "I guess this might have been why. The kidnapper must have been someone from the Lumen…"

"Did you notice the date in the corner of the video?"

"I was busy watching the kidnapping of innocent children."

The hint of a smile tilted on his lips. "You feel pity for the people who murdered your husband and tried to kill you?"

"They had something horrible happen to them, too." She took a breath, her determination unwavering. "But it doesn't change what they did. I will avenge Thomas. That much hasn't changed."

A grin widened on Kai's face. Finally, he crouched in front of the console and pressed the play button. "From the way the camera is steady and does not shake, we can assume it was placed on something to film all this. Meaning the kidnapper works alone."

"Why was it even filmed in the first place? Did they know someone would come for their kids and put it there in case? And how did Thomas even get the recording?" The questions tumbled out of her one after the other, but Kai didn't comment.

He pointed to the top right corner of the screen. "Someone filmed this about a month ago. Meaning this happened after your husband spoke to Adam, inquiring about a church. Did your aunt not find him in the church she attends?"

Something snapped together in her mind, and she headed to the door. "Let's go talk to Adam again."

"The sun is rising, he will be—"

"I don't care." She strode out the front door toward her car. "He can drink coffee while we chat."

"If the authorities ever have probable cause to come here…" Kai called out. She froze. "Are you happy to leave that disk to be found?"

Her jaw clenched. If the police found it, they might try to link Thomas or even her to the kidnapping of the boys.

"No. We'd better bring it along and get rid of it." Celina didn't know what kind of technology could put it back together if she destroyed it. The safest bet would be to get it out of here and then try her luck at disposal.

"I will take care of it." Kai vanished, only to reappear a few seconds afterward.

Things were falling together at last. Thomas had visited Marie, so maybe he'd been investigating a church. Maybe that was what he'd done instead of working.

"We should wait for night before going to The CrowBar since—"

"Like I said, he can drink coffee for all I care."

He sighed. "While Sanguis demons can digest human beverages, caffeine has no effect on them."

"Then Adam can suck my blood to stay awake."

"I will rip him apart if he touches you." His irises darkened as they did when he got angry, and she couldn't help but resent him.

Kai didn't care about her—he just didn't like others touching what was his.

"Is that what you're keeping me awake for?" Adam asked.

The Sanguis demon looked tired but not as much as Haku and Linda, who stood by his side. They were inside the main room of the now-empty club as it was early in the morning.

The few remaining lights did nothing to quell the eerie darkness, the sticky floor, or the smell of alcohol lingering in the air.

"I want you to give me the same blueprint you gave to Thomas Leviet." Celina saw no reason to ask nicely. He'd given it to her husband, and he would give it to her, or she would turn her demon loose on him.

Adam raised one eyebrow.

Linda's fingers curled into fists as she advanced on Celina. "How dare you speak to our master like that?"

Kai's eyes flashed red, and her face paled. She closed her mouth, her lips compressing into a thin line as she stared away from her king.

Adam sat straighter in his chair. "The price would be the same as Mr. Leviet's."

"What was the price you two agreed on?"

What price had Thomas put on the value of the blueprints?

"His life."

"Thomas wouldn't have given his life for a blueprint."

"Are you calling me a liar, human?" Adam's eyes glowed red in a menacing stare.

Celina leaned forward in her chair, staring right back at him. "Yeah, I'm calling bullshit, demon."

Kai sighed as though he'd grown bored by explaining to her the intricacies of his world. "He doesn't mean giving his life with death. Your husband promised to provide Adam blood. Human blood is a Sanguis demon's food source. Unfortunately, it isn't available at the convenience store."

Celina ignored Kai's attempt at a joke and focused on Adam. "For how long?"

His cold smile chilled her. "It depends on the contract. Mr. Leviet agreed to ten years of being a blood slave. You can imagine my disappointment at his death."

She could have lived happily without all the demon sarcasm. She glared at the demon. "Blood slave?" She couldn't imagine Thomas agreeing to that for any amount of time.

Though, after what she'd discovered about him so far, Thomas wasn't the man she thought she knew. Not by a longshot.

"Well, our slaves amuse us with more than blood." Adam licked his lips and winked.

"Would you agree to a deal that involves me taking the blueprint if I bring you another human in my place?" A plan formed in her mind as she spoke the words.

"It would be a risky deal for me. If you were to fail in bringing me a human, I couldn't take you since you already belong to another."

Kai put his hand on Celina's elbow, drawing her back toward his body. "I will bring you a human if she fails."

"I have one last question." Celina jerked out of Kai's grasp.

Adam stared at her, his eyes holding her captive. "Naturally."

"Did Thomas tell you why he needed the blueprints to the church?"

"He did, but that information has an extra price."

Kai stood, and Haku and Linda shrunk away. Adam glanced up at him, the muscles in his face stiffening. Kai leaned his hands against the table and stared down at the Sanguis demon. "You are trying the patience I already do not have."

Adam glanced at his children and drew a deep breath. "You have imprisoned Shiriki."

Celina's hands grew clammy at the mention of the name, and she glanced at Kai.

"He holds the link between here and the dark realm. And since his imprisonment, we've had a hard time drawing energy from the realm."

"You want me to release him?" Kai tilted his head to the side.

Celina nodded. "Fine."

Kai stared down at her, his eyes gleaming, and then straightened and waved his hand.

"Done. Though, give Shiriki time to heal. I am afraid he will have lost the function of his legs for some time." The smile on his lips burnt the air with cruel satisfaction, and for a moment, she almost felt bad for Shiriki.

"So? Who sent Thomas?" She surveyed the Sanguis demon.

"Mr. Leviet said he needed information that could be found within the church in a certain section hidden from the public," Adam spoke with the hushed voice of a man with a secret to tell. "He mentioned he needed this for his investigation into a church group called Lumen—all this for a man named David Corval."

Her lips curled into a triumphant grin. *So, Corval had a part in this mess.* "You have no idea how happy I am to hear that."

"Oh?" Adam looked curious.

"If he's involved, it means I get to watch him die." The bastard had flirted with her at Thomas' funeral. His death would not be swift or kind.

David Corval had stared her straight in the eyes and told her he was sorry for her loss.

Fucking liar.

Adam's laugh, real and warm, took her by surprise. "You've tainted her soul well… and in such a short time." He nodded with the smile still on his face. "Haku," he called out, "get the blueprint for the old Yonah Church."

Haku bowed and moved so fast that his shape blurred as he disappeared.

Why were the Lumen kidnapping children? How did Thomas get involved with all this, and what did Corval have to do with it?

After Celina's parents died and Marie became her

guardian, she'd attempted to bring back Celina into the church. Celina went to great lengths to be elsewhere every morning. After all her mother's warnings about how dangerous that particular group of people was, Celina hadn't wanted to go near the place.

Kai sat down next to her again, his fingers drumming on the armrests. She leaned into him and for a split second, his eyes widened, and a flash of vulnerability gleamed in them. As though her willingness to get close of her own free-will surprised him.

"Can I choose which human we bring to Adam?" She could practically taste the anticipation behind her choices.

He nodded, the corner of his mouth curling. Adam's words repeated inside her mind; her soul was tainted—already? Could Kai drag her to his realm and claim her as his before she'd even settled anything for Thomas?

He chuckled. "Your soul needs to be a lot more tainted than thoughts and promises of death and sacrifice." His eyes met hers. "You will need to kill them yourself."

"I'm the one who'll kill people?" Surprise raised the pitch of her tone. She always figured it would be Kai doing the killings, not her.

"I will help you hurt them enough so they cannot get away. However, you are the one who will rip their lives from them."

Haku returned and bowed as he handed a rolled-up paper to his master. Adam unrolled it and placed it on the table.

"This is a copy of the blueprint." He scanned it with his red eyes. "Here is the room Mr. Leviet inquired about." He pointed at a tiny section with one entrance.

"Let me guess. Basement?" Kai looked up from the paper to the demon, amusement glittering in his eyes.

Adam nodded.

"So, we can get in the door here." Celina traced her finger along the blueprint.

"Mr. Leviet was skeptical it would be that easy. He mentioned something about possible traps." He shuddered and drew away from the map as though it contained the traps he spoke of.

"Traps? What traps? And how would Thomas know anything about that?" At the silence of the two demons before her, she huffed out a breath. "All right then, is there another way in?"

Haku said something in Japanese, but Kai cut him off with the Demos language, his tone commanding, and a shiver prickled across her skin.

He knows I understand Japanese.

All she caught from the Sanguis demon was one word. *Journal?*

Adam cleared his throat but glared at Haku before speaking. "Older blueprints of the church showed access by a sewer system. I suggested he ask a member of the church."

"Member of the church…"

That's why Thomas visited Marie. It all fits together.

She stood.

"I suppose you have a plan in mind?" Kai asked.

"Yes," Celina said, thinking fast as she regarded each of the Sanguis demons. "I have one more question, and as all answers have a price," she lifted her arm and rolled up a sleeve, "will you accept blood from me?"

Kai grabbed her wrist and squeezed it. "No one tastes blood from you, dove…except me."

She wrenched free. "You may own my body, but until we finish this deal, I can still decide what I can or cannot do with it."

All three Sanguis demons' eyes widened as crushing darkness pressed around them. Kai's lips pulled back over his pointed teeth, and he muttered something in Demos. He turned to Adam and the Sanguis demon jumped, shrinking back from his king.

Her neck prickled at their fear, but as she recalled the terror of being trapped with Haku and Linda, Celina's lips twitched.

How do you *like feeling terrorized?*

Adam's mouth twisted as he stared back at Celina, "What's the question?"

"Did you hire the people to murder Thomas Leviet?"

The whole scene replayed inside her head like something stuck it on repeat. Thomas' eyes widened as he begged for Celina's life, ignoring his own safety as the gun pointed at his head. The explosion as the man pulled the trigger and took away her husband. She curled her hands into fists, staring at Adam and waiting for his answer.

He cracked his knuckles, his eyes turning cold. "I prefer to do my own killing, thank you. Besides, he was to be my blood slave."

She nodded and left, certain Kai's glare would bore a hole right through her.

15

CONFESSIONS

They came out of the club as Celina's car, hooked to a big red tow-truck, drove away.

"Fuck!" People turned to stare at her outburst, but she didn't care.

The urge to rip someone apart surprised her. She'd been around Kai for too long. He was rubbing off on her, and that idea alone inched her away from him.

"I warned you not to park in a no-parking zone." A cocky smile tilted on his lips.

Celina groaned, and Kai's attitude worsened her frustration. "If you've got nothing helpful to suggest, don't speak."

"Humans have other means of transportation, no?" Kai asked.

The calmness of his tone reached within her core like a wave of gentleness putting out a fire. She softened her own voice. "We could take the bus."

"Then, shall we?" Kai continued walking as if nothing were unusual, his hand brushing against hers as though reaching for it.

She pulled away and frowned at the disappointed look that flashed across his face. "Are you okay?"

"Do you know where the church is?" He glanced at her, acting like nothing had happened.

"Kai," she spoke quietly, "I just really want to get this all over with. It's been eating at me, and this feels like this is the first break we've had, but—"

He wrapped one arm around her, gentle maroon eyes gazing down at her. "You'll get your revenge. You have my word."

They headed downtown and waited at the bus stop. Celina glared at any women who smiled at her demon.

Get a hold of yourself.

He drew her closer to his body, and her cheeks grew warm.

"What are you doing?" Her skin tingled at his touch, and her voice was barely a whisper.

"Giving the message to others around that I'm not interested." He leaned in and pressed his lips against hers. Heat washed over her even as goosebumps rose on her arms. She couldn't think of anything other than the caress of his lips, the hand cradling her waist, the heat pooling in her stomach. By the time he withdrew from her, the women were no longer gazing at Kai. One shot her a dirty look instead.

Before she could make sense of her emotions, the bus pulled up next to the sidewalk.

She sat down on a seat that had another available one next to it. "Here."

As her heartbeat neared its normal beating range, she reminded herself what Kai was, and that the kiss meant nothing. He could never be to her what Thomas had been—gentle and affectionate.

"I can be gentle." Kai's whisper tickled the shell of her ear as he sat next to her. "I can be everything you dream of."

She crossed her arms. "Stay out of my head."

He grinned, and the bus stutter-stepped along with the morning traffic. Three stops later, they stepped onto the busy sidewalk. The sunlight outside lent the air its warmth, the promise of better days to come. Her heart ached; when this was over, she would never again feel the warmth of summer, the breezes stirring along her skin, the rays as she bathed in a golden glow of light.

She drew in a breath, but it shook with the tightness of her throat.

"Something on your mind?" Kai's voice pulled her from her thoughts.

"Nothing." She knew he'd just comment about how hot the dark realm was or something like that.

"It can be cold, too."

"If you go into my head one more time, I'll—"

He turned his body toward her, honest curiosity reflected in his eyes. "You'll what?"

Celina bit her tongue. She didn't have an answer.

Before long, they'd walked the four blocks from the bus stop, and arrived at the church.

"There's a side door to the administration office." She moved around the side of the building. "I'd rather not go into the sanctuary."

They walked to the door, but she stopped and observed Kai from head to toe.

"If you'd like a better look, just ask." His hands moved to the top button of his shirt, and a wicked smile spread over his lips.

She rolled her eyes and ignored him, wrapping her arms around herself. "Can you go into a church? I mean, since you're—"

"A demon? Yes, I'm aware." He tilted his head to the side.

"Are you going to be okay in there?"

As much as she hated him—going inside her head, invading her personal space, ordering cruel experiments, and even threatening her—a part of her wouldn't be able to bear it if something hurt him. It was a part she'd rather not know about, but it existed.

His eyebrows rose, but a gentle smile appeared on his lips. "I knew you'd be interesting to work with. I see I wasn't mistaken." He grinned. "I may burst into flames—"

"Are you serious?" Her fists clenched as she took a few steps closer to him. "You were going in there without saying anything? What if something happened to you? I wouldn't even know what to do." She grabbed the front of his jacket, panic seething in her veins. "You aren't allowed to die on me."

His gaze shone with such fondness it brought tears to her eyes. Celina bit the inside of her cheek. She already felt weak and stupid and didn't want to add weeping to her list.

"I won't burst into flames. That was a joke. And I'm immortal—always have been and always will be. I can't be killed."

She let him go and backed away, smoothing his jacket. "I'm sorry I overreacted. It's been a strange day." She couldn't take her gaze off his face.

Kai slid his hands along her waist and advanced, forcing her to stumble back. She opened and closed her mouth, her breath hitching as he pinned her against the stone wall of the church, and her blood ran cold, freezing her in place. "You know what you're feeling, but your human consciousness can't accept what your heart already knows. Stop fighting yourself and give in to me."

"What I'm feeling—or not—doesn't matter. We both know once you've completed your end of the deal, it will be all over for me."

And I still love Thomas; I won't betray him. But…

He kissed her, this time using her passion against her, drawing the feelings from her as his tongue slipped inside her mouth and caressed her own. She threw herself into the kiss, body…and soul. When she shuddered, he withdrew from her and flashed his mischievous smile.

"Shall we go inside then?"

She took a breath to steady herself. "And nothing bad will happen to you?"

"If anything, the church may burst into flames."

"Stay with me. Promise you will." An eternity of torment awaited her at the hands of this demon, but he was *her* demon.

"I promise." He held the door for her.

A woman sat at the reception desk, a large cross hanging behind her. Celina glanced sideways at Kai, still half-expecting a giant fireball to take his place.

The woman gave an over-polite smile. "Good morning! May I help you?"

"I was wondering if my aunt's volunteering today? Marie Tayen."

"I believe she's here, as a matter of fact." The woman grabbed a sheet of paper, her finger inching down the page as her eyes scanned the words. "Ah, yes. Just follow this corridor down, turn left, left again, and you'll come to a door that says 'staff.'" She waved her hand behind her.

Celina thanked the woman and walked alongside Kai. "Did you memorize the blueprint?"

"I did."

"Do you know where the room we're looking for would be from here?"

"Yes."

"Okay, here's the plan then." She glanced at Kai, remembered the kiss, and heat made its way up her cheeks. "You find an entrance to that room, and I'll go find my aunt to ask her why Thomas was here." Her chest tightened as she thought of her husband's lies. She hated him, but still loved him. Was this why she was drawn to Kai?

Am I taking my revenge out on Thomas the only way I can now that he's…gone?

Kai glanced away from her. "I'll fetch you when I'm needed again."

Her eyes narrowed, but he'd already vanished. "I swear, men are all alike, whatever species."

She leaned against the wall and closed her eyes, breathing deeply through her nose as another dizzy spell hit her. Her hand went to where Kai's brand was burned into her flesh, and she traced it.

It's taking a toll.

Voices caught her attention, and she opened her eyes, staring toward an open door. With a sigh, she straightened and walked toward it. Celina spotted her aunt, chatting with a couple of other church members while packing boxes. As soon as their eyes met, the blood drained from Marie's face.

"What are you doing here?" Her hissed whisper conveyed her displeasure and surprise.

Celina's eyebrows rose, but she remained calm knowing she'd get more information than if she blurted the questions out. "Can we talk?"

"Did you come with the devil?" Her aunt glanced to the door like he might be hiding behind it.

"Look, I need to speak to you in private."

All gazes rested on Celina. One man even crossed himself as though he expected a giant hand to reach down from the sky and pluck him to eternity.

"So that your devil can attack me and drag me to Hell?" She grabbed onto the box in front of her with shaky hands.

Celina sighed. "Please, I need to ask you questions."

"You're desperate for answers?"

"I am, yes." Celina was sure her aunt would ask her for something in exchange. "Will you come speak with me? We can go where you—"

"Follow me then." Her aunt stopped at the entrance and poked her head out to look both ways down the corridor.

Celina followed her upstairs until they came into the central part of the church. It was as dark and stuffy as she remembered.

From the time Celina was born until she turned nine, she'd been forced to attend this church with her mother and aunt every morning. She'd begged her mother to leave her at home, but her mother insisted Celina attend. Only when her mother remarried did they stop going. As far as she knew, her mother and her aunt never spoke to each other after that. That her mother had stopped attending was strange, considering her parents had a connection to a demon.

A knot tightened in her stomach at the thought of Shiriki.

"We can sit here." Her aunt's voice jolted her out of a past she didn't understand.

Celina sat next to her on the long wooden benches at the front. "I need to ask—"

"I will answer your questions on one condition."

"Of course."

Her aunt ignored her muttered reply. "I am concerned for your soul, and I want you to go to confessional right after I answer your questions. It may redeem you. I wasn't able to convince your mother or stepfather. Then they died, and it was too late."

"Don't talk about my parents."

Celina had never known her biological father since he left before she was even born. To her, the man her mother married when she was nine years old was her father, and no one could ever tell her otherwise.

"I suppose the answers you seek aren't as important to you as I thought." Marie's lips pressed down together.

"Fine. I'll go confess to the priest right after you answer my questions."

"Thank you." Marie stared at her and let out a small sigh.

"I just don't understand you. I was good to you after your parents died. Took you in, cared for you as though you were my own. What thanks do I get?"

"I'm not here to talk about that. The past is the past. Let's leave it there."

She had no intentions of making up with her aunt, not after what she'd discovered about Audrey—the aunt she once had and would never meet.

"If you wish. However—"

"You mentioned at Thomas' service he came to visit you here. Why? What did he say? Was there anything strange about his behavior?"

Her aunt pressed her lips together at being cut off, but a shadow passed over her face. "He came to find me. It surprised me since we'd only spoken once on the phone. He must've seen a photo of me because he recognized me when he came."

Celina's mind raced. She had no photos of her aunt. Her mother had thrown them all away. Maybe it was a coincidence but knowing Thomas—and what she had learned recently about him—she doubted it.

"And?" Celina encouraged her to continue.

"He talked about the church and how beautifully built he thought it looked. Said something about old churches and secret rooms. Your husband asked if there were any in this church."

"Are there? I mean, secret or hidden rooms?" She kept the urgency of her tone in check.

Her aunt wrinkled her brow. "I told Thomas if there are, I don't know where."

"I also noticed you were talking to David Corval at the funeral. Do you know him?" Adam mentioned Thomas exchanging the ten years of his life as a blood slave to the Sanguis demons, all for a blueprint on behalf of that man.

"David Corval?" Marie's eyes widened. "Yes, he used to

be a member of this church, but he renounced the truth and left. Such a pity, he was a good man." Her aunt spoke in the past tense as if he'd died.

"Was there anything else Thomas mentioned while he was here?"

"Come to think of it, he asked something strange." A faraway look glazed her aunt's eyes.

"Strange?"

"He asked if the disciples of this church still had the original Lumen within."

"Original Lumen? What exactly is the Lumen?"

"A name we call ourselves, but I don't know what he meant by the original."

"I see."

"After I told him I knew nothing about it, he left. That was the first and last time I ever saw him." Her aunt stood. "Now, time for your confessional."

Celina sighed but stood. She'd never done a confessional, but what could it hurt?

"Can priests divulge what you confess to them?"

"No. It would be against—"

"Even to the police if it was something against the law? Or if it was something that could endanger the lives of others?" she cut in, wanting to know for sure.

Marie almost ran in her hurry to get Celina to the confessional.

"Father Christopher would never betray the holy order. He doesn't even know who you are if that's any reassurance to you. Being a heathen, I wouldn't think the promises made by the church would mean anything to you." She pressed her hand against Celina's back and gave her a shove. Celina stumbled forward into the small compartment of the confessional and said nothing as her aunt closed the curtain.

She sat on the small wooden platform and studied the

cramped space. *This is what being buried alive would be like.* Her chest tightened at the thought.

The priest opened the partition. Her mother and aunt had talked about their first confession, comparing what mistakes they'd made, and sometimes discussing what the priest recommended they do. Overwhelmed ever since Thomas' murder and the deal she made with Kai, the weight of her solitude ached within her. The only person she could talk to at this point in her life was the demon, and he wouldn't or couldn't understand human emotions.

"Forgive me, Father, for I have sinned." She remembered the first part well, but then a small smile came to her lips. "Well, I've never confessed."

"It is never too late to start, child," Father Christopher said.

The resonance of his voice reassured her, and words poured out. "After my husband was murdered, and the murderers tried to kill me, I met a demon in the forest behind my house." She never realized how ridiculous it sounded until she heard herself say it.

"A demon? You mean someone of ill mind?"

"No, no, an actual demon. I made a deal with him. Revenge for the people who'd wronged me and my husband in exchange for my life and soul."

"My child, what you are saying is—"

"Crazy? Yes, I've said that myself before. And yet here I am, confessing to a priest because my aunt wouldn't give me answers I need until I promised to. Besides, who else could listen to me ramble about my choices? Or sins as you'd call them, I imagine." Bitter amusement tinged her voice.

"Tell me, my child, why you exchanged something as precious as your life and soul." Disbelief lifted his voice.

"Because my husband had just been murdered, and I was injured and pissed off. At the time, his offer made sense."

"At the time? You have regrets, then?"

"I have some regret because everything I thought I knew before my husband died is wrong. But it doesn't matter. I can't go backwards. Still, that's not the worst part."

"In confession, we start with the sins we need most forgiveness for."

"My greatest sin…" She paused. "I think I'm falling in love with the demon." She wiped the tears from her eyes before they could roll down her cheeks.

After a few seconds of stunned silence, the priest cleared his throat. "Anything else, my child?" Father Christopher's voice wavered as though nervous about her answer.

"To be honest, I've done so many bad things, I'd be in here for a long time. Besides, if there is a God, I don't think he'd forgive me."

"God forgives all His children even if they don't believe in Him."

"How does this sin thing work? I might need to confess for someone else. Can I do that?" Without waiting for an answer, she plunged forward. "My husband isn't the person I thought he was in all the time I've known him. The last five years…since we got married, has been nothing but a lie. Even before that, probably. And now he's gone and can't confess for himself."

"Would your husband's lies be the fault of the demon then?" Skepticism dried his tone.

"I find it strange you're willing to believe in God, but I'm the crazy person because I said I made a deal with the devil."

"Devil? I thought you said demon?"

"I did, but since he's the king of the dark realm—"

"Mekaisto." His voice trembled.

Her back tensed, and she caught a blur of movement as he disappeared from the partition. Father Christopher drew back the curtain and grabbed her by the arm, beads of sweat on his forehead.

She swallowed hard. "You've heard of him?" How was it possible for another human to know about Kai?

Unless the priest wasn't human.

"Mekaisto is darkness itself."

"How do you know about him?"

The priest's shoulders tensed, and he glanced around. He let her go and backed away. "That's a long story." The lines around his mouth tightened. "Is he here?"

"Father, please, tell me how you know Kai."

"Kai?"

"Only my dove may call me that." His voice startled her, and she turned to find Kai lounged against a wall, listening.

Father Christopher followed Celina's gaze, his eyes widening. Kai had taken the demon form she'd seen him in most often so far—more intimidating than ever.

"Mekaisto," the priest whispered.

The smile on Kai's lips sent a shiver down Celina's spine. "How interesting. I have not seen an original Lumen leader for a while."

16

ANCIENT TRAPS

"Original Lumen?" Celina took a few steps forward.

Father Christopher scrubbed a hand over his face before turning to her. "You sold your soul to the darkest and most dangerous demon." He crossed his arms while focusing on Kai. "And you, Mekaisto…you don't make deals with humans. Why her? Why now?"

"That is not the business of a priest, but my private affair."

"Would one of you please explain what an original Lumen is?" An exasperated sigh at being left out of the conversation blew between her lips.

The priest glanced at her, but Kai was the first to answer. "I will explain later." He walked away, heading to the main doors.

"My child, you mustn't go with him."

"I have to. I need him." She turned away, but the priest caught her arm in a meat-fisted grasp, yanking her to a stop.

"Be careful around him. He manipulates humans to get what he wants. Mekaisto has existed for so long that even his secrets have secrets and—"

"Your point?"

"Don't you wonder why the evilest demon, one who has

existed since before the beginning of time, a demon who has never made a deal with a human, would betray the only code he exists by to take *your* life and soul?"

Celina stared at Kai. "He won't tell me," she confessed, "and it's not as if I have any other ways of finding out."

The demon's voice rang out. "We are leaving."

She gave Father Christopher one last glance, yanked her arm free, and moved toward the demon. Once outside the church, she turned to Kai. "Did you find the room?"

He had switched back to his human form again, but he looked no less intimidating as he shot her a narrowed glance. "The door is well protected. We will only gain entry by using the tunnels of the old sewer system."

"Even from you?"

"I could go through. However, the room has a fail trap that would set it on fire and destroy whatever is inside."

"Sewers then."

"You're not coming." His voice hardened. "I'll bring back whatever is relevant. Did your aunt answer your questions?"

"Yeah, but at some cost to my faith." She pushed the secrets she'd confessed to Father Christopher to the back of her mind.

He grabbed her arm and spun her. "Trying to block something you don't want me to see inside your mind will make me dig without being gentle."

"Sometimes, I wish I could go inside your head to see what you're thinking." Her resentment made her petulant, and she crossed her arms.

His eyes flashed despite his human appearance. "Be careful what you wish for. My mind contains more evil than the dark realm itself."

Nausea knotted her stomach, and she pressed her hand over her mouth as her steps faltered. Kai grasped her shoulders, steadying her as her body shook. He stayed silent as she stared at him, his eyes lightening into hints of red as though unable to control his form.

She blinked a few times, and her breathing relaxed. "I'm fine," she breathed. "Could we stay outside a bit?"

The afternoon sun brought her back to peaceful times in her backyard where she used to sit. Besides, she needed to organize everything inside her mind. They found a small restaurant with a terrace and sat.

"Are you going to tell me what an original Lumen is?"

"They used to go by a different name—Venatores. That's why I wasn't sure about the word at first. The members are a group of humans who have existed for many generations. They are demon hunters, and although they had many descendants, their line is dying out. The priest you were confessing to is a leader, an expert among his group."

"I used to be a member. My mother's family were all considered Lumen, but none of us were any kind of hunters." She frowned. "Though I guess you already knew that."

He grinned but didn't comment on her assumption. "All the members of this faith have the blood of Venatores running through their veins, even if most aren't trained in the art of demon hunting anymore."

"Why are they dying out?"

He shrugged. "Because I send demons to kill them."

A horrible feeling seeped through her, but she couldn't pinpoint why her stomach clenched at his words. Not sure how to reply to what he'd said, she changed subjects and told Kai what her aunt said about Thomas.

"So, it's weird Thomas went there asking about the original Lumen members, right? I mean, do regular human beings even know about them?" She leaned forward, wanting his thoughts on the mystery.

He narrowed his eyes, and for a second, they flashed red. "It's not impossible. Some know more than they're supposed to, particularly if they find old texts Venatores were careless with."

"I guess we'll know more once we get into the room."

His jaw clenched. "Once *I* get into the room."

She scooted to the edge of the chair to get even closer. "I made it clear that when it's something that has to do with my plan for revenge, I'm not left out."

He gritted his teeth. "I'll bring the information to you. You won't be left out or—"

"I'm coming with you, and that's final."

Kai considered her for a few seconds before a smile appeared on his lips, his eyes gleaming. "Taking charge with a demon? You fascinate me."

A waiter came to their table, and they ordered. Celina nibbled at her food, her mind stuck on Father Christopher's words.

"Instead of trying to figure out the answer," he drummed his fingers on the table's edge, "why not just ask the question?"

"Will you answer it?"

"Maybe."

"The priest reminded me of something. I asked, but you didn't want to answer."

"And you're still trying to get an answer from me? What a brave girl you are."

She narrowed her eyes into a glare but continued. "Why did you make a deal with me?"

He cocked his head. "That again?"

"Yes, *that* again." She crossed her arms.

"I've already told you. You fixed the branch of my tree, and I only wanted—"

"To return the favor. Yeah, I got that," she said, "and I know you don't lie. Or at least I've heard nothing that says otherwise..."

"You're circling around the point."

"That's a weak reason, don't you think?" Celina issued her words as a challenge, but when he clenched his jaw and his eyes lightened to a shade of red, she added, "I mean, it might be one reason, but I think there's a much bigger picture you're not telling—"

"How about another little deal, Celina?" When her posture became rigid, he continued, "An informal one."

"And what's this informal deal?"

"If you stop asking me why I made a deal with you, I promise to answer that before I claim your soul. Deal?" He winked.

She tilted her head. His anger had dissipated, but he shoved a forkful of food into his mouth, so it was clear he didn't intend to answer further. "Deal."

Kai smiled, his eyes softening.

They stood near the church, darkness surrounding them with only the streetlights for illumination. Kai had switched back to his demon form since, at this hour, the odds of meeting anyone were slim.

"Which sewers are we using?" Celina imagined herself swimming inside murky waters.

"The building behind the church is being renovated. The tunnels go right under it, so we will reach the room that way."

"It'll be dark." She held her body rigid to suppress a shudder.

"I would worry less about the dark and more about the traps down there." Kai strode toward the building.

Celina ran to him, drawing in rapid breaths. "Traps? What traps?"

"To stop demons from entering the room."

"But it won't work on you, right? And since I'm human—"

He glanced at her and his shoulders tensed. "The Lumen fight fire with fire. They will have tame demons, illusions, and all manner of dark curses in those tunnels."

She blinked several times. "Can demons even be tamed?"

"Sanguis demons, yes."

He threw open the door, leaving splinters of wood hanging from the doorframe. They located the basement quickly since only one door in the room creaked open to a flight of stairs leading down to darkness and the smell of dampness. Kai descended the steps first, Celina following closely. She clasped her hands tighter with each step, glancing back to the only source of light.

They stopped in front of a large brick wall, and Kai smirked as he passed his hand over the rough surface. "When will humans learn that keeping something forbidden only makes others crave it more?"

She eyed him, her heartbeat quickening.

Those words seem to have a deeper meaning than a brick wall.

His fingers pressed against it and cracks split the bricks apart like an earthquake shook them. It crumbled to his feet, and she closed her eyes as the dust flew all around the basement.

They stepped into the hole, the dripping of water haunting the old tunnels.

Waving his hand, a white light grew larger until it illuminated most of the tunnel.

He stared ahead. "Stay close."

She nodded and kept her lips pressed together.

A high platform ran into the darkness straight ahead, murky black water flowing next to them. She rubbed her arms at the sound of the drainage suction combined with the dripping; it gave her the creeps.

The tunnel changed toward the end, the water no longer

taking most of the space, but a low rumbling sounded threatening as though the ceiling might crumble any minute.

"I have not seen Lumen traps in some time. This will be amusing."

"I fail to see the fun in this," she muttered with a shiver.

"I am interested to see if they have changed their methods throughout the centuries."

"Did the traps work before?" She kept closer to Kai, trying to ignore the sound of breathing resonating in the distance. What was down there?

"They worked on many demons, yes."

"Well, if it ain't broke, don't fix it."

Kai chuckled, his footsteps echoing along with hers as they continued down the straight path. Celina froze and grabbed on to him, her eyes catching movement up ahead.

"I do not suppose you ever thought you would hold on to a demon for safety," Kai quipped as he glanced ahead.

"What is that?" Her voice trembled, and her fingers clutched tighter; she tried not to notice the muscles in his bicep.

The thing came into view. It looked human but shuffled on its knees, the lower legs dragging behind like they were no longer connected with ligaments. Its skin was pale with large gaping holes oozing of thick, dark liquid across its body. With the jaw and eyes missing, it was horrifying.

"This," Kai pointed toward it, "is what happens to a human caught by Sanguis demons."

Celina let go of him and gaped. "That thing is human?"

"*Was* human," Kai corrected.

A shiver ran down her spine. Would this be what she'd look like once Kai took her life and soul?

"Is it dangerous?" she whispered as the monster came closer.

Its face lifted as it sniffed the air.

"Not to me." Kai stepped forward.

She tried grabbing his hand to stop him from going closer, but her fingers brushed along his sleeves as he moved away, and a lump formed in her throat.

I don't want him near that.

Her eyebrows rose in surprise when he crouched in front of it and caressed its hair, like a pet. "Please tell me you're not going to adopt it." She forced her mouth into a smile.

"It has been down here for some time."

"How long?"

"A few hundred years." Kai stood, and the monster climbed the wall and hung upside down on the ceiling.

She ran to Kai and grabbed his arm again. "Will it—?"

"It will not hurt you; it knows who you belong to." He took her by the hand and continued down the tunnel.

She twined her fingers with his without arguing, her gaze lingering on the monster.

"Where is the entrance to the room, anyway?"

Kai stayed silent and continued walking. After a few more steps, he pointed at a metal plate in the ceiling. "Above."

"Of course, it couldn't be easy."

"I will go inside first, make sure there are no traps that can hurt you."

"You're leaving me here alone? With that monster wandering around?" Her voice screeched from her throat.

"It is not alone, and there is far worse here. Stay put. Nothing will hurt you. They can sense my brand on you."

She caressed the uneven skin on her abdomen, unconvinced the demonic tattoo could help her. Celina opened her mouth to argue her fears, but he'd already vanished. Footsteps ran behind her, and she spun. Clutching her throat, she gasped for air as fear pulsated inside her, but the runner raced by so fast she couldn't see it.

"Hello?" she whispered.

Again, someone ran behind her. This time, she stared down at a small girl, and her breath caught in her throat.

Oh shit. That's me when I was three.

Her body stiffened.

"Where's my mommy?" the little girl asked in a small voice, tears filling her eyes.

"Don't be scared." It was difficult to reassure someone while her chin and lips trembled so much.

"Mommy doesn't want me to see daddy."

"Why not?" She searched for the memories she had about her father. At this age, it had been only Celina and her mother, so she was speaking about her—their—biological father.

"Mommy cries when I ask about daddy." Tears rolled down the little girl's cheeks.

Memories of her mother crying when she thought Celina couldn't see washed through her mind. It had been so long ago, she'd forgotten those moments.

The tears changed into blood, and the girl melted into a puddle of oozing flesh on the ground. Celina backed away in jerky steps, wrapping her arms around herself, and when she bumped into something solid, she stiffened. Whispers came from behind her, and when a hand rested on her shoulder, she gagged on the reek of decay.

Another monster resembling the first one they'd seen slithered in front of her and jerked in quick movements. It sniffed at her hair, and Celina tried to control the shaking of her body, as its hand touched her abdomen where her brand was. The head spun all the way back, the tendons stretching under the rotting skin and snapping.

Kai reappeared inside the room, and took a step toward her, his eyes glowing red. "Come with me."

Celina didn't move. Her legs locked, and she whimpered as she gasped for air.

Kai came forward, patted the new monster on the head with affection, and then took Celina around the waist. He guided her under the hole in the ceiling and waved his hand.

The trapdoor opened, revealing light. Wrapping his arms around her, she blinked once and found herself inside the secret room.

"What the hell happened down there?" Celina glanced at Kai, still shaking, "I saw myself when I was three years old! Do you know how unnatural that is?"

He shrugged as he searched through the books. "I am not human, so I would not know."

She peered through the exit into the tunnels, not wanting to go back out that way. "Can we use the door after we're done in here?"

"The room may react, as I explained earlier."

"That's fine since we'll have what we came for," she said, determined never to go down into those tunnels again. "How do we find what we're looking for?"

The room was much smaller than she'd imagined. The walls had dark gray shelves lined with papers, books, documents, and strange objects. Some looked like hollow globes with clock-like wheels spinning fast inside. Others were boxes that rattled with occasional whistling sounds. Celina jumped at the clicks and bangs coming from large glowing stones.

"Touch nothing that emits any kind of light."

"Like I'd do that."

Stop lying to him, he can see right through you.

Kai put his hand up and moved across the room until he stopped in front of a thick folder. He took it and moved to the door. "We can go."

Again, he lifted his hand, but this time waved it to the side. The door exploded, fire sparking within the shelves, destroying most of the objects.

They left the burning room, but he stopped, his gaze sweeping the inside of the church. Kai handed Celina the folder and gave her a smile.

"You will wait for me to return."

She opened her mouth to protest but froze when footsteps

ran in their direction. Kai touched her shoulder and she staggered backward, staring around their hotel room. He'd sent her back alone.

After a few hours, when Kai hadn't returned, Celina's heart throbbed as though it would break through her chest. She paced, wondering what the hell to do.

The door opened. "It's about ti—" She stopped when Father Christopher stepped inside, a gentle smile on his lips.

"Hello, my child."

"No, no, no! There are no hellos until you explain what you're doing here. How did you even—?"

"I asked the hotel reception for your room number."

"They wouldn't have given it. They would have called for Kai or me and asked if—"

"I didn't phrase that right, apologies." He gave a small bow and smiled sheepishly. "I meant that while a member of my group distracted the receptionist at the desk, I looked up your room number."

"But you don't know my name and besides—"

"Your aunt is a member of my church. Did you think she wouldn't tell me your name, Celina?"

"Okay, fine, but you still haven't told me why you're here."

Did this have to do with Kai? Did Father Christopher know they had been inside his church?

"After your aunt told me what you were asking about, I made plans."

"Plans?"

"Yes, I knew the demon would come back to the church, after hours." Father Christopher held a note of excitement in his voice she didn't like. A chill ran down her spine as she imagined the worst. "We caught him in the most powerful demon trap we've ever created, and he's now imprisoned there."

"You imprisoned Kai?" Her heartbeat sounded in her ears, and her balance faltered for a second.

"I wanted to come to tell you the good news so—"

"The good news?"

His features softened. "Your life and soul no longer belong to Mekaisto. You're free."

I'm free.

She could live and keep her soul. Millions of dollars waited in a bank account. At twenty-five, she could do whatever she wanted.

None of it sounded appealing, though. Her husband was dead, and his memory was tainted with his lies. She made a deal for revenge, and although the circumstances had changed, she wanted it. How would she achieve it without Kai?

I don't want to be without him. He promised he'd stay with me.

"You said he's the most powerful demon. What makes you think you can keep him imprisoned?" What would Kai do once he got free?

"Mekaisto would have gotten out already if he'd been able to."

"So, is that all you came to tell me?"

I have to get to him. I have to save him.

"Celina," the priest said with a smile. "Don't you understand you have your whole life ahead of you again?"

Perhaps he wouldn't leave until he'd convinced her of the great news. She pushed thoughts of Kai being imprisoned in a horrible trap away to put on a fake smile. "You're right. I get to live my life—a second chance at it."

His smile widened. "I'm pleased you see it. We'll do everything we can to kill him, or at least keep him trapped. Please try not to worry."

The door closed behind the priest, and she was left alone inside the room.

Kill him? Kill Kai?

She pictured herself without Kai, and her chest tightened. Tearing her heart out would have hurt less than the thought of him being killed. Did the Lumen have a way to rip away his immortality?

Celina couldn't lose someone again. She couldn't bear it. She wouldn't leave Kai to remain imprisoned either.

It wasn't just about her revenge anymore. It was more than that.

She wanted him to keep his promise and stay with her.

17

WITHIN REACH

The sanctuary in Yonah Church was in lockdown, but the rest of the holy grounds remained opened to the public to avoid attracting suspicion. Kai stood in the middle of a circle of blue flames, four metallic pillars about his height surrounding it, electricity sparking between them.

Father Christopher stared at him from head to toe, a frown wrinkling his forehead. "I still can't understand why you've made a deal with a human."

Kai swept ash from his sleeve. "Does it concern you?"

The priest held his head high. "Of course, it does. Celina may not have attended the church in a long time, but she remains a Lumen member."

The room illuminated in purple color for a split second as Kai's eyes flashed red, mixing with the blue light around him. "That is where you are mistaken."

Father Christopher glanced down at the floor, took a deep breath, and then stared back into the red eyes. "Her mother's family were Lumen and descended from one of the greatest Venatores. She is—"

"What did your predecessor tell you about why her

mother left the church?" Kai smiled to reveal his pointed teeth.

"It was a personal choice, that's all." His voice shook a little. "A temporary loss of faith after the tragedy that befell—"

He chuckled. "Elizabeth Tayen had better reasons to leave the church, and Father Robert knew them." Kai inspected his fingernails, his glowing eyes lending a red tinge to his skin. "I suppose he did not trust you enough to confide in you the details."

Taunting humans had never once changed throughout time; it was always so easy.

The priest's hands curled into fists as he stomped forward. "And why would you know any of this, Mekaisto?"

Another Lumen member came forward and placed her hand on Father Christopher's arm. "The others have arrived, Father."

Drawing in a breath, he nodded. "I..." He glanced at Kai. "I'll go see to them."

The girl, in her early twenties, stared at Kai with wide eyes.

He grinned. "It is impolite to stare, Kelsee."

She glanced around the room, her heartbeat accelerating. "I should join the others..."

Kai crossed his arms and gave a low chuckle at her increasing terror. "Uncertain you should speak with me? And yet," he stepped forward, "you have so many questions swirling inside your mind."

She bit her lower lip. "You're the devil?"

"If you are still being trained as the Venatores once were, then you know that is incorrect."

"They haven't taught me everything...yet. Most are busy with their own lives, and there aren't many left." She tugged at her gray cloak, the standard attire for all Lumen hunters.

"I have noticed, yes." He stared at the pillars surrounding

him. "The last time I infiltrated this group, there were about fifty thousand members."

She let out a small gasp. "I never knew there were that many. When was this?"

"In the late fourteen-hundreds."

She shuffled a little closer to the trap, and Kai couldn't help a smirk.

Keep asking questions, curious little thing…

"Then, you've existed for a while…" The light in her eyes further faded away the more she asked questions and revealed her mind to him.

"I smell the question that burns through all Lumen at the moment." He leaned in toward the edge, his voice barely a whisper. "Ask it."

Her heart hammered, but the rest of her body numbed. "Why make a deal after all this time?"

"Why so curious about that? Is there something you need?"

Kelsee took a step forward. "No."

The electricity sparked angry blue colors as he traced his sharp fingernails against the invisible wall. "Are you certain?"

Some humans are too easy to hypnotize.

Entranced by his piercing red eyes, she stepped closer. The thirst for knowledge filled her mind; it was the first thing he noticed, and all he had to do was respond to every question.

Kai put out his hand over the electricity. It sparked around his wrist, but he ignored the tingling sensation, keeping his eyes locked on his prey.

Take my hand.

"I…" She reached out to him, and Kai drew her in close, the glowing of his eyes reflecting in hers. "I want…"

He leaned in a little closer, searching into her emotions and feeling her fear radiating through. His sharp fingernail traced around her throat, her terror feeding his darkness. Her body trembled, and his lips curled into a cruel smile.

Tell me what you wish for.

The other members walked in, accompanied by Father Christopher, and they froze at the scene. Kelsee stood inside the trap with Mekaisto, a blank stare on her face. A few of the members ran toward the pillars.

"Get her out!" One of the Lumen scrambled to the front of the sanctuary, digging old texts out from the bookcase against the wall.

"Kelsee..." the priest muttered.

Kai broke the spell keeping her in a trance, and her eyes widened as she fought to wrench free of him.

Such terror... almost too delicious to pass up.

He turned his stare on the Lumen who stood still, glancing from Kai to Father Christopher, waiting for orders.

The priest took a few steps forward. "Please...she's young. She doesn't—"

Kai chuckled. "Yes, and she is innocent." He bent down and breathed in the air around her while she cried out. "If you do not stop crying, I will rip off most of your skin and fill your throat with it." His smile widened. "A lesson for you, Kelsee; human flesh makes for an interesting gag."

She pressed her lips together, her entire body trembling while tears continued to roll down her cheeks.

Father Christopher strode to the edge of the trap, his jaw clenching. "Mekaisto."

Kai grabbed her by the hair, holding her against him as he addressed everyone in the room. "You are all pathetic and weak compared to what you used to be. You let time modernize your ranks and forgot what exists in the darkness." He yanked her head back, and she screamed. "Well, allow me to remind you."

"You're the one killing everyone in our ranks," the priest spat, as though forgetting who he spoke to.

Kelsee reached into her cloak and tried to slash at Kai with a blade, but he grabbed her wrist, the smile never leaving his lips. "That was unwise." He waved his hand to the side, and Kelsee brought her hands to her own neck, eyes wide.

"Help…" She barely had the word out when her head turned to the side, slow and steady, forcing her skin to stretch, the tendons to twist. The bones cracked until her flesh and muscles ripped, her head continuing to twist all the way around, her shriek ending in a bubbly gurgle. The final twist ripped her flesh, and the girl's head rolled out of the trap, stopping at the Lumen members' feet.

Gasps and retching noises filled the sanctuary as Kai dropped the decapitated body.

Playtime…

18

CHOICES

Celina marched out of the hotel after changing her clothes, even more determined than the night she told Kai one simple word: Deal. The air was cool, and hardly anyone was out this late. She jogged almost all the way and stopped only once she stood in front of Adam's goth club, The CrowBar.

She stepped inside, out of place in her blue jeans and white top. "I need to talk to Adam," she told the bartender.

"Sorry, but he's not—"

"Tell him it's Kai's friend."

The bartender's eyebrows furrowed, but he stepped behind a curtain, disappearing from sight. She waited by the bar until someone tapped her shoulder, making her turn. Celina found herself face-to-face with Haku.

"Look at what the cat dragged in." He smirked.

She rolled her eyes. "Always nice to see you."

"What are you doing here?" He leaned against the bar.

She let out a sigh, restraining from tapping her foot at this point. "I'm here to talk to your master."

No wonder Adam's annoyed with me whenever I ask all my questions. Bet he'd love hearing me admit to that.

"Talk to me about what?" Adam stepped out from behind the curtain, followed by the barman.

"Can we talk in private?" Celina crossed her arms and added, "Somewhere other than the basement?"

He nodded and then walked to the back room.

"Maybe I'll see you later," Haku called, but she ignored him.

Adam sat on a loveseat placed further inside the room and patted the space next to him. She stared around what looked like a small living room, her skin prickling at the dim lighting that set a mood she wanted nothing to do with.

He looks human, but he's the first Sanguis demon; don't let him trick you into anything.

She forced herself to sit. "I need to ask a que—"

"Humans are always full of useless questions, but you're the limit." Although he sounded annoyed, his lips twitched.

She shrugged. "Is there a deal I can get from you to guarantee my safety, my life, and my freedom from you and your demons?"

Adam's brow furrowed. "You already have that because you belong to Mekaisto."

"I need something more than that." She stayed as calm as she could.

Hope they can't tell Kai's cut off from me, or I'll be on the dinner menu.

He arched an eyebrow. "If it's keeping you safe from whatever you got yourself into with my king, then I'm afraid—"

She shook her head. "Nothing like that, but I'm not telling you why until you guarantee me what I requested."

He stared at her, eyes gleaming. "Would my word suffice?"

In your fucking dreams. "I don't know you well enough."

He ran his tongue across his lips. "A contract signed in

blood then?" He spread his hands. "It's the normal demon way."

Celina's chest tightened, but she nodded. *Kai needs me.* "Okay."

"Done." He smiled and closed his eyes for a few seconds. When he reopened them, Linda strode in.

"Yes, master?" She bowed, her glare focused on the floor.

"If he's up to it, get Denzel to draw a contract for safety and bring it to me once he's finished," Adam instructed.

"Safety, freedom, and my life. And from all Sanguis demons," Celina added.

Linda's mouth opened, but no sound emerged.

"Tell him to add those."

"Yes, master." Linda bowed again and moved in a blur of movement, disappearing from the room.

When the contract was brought to them, Adam's lips curled to one side over his pointed teeth, his eyes burning red. "How should we do this, then?"

Her hands curled over her lap. "What do you mean?"

"Would you like me to cut you with a knife or would you prefer I use my teeth?"

Alarm bells rang inside her ears as her heart pounded, but Kai had already been inside of that trap long enough. "Just use your teeth and let's get on with this."

Adam's eyebrows shot up, but he nodded. "As you wish."

The Sanguis demon brought his index finger to his pointed teeth and punctured his skin. A large bead of ruby red blood formed on the tip and Celina's stomach hollowed. He pressed down onto the paper, leaving a fingerprint, and then turned to her with a smile. Adam took her hand and brought her finger to his mouth, and her muscles tensed.

Celina gasped when he punctured her skin, but she withdrew and left her own mark on the contract. If Kai ever found out Adam even touched her, let alone drew blood…

Well, the last time someone harmed her, they ended up with the skin ripped off their face, hanging over a roaring fire.

Adam handed her the paper. She folded it, stuck it into her jeans pocket, and told Adam about the Lumen's trap. "I need to know if there's a way to get him out, but I won't be able to do it alone. I need help."

She'd kept her voice as steady as she could, but her mind raced with all the torture devices the Lumen had in that church, just waiting to be tested out on Kai.

If they hurt him, I'll slaughter them all.

Adam listened the whole time without interrupting, but when she fell silent, he smiled. "I understand why you wanted a guarantee of safety now. Without Mekaisto, you're vulnerable."

"Yes, I know. So, do you know anything about the Lumen? Or their traps? Anything? Can you help?"

"I can help, along with two of my children, but there's one we'll need to speak to." He glanced away from her, and his shoulders slackened.

She held her breath, waiting to find out why he looked like he needed help from his worst enemy.

"I believe you've already encountered the demon Shiriki?"

Her insides quivered. "Are you kidding me?"

"He's the keeper of information. If anyone knows about the Lumen and their traps, it would be him."

"I can't! Do you have any idea what he did the—"

"I know all too well what he does." Adam's eyes glowed. "You've asked for help, and you signed a contract in blood. You can't turn back now."

Her heart drummed against her ribcage. "What the fuck do you mean by that?"

A smug smile appeared on his lips. "We signed a demon contract that guarantees your safety because you need help, and you aren't allowed to stop until we conclude our business. In your case, saving Mekaisto." He grinned. "There are no early withdrawal clauses."

She opened and closed her mouth, her hands curling into fists.

I fucking hate them all with their tricks.

"This night keeps getting better and better." Celina gritted her teeth as she stood.

"As you're always so fond of asking questions, I believe it's my turn."

She already knew what he'd ask. "Why am I trying to rescue Kai instead of saving my life and soul?"

Adam nodded. "Indeed."

"Kai rescued me. And I know it was because he wanted what was his at the end of this deal, but he didn't abandon me. I'm just as selfish. I want my revenge, and I won't get it without Kai, so I won't abandon him, either."

She was about to leave, wanting to get a visit to Shiriki's over with, when Adam grabbed her wrist. "The contract we signed in blood guarantees your safety from Sanguis demons," he reminded her. "I have no control over Viscus demons, so be careful."

"Viscus? What's the difference between that and Sanguis demons?"

"We're Sanguis demons—second-class demons, you might say. Humans often refer to us as vampires, but while they exist, we're different." He snorted. "Shiriki is a Viscus demon —an upper-class demon, right hand to Mekaisto, and the first of his kind. Meaning he is also one of the most powerful."

"Oh." Celina shivered; that demon was already terrifying enough without knowing he was right under Kai in the power hierarchy.

Shit.

They returned to the main part of the club and found Linda and Haku chatting with a group of people farther away. Both demons stiffened and moved toward their master without Adam even opening his mouth. He explained the situation, and Haku's smile vanished while Linda gaped from Adam to Celina.

"Well, let's get this over with." A small muscle pulsed beneath Haku's eye as he spoke.

They strode out the door and headed for the one place Celina never wanted to go back to.

Linda glanced at the building across the street from where they stood, hugging her arms. "Are you sure we need to go in there?"

Adam let out a small breath. "We have little choice. Shiriki is the only one with the information we need."

Celina didn't like the demons' reaction to this; they appeared as terrified as she felt.

Why can't I leave Kai to rot and start a new life?

"Will he even want to help?" Celina's gaze darted around. "If Kai is out of the way, and he's his right hand, wouldn't that mean Shiriki would become the king of the dark realm?"

Adam shook his head. "If Mekaisto remains imprisoned, the dark realm's energy will fade, and so will we. Sanguis and Viscus demons alike."

"I still can't believe you're going in there. And to rescue Mekaisto." Haku fidgeted with the piercing in his eyebrow, his hand trembling a little.

"Why do you care if I go in there?" What she was doing was stupid, but what choice did she have? *Revenge isn't the reason I want to save Kai. I'm lying to myself.*

"You're a strange human. One would think you seek danger." Haku sighed.

Celina's gaze rested on the seventh floor, a chill coursing in her veins. "We're wasting time." She crossed the street, leading the three Sanguis demons. The security guards opened the door without a word. It took a few seconds for the woman to come rushing from the foyer to the grand entrance hall, and Adam didn't wait for her to halt.

"We need to see Shiriki."

She pointed to the staircase as she did the last time Celina was here.

Celina, Adam, Haku, and Linda climbed to the seventh floor and crept down the hallway to the door. Celina froze. She knew what waited for her behind the door this time, and as much as she needed the demon's help, fear wouldn't let her approach it.

"Easier said than done, isn't it?" Linda let out a small laugh, twirling her finger around a lock of blonde, curly hair.

"I'm only human." Celina's voice barely left her mouth, as though her throat squeezed every word.

"What a pleasant surprise." A cold voice spoke from behind them.

All three demons turned and bowed their heads.

Celina chilled from the outside as if someone poured a bucket of ice water over her. A hand pressed on her shoulder, and she kept still as her heart rate sped up. She took a breath to calm herself before facing Shiriki, but as soon as she locked eyes with the white-haired demon, her trembling returned.

"We're here for information." Adam's voice cracked, and the Viscus demon smiled.

"I am rather disappointed. I thought you brought me a gift to play with." He grabbed Celina's chin and lifted her head.

Her eyes watered but she blinked several times, willing the tears not to fall.

Linda spoke in a small voice. "We're here about a situation involving Mekaisto."

Shiriki's gaze traveled to her, and he released Celina as he moved to Linda.

The Sanguis demon's gaze remained focus on the floor as

he leaned in. "You have not visited me for a while. Does Adam no longer wish to share?" He stared in her master's direction.

Adam's body stiffened, and Celina couldn't help the shudder at Shiriki's icy tone. Linda muttered something in reply, and the Viscus demon chuckled.

Shiriki walked around them and opened the door. "Come inside."

Celina glanced at Adam and stepped in, her heart beating faster. The door slammed, and she jumped. Shiriki passed her and continued farther into the room without another word. The wooden floor creaked under Celina's halting footsteps, and every breath hurt as though she lacked oxygen.

She followed Shiriki and the Sanguis demons as they sat on the numerous armchairs in a room filled with mannequins. Only a few of the lifeless objects were bare, but the others had white sheets covering them. Most stood on pedestals, while some leaned up against the wall and others were piled on top of one another. She shuffled in between the hidden figures, the sheets fluttering as though reaching for her. Celina closed her eyes, trying to compose herself, and looked toward where the demons sat.

Shiriki stared at her, his smile filled with pointed teeth. He waved his hand to the other armchair facing him. "Sit."

She obeyed as Adam told Shiriki of the situation.

"And you know this how?" The Viscus demon brought his fingers to his mouth and used his teeth to rip the skin from the ends. His vertical pupils stared right through her, and she fidgeted in her seat. Kai did that often, but something in Shiriki's cold gaze scared her more than when it was the demon king.

She took another breath. "The Lumen leader told me he imprisoned him."

Shiriki's smile widened, and her neck prickled. "Ah." He

leaned forward and tilted his head to the side, "So you came to my lair to rescue a demon far more dangerous than me?"

"I need help—"

He grabbed her knee, his sharp fingernails digging into her skin and forcing a scream up her throat. Celina's hands gripped the armrests, fighting back tears as she stared into the demon's eyes. Adam shifted in his seat while the other two sunk deeper into theirs.

"I wonder…what has Mekaisto told you about me?"

"That you're cruel. But he didn't need to tell me—I saw it for myself." She winced, pressing her back against her chair to keep from shaking any more than she already was.

The demon loosened his hold. "Oh, you have no idea, pet."

Celina concentrated her thoughts back to Kai. "Do you have information about the Lumen that could help?"

"You should worry less about your questions and more about your safety." Shiriki let her knee go and stood.

Adam spoke, and this time, his voice shook less. "I guaranteed her safety. Though, I'm aware that doesn't include from someone as high as you. However, I request you to honor my contract with her."

Shiriki stared at him. "Your contracts mean nothing to me, Adam; I could do anything I like with her and could even make you take part, annulling your useless piece of paper." He strolled to one of the sheet-covered mannequins.

Buckets of ice couldn't have made her skin crawl more than this demon.

She swallowed hard and glanced at the Sanguis demons before returning her stare on Shiriki. "I still have my deal with Kai. He'll be pissed if you hurt me again."

Unless he's dead. Then I'm stuck with this twisted sociopath.

She wiped her sweaty palms on her jeans.

He's not dead—he can't be. He promised he'd never leave me.

"I already had that information when you first came to

me." He stared at her up and down with a cold smile. "That did not stop me then, why would it this time?"

She curled her hands, so her fingers pressed hard against her palms. "Because I saw what he did to you."

"I would take Mekaisto's punishments if it meant spending time with you."

She stopped circling around the subject, not wanting to stay in the company of this demon any longer than necessary. "Will you help us? Please?"

Shiriki's smile widened and he pulled on the fabric, leaving it to pool on the floor and revealing the mangled corpse of a young girl. Celina brought her hand to her mouth and turned away so it would be out of her line of sight. The demon had mounted her on a base with a large metal rod through her spine. He hummed another tune that sounded like something she'd heard before, and her heart pulsed in her ears.

Where have I heard that?

Celina glanced back to him, and her stomach churned as he caressed the dead girl's cheek. Her sanity almost went over the edge when the girl's chest moved up and down, and her gaze darted from side to side.

"That's impossible," Linda murmured. Adam and Haku stayed silent, their gazes fixed on the contorted body.

"I put in a demon's lungs and eyes. But she is an empty shell, and less amusing than a live subject."

He locked eyes with her, and Celina jumped up like an electric shock surged through her, wanting nothing more than to run. He prowled toward her, and she backed away until her knees hit the seat of the armchair and she fell into the moldy fabric. Shiriki placed his hands on the armrests and bent over her, his cruel smile making her wish she could disappear.

Adam edged forward in his seat, but Celina spoke first. "We need to free Kai. Are you helping, or not?"

Shiriki laughed, backing away until he sank into his armchair. Celina forced herself to sit up in the chair.

What's so fucking funny?

His gaze pierced through her as though searching her mind. "The ruler of the dark realm gets imprisoned, and you—"

"I know it sounds crazy. I'm well aware of that, but I didn't come here for your approval." She pressed her lips together, waiting.

"Crazy is not even the correct word. I suppose this means Mekaisto was right," Shiriki muttered but nodded and straightened. "The information I have about the Venatores or Lumen is vast, but there is one thing, and *only* one thing, you all need to know."

Linda leaned forward in her chair. "And what's that?"

"They cannot imprison Mekaisto."

His words rang inside Celina's ears. "But the—" she started.

"He is playing with them." Shiriki's eyes grew cold.

"I can't take that chance and leave him." She straightened. "Are you helping us or not?"

"The Lumen are mortal and weak." His eyes fixed on Celina again. "Even you can kill them with whatever you would like. Let your imagination run away." He leaned in toward her, and she tensed. "I know you have it in you."

"Just kill them?" Linda sounded surprised.

"Yes. But remember they can also defend themselves against other humans and Sanguis." Shiriki stood, and all four of them flinched at his sudden movement, but he sauntered away, disappearing from sight.

After a few seconds, the three demons stood, and Celina sighed as she followed them to the main entrance of his apartment. Passing the covered mannequins sent shivers through her.

Are they all corpses? Or still alive?

She fought the morbid urge to peek under the sheets and find out.

Shiriki slinked back into the room, glancing toward Celina like stalking a juicy prey before turning his attention on the three demons. "Wait outside."

They bowed and left. Celina wanted to follow them, but stayed put, rubbing her arms. "What?"

He held out a pistol. "Sanguis can kill humans without the need for weapons, but I have not yet assessed your strength. This shoots bullets that will set people on fire."

"I'm not like you. My goal isn't to cause them pain, just to kill them."

"Lying to yourself is as pathetic as trying to lie to a demon." He took a few steps toward her. "You have never taken a life; I can tell by smelling you. And you think you will kill them without causing pain?"

She gritted her teeth, willing herself not to back away from his advance. "I didn't say I wouldn't cause them pain. I said it's not my goal."

He chuckled. "Ah yes, the *Mens Rea* humans are so fond of." She arched her eyebrow but yelped when he materialized inches from her face. "It means guilty mind, pet. However, I believe the guilty act is enough."

She stared into his silver eyes, standing still while her grip on the gun tightened. "I have to go."

Something flashed across his expression, but before she could identify whatever it was, it vanished. He took her hands and raised them, so the pistol aimed at his chest, and she shuddered at his smile. He showed her how the weapon worked, all the while his gaze dared her to fire it.

A slight smile touched his lips as she tucked it in the back waistband of her jeans. "You realize that you are not like most humans?"

"Thanks for the pistol." She ignored his comment. "When we free Kai, I'll tell him you were extra helpful."

"Have you figured out why Mekaisto made a deal with you?" Shiriki held a gleam in his eyes as he approached her.

"No, but he promised to tell me, eventually."

He shoved her against the wall. Her eyes widened as he traced his fingernail above her upper lip. "If I skinned you, then stitched you back together…would your soul show itself?"

She reached for the gun he'd given her, but he slammed his hands on either side of her, and dust fell from the cracks in the wall. "Please try. It would bring me such pleasure to see your pained expression again." The way he spoke her name sent her body into a trembling terror, but he sneered and drew away.

She inched along the wall and darted out of the room as soon as she reached the doorway. The demons glanced up when she rejoined them in the hallway, and all four descended the stairs to the reception area of the building. Celina hesitated when the old woman approached, her small eyes narrowed in curiosity.

"Thank you for letting us see Shiriki," Celina spoke to ward off any further interaction.

The woman nodded and vanished in a wisp of silver smoke.

Celina's eyes widened. "Ghosts, now?"

A chill ran inside her when whispers hissed across the room. Were these the ghosts of victims Shiriki let die, but who remained trapped within the building? With a shudder, she hurried and caught up to the demons, all on their way to the church.

19

TRICKS

Celina stared up at the sky as she and the three Sanguis demons huddled in front of Yonah Church. "It'll be morning soon, so we can't take too much time in there. There are more chances of people hearing gunshots or screams while they're heading to work."

She hoped it wouldn't come to her firing any shots.

"Do you always take charge with Mekaisto like this?" Haku's eyebrows rose.

"I try." Her answer sent him into muffled chuckling, but Celina stayed serious. "I'll go in alone at first, just so we don't raise any alarm. Even if you all change to look less demonic, it'll still look suspicious if four people come into the church at this hour."

"Worried about attracting the police?" Haku stared around as though expecting them to appear.

"I'd rather avoid that, yes." She turned her attention on the demons. "The church has a homeless shelter inside, so there's round-the-clock staff. Don't attack anyone who's not a threat."

Linda placed her hands on her hips. "I don't take orders from humans."

Adam curled his lips into a snarl. "Do I need to remind you she is under our protection?" He shot her a sideways glare. "Or that she belongs to Mekaisto?"

Celina didn't wait to see where the conversation would go. She strode to the side door of the church and opened the door. The receptionist she'd met before sat at the desk. "Oh, hello again. You're here late!" Her polite smile hit Celina with guilt. "Are you here looking for your aunt? I think—"

The woman stopped talking when Celina pulled out the pistol and pointed it at her. "If you scream, I'll shoot you."

The receptionist's jaw dropped.

Is this how weak I look to Kai?

"Please don't hurt me, I—" Her voice shook, tears filling her eyes.

"Turn around."

Once the woman faced the other direction, Celina walked over and smacked her in the back of the head with the pistol handle.

"Ow!" The receptionist's hands flew to her head, pressing hard.

It looks easier in the movies.

Celina hit her again, but this time, there was no hesitation in her swing. The woman fell unconscious to the floor.

She opened the front door, and the demons crowded into the room. They continued through the corridors and up the stairs she'd used during her previous visit. Once at the wooden door to the main sanctuary, they stood ready, listening. Raised voices argued on the other side, urgency in every word. With her heart hammering fast and the pistol at ready, she turned the doorknob and opened the door a few inches.

Kai stood, surrounded by metallic pillars, electricity linking lines of white energy between them and sparking over the blue flames circling around him.

"That's a powerful trap." Adam breathed.

About a dozen cloaked people stood inside the sanctuary, and most were arguing.

"We can't leave it here." A woman pointed at Kai.

"Obviously not, Sarah." Father Christopher ran a hand over his face. "But moving it is much too dangerous. We risk setting it loose."

A half-smile hovered on Kai's features. "*It* is standing right here."

Celina couldn't help grinning at his attitude as Shiriki's words echoed through her head.

They cannot imprison Mekaisto.

"Besides," the priest said and pointed at what looked like a lump in the middle of the trap with Kai, "look at what happened when Kelsee got too close."

Celina squinted and realized with a jolt that the lump was a body, its head missing. She pressed her lips together and breathed through her nose.

For fuck's sake, Kai, did you have to?

"Why hasn't our magic killed it?" Another man came closer to the blue flames and folded his arms.

A murmur of apprehension swept across the large room.

"Our magic kills Sanguis demons and, if we're lucky, Viscus demons. Any of you know what kind Mekaisto is?" Father Christopher surveyed the members. When all remained silent, he let out a sigh. "I didn't think so since it's not in any of our documentation."

"We're the Lumen. Demon hunters." The one Father Christopher called Sarah raised her head high. "Shouldn't we know how to kill their king? Isn't it written somewhere?"

"He hasn't been on earth for centuries, so no, there wouldn't be any mention—"

"Actually, you are wrong." Kai took a few steps to the edge of the blue fire. "I have been on earth for a little less than thirty years now."

"Impossible!" Another man from the Lumen group strode forward. "We would have known!"

Kai raised an eyebrow. "Not if I did not want to be found."

"Enough!" Another woman gritted her teeth as she stared at the demon. "We've tried a few ways to kill it already. Maybe if we combine them all, it could work."

At the mention of even trying to kill Kai, Celina straightened and, without waiting for the demons' approval, burst into the room. When the last demon, Linda, joined them, the door slammed shut.

The Lumen whipped around at the sound, most with their mouths open. Kai, however, had a slow smile tugging at his lips.

Celina pointed the pistol at Father Christopher, guessing that threatening their leader would be her most effective option to get what she'd demand.

The priest blinked several times. "Celina? What are—?"

"I'm here for Kai." She took a few more steps toward him. "You can either set him free from that weird-looking bonfire, or the demons behind me will attack."

His gaze darted over her shoulder. "I don't think you realize what you're doing."

"Why is a human accompanied by these creatures? Who are you?" Sarah's eyebrows rose so high they disappeared in her bangs.

Celina aimed the pistol at her now. "I'm Celina Leviet, and I'm here for my demon."

"This is madness, my child." The priest stepped closer to her. "You're free from him. You don't have to suffer anymore."

"Don't presume to know my situation." She spoke through gritted teeth and returned the aim of her pistol on him.

"Is this about what you shared with me in confessional?"

His voice softened, but her heart pounded faster, and no longer from what she was doing, but from what Kai—all the demons, everyone in the room—would hear. "Mekaisto is strong, but I never realized how strong until you told me—"

"You're not allowed to repeat what I confessed!"

"Celina." Kai's voice rang out. She stared at him, the pistol trembling in her hand. "Is that what you tried to hide from me?"

"Shut up, Kai." She tried to steady her hand.

Linda sucked in a breath.

"You won't kill us. You're just confused. Let me help you." Father Christopher held out his hand for the gun.

Celina lowered the weapon, her heart pounding. The priest was right; she didn't want to take these peoples' lives. But the demons wouldn't hesitate, and she didn't have control over them. A quick movement to the left caught her attention. Sarah lunged at her, and before she could react, Adam grasped the woman by the throat.

The Lumen's shrieking screams echoed across the sanctuary, and Celina's stomach churned. Adam moved aside, revealing the sight of his victim's mangled throat pouring blood into a pool under the twitching body.

Celina stared at the priest, tensing to control her stance. Two other Lumen members ran at them, throwing small knives, and this time, the two other Sanguis demons moved into action too. More screams followed, but Adam stayed near Celina, guarding her.

"You'll let these demons kill us? Have you no respect for the church and everything we stand for? For life?" the priest shouted.

"Tell the Lumen to stop attacking!" She'd panicked at the shredding of the other woman, but if the Lumen kept coming at her, the demons wouldn't stop until the threat subsided.

She moved toward Kai's prison, all the while keeping an eye on the church members and the demons.

"That's one of the old relics…" Another woman took a step away as she spoke. "Where did you get that pistol?"

"Oh, right. I forgot to mention." Celina stared at Kai. "Shiriki gave me this so I could protect myself."

His face went blank for a second before a look of overwhelming pride softened his features into a less threatening smile. Still threatening, just a little less.

At the sound of footsteps behind her, she spun. The woman who'd asked about the gun lunged at her, but darkness wrapped around her form in a matter of seconds. A loud crack echoed through the sanctuary, and as the smoke dissipated, a pile of flesh and organs mixed with fine white dust landed on the floor in a splatter.

Celina's eyebrows rose as she took a few steps back, and she glanced from Adam to Haku to Linda. They hadn't done it. She narrowed her eyes at Kai. "Shiriki was right. The Lumen can't hold you prisoner." She gritted her teeth. "Do you know what I went through to get you out of here? You owe me big."

"Oh, I will give you something in return." His eyes gleamed with unspoken promise as he stared at her before turning his attention back on the Lumen. A cruel smile curled on his lips as he waved his hand, the pillars crashing to the floor and electricity sparking all around. The circle of blue fire changed to regular flames and lit around Kai, the glow inside the room turning to a sharp red color.

Haku looked both excited and terrified. "Here we go."

"It can't be." Father Christopher stared through the smoky glow at the demon he'd trapped.

Kai took on a more demonic appearance and the surrounding flames illuminating his red eyes and his smile so wide his pointed teeth gleamed more menacingly than ever. The Lumen ran forward, muttering strange words and holding their hands above their heads. Fire soared up to the cathedral ceiling, hiding Kai from view.

"No!" Celina darted toward the flames, but something hard smashed into her.

She landed on her back, losing what wind she had left in her lungs. The tackler grabbed at her, but she raised the pistol and fired.

The room whirled out of focus as the man burned from the inside out, her ears ringing as they had the night Thomas was murdered. His charred body fell to the floor, and she stared at it through a blurred vision.

She'd taken a human life, and it hadn't felt like anything she'd imagined. Instead of satisfaction, guilt warred inside her, despite it being in self-defense. Numbness pushed away the shame, and the idea of rescuing Kai and seeing those responsible for Thomas' death coming to a painful end snapped her back to reality.

She stood. Most of the Lumen lay mutilated on the floor. Father Christopher was the only member of the order left standing.

"Celina, please..." He raised his hands higher, trying to hold the fire back.

"End this now."

He shook his head.

Her inner battle waged on. She'd killed a person, reacted in the heat of the moment. But she couldn't raise the pistol to shoot the priest when he wasn't attacking her.

A shadow fell next to her. She spun her arm sideways to point the pistol in the direction but froze.

Kai.

He brushed his hand through the air, and the fire lifted to the ceiling, setting the wooden beams alight.

"H-h-how did you get out?" Father Christopher wrung his hands as he stared at Kai.

"I could always get out...Venatore." He hissed the word. "I just wanted to see how many of you were left."

The priest ran, but Linda blocked the door, cutting off any chance of escape.

"Someone will find a way to kill you, Mekaisto." The priest backed away from her and turned to glare at the demon king.

Kai shrugged. "Others have tried through the centuries. And yet, here I am."

Celina glanced up at the ceiling as the fire spread to the walls. "We should get out."

"I need you to close your eyes again." He licked his lips, his stare fixed on the priest.

She crossed her arms, opening her mouth to argue, but Haku dashed to Linda and grabbed onto her arm. "I'd rather not stay for this."

Adam stared at his king. "Do you want me to take her along?" He motioned toward Celina.

"No," she answered for herself.

The Sanguis demon lingered until Kai nodded, and then they bowed before vanishing in a blur.

Kai sighed. "You should not be here when I—"

"He might have useful information." She tried hiding the plea in her voice.

"You have no say in this matter. He is my kill." He took a step closer to Father Christopher. "Close your eyes, dove."

She flinched at his harsh tone and did as he ordered.

Evil slithered to her core as if all life rotted around her. Someone grabbed her from behind, and she guessed it was the priest before he spoke.

"Look at what you made your deal with, my child."

Instinct took over, and she opened her eyes. Kai's appearance might have shocked her before, but no longer did the jolt of surprise shake her. Instead, numbness took over.

A strange aura fell on the room as though the darkness devoured everything in its path. Kai stood in his true form—a tall figure emanating brutal strength—and a hint of far-off fear trickled through her. She stared at her demon. The wings in his back were as black as his hair, and each feather floated as though composed of pure smoke. His eyes glowed red as they always did when his pupils turned into vertical slits, but it was the look inside them that laced ice through her.

He took a few steps toward Celina and the priest, an evil smile on his lips. "I enjoy it so much more when my prey fights back." His voice exuded, almost commanded, terror, and she pushed down admiration for him as she stared.

"You'll have to kill her if—"

It took only a few seconds as Kai materialized next to Father Christopher and grabbed one of each of the priest's arms in a clawed grip. He yanked them from the shoulders they were attached to as though the priest was no sturdier than a sheet of paper. A gut-wrenching shriek escaped him right as Kai split his body in two. Blood sprayed in a gory fountain, but Celina's only reaction was to blink even when the hot liquid hit her face.

She shrank away when Kai approached.

Unsure of his true nature when in his most demonic form, she shuddered with fear. "Are you going to hurt me?"

"Would you like me to?" He stopped in front of her then lifted his hand, his fingernails long and pointed claws cupped her face. When she flinched, he smiled. A glimmer of light reflected off his fanged white teeth, and her heart sped up.

Her lips trembled. "Still answering questions with questions."

Part of her sagged with relief that his personality didn't change, but her mind couldn't process seeing him in its truest form. She glanced at the long black horns on his head, focusing on their etched arcane bright red symbols.

"You made it sound like you went through quite a lot to rescue me." His voice hummed with more than curiosity, less than malevolence, and her gaze darted to his. "Do tell."

Outside the room, over her shoulder, someone or something pounded hard, rattling the remains of the crumbling building. She spun, and her heart hammered so hard against her ribcage she feared it would shatter a bone. Through the window in one door that led to the homeless shelter inside the church, Celina's aunt pounded, trapped, her eyes desperate and her face drawn in the terror of impending death.

That half of the sanctuary was ablaze with flames licking the walls.

"Marie!" She stuck a foot out, ready to run, but Kai slithered an arm her around her waist and held her firmly against his body.

"It is too late for her."

Her lungs burned with the exertion of fighting his grip and the smoke billowing around them. She stared at him, grabbing his arm hard. "Please, help her."

His eyes softened, despite the darkness flowing around him like smoke. "It is over, Celina."

She struggled to break free of his grasp. "You fucking monster! I won't let her die."

Only when she turned toward her aunt again did she realize what he'd meant. The room had nothing left. Flames flickered up the door, melting the window and leaving no chance for survivors. Celina stilled as tears streamed down her cheeks. A wail welled up in her throat, and she gave in to its pressure.

Kai turned her and tightened his grip as she buried her face in his chest with a sob.

20

LOVE AND DEATH

Kai threw Shiriki against a table and shoved a clawed hand through his abdomen. Blood streamed down Shiriki's chin, but he didn't lose his smirk. "It seems something has upset you."

"You should have stopped her from coming." Kai's growl intensified as it burst through his pointed teeth.

"She does as she pleases when she is determined. The only way I could have stopped her would have been to use force. Did you want me to do that?"

Though Shiriki's tone mocked him, Kai withdrew and continued to glare at his second in command.

Shiriki wiped away a droplet of blood near the raw flesh Kai had torn, already knitting together. "There is more to why you are so upset, Mekaisto."

Kai stayed silent for a few seconds. The laboratory emitted its usual clinking sounds, and Shiriki's victims' whimpering faded. "She saw me... like this." His voice started quiet and then turned into a hiss.

She will never look at me again without seeing a monster.

Shiriki didn't bother looking up from the jar he'd shoved his hand into, but the corners of his mouth curled. "I told her the Lumen could not trap you. I would have thought it enough to keep her here, keep her safe while awaiting your return." The Viscus demon caught an eyeball in his hand and pulled it out. "Squirmy little thing..." He stared at the wiggling organ.

Kai glanced at the long robe he wore. "Are your legs healing?"

"I have a few blisters. Why? Are you concerned about your only friend?"

Kai chuckled. "Concerned? No...just curious." He calmed and let his mind settle on the demon. "Viscus demons heal fast, but you have always been an anomaly."

He shrugged. "Well, I suppose it comes with being the first Viscus demon."

The tenuous hold Kai had on his patience snapped. "I think you are more than that." The darkness in his tone fissured the wall behind Shiriki.

"Who knows?" He caught a few more eyeballs and placed them in a smaller container. "Tell me, my friend, why are you upset because she saw you in your demon form? Could it be because you care what she thinks?"

Again, his tone taunted Kai.

"We do not feel those kinds of emotions." Kai stopped and glanced to where a human male lay on a surgical table, struggling against the restraints holding him secure. Against his better judgment, Kai turned to Shiriki. "What happened when you did?"

Shiriki moved to the male and grabbed a curved blade with a razor edge. "You mean when I felt what humans call love?" He tapped the human's chest with the tip of his knife. "You assured me we were unequipped to feel that emotion; could it be you were wrong, my king?"

"You are trying my patience." He dug deep for a growl that equaled his building rage.

"We are not *supposed* to feel the human weakness of love."

Shiriki spoke the word as it was toxic. "For us, our passion is consumed by our hatred, feeds on it, even." Shiriki pushed the knife into his prisoner's abdomen and cut out a chunk of skin, almost in a perfect circle, as the man bellowed and writhed in pain. "Love grew to possession, to violence, and eventually…"

He stopped talking when he shoved an eyeball into the new hole, and the victim's shrieks split the calm of their conversation.

Kai moved to the table and leaned the man's head back a little. "Hush." He opened his fist near the man's neck, and tiny spiders erupted through Kai's skin, crawling out of his veins.

As the creatures forced their way into the man's neck, tearing flesh as they burrowed inside, an inhuman howl screeched from the man in wave after wave. A dark, creamy liquid dripped from his mouth until the screaming cut off in a wet gurgle as spiders spun webs across his vocal cords. The room became quiet once again with the man merely able to squirm.

"I am rather jealous of your pets…though I find such pleasure in using my hands." Shiriki's smile broadened the lines of his face, and he continued digging holes into the man's torso to insert more eyeballs.

The Viscus demon stood back to admire his work.

Kai didn't understand Shiriki's obsession with humans but didn't much care to, either. He glanced down at the multitude of eyes looking back at him from the holes in the man's body.

Kai stared back at Shiriki. "What happened after your love turned to possession?"

"It is the only memory involving pain I do not wish to remember."

How much love will I be able to give her before it turns to a death sentence?

21

CLOSER TO THE TRUTH

Celina pressed her hands on either side of her head to hold it together. While the pressure took away some pain, the throbbing didn't cease.

She slid out of bed and trudged to the bathroom. The bright light aggravated her headache, and the memory of the church snuck into her mind. Her stomach turned and bile rose in her throat, forcing her to her knees. In a painful smack of bone against the tile, she jerked her head over the toilet as she threw up. Her body trembled and tears ran down her cheeks, but she wiped them away and stood.

Her stomach twisted again as she held her hand in front of her face. Dried blood…so much of it. She stared in the mirror at all the blood splatters dried on her face. With her red hair matted and dark circles under her gray eyes, a quivering girl stared back.

She glared at her reflection. "Murderer."

She twisted the faucet and plunged her hands beneath the spray, watching as the water turned pink. She couldn't save her aunt… the last of her family.

I'm so sorry, Marie.

She stepped into the shower, hoping to wash away the

guilt as easily as the blood. With the burn of shame rushing through her, she stepped out and wrapped herself in a towel.

Rummaging through her clothes, she picked the only one appropriate for the hot summer day she felt through the open window, a navy-blue dress with a pattern of white flowers. She slipped it over her head and tiptoed into the kitchen.

No sound came from anywhere inside their room, but she remained silent as she went to the countertop. A thick folder caught her attention, and she flicked through the pages with a frown.

The sound of the floor cracking prickled her skin, and she spun.

A black hole opened in the floor, blasting with heat, and a cloudy abyss of black and gray swirled in wide circles before her. The sounds—screams and howls—she imagined in the pits of Hell squealed from the depths of the darkness within the space. A bright flash blinded her, and when her vision cleared, Kai stood where the hole had been, as familiar as she'd ever known him. His gaze lingered on her dress long enough that she cleared her throat.

"So, I went through a few of the papers inside the folder, and I don't understand why you took those out of everything in that secret room."

Above all else, she didn't want, couldn't talk about anything that had happened at the church.

"Hello to you, too, dove."

"Yes, fine. Hello." She ran a hand over her hair. "So, care to explain?"

He came to stand next to her and opened the folder. "I sensed its energy."

She rolled her eyes, and he smiled in that damned condescending way that said he enjoyed explaining what she didn't know of his world from time to time. Her rage and grief mixed, forming a ball of something she could barely contain. "Explain it."

"This was the only document looked at by someone other than a Lumen member in the past few years." He looked up from the paper and searched her eyes with his gaze.

She glared at him for a moment and then centered her focus on the floor in front of him.

"Did you look at the papers in the back?" He thrust the folder out.

She yanked it away, flipping through one page at a time. "What are these? What does it mean?"

"These are the Lumen member family trees, dating back to when they were called Venatores."

"Family trees?" She glanced down. "There are so many names. Why would Thomas have looked into the ancestry of a bunch of people he didn't know?"

"It was thought by some that Venatores held great power in life and even more in death."

She scanned down the names with her finger, trying to piece together what was important. "I don't get it." She shoved the folder toward Kai and then put a hand on her head as the throbbing came on with greater ferocity.

"Side effect of seeing me in my true form."

"I won't let it stop me, so I don't care." Her words were as much a vow to herself as it was to him.

His smile turned gentle. "It pleases me to hear you say that."

An odd sensation tickled at her senses. As a demon, in his true form, he terrified her, had her trembling in her own skin. But in the rare moments of his kindness, she grew warm in his presence.

"Wait." She held her hand up as he tried approaching her. "Apart from the main door with the trap, was there another way to get to the tunnels we used to access the secret room?"

"No." But he looked out the window instead of at her.

She arched an eyebrow. "Then how did Thomas get in? I

mean, you had to break down a brick wall. I doubt he could do the same."

Kai stood silent for a few more minutes, and Celina's frustration turned to rage. She wished for the power to invade his thoughts to take knowledge from him. Instead, she waited as patiently as she could.

He turned his attention back to her. "Perhaps he found a way through the main door within the church without triggering the traps inside the room."

"Maybe." But as she rolled the idea around in her mind, the ball in the pit of her stomach gave a slow roll. It couldn't be so simple as walking through a damned door.

Maybe Thomas got in because Father Christopher let him in and disabled the traps? Maybe they'd been in on something together?

She glanced at the folder between them. "Why do you think Thomas wanted this information?"

"He was investigating the Lumen, and the video evidence might have something to do with all this." His overly-sugary tone made it sound like he was explaining something simple to a child. He might as well have been describing how to tie a shoe.

She sucked in a breath. "How does this all connect?" She'd reached her limit for tolerance.

He grinned. "While I was a guest in the church, they accused me of corrupting someone within their group. They mentioned a few Lumen parents were victims of a crime involving the kidnapping and suspected murder of their male children. The priest believed it was a Lumen member who hired someone to do the killings since it involved a ritual." He shrugged, and the bitter acid of disgust crept up her throat.

"Ritual?" Instead of answering, filling in a blank she needed to understand, he shrugged.

He drummed his fingers on the counter, a small smile appearing on his lips. "Lumen leaders have access to magic. It

is meant to hunt my kind, but perhaps your Father Christopher used his powers for evil rather than good."

"Like what?" Talking about the priest who had been
ripped in half unnerved her.

"Maybe he turned the magic against them? Maybe he was
looking inside his people to see who went rogue."

Again, she doubted it. The muscles of her face tightened,
and she didn't bother to hide the grimace that resulted. "Is
there anything you can explain without riddles? Just once,
can't you be clear?"

"Spells created by the Lumen have flaws." He smirked. "A
perfect spell requires dark magic, and most do not dare use it.
Without that kind of magic, he could not search for a guilty
mind."

Guilty mind. The *mens rea* Shiriki had mentioned flashed
through Celina's head.

She crossed her arms, glancing from him to the folder and
still not buying any of it. "You're saying a Lumen member
hired someone to kidnap and maybe kill male children. Then
Thomas, in some ridiculous matter of other-worldly insight,
investigated this and somehow got a hold of the video
showing one of the crimes? None of this explains why he
needed the family trees you found important enough to steal
and get captured for." She gave him a sideways glare. "Well,
pretended to get captured anyway."

Family trees.

She restrained a scoff. Of all the papers, books, documentation in every form, Kai stole a bunch of names connected by
boxes and lines. And he couldn't even seem to be bothered to
giving her a clear reason.

"Your husband might have needed them to find out who
had sons. He needed to find the victims to discover who had
done the kidnapping." His lips curled into a smile. "And
perhaps murders."

Her attention rested on the page, and her heart hammered

faster against her chest. Finally, it became clear. "So, I'm holding the names of the parents in the video. The ones who murdered Thomas and tried killing me." At Kai's nod, her heart sank. "There must be hundreds and hundreds of names. This will take forever."

Her headache worsened, and she massaged her temples.

"We will eliminate the ones with daughters and less than two sons."

Celina sighed, but she knew it had to be done. She flipped through a few pages, and her heart skipped a beat when she saw a familiar name.

Elizabeth Tayen.

Mom.

The little box where her biological father's name should have been remained empty. Celina Tayen was the product of her mother and an empty box.

Perfect. And fitting, considering he'd been an empty space in my life.

She continued down the page. Next to her mother, Marie. Again, her chest tightened, and guilt flowed through her.

It's not time to think about that. Not yet.

He chuckled. "If you do not feel like going through the rest of the genealogical histories of those who wish me dead, there *is* something else we can do in the meantime." Kai traced his pointed fingernail down Celina's arm.

Her cheeks burned, and she swallowed hard but didn't try to block her imagination from conjuring what he would look like stripped free of clothes. "I—"

"We could go to a few banks and check if any of the Lumen members have accounts there. We need to see if one of them had a large amount of money disappear. The kind one would require to, say, hire someone to kidnap children." He grinned. "All these Lumen called me a monster, while they have evil inside their own ranks." He clucked his tongue against his teeth. "Such wasted opportunities."

She sucked in a ragged breath, grateful his suggestion hadn't paralleled the mind-movie playing on repeat in her consciousness. The heat passing through her body didn't cool, even with the implication of his added mutterings.

I wouldn't say no. Shit, what's going on with me?

She took a step out of his reach but held her chin high, as though daring him to say anything about her passing thoughts. He smirked but remained silent.

"The bank is a great idea, but there's a flaw in your plan, Kai."

He took one step closer. "I see no flaw."

"Oh, it's there." She stayed still, stiffening her muscles until they hurt. "The banks aren't going to just invite us behind the counter and give us access to random people's accounts. There are security measures we'd have to bypass somehow and—"

In one movement, he took the back of her neck and gave a gentle squeeze. "You forget I can be persuasive." His lips pulled over his pointed teeth, and the result was a malicious smile that Celina leaned toward.

She stared at him, desperate to keep her mind from wandering to the more appealing parts of her demon. "How…?"

"Hmm. I have ways." He traced a finger along her neck, his eyes focused on hers and the weight of the conversation forgotten under the intensity of his gaze.

"I guess this is why I need you." Her voice cracked, and her pulse traveled south. She almost whimpered at the power in his knowing smile.

She ripped her gaze away, and grabbed a paper, inspecting the information.

"My aunt…" Her stomach seized again at the thought of Marie, but she pushed it aside, hiding her emotions behind her thorough investigation of the names that blurred before her. "She used a bank down the street from the hotel. It's close to the neighborhood and the church. We could start there."

He leaned in, pressing his lips against her throat, smiling against her skin when she shivered. "Anything you want, dove."

Once outside, Celina let out a sigh of relief at no longer being trapped in the hotel room. It was a beautiful day, but her thoughts focused on avenging her husband's death, finding the truth behind the mystery she'd never known existed but now had her trapped.

As lust slithered over her, she shook it off with a literal shake of her head.

Stop thinking! He can read your thoughts!

Kai's lips curled in the knowing smile that infuriated her. He pulled the door open for her. "After you."

"May I help you, sir?" The man at the counter looked past Celina to address Kai.

"Would it be possible to meet with a financial advisor today?"

The man typed on his computer. "We have a space available in about ten minutes, with Ms. Rosand." He stared at Kai with a smile. "If you wouldn't mind waiting?"

Celina moved to the seating area without him and waited in front of a poster, keeping her mind focused on anything but her demon.

Kai joined her and stretched his long legs in front of him as he sank into a well-cushioned chair, but Celina remained standing next to him.

"You can sit next to me. I won't bite." Kai said in a teasing voice. "Unless you ask me to."

"That is not an original line. I expected better from the king of the underworld."

"Should I wait until we're alone, or would you like *better* now, dove?"

The suggestion in his voice had nothing to do with pick-up lines or banking, and Celina's skin heated from her forehead to her toes. "This is why I have no clue how to act around you."

His attention swept the large room, a smile curling his lips. "When they call me into the office, go to the hotel restaurant and eat something. I'll meet you there."

She crossed her arms. "Why did I come here, then? I could have just stayed at the hotel."

"It's important you eat." When she opened her mouth to argue, his eyes flashed. "Do not test me; I will force feed you if I have to."

Before she could form a retort to satisfy her anger, Ms. Rosand approached them and smiled. Her gaze lingered on Kai longer than Celina appreciated.

"I'll see you now, Mr. Markham."

Celina arched an eyebrow, curious as to whether or not that was one of the last names he'd used for centuries, or if he'd just made it up.

Ms. Rosand walked to her office, and Kai grinned at Celina as he followed. As soon as he disappeared from view, she stood and left the bank.

As she walked, her mind whirled…blood splatters inside the church, demons killing the Lumen members, murder on her hands, Marie fighting for her life only to die in a flaming ball of agony. Celina's craving for revenge wavered. Violence left a scar larger than she wanted to admit. What would taking the lives of others gain her? Did she have it in her to kill for the sake of what she thought was justice?

I still love Thomas, despite all the lies and secrets.

But, if that was true, what did she feel about Kai? How could she fall in love with a demon? And so soon after her husband's death?

I can't be in love. It must be confusion. A rebound or something.

Celina stopped. How had she gotten to the hotel so quickly? She'd been lost in thought and hadn't even noticed her surroundings. She sighed and opened the door, making a line for the restaurant.

Her meal had just arrived when Kai joined her at the table. "I found something interesting about one of the bank accounts."

"Which one?" She put her fork down next to the plate.

Kai handed her the paper and the letters blurred in front of her; ten thousand dollars withdrawn from Marie Tayen's bank account six months earlier. Her aunt's untidy signature was scrawled on the bottom of the withdrawal, confirming she was the one who took the money out.

Her hand shook as she held the copy. "Six months ago."

"She might not have hired the murderer right away."

"I can't…I mean, why?"

"The Lumen had old texts with lists of rituals that were never meant for their eyes. One of those rituals exists to gain immortality and requires an original Venatore family with three sons. It is performed by killing the eldest son and hanging his corpse over his youngest brother, who is driven to madness, so his soul becomes tainted beyond repair. Then a demon is summoned, the human kills the youngest son and drinks his blood to gain immortality."

She squinted at him, the suspicion in her heart seeping into her voice. "It sounds demonic."

He scowled. "If you're suggesting demons have something to do with this beyond being summoned, do remember we're already immortal. This ritual would be useless to us."

She lowered her gaze. "Right."

Kai put his hand over hers and squeezed, giving her a gentle smile. "You rarely shy away from an argument, dove."

She pulled away, ignoring the thrum of passion inspired by his touch. "So, my aunt paid someone to kidnap Lumen male children to gain immortality?" Her mind raced until dizziness swayed the room around her.

"It is a possibility."

She let out a sigh. This wasn't how she wanted to remember her aunt.

"But why did those people murder Thomas? They weren't the kidnappers, so it couldn't be as simple as escaping prosecution by killing the man with the evidence. Did the person who kidnapped these children find out what my husband was doing and use the parents to get him out of the way?"

"Eat."

She picked up her fork, but only brought it to hover over her food when she remembered. "They said something about a letter." More and more of a memory formed in her mind. "Something about killing Thomas to get their son back. I guess this is what they meant..."

Kai gave her another glare, and she took an obligatory bite out of her salad. He nodded his head as though satisfied with the single leaf of lettuce she'd shoved in her mouth.

"We'll go through the other bank statements I took. We might find the parents who murdered your husband and tried to kill you."

Celina stayed quiet, her mind protesting against more questions. The aunt she knew would never have hired someone to murder children.

Don't be too sure; she had encouraged her own sister to commit suicide.

Celina slammed the pile of papers onto the table. "I'm tired of waiting." Searching through the records of every Lumen member would take time, and she felt it was a waste.

"Would you prefer to kill them all?" Kai sounded almost hopeful, and Celina shot him a glare.

"We have addresses. Let's pick one and see if it's them. I mean, we know what they look like from the...video." She still cringed at the memory, and finished with far less enthusiasm, "Maybe we'll get lucky."

He caressed her knee. "I love that you are in such a hurry to bring our deal to its resolution."

She stood even though her body tingled from his touch. "I need to finish this."

They left the hotel in silence, and only once seated on the bus did he speak. "Are you angry with me?"

Celina ignored the question, lifting her foot off the sticky surface of the floor, and grimaced. "Why can't I get my car back yet?"

"You can, but we wouldn't be able to use it," he said.

She pressed her lips together and narrowed her eyes.

"Think about it, dove. Do you want your license plate reported for snooping around?" He stared down at one of the bank statements they brought. "And you didn't answer my previous question."

This time, instead of ignoring the question, she chose not to answer. In her book, those were two very different things. He didn't push the issue, and soon, they stepped off the bus into a neighborhood of historic homes, lined with stone walls and flower beds that wouldn't dare show a weed.

Kai grabbed her arm and led the way to a wooded area behind the bus stop. As she opened her mouth to ask what was going on, he pinned her against a tree.

"What the hell, Kai?"

His eyes morphed to bright red, the vertical pupils glaring at her. "It will be difficult to work together if you insist on not speaking to me."

"I don't have much to say."

"You are a strange one." He took her in his arms and held her. "You are either much too comfortable with me, considering what I am, or you stay silent and seem to be so fearful or angry with me."

She flattened her hands against his chest and shoved with

all the strength she had. "You're one to talk! You go from attacking me to holding me in less than point-three seconds!" She fought to keep her resentment contained. There was no need to pick at that scab until she investigated what to do about it. "Besides, I'm feeling a little…well, I'm not sure what I'm feeling." Her brain and her mouth hadn't coordinated a plan of attack, and she confessed before logic could stop her.

He traced along her shoulder, his expression unreadable. "Revenge is complicated."

If only he knew.

"Ever since…" Celina turned away from him, blinking back her tears.

Since she'd pulled that trigger and committed murder —*murder*—then watched her aunt die, guilt ate at her core. No matter how hard she tried to focus on her revenge, it was there…in her face… She blinked the thoughts away, once, twice, hoping Kai would, for once, stay out of her head.

He rubbed her back. "Yes?"

"Can we talk about this later? We're standing close to a public street talking about things that, if anyone overhears, will have me locked in a cell for the rest of my life with a jacket that snaps in the back." She stalked to the sidewalk.

He grabbed her wrist and spun her around, her eyes widening at the scowl he gave her in public. "We *will* finish this conversation later."

She yanked away, visualizing pictures of running puppies, pouncing kittens—anything to push away the guilt, keep the lust buried, hide her uncertainty about the revenge that had once driven her. She could almost feel him digging around her thoughts. "Stop."

As physically as she'd felt him enter, she knew when he left, and she let out a breath. Her attention wandered to the number on the front of the first house.

He glanced at her. "We appear to have a little walk ahead of us."

"Wow. All those demon powers make you observant."

He probably kept a tally of her sarcasm, snide remarks, and biting insults for later punishments, but at least he had the decency to keep it to himself as they continued along the street.

As they neared the house, her heart skittered and missed a beat. The woman from the video, as though summoned by Celina's own thoughts, strolled to the edge of the driveway to pick up the morning paper.

As soon as anything that resembled compassion seeped into her mind, Celina booted it back out with a firm mental kick. Morals were for the weak, people who let murderers get away with ripping people apart. If these people hadn't killed Thomas, hadn't shot her, she wouldn't have had to take Kai's deal.

She clutched Kai's arm as she fought for a steady breath.

He pulled her in close to his side and stroked the back of her neck. "Do you have a plan?" A hungry growl erupted from his chest as though he'd spotted a tasty morsel of a prey.

She couldn't let go. The muscles and tendons holding her upright had evaporated as soon as she eyed the woman, and now, she relied on him to hold her straight. "We can't question them here. People would hear the screaming."

Since when did questioning involve screams? The part of her not destroyed by Thomas' death lodged its protest, and Celina silenced her inner voice with a growl of her own.

"Oh? You're planning on making them suffer loudly?"

"Thomas begged them not to kill me. He screamed when he knew they didn't care and would go after me when they'd be done with him. I'm only here to return the favor."

"Nothing like a good maiming." His voice rang with excitement, and a shiver shot through her spine.

She turned her head a little to look at him and then shifted to watch the house once more. "Look! They have a car." Her mind whipped up a plan at a speed that both frightened and delighted her. "Once it's night, and most people have gone to bed, we can put them in the trunk. The two of them will fit in there together." She didn't care if they were bent until bones broke, they would fit.

"If this were part of the ritual I told you about, it would mean they still have a middle child." His eyes gleamed. "If that's the case?" A hopeful smile twisted his lips.

She stayed as calm as she could. "We're not hurting a child. We'll leave him here, tied up, and call the police on the way to The CrowBar."

"Why the club?"

"I promised Adam a human, remember? And I need the dungeon of doom basement he has underneath the club."

If he mentions using Shiriki's laboratory from Hell, I'll hit him.

His hands wrapped around her waist as though reacting on their own. This was as close to happiness as she'd seen from him, a genuine smile curved his lips and lines crinkled at the corners of his eyes. "Are we waiting here for the night to come?"

His giddiness and what it meant caused her guilt to erupt. A vision of Thomas tied to a chair became her go-to image when she thought of sparing them out of compassion. "Out here, but we can't stay in front of the house like this or we'll draw too much attention." She scanned the surroundings.

A small playground stood empty just across from the target house. It would do. A bench had a clear view for observing her subjects.

As they sat, she fidgeted with her fingers, with the hem of her dress, with a strap that insisted on sliding down her arm. But nothing stopped the realization that she'd held on to Kai when panic spiraled through her. When she should have been strong, she clung to him.

Was it self-loathing or the damnable lust? Was it weakness and need, or longing for a demon that let him slither his arms around me? Again.

"The confusion you're feeling is normal."

Celina glared at him. "I didn't give you permission to poke around in my head."

He matched her snappy tone. "It's difficult for humans to sort their emotions about certain situations. You feel guilt over what happened at the church, all the while managing your thirst for violence." He paused before turning to face her and gentled his voice, his touch on her face sending fire to her core. "You've also fallen in love. But it's difficult to accept because I'm a demon who has every intention of taking what's mine at the end of our contract."

"You don't know what you're talking about." She stared at her feet, not wanting to talk about feelings with him.

"You don't believe it would—"

She stood and glared down at him. "Why not just say you have no interest in a vengeful human except for the taint on my soul?"

Kai's eyes flashed, and he stood. She wished she had that kind of effect. "Why would I say that?"

"You—"

He grabbed a fistful of her hair and tilted her head back. "You're much more than a life and a blackened soul." He pulled her closer to him, his body pressing hard against her own. "And I guarantee if it's affection you seek from me, you'll have an eternity."

He let her go, and she backed away from him, furrowing her brow.

"I doubt you'll cuddle me to death." She kept her tone as passive as she could to avoid antagonizing him further.

He smiled and sat down, not through with the promises. "Torture, agony, pain," the gleam in his eyes resembled a leer, "can all come from affection."

Celina stared at him. For being the most eloquent of demons, his statements often left her confused, shaking her head and wondering. After some time passed, it occurred to her staying in the park all day could draw just as much unwanted attention as standing in front of the house.

She jumped up, the dress swirling at her knees as her forward motion came to an abrupt stop. "We can't stay here. We'll come back later, once we've planned better."

"And in the meantime?" Kai followed her to the bus stop.

She sighed, blinking back tears over all her mixed emotions. "I don't know."

The bus arrived, and they stepped on. Her gaze landed on some advertisements for traveling for great deals, transferring college credits, and her shoulders stiffened. Every single thing she'd never get to do flew through her mind; fly in an airplane, drive across the country, get a degree. There was an entire world she'd never see because her husband had kept her locked up in a beautiful cage she'd called her dream house.

Soon, her life would end, and all her missed opportunities with it.

Kai pushed the button to get off at the next stop, and she jerked her head toward him, her eyebrows rising. "This isn't our stop."

He took her hand and pulled her toward the exit. "Follow me."

They stepped off the bus in the middle of a neighborhood she didn't recognize.

"Why are we here?" She caught up to Kai as he strode between two houses.

He wrapped his arms around her. "Don't you like surprises?"

Celina opened her mouth to say something, but in the second it took her to blink and turn her head, their surroundings changed.

A DAY TO FORGET

Celina stood shoulder-to-shoulder with Kai in a large parking lot. Her eyes settled upon a sign. *Six Flags—La Ronde.*

He leaned toward her ear. "I'll give you twenty-four hours to do anything you like, and not to think of the emotions eating away at you."

They walked to the park's entrance, and her heart lightened as her gaze darted back and forth among all the rides. Colors flashed as hundreds of sounds rang through the air. The last time she went to an amusement park was before she and Thomas were married. It had been a small seasonal one and felt so long ago.

She stared at Kai with a small frown. "How did we go from Ottawa to Montreal in less than a second?"

"I have many talents." A cocky smile tugged at his lips.

"Why can't we always do that? Wouldn't we waste less time?"

"Because it opens rifts to the dark realm and releases all kinds of monsters. They become difficult to control here."

"Monsters?" The image of her encounter in the hidden

tunnels beneath the church raced inside her mind. "Difficult to handle? Even for you? Does—?"

Kai chuckled as he took her hand and brought it to his mouth. "No need to worry, dove." His lips brushed against her skin in a small kiss.

He tugged her forward to the front of the queue, and the people they passed ignored them as if they were wisps on the breeze. He bent his head to look into the small booth, and the teen with the dirty blonde hair held out her hand for his money. No reaction. No gasp of shock or recoiling as Kai smiled. Just an ordinary couple on an ordinary date. Excitement welled in Celina. They wandered through the entrance, and she glanced down at the asphalt.

"Well...this is weird." Heat prickled over her cheeks as she studied her sandals.

"Oh?"

"Having fun with you is strange, you know? You'll be taking everything from me soon, so it'll be hard to not think about my future."

A flicker of disappointment seemed to flash across his face, but it vanished so fast, she was sure she'd imagined it. "If you'd prefer, I can leave and come back for you later. Perhaps you want to be on your own?"

She grabbed his arm, afraid he'd disappear. "No." Her eyes widened a little at her own reaction, and she relaxed her grip. "I think it...it would be worse if I stayed here alone with my thoughts. I just need you to be...well...normal for a day."

"Normal is boring." His eyes gleamed. "Come." He strode to an ice cream shop.

"Kai."

He turned.

"Thanks for doing this for me."

He smiled, and she warmed at the fondness shining through his eyes.

Grateful that each lick of her ice cream allowed another

moment to compose herself, she took the time to look around as they strolled farther into the park. Kai squinted at the map. "So which ride would you like to go on first?"

The roller coasters roared, screams echoing in the air. She wanted to start small and build from there. "The Ferris Wheel."

"Any chances of going into the haunted house at some point?" He grinned and rested his hand on the small of her back.

"Oh sure, because my life isn't enough of a horror show?"

"We should save the Ferris Wheel for when it's dark." He traced his fingers along her skin. "The lights are beautiful from high up."

She whirled around at the sound of splashing water. "All right, then how about the log ride?"

"If you want to get wet, all you have to do is ask."

"Kai!" Just the thought of his lips, his touch, across her skin...she shivered, and he pulled her more tightly against him as if to shield her from the cold.

Kai's grin widened with every ride, and his ready laugh became infectious. Wide-eyed with fear in the haunted house, with Kai...caught in sprays on the log ride, with Kai...arms above her head and screaming on the roller coaster...with Kai. Always with Kai, always happy.

Without dwelling too much on her shifting feelings, she grabbed his arm as they stepped from the ride exit and into a food court. Her stomach growled as they passed each food stall, and the smells of grease and sizzling vats of oil teased her nose.

"Next time, tell me when you're hungry instead of waiting for your stomach to notify me." He grabbed her hand, and she winced when he squeezed hard.

She tried pulling from his grip, and only once he relaxed did she yank free. "Why are you biting my head off for something as stupid as that?"

Balloons popped nearby, and she jumped. Despite having had so much fun, fear still lurked in her thoughts about what was to come. Murdering, even for revenge, was not something easily resolved with her morals.

Kai's arms wrapped around her, and he rested his cheek against her hair. "I'm sorry. Let's get you some food."

She focused on the popcorn strewn on the ground among all the garbage, wrappers, and cigarette butts while her vision spun. Her head pounded from the loud music and cheering from a nearby game stall, and she closed her eyes, willing herself calm.

The smell of French fries returned, and she smiled. "Can I have a hot dog and fries?"

He withdrew, and his lips curled into a mischievous smile.

She pointed her finger at him. "And before you make any kind of jokes about hot dogs, don't."

Kai laughed. "Ah, you know me too well."

After she finished her lunch, they continued to stroll around the park as she picked at stringy pieces of her cotton candy and then sucked the residue from her fingers when they stuck together. He grabbed at the pink cloud, but she held it out of his reach.

"This is one thing I'm not sharing with you." She grinned.

He pulled her close. "Everything else is up for grabs then?" He looked so serious she couldn't utter a single word.

A hawker called out to them, and relief brushed through her for the interruption. Kai shifted his hand into hers and led her to the carnival game dumbbell strength meter.

"Don't you dare." She muffled her laugh behind her hand. "You'll break it."

The employee offered a practiced smile. "Gonna test your strength to win something for your girl?"

Not half as charming as Kai's.

"Which prize do you want?" He wrapped his arm around her shoulder.

"Seriously, you're going—"

His gaze pierced her. "Celina."

She bit her lower lip, scanning through all the stuffed animals, toys, and glittery accessories. Her smile widened. "The stuffed animal there. The dove."

Kai took the hammer and leaned it against his shoulder as he looked at the top of the game where the bell hung. He turned his head to the side, his eyes locking with Celina's. His mischievous smile did nothing to reassure her, but she kept quiet.

With one quick swing, Kai brought the hammer down, and the machine exploded in a spray of sparks. A few people around jumped and stared, their mouths opened wide.

I knew it… He broke the damn game.

The man gaped at Kai, but his eyes narrowed, and his lips flattened into a thin, straight line across his face when he requested his prize. Celina had to hold his arm so he wouldn't attack the game host, and Kai relaxed in her grip. She turned her head, trying to glimpse his expression, and fell back as she recognized the harsh planes of his face, his angular cheekbones and the darkness in his eyes. He murmured, the cadence familiar, the words in his Demon language. The stall-holder paled and held out the dove in a trembling hand.

"I should stuff that man and put him up as a prize in my realm. We love to win things like that."

A shiver chilled her, but she stiffened her muscles and held the stuffed dove closer. "It'll be dark soon. Should we go to the Ferris wheel now? I think there's a long line."

He gave her hand a gentle squeeze, and they made their way toward that section of the park. They passed a small girl on a bench, fat tears rolling down her face and dripping from her chin. She sucked in a noisy breath, and Celina drew Kai to a stop.

"What is it?"

"I think she's lost." Celina let go of his hand and went toward the girl. She bent a little and smiled. "Hi. Are your parents around?"

The girl shook her head, crying louder as she used her arm to wipe her nose. "I... can't find...Daddy."

Celina gave her the stuffed dove. "Here, you hold on to this, and we'll look for your dad, okay?"

The girl looked over Celina's shoulder, her eyes widening. Kai crouched next to her, glanced around, and put his hand out in front of him. A red butterfly appeared over his palm, its wings glowing as it fluttered in front of the child's face before landing on the tip of her nose. She giggled, and the butterfly lifted into the air again, hovering closer to Kai. He swept the crowd with his gaze, irises flashing red for a second before he straightened. The butterfly flew around people, a glow pulsing each time it approached someone.

Celina stayed quiet, no idea what to say or think about the whole thing but wondered if other people could see the glowing insect.

It touched a man looking around wildly, and he turned toward Celina and Kai. The girl met his gaze and screeched as she pointed. "Daddy!"

She ran to her father, and he picked her up, holding her against him so hard, as though he'd never let go again.

"That was nice of you." Celina slipped her hand into his. "But why did she look afraid of you at first?"

He chuckled. "Children can feel things. You knew what that dark silhouette in the woods was before you met me, but, as you got older, your adult mind blocked it with reason and logic."

"I'm sorry I gave away the prize you won for me."

He shrugged while staring straight ahead. "I'll get you a stuffed human next time."

She narrowed her eyes, but the corners of her mouth curled as they headed to the Ferris wheel. "How can you switch from kindness to cruelty so fast?" She avoided his gaze.

"Cruelty is my nature, and it often suppresses any other emotion."

But he tries.

Their turn for the ride finally came, and they stepped inside the compartment for two before sitting side by side. The city lights sparkled and glowed, and she sighed, staring into the night. The ride stopped right as they reached the top and she turned to Kai, taking in his softened features, the fond smile on his lips.

She smiled back. "What?"

His fingers pushed a strand of loose hair behind her ear. "You're so beautiful."

Her lips parted, and she glanced from his eyes to his lips. He drew closer, and without waiting for him to act, she kissed him.

He licked her lower lip, and she opened her mouth, taking in his tongue as heat threatened to burn through her body. She squeezed her legs tighter as her pulse throbbed so hard it became almost unbearable.

The motion of the wheel shook her, and she drew away, panting. For the rest of the ride, she leaned against him to watch the lights, but all too soon, it was over. Dark storm clouds covered the sky. Her fun was over, and it would be back to thoughts of revenge, guilt, and the conflicting emotions she felt for Kai.

He took her hand and led her to the park exit. "Come with me."

She hesitated when they came to the escalators going down into the metro station. The underground resembled the sewers, and her body tensed at the thought of the creatures down there. Would anything appear with Kai present?

She'd never been to this city, so the names of the destinations were unfamiliar. "Where are we going?"

A small bell announced the metro, the sound echoing in the dark tunnels as lights appeared at the end of one.

"I said I'd give you twenty-four hours." He winked as he pulled her inside the carriage.

She glanced at her hand wrapped around Kai's. If she let go, it would mean her normal day would end, and he'd become her demon again; she wasn't ready.

Once they were off the metro, and out of the underground station, he came to a stop in front of a centennial-looking house and opened the door. "Here we are."

Celina stared up at the sign. *Old Port Inn*. She frowned. "Why are we here?"

"We can't go back to Ottawa just yet. Opening another rift so soon after the first one would be catastrophic for this world."

She crossed her arms over her chest and walked through the grand entrance doors. "This looks expensive and busy. They won't have anything available last minute." She looked at her clothes, and warmth flushed her face. Everyone dressed so fancily in comparison.

"I'll be right back." Kai moved to the reception desk and spoke with the man there.

A few moments later, he closed the door behind them as they stepped into their room.

It had a rustic style to it, but her attention went straight to the king-size bed. Heat surged through her as she took in the iron bars. She imagined Kai tying her wrists, and her heart pounded in her ears. She rubbed her arms and let out a breath. They'd shared a hotel room ever since they made the deal; this wouldn't be any different.

Celina tried shoving those ideas out of her head. "How did you get this room? I know there weren't any; I heard a woman complaining about it as she left."

"Someone already had a reservation, but I pretended it was me."

"Are you insane? They'll show up here, and we'll be—"

"I cloaked the building for the night. No one will find it."

Every exposed brick in the room's decoration pressed against her chest as images of Shiriki's dungeon flew through her mind. She was trapped all over again. Just a different demon.

"I need some air."

She stepped around him and through the door without giving him a second glance.

Dashing down the hall, she marched through the lobby until a warm breeze tickled her skin. She left the inn and walked away from the building as fast as she could, unsure where she was heading. She'd been good at keeping the torture out of her mind, but now the vivid images wouldn't release her. The pain had been horrifying, but her stomach quivered at the memory of the satisfied sneer Shiriki had shown her after cutting her leg open.

An hour passed, and she didn't know where she was anymore. The city was huge, and none of the streets or buildings were familiar. The night sky blazed as lightning flashed across it, and Celina stopped. Her breathing grew shallow and rapid when a vision of Thomas' murder replaced the memories of her torture.

Rain poured down without warning, soaking her in a matter of seconds. She smiled as the smell of the crisp scent in the air filled her nostrils. She'd enjoyed storms in the past, but it had been so long ago.

"Celina?"

She'd expected Kai to find her, and her heart fluttered when he did.

I love him.

Celina clutched her chest and squeezed a little, a smile appearing on her lips. "This might be the last time I feel the rain." Her hair stuck to her face as her eyes blurred with water—or were those tears?

He took a few steps toward her, the rain soaking through his clothes. "We'll go somewhere else for the night."

"Thank you for everything today, Mekaisto." She put her hand on his cheek and caressed him with gentle fingers.

He blinked twice and then his eyes widened as though he'd seen her for the first time. His lips curled into a smile. "My pleasure."

Kai took her to a simpler hotel—one without bricks or stonework, one with so many rooms they didn't have to lie to get one. She shivered in her wet clothes as they got off the elevator to the fifth floor.

"You're lucky. You don't seem to get cold at all." She stepped inside the small room. It had a queen-size bed, an open door to a tiny bathroom, and a small kitchen area.

Kai put his hand on the wall, a strange red glow shining over it for a few seconds before disappearing. "I've created a sound barrier within the room, so you may speak freely, or make any kind of noises you want." He leaned against the door with a grin and then pointed toward the bathroom. "You should change."

A fluttery feeling invaded her stomach. "These are the only clothes I have."

"Take a warm shower, and I'll have dry clothes ready by the time you come out."

She locked the bathroom door, even though pretending to keep him out was useless, and stripped off her clothes. The hot water from the shower warmed away the goosebumps she'd received while walking in the rainstorm, but every so often she'd glance at the curtain, wondering if Kai was inside the bathroom with her. When she stepped out, the only things folded on the counter were her underpants and Kai's dress shirt.

She left the bathroom, uncomfortable at how few clothes she wore, and her pulse raced as she spotted him. He'd given her his shirt, and she couldn't seem to take her gaze off his toned upper body. "If you can dry clothes so quickly, why not just do that for mine?" She swallowed hard, focusing on her bare feet instead of him.

Kai leaned his hand on the wall next to her, and she jumped. His other hand slid down to her legs, his fingers gliding over her skin. "You're lucky I haven't ravaged you so far." His heated whisper inspired a shiver. "Unlike most of my kind, I desire you to want it. To beg for it."

"Well, I…" Her voice broke as she tried to form words.

Kai leaned into her neck and pressed kisses against her skin, and she quivered. When his tongue flicked across her skin, her breath caught in her throat but escaped in a whoosh as his hand moved higher up her leg, his thumb tracing her inner thigh as it continued.

"Kai, no!"

He withdrew, the pain in his eyes almost overwhelming. "You want me to stop?" His head tilted to the side.

As she struggled to fight between guilt and her desire to give in, tears rolled down her cheeks. "I still love Thomas. I can't betray him."

He pressed his forehead over hers and cupped her face. "I know you still love him, and I'm not asking you to bury those feelings." Despite his human appearance, his eyes glowed a little. "But he would've wanted you to be happy."

Her chest squeezed at the continued gentle expression on his face. She touched his cheek and stared back into his eyes.

He kissed her, gentle at first, but passion slipped through, and his lips became more insistent. He traced his fingers from her neck to the first button on the dress shirt she wore. Leaning back a little, his gaze remained on her, warming her, as he freed one button at a time. Her breathing quickened; she wasn't wearing anything else except for the underpants.

She placed her hand on his chest. "Kai—"

He grabbed her wrist and pressed it against the wall. "If you fight back, my instincts will react, and I'll continue with no mercy to you." He released her but continued to caress her skin. "If you want me to stop, say it. A clear 'no' is all I ask for."

"I...I'm scared." She gasped in surprise when his fingers spread across her inner thighs and rested between them.

"What I offered you today was an opportunity to forget about your revenge. What I'm offering you now is a means to escape reality. Wouldn't you like that?"

She wanted to escape, to forget. Her body begged for release, ached for abandon, and knew Kai could give that to her.

Thomas always had made love to her with the lights off and, being her only lover, she had experienced nothing different. Kai always took what he wanted so far...no hint of shyness in that demon. She knew he would give her the deepest and darkest fantasies she craved.

"Can you make me forget?" Her voice sounded small.

Kai took this as an answer, a smile curling his lips. "It is difficult for humans to think of anything when they are experiencing an inordinate amount of pleasure."

Her cheeks burned like fire when he parted the front of the shirt and cupped her breasts. She drew in a breath, and her panties moistened at a sight she'd never seen—her breasts in the hands of a man. He kissed her again, his tongue slipping inside her mouth. His fingers drew circles around her nipples, and she gasped. He pulled away the shirt and slid his hands around her back.

His gaze hovered over her body. "So beautiful..."

She pulled him to her and kissed him, pressing her breasts against his chest, so their warmth passed from one to the other. Taking her in his arms, he carried her to the bed. Celina brought the blanket up in front of her, but Kai grinned and drew it away. She protested, but he lifted her onto him, so they were face-to-face.

"I find it amusing how shy humans can be about being

naked." He tugged her wrists, removing the shield hiding her breasts. "What is it you're trying to hide?"

She turned away, embarrassed that she was sitting on top of him in only her panties. "A lot of things."

"Let me explore all of you." He cupped her breasts again.

He leaned in and took her nipple inside his mouth, making her head jerk back. She sucked in a breath when his tongue flicked at her nipple while his fingers pinched the other. He withdrew, and his eyes glowed bright red, but the rest of him remained human.

She gazed into the glowing eyes. "How does that happen? I mean…"

"Intimacy makes it more difficult to control constrictive forms."

He drew her even closer, his tongue lapping between her breasts. She ached for more, and when their gazes met, her cheeks burned. With a wink, he laid her on her back, his fingers gliding down her belly, tracing her skin. When he reached her panties, he yanked. She ached for him to touch her, and as he unbuckled his belt, his eyes burned her with lust that spread like fire through her veins.

He kneeled in front of her, and she swallowed hard at the sight of his erection. She'd never seen a naked male form so close, and he was just… breathtaking. His muscles rippled as he moved, built to take possession of whatever he wanted.

He wants me… Why?

"You already know the answer." Using his fingers, he drew a path up her thigh, climbing higher as her breathing grew into begging moans. "Open your legs, Celina."

Her whole body burned, but with her heartbeat pulsing between her legs, they seemed to open by instinct alone. She arched back as his fingers slipped between her wet folds, a gasp escaping her mouth as she rocked her hips so he'd penetrate deeper. He groaned as he leaned over her, his lips taking the hard peak of her nipple in his mouth again.

She whispered his name somewhere between a moan and plea.

He massaged her clit, gentle at first, then faster with every pleasured sigh that escaped her. She clutched his arm, wanting safety, her whole body vulnerable under his touch. Heat radiated through her body, and she screamed as pleasure tore through her core.

He moved down her body, kissing along her stomach until he reached her sex. His tongue entered her center while his fingers continued playing with her, and she threw her head back with a wail, her breath coming in ragged pants as another surge of pleasure crashed in waves. Her hands latched on to his hair, and her body shuddered. "Kai...I want you."

His voice came out in a growl, vibrating against her wet opening. "Patience...I plan on savoring you."

She looked at him, and her heart hammered against her chest when his stare said he'd devour her sooner.

He licked her clit again, but when he sucked, her moans turned to cries of overwhelming bliss. His tongue trailed toward the upper part of her body again, and she locked eyes with him as he pressed his erection between her legs. He leaned into her ear, his hand closing in around her throat gently. "Do you want me to stop?"

"No."

She moaned as his cock filled her, stretching her with his thickness. He went in slow but didn't stop until he was balls deep, his crown hitting the end of her insides. A whimper escaped her, but his lips found hers, cutting it short. He slid his tongue inside her mouth, and she tasted herself, driving her excitement further.

Her nerves quivered with ecstasy as he slid out and back in, hard. Another moan mixed in a gasp escaped from her, forcing their mouths apart. She ran her tongue over her lips, missing the taste of his mouth. He grabbed her hips and went in hard and deep again, every thrust throwing her back.

He took a fistful of her hair and became rougher. She writhed and squirmed under him, biting down on her lip and trying to stifle her moans.

"Don't hold back." He took hold under her knee and lifted her leg, driving himself in again.

She cried out, her hands tightening their grip on his arms, her back arching higher. He sat and pulled her over him. She licked her lips again as she wrapped her legs around his waist. He squeezed her ass, lifted her, and slid his cock inside her again. They moved slower, their hips rocking back and forth into each other, making her gasp.

She pressed her forehead against his. "Don't stop…please."

He brought her breast to his mouth as she kept moving, his hand gripping her ass tighter, and her moan turned into a stifled whimper.

He laid her on her back again and thrust inside, rougher. Another scream left her mouth as her pleasure peaked, and her muscles clenched around his cock. Her legs twitched, and her body shuddered.

Kai lay over her, cradling her as his hands caressed her shoulders. His eyes met hers, and she surprised herself with thoughts of how gentle he could be.

"Did you… I mean…" It felt stupid to be shy after all that. "Did you come?"

"I am not even close to being finished with you. Remember what I told you? We make intimacy last." He kissed her neck. "We take our time."

"Would it be the same if you weren't in human form?"

His mouth curled to one side. "No, it wouldn't."

She blushed and turned her head, tracing his arm gently. "What would be different?"

"Demons aren't anatomically the same as humans."

She met his eyes. "What…parts?"

"Ah, you're a curious one, aren't you?" Amusement rang out in his voice.

His hand traveled to her sex again, wetting his finger inside her before continuing down, and slipping between her ass cheeks.

Celina's gasp turned into a moan. "Kai…"

He chuckled. "You enjoy it there too, no?"

She blushed and tried turning away, but he held her face.

"Why are you embarrassed about it? Humans have so many pleasure receptors. Why not enjoy them all?" He pushed his finger inside, and she let out a shuddering breath.

She wrapped her legs around his hips. "Is it possible…? I mean, would you? I want you to take me in your true form…please."

Kai sat up, and his gaze pierced through her. "I will not be gentle nor show you any mercy. I'll play with every single pleasure nerve in your body." He bent toward her ear. "Are you certain?"

"Yes." She sat as well, and a flicker of fear ran through her. "Will…will it hurt?"

He smiled. "There is a fine line between pain and pleasure. The middle is so blurry that the two are part of the same bliss." He stood and stepped away from the bed. "Let me take you there."

Darkness fell across the room, the only source of light coming from his glowing eyes. The same horrible feeling of death she'd felt when he rescued her from Shiriki's dungeons, the same as inside the church, washed over her and she shivered. The lights flicked on again, dimmer than before, and her eyes widened as she stared at his naked form. And both of his cocks.

Kai's black wings folded as he took a few steps and sat on the bed in front of her. Without waiting, she faced him, staring into his eyes—the red glow more pronounced than ever. Moving her hand to the black horns, she traced the rune-like inscriptions that glowed a deep red. She drew out her touches, feeling their texture, but also to test his patience.

He groaned, his eyes closing.

Her curiosity grew as she followed the horn down to his hair. Silk was never so smooth. In his true form, his jet-black hair fell all the way to his middle back, but she followed it only to his ear where she tucked the black hair behind it.

His hands gripped her hips with a squeeze, and he lifted her. His cock pressed against her slick opening, but this time, around the tightening of her ass as well.

Oh… Does he have lube?

He licked the side of her neck. "No need for that."

Before she could question him, he kissed her, cutting off her thoughts.

Her body trembled in anticipation as his slick cocks slid inside her, their lips parting as she gasped. Her hands squeezed and dug into his shoulders until he stretched both her holes and filled them. Kai let out a chuckle, and her eyes flew open.

His vertical pupils had become tiny slits, and the smile curling over his pointed teeth turned her blood to ice. "You are mine." He flipped her on her back again. She opened her mouth for a scream trapped in her chest as he grabbed her ankles and rested them on his shoulders. "And I will," he slammed his cocks into her, and she screamed this time, "claim every inch of you."

"Kai, please!" She didn't know if she was begging him to stop or to keep going, her mind blocked by her nerves being set on fire.

"Keep begging, dove." He lifted her legs higher on his shoulders and plunged deeper.

She fell into fevered ecstasy, wailing. He put her legs down again, and grabbed a fistful of her hair, wrenching it back and using it to drill inside her deeper than she thought possible.

He drew away and spun her flat on her stomach.

Glancing back at him, her eyes widened. "Wait…what?" She'd never done it like that.

He closed his hand around one cock, stroked once, and did the same for the other. As Kai leaned over her, he pressed against her openings again. "Take a deep breath."

When he entered her again, she cried out so loud someone should have heard her—soundproof spell or no. Like a protective cocoon, his wings came down on each side of her, his breath warm on the back of her neck. His tongue slipped across her back as he thrust faster, and she moaned louder.

After what seemed like hours, he grunted as his cocks stretched her insides, a searing hot liquid causing her to cry out. Her hands gripped the blanket tighter, and her toes curled as her orgasm flooded her repeatedly.

He slumped over her, panting as his grip loosened around her hair. Her thighs twitched as his cum, and her own, streamed out of her. Goosebumps crawled on her skin as their scents mingled.

He turned her on her side and held her to his chest, one of his wings resting over them both. Tears rolled down the side of her face, and she blinked, unsure why she was crying. Kai leaned on his elbows so he could look at her, and she half-turned her head away, wanting to hide her shame. He kissed her, his tongue pushing its way inside her mouth again, and another set of moans escaped them.

Her body shuddered, and he withdrew. "Are you all right?"

She nodded, but her eyes widened again when he sat up, both his cocks erect. He took her by the arm, turning her on her stomach, and lifted her thighs, so she was on her hands and knees. She let a whimper, both in protest and lust. Kai entered both holes, slow and deep, and she gasped. "Oh, God..."

"Not quite. I am the other one." He leaned over her, the angle of his cocks changing, and she cried out louder. "Did you really think I was done with you?"

She pressed her forehead against the mattress and moaned.

A DEEP CONNECTION

Kai drifted in and out of sleep—a rare thing for him, to slip so deep into his subconscious. He smelled Celina nearby, her scent sending his hunting instincts into overdrive.

She walked ahead of him, naked. Her muscles tensed as she entered a large room decorated in black tiles, with a tub in the middle. Every breath she exhaled echoed from the smooth surfaces and called out to him.

His wings flapped, and he rose into the air, hovering above and watching his prey as she tiptoed toward the old roman bathtub. The white of it was almost blinding in the gloom, forcing her to squint. She leaned over it, her breasts swaying as she stared into the black liquid filling the tub.

He swooped down behind her. His claw-like fingernails reached toward her, but as he touched her skin, he gentled under her warmth. Spinning around, her whole body shivered. "Shut your eyes and look away, the shadow monster will not stay," she whispered the words, her eyelids closed tight.

The evil within him pushed forward, and he grabbed her by the hair, pulling her toward him roughly. She had shown fear, and the monster within him would oblige. "I will stay, dove…inside…" He grabbed under her knee and lifted it, penetrating her harder than ever.

She gasped, and her eyes flew open. "I'm not scared of you, Kai," she whispered as he thrust in deeper.

She caressed his cheek as another moan escaped her lips.

"You are supposed to be afraid of nightmares."

Kai opened his eyes, and he gazed at the hotel room plunged in darkness.

Even in my dreams, I want her.

Celina jerked awake, and she sat on the edge of the bed, silent. His blood boiled as he stared at the claw marks on her once smooth back; he would heal those later. A few more seconds passed before she stood and wobbled to the bathroom. The door handle provided stability as she gripped it tightly, but she let it go and closed the door behind her. The light appeared around the doorframe, and Kai couldn't help the frustration building inside.

I still want her.

The sound of water from the shower caught his attention, and he peeked inside her head to make sure everything was all right.

Pain. Sorrow. Despair.

He materialized inside the bathroom, his eyes narrowing on her. The curtains were left open, and Celina kneeled in the tub while water poured over her. She sobbed, her hands pressed against her face.

If he'd had a soul, it would have ripped apart at the sight…even still, his core shook.

I was too rough…

He stepped inside the tub, and crouched in front of her, the water spilling over his wings. Her head shot up, and she gasped in surprise. She covered her breasts and turned away.

"I…"

You regret it this much?

He strained to keep his voice steady, not wanting to scare her further. "You do not have to—"

She locked eyes with him. "I betrayed him." More tears streamed down her face. "What else can I call it since I've fallen in love with you?"

His hands curled into fists, and he opened his mouth, ready to tell her the truth.

No. Not yet.

"Everything will be explained soon." Kai muttered the words more to himself as he drew her into his arms, unable to stop his lust from hardening against her abdomen.

She let out a nervous-sounding laugh. "It's always later with you."

He withdrew a little. "Not everything." She gazed down, her cheeks flushing, and he took her chin and forced her to look at him. "It pleases me when you blush, but it provokes me to do much more with you."

She wrapped her arms around his neck and pulled him closer, so her lips rested on his. "Then do more." Her eyes filled with lust, sending all his instincts surging forward until the light bulbs inside the bathroom burst.

She let out a small scream and held on tighter to his arms. He could see, even in the darkness, but the glow of his eyes kept some illumination inside the room. The evil inside him stirred again as a shiver ran down her spine. "You only need to beg."

He waited as he followed her thoughts. Her mind rang with alarm bells, but her heart beat faster, and the throbbing between her legs demanded more. She lifted herself a little, still on her knees. "Please."

He chuckled, his hand tracing her skin and feeling every single goosebump he'd caused. "I know you can do better than that, dove. You did it more than once when I was inside you."

Her breath came faster, and he could smell what she

wanted before she even knew what it was. "Please, Kai, I'm yours. I want more. I want everything you can give me."

The wave of lust heating his body could have burned a city to the ground.

"Well, now," he whispered in her ear as he stood, lifting her up with him, "I need to oblige such begging with a reward."

Her nipples rubbed against his chest, sending him beyond clear thought. The demon inside roared with want, forgetting who he dealt with. He let everything go, including the limits he'd put on himself from fear of hurting her, and watched as the darkness slithering from him wrapped around his prey.

He focused on her eyes, following her thoughts, wanting to hear fear and panic inside her. But what he found was animalistic lust, ripping away the fragment of control left in him. She stared down at her body, following the smoke she could barely see.

You do not need to see it. Feeling it will even be too much.

She took a step back as it slipped around her wrists and ankles, and before her scream ever left her mouth, he lifted her with his natural energy, pinning her against the tiles. He felt her through the smoke as much as with his bare hands since every inch of that darkness was a part of him. Her muscles tensed, and his smile widened.

"Kai?" Her voice was barely a whisper—music to his ears.

The smoke around her ankles spread her legs open to a display he would never tire of. He leaned in, his hands grasping her inner thighs. "Yes, Celina?"

A gasp escaped her when his fingernails pressed harder. "Is—?"

He chuckled, already knowing what she wanted to ask. "I will stop if you tell me to." He stared into her beautiful gray eyes. "At any time."

Her muscles relaxed a little, and she wet her lips. "Okay."

He slid inside her, and the wetness and tight squeeze

invited him in with such need that his smile widened. Her moans filled his ears, but it was her gaze that sent more fire through him than anything else. He thrust slowly, taking his time with her, feeling her every tremor, each heartbeat. Even the sound of her blood pumping through her veins screamed for more.

Or is that her *screams?*

She turned her head away, biting down on her lip again, but he took her face with his hand, holding it steady to see every changing emotion flashing through her.

He caressed her breasts as he continued thrusting into her. "Celina." He grunted her name, and her lips parted in a silent whisper of ecstasy.

"I want more..." She twisted her wrists inside his shadows' grasp, clenching her fingers.

He smirked and slithered the smoke along her body, so it would replace what his hands had been doing. It pulled at her nipples, and she moaned louder. Folding his wings around them, he brought her closer to what she needed, never once stopping his exploration of her body with more than just five senses.

He slithered his darkness between her lips, suckling on her clit, her nerves burning so hot he could smell them. She tightened around his cocks with a piercing scream, and he let out a groan as her orgasm thundered through her—in her body, in her head, in his head—driving him on until he climaxed himself. Her whole body shook, and he stopped, listening to her heart, pumping blood faster than he'd ever heard it in her life.

He chuckled, pushing her wet hair from her face as her head lolled on his shoulder. He carried her out of the shower and back into their bedroom. She didn't wake when he laid her on the pillows and pulled the scattered blankets over her, so she'd stay warm.

She mumbled a few words, but one was clear. "Thomas."

A heaviness weighed on him as the name seemed to linger in the air. Leaning in to nuzzle her neck, he breathed in her scent. "Sleep."

Kai materialized to where he had to be in the early hours of that morning. The park and its surroundings were empty as he sat on the bench. He stared at the telephone pole across the house, knowing he'd get a better view of the murderers if he perched there, but he didn't want a constrictive form so soon.

Shiriki appeared and sat next to him. "Did you hurt her, then?"

Kai hissed through his teeth as he spoke. "I nearly broke her."

She lasted a lot longer than I expected...

"I am sure she is fine, Mekaisto. You worry too much."

Kai stared at the house as the man's shadow crossed the kitchen window. "She still loves her husband."

"Did you expect her not to?"

He smirked. "With the way people react to being lied to, I expected it to some extent."

Shiriki scooted closer to his king, a smile on his lips. "I request your permission to end Plan A."

Kai's eyebrows rose. "I thought you enjoyed it."

"Plan B worked better." Amusement rang through Shiriki's tone. "And I would like to move to other things now. My research on the secrets of the soul has been neglected for some time."

"As long as you follow my laws, you can research what you want."

"Generous as always." Shiriki eyed Kai as though determining his mood, and when he grinned, the Viscus demon relaxed. "Has she asked you what the connection is between her parents and me?"

"You know how humans are. They burn with curiosity but are too frightened of what the answers could be."

"Will you tell me if things change?"

Kai turned away from his prey and faced his second in command. "Why?"

He shrugged, but a sinister gleam shone in his eyes. "Oh, I simply would like to speak to her freely."

"All in good time, Shiriki…"

INTERROGATION

Celina continued thinking of Thomas, and every time she did, her chest tightened. She felt she'd betrayed him.

What the hell was I thinking? I'll die soon anyway—what's the difference?

After watching the murderers for a whole day, Kai returned to the hotel with a clear plan. Once most of the neighborhood went to sleep, he would go inside the house, and after silencing them, Celina could join him.

She stood at the back door of the house, counting from the time Kai vanished to when he opened the door.

She reached thirty.

"The child is tied up in his bedroom, and the parents are in the living area." He closed the door behind her.

"Are they all gagged?"

"Yes."

She turned to him, avoiding his gaze as she processed what had happened between them. "You were gentle with the kid, right?"

He lifted her chin. "Only because you asked so nicely."

His eyes gleamed, and her cheeks burned. "And you know how kind I am when you do anything close to begging."

Concentrate on what you have to do! Stop thinking with what's between your legs.

His smile widened, and she walked past him, knowing he'd read her thoughts. She stepped into the living room where the parents sat on the floor, hands and mouths bound. Déjà vu—a perfect reminiscence of the video Thomas marked as Lumen evidence. The mother had tears streaming down her cheeks while the father's attention darted from Kai to the floor. Celina crouched in front of them, the murderers who started it all.

All other thoughts, including lust, left her, and it filled her with hatred.

"Do you know who I am?" They both shook their heads and something inside her heated with even more anger. "I'm Thomas Leviet's wife."

I was nothing to them…

The father's gaze lowered, while the mother's muffled words caught in her gag.

"I have questions, but we'll be going somewhere else to talk." She studied them, even though inside, she was eager for their blood. "If you try anything stupid, I guarantee your son will be the one to suffer. Understand?"

They both nodded.

Once Kai shoved both parents in the trunk of their car, he came back into the house. "Are we going to leave the one person we can use against those two?"

She glanced toward the kid's bedroom. "What do you suggest?"

"Bring the boy along. It'll help if they know we can hurt him." He spun the car keys around his fingers, eyeing her with an arched brow.

"I don't want the Sanguis demons to hurt him."

"They won't if I tell them not to."

He had a point about bringing the boy, but it didn't make the decision any easier. "Okay."

Kai moved toward the bedroom and shot a backward glance at her. "I like it when you listen."

She rolled her eyes but said nothing as she left the house.

Not long after she'd climbed into the passenger side, Kai put the child on the back seat. She glanced to the boy, gagged and blindfolded. "Why did you cover his eyes?"

He stuck the keys in the ignition. "No point in him seeing any of this."

"Your thoughtfulness is strange sometimes." She gazed at him, trying to truly see who this demon was on the inside.

He shrugged. "Just like humans can be cruel."

Celina remained quiet as they drove. A tingling sensation ran through her, and she tightened her fingers against the hem of her shirt.

It'll be over soon—I'll finally get my revenge.

Kai pulled up in the alley behind The CrowBar. Celina stiffened when she spotted Haku and Linda already waiting for them.

"How did they…?"

"I told Shiriki to come and instruct the Sanguis demons to be ready."

"Shiriki? Why is that sicko invited?"

"I ordered him here to watch the boy in another room while we question the parents." Kai stepped out of the car.

"Are you insane?" She raised her voice, her terror flaring just knowing that Shiriki was here. "You're going to let that demon watch a vulnerable—"

His eyes narrowed. "I give orders to all demons. If they disobey, their suffering is excruciating."

"He is not exaggerating." Shiriki materialized next to her, and she jumped at the sound of his voice.

She grabbed on to Kai's arm and semi-hid behind him as the white-haired demon stared at her with his cold silver eyes. "That didn't stop him from breaking your laws and torturing me," she muttered.

"No demonic forms right now." Kai's voice had a commanding tone, and she flinched even though the order wasn't directed at her.

She considered his use of the words *right now*, curious about what he meant, but by the time she faced Shiriki again, he'd already changed. His hair gleamed white blond under the moonlight, and his gray eyes searched hers.

He never seems to lose his demon appearance...

Haku stepped forward, yanking Linda into line alongside him. "Where are the ones we're to bring to the torture room?"

"Torture room?" Celina repeated, glancing from Kai to the Sanguis demons.

"It's the best way to get answers." Linda winked.

Shiriki passed Celina and hefted the boy over his shoulder. She swallowed hard. No child should suffer what that monster could do.

"He won't harm him." Kai trickled a fleeting touch over her arm.

She didn't bother to ask how he knew what she was thinking. "Promise me he won't."

"I promise." He breathed the word into her ear, and she shivered.

Celina jerked her head in a nod of assent and followed as Haku and Linda escorted the parents to the basement. The room was a perfect replica of a medieval torture room—she even recognized some devices from the Lumen's teachings. She pushed the bile against the back of her throat as she stepped farther inside.

I'm in a torture room with hundreds of devices to cause pain, there are three demons, a fourth not far, and the only two other humans are tied. This could all turn around on me, and I'd have no one else to blame but myself.

She jumped when Kai wrapped his arms around her, holding her tight against him. Haku's and Linda's eyes widened, but they turned away quickly to avoid, what she imagined, was a burning glare from their king.

"I'm here, dove."

A sense of calm washed over her at his touch, but she wanted this to be over. Yet her stomach churned at the thought of point-blank murder. The memory of killing at the church taunted Celina with own her capacity for evil.

Once the parents were tied to chairs next to each other, Celina detached from her demon and sat in front of them. Kai stood by her side while Haku and Linda leaned against the back wall between the multitudes of hanging chains, near the table of torture devices.

Adam strolled inside the room and clapped his hands together, a smile curving his lips. "Which of these is mine?" He stepped closer to the couple and leaned forward.

Thomas' murderers shrank in their chairs.

"That'll depend." Celina's pulse sped as she glared at both parents. "Ungag them, please."

Kai moved forward and yanked the bindings from their mouths. The mother screamed, and Kai backhanded her across the face. Celina jumped but bit her tongue. She needed to look as though she had control over what was happening, so when she threatened them, they wouldn't doubt her.

The husband's face contorted with rage. "Don't you dare hurt her, or I'll kill you!"

Kai ignored the empty threats and stood next to Celina again. Adam crossed his arms and smiled.

Her jaw clenched when she stared down at Thomas' killers. They were at her mercy, and this time, she would be the one to deny their pleading, ignore their begging.

Vengeance was finally hers, and she could taste it on her tongue. She would tear them apart before giving one up to the Sanguis demon and killing the other.

She pulled out their family tree. "Wayne and Emily Pierce," she read aloud. "Parents of Cedric, eleven years old, Henri, nine years old, and Simon, six years old."

The mother burst into more tears. "Please, we didn't have a choice. They took Cedric and Simon."

Celina shuddered, the kidnapping fresh in her memory. "I know what happened."

They raised their eyebrows at the same time.

Wayne tried pulling harder on his restraints. "Then why are you doing this?" He glanced around the room. "You must understand why we killed your husband—"

"Understand?" She threw the papers to the floor. "No, I don't understand why you had to murder my husband, why you tried doing the same to me!" She leaned back, tensing her muscles to keep from shaking, and waved her hand. "Go on, then. Explain."

Wayne's eyes flooded. "Someone told us that if we didn't kill him, they would torture our son, Simon." He blinked several times as though trying to keep the tears from falling. "They sent us a photo of Cedric…they killed him and would've done the same to our youngest. Simon hasn't been returned to us yet, but we still have hope."

Celina let out an impatient sigh. "I don't—"

"What would you have done if someone threatened your child?" Emily's tone pleaded. "Someone ordered us to kill a man for snooping around. If we did it, we'd get our son back."

"So, you murdered my husband in the faint hope that whoever kidnapped Simon and killed Cedric would return him to you?" Celina clutched the seat of her chair.

Kai's hand rested on her shoulder, and she glanced up at him. "Perhaps you should ask your questions."

Wayne raised his head high. "We're not answering anything."

"But...but what about Henri? They have him!" Emily stared at her husband, tears rolling down her cheeks.

"You heard that man." He glared at Adam. "They'll kill us either way. And Henri is probably next."

Time to bluff.

Celina glanced at Kai. "Tell Shiriki to bring Henri in here."

A few seconds passed before the metal door opened. Footsteps shuffled outside the door, and Shiriki came inside, holding the young boy by the shirt. Seeing Henri still blindfolded, gagged, and tied, but alive, reassured Celina he hadn't been hurt.

His parents begged for his life, but when Celina stood, they fell silent.

"Here's how this will work." She moved to the boy and the demon holding him. "You'll answer my questions, or I'll let Shiriki here have fun with your son."

Both parents trembled.

Shiriki's cold stare was enough to make Celina flinch. "The day I take orders from you—"

"Do as she says." Kai's tone sliced through the air like a knife.

Shiriki bowed, quiet.

Emily's face flushed, starting from one person to the other. "Why would you hurt an innocent child?"

"My husband was innocent, and so was I!" Her hands balled into fists. "Shiriki," her voice turned deathly calm, "I don't think they understand how vulnerable their son is in your hands. Maybe you should show them."

He chuckled, and gray smoke swirled around him and the boy. When the mist disappeared, he stood in his demonic form. Henri's parents screamed, the blood draining from their faces as they studied everyone in the room.

Shiriki grabbed the boy's throat, and he whimpered. "Do I get to hurt him?"

Her stomach churned at his action, but she stayed calm. "For every lie they tell me, yes. Kai will let you know, and you get to make one cut into the boy."

Shiriki's smile widened. "I wonder what would happen if I put the soul of a child inside the body of a demon?" He winked at his king and dragged the boy out of the room.

The door slammed, and the parents' faces paled further. Celina, stiffening her muscles to stop herself from trembling, moved next to Kai.

I lied to get them to talk. Please don't let him hurt Henri. I'm begging you, Kai.

He gave her a gentle smile and nodded. She drew a deep breath through her nose, relief flooding her. The last thing she wanted was for a child to suffer.

She sat down on the chair again and stared at her captives.

Wayne's shoulders dropped. "We'll answer your questions." His wife nodded.

"Who hired you to murder my husband?"

"They sent the instructions in an unmarked envelope. There was no name! We swear it!" The father's eyes widened.

Celina glanced up at Kai. "Can you confirm it?"

He smiled and transformed to his lowest demon form, his shoulder-length hair blending with the blackened stone walls, and his irises burning red. The parents trembled, their eyes bulging as they stared at the demon approaching them. "They are not lying."

If they're scared now, I'd love to see them when he's his true self.

Disappointed at the lack of information, she tried another angle. "My husband seemed to have been investigating Lumen members. He came here for information about Yonah Church, asking about blueprints and secret rooms. Apparently, he was getting the information for David Corval. My aunt..." The memory of the burning church still hunted her.

"Your aunt?" Wayne squinted at Celina as though trying to find a resemblance.

"Marie Tayen."

"Then…you're a member of the Lumen as well?"

"That's beside the point." She crossed her arms, wanting to steer clear of that subject. "My aunt mentioned David Corval used to be a member of your church but, at my husband's funeral, he claimed to be a business associate."

"David Corval?" Emily repeated. "He left the church some time ago because he came into a lot of money."

Celina's eyebrows shot up. "What?"

"Yes, about five months ago."

Emily shuddered. "Before our boys, there were others. David Corval came to see us not long after a few murders took place. He said someone was kidnapping and killing children of the Lumen families. He mentioned something about that same person coming after every member as well."

"I knew someone had been kidnapping them. That's what my husband was investigating."

Wayne glanced around the room. "Well, that's why the church was burnt down with all the members inside, isn't it? Cedric and Simon were taken, then they…murdered our eldest. And now the only members left from Yonah Church are Henri and Simon, my wife, me, and David Corval." He frowned, staring at Celina, "I suppose you as well."

She pushed that unsettling thought away. "I thought you said David left the church?" Celina said in surprise. "But I still don't understand what—"

"Someone is trying to kill off all the Lumen." Emily swallowed hard. "Starting with this church and probably planning to go to Giona next."

The fire at the church was her doing, but if someone planned on trying to exterminate those members, they might head for David next.

Am I still considered a member of the Lumen if I haven't attended for years?

"Let me get this straight." Celina paced the room, Kai's gaze following her as she did. "A rogue Lumen member hires someone to kidnap children. My husband investigates it, gets evidence on the kidnapper, and then the rogue member threatens your child's safety unless you murder my husband?"

"We didn't want to kill your husband or harm you! We're so sorry!" More tears streamed down Emily's face, making it look almost like it was glowing.

"I believe that is all the information they have." Kai's tone resonated against the dungeon-like room, making them flinch.

Celina nodded. "Well, let me reassure you, I have no intentions of hurting Henri. He'll be safe, dropped off at the nearest police station. But, for one of you, your life ends here. While for the other, a life of torture begins."

"Have you chosen the one you're giving me then?" Adam considered them both, his lips curling over his teeth in a snarl.

"What kind of company do you keep?" The mother's wide stare darted around, and though she'd whispered her question, the vast open space of the room amplified it.

"Him?" Celina asked, pointing at Adam. "He's a Sanguis demon—does business with humans willing to become blood slaves for certain favors." She smiled as Emily blinked several times and Wayne looked away. "As for him," she continued, pointing at Kai, "he's the demon I made a deal with the night you murdered my husband. I exchanged my life and soul to get revenge against the people who had anything to do with the murder. I should have died, but he saved me, and that's why you're both here."

"Have you chosen, dove?" Kai's eyes glowed red.

She hesitated and turned to Adam. "Do you have a preference?"

Adam snapped his fingers, and Haku and Linda came forward to carry off the father. He screamed while kicking and trying to wrench free, but Haku sank his pointed teeth into his neck on one side while Linda mirrored the action on the other. The mother screamed as her husband went limp before the Sanguis demons dragged him out.

"Pleasure doing business, Mrs. Leviet." Adam bowed to her and then joined his children and their new blood slave.

Celina stared at Emily, ice surging through her veins. "As for you." She took a few steps to the woman who'd tried to kill her. "I did nothing wrong, yet I paid the greatest price."

"Wait!" Emily's face shone with tears. "Please don't kill me."

"If I had begged for my life that night, would you have spared me?" Her curiosity piqued, but she kept her voice cold, heartless even.

"Please…I don't want to die," she sobbed.

Celina stared at the mother and saw herself on the night she made the deal with Kai. She hadn't wanted to die either. "All right, I'll let you live."

Emily nodded her head and sighed in relief. "Thank you."

Celina walked over to the table, perused the torture instruments, and picked up the pistol. *This way, she won't be scared before she dies…I can do that, at least.*

She pointed it at the back of Emily's head, darkness surging inside her like the night she made the deal. "Thank you for all the information."

She fired the pistol, the deafening bang echoing in the vast space.

BANKRUPTCY

Celina turned and pointed the pistol at Kai's face. His eyes narrowed, but his lips curled into a venomous smile tinted with pride.

"Someone is trying to kill off all the Lumen."

Including me, if I'm still considered one of them...and you're taking my life real soon.

Her body trembled, but she stiffened her muscles to keep her hand steady. No way would she show weakness in her current position.

Kai's head cocked to the side. "It seems that way."

She kept her guard up while sorting the information. "You said you sent demons after them to kill them off, that's why their bloodline was disappearing. I have the feeling you've something to do with this." She stared into his red eyes. "If I find out you did, I'll—"

His eyelids lowered. "You will what, Celina?" He took a step forward and reached out toward the pistol.

She backed away until she hit the nearest wall and flinched when his finger slid along the metal of the weapon. His red gaze burned into her as he held her hand steady against the pistol and pointed it against his chest. He pushed her finger against the trigger, and she screamed as another resonating explosion echoed inside the room. Blood poured from his wound, but his lips held his smile.

"No! Kai!" She threw the weapon on the floor and pressed her hands against the bleeding, her mind racing. "I don't know how to…" Her breath caught inside her chest as she stared around. "I need to get Shiriki, or Adam—they can—"

Smoke seeped from the gaping hole, and she took her hands away in surprise. The shattered sternum repaired itself, muscle formed over the bones, and flesh stretched across his insides. After a few seconds, it was as though he'd never been shot.

"Empty threats are as useless as firing a weapon on me." He waved his hand in front of himself, and his clothes returned to normal.

She opened and closed her mouth, her bloodied hands twisting together. "I'm…"

He leaned against the wall, his stare boring into her as his vertical pupils thinned. "Why even threaten me in the first place?"

Her body shook. "Because the more I find out about what's going on, the more I see your name written all over it. Tell me I'm wrong!" She didn't want to believe he had anything to do with her situation. He'd saved her from dying, and even though it was wrong and twisted, she loved him.

He took her face between his hands, his eyes searching hers. "Never. Do that. Again."

She stared at him, blinking back tears. The lump in her throat threatened to free her emotions, so she pressed her lips together. She focused on her feet and dug her fingernails into the palms of her hands.

He wrapped his arms around her, and she sobbed into his chest, choking on her lack of air. "I'm so…sorry."

He sighed, and when she tried looking up at him, he held her tightly in place. "A demon's love can only turn into violence. Imagine what happens when you threaten one." He rubbed her back. "Remember that next time you make an unwise choice."

His words burned through her like an unforgiving fire, and yet they were cold as ice, as though he hated the fact.

Her breath stuttered as she glanced at the corpse of the woman who'd tried to kill her. She hadn't killed Emily in self-defense, or to rescue anyone. She murdered her for revenge, and it left a bittersweet feeling inside.

"We need to find David Corval. I've got questions for him." She brushed her hair from her damp cheeks. "Let's go."

His eyes glazed, as though lost in thought, but a smile curled his lips. "Of course."

When he opened the metal door, Celina stepped out and waited for Kai so she could follow him out of the maze-like basement and back outside.

Shiriki stood in the alleyway, Henri still in his grasp.

"I had no fun with this one." His tone held a hint of disappointment.

"Kai." She spared the briefest glance over her shoulder. "Could you bring Henri to a police station and make sure they help him?"

Unlike me, he'll never get the chance to avenge the deaths of his parents and brothers. Nothing is fair.

Shiriki sneered. "Poor thing has no one left."

"A little like me, but he's worse off." She stared at Kai. "At least I don't have to live with nothing left. I have a demon."

Kai chuckled. "Lucky you." He eyed the vehicle. "What about the car?"

She didn't want to draw attention to the Sanguis demons by leaving a stolen car in the alleyway of the club, so she glanced at Shiriki. "Do you drive?"

"I have been much too busy learning how to dissect humans in the most painful ways possible."

She crossed her arms, feeling a little braver because Kai

was close. "Fine. Ask Adam if one of his demons can dispose of the car."

"Only because Mekaisto ordered me to do as you say." He let the boy go and disappeared.

Henri staggered around, blindfolded and gagged. Kai took the child into his arms. "I have business to take care of in my realm again. Go to the hotel and wait for me there, however long it takes."

He disappeared, and she swayed on her feet. She still needed to visit David Corval, but for once, she'd do as Kai ordered.

With part of avenging Thomas complete, a weight lifted off her shoulders. But mixed emotions flooded her from the murder she had committed. There was still the matter of a kidnapper and a murdering Lumen member though. Emily Pierce said the only members left were Wayne, Henri, David Corval, and Simon if he was still alive.

It has to be David. Unless there's an unknown member. Maybe he knows who it is… And I'm still left, for now.

Linda came from inside the club with a sweater for Celina.

"What for? It's not cold."

With a smirk, the demon pointed at the blood splatters on her clothes. "I think you'll attract some unwanted attention, no?"

Without another word, she slipped the sweater over her bloodstained shirt.

As soon as Celina returned to the hotel, she showered and changed her clothes. A knock on the door startled her, and her heart pulsed as though inside her throat. Kai wouldn't knock, and she hadn't ordered room service.

She opened the door, and her eyes widened. Thomas'

lawyer held a sealed cardboard box, sweat rolling down his face.

What is he doing here?

"Yes?"

He gave her a pleasant smile despite the heavy box. "May I come in?"

"How did you know where to find me?" She did her best to hide the accusation behind her words but couldn't help frown.

"The contact information you provided had your room number." He glanced over her shoulder and shifted the box in his arms.

Celina opened the door wider, but she couldn't shake her unease.

Lawyers don't come to deliver things like this. Why didn't he go to the front desk and have them call me?

She sat next to him on the sofa. "Is this about my husband?"

He set the box on the coffee table and took a piece of paper from his inner pocket. "No, no," he said hesitantly. "I'm afraid it's about your aunt, Marie Tayen."

"Oh…"

He nodded. "I take it you've heard of the tragic fire that took place at the Yonah Church?"

Her stomach clenched. "Yes. I don't know why she was there at that hour…"

"Ah well, I suppose your aunt didn't tell you she declared bankruptcy about six months ago." He furrowed his brow. "After your uncle died, she discovered he had large debts she knew nothing about. The few thousand dollars she'd saved up went to the bank. Your aunt had nothing left, save for the debts, so she lived at the church under a temporary arrangement with the priest there. I believe a Father Christopher?"

So that was why there'd been a withdrawal from her bank account. She was paying into the bankruptcy, not hiring a hitman.

Celina squirmed. "I see."

"This box contains the last of her possessions, and, luckily, was stored away from the fire. Your aunt left everything to you, Mrs. Leviet."

He handed her a piece of paper and a pen—a receipt as proof she accepted the contents of her aunt's personal effects. She signed it, her hand rubbing against the paper as though moving on its own. The lawyer gave her a copy of the receipt and then left. Once alone, Celina stuffed the paper into her back pocket, and sat in front of the box, staring at it.

Marie is dead. I killed her. This whole time, she was living at the church because she couldn't come to me. When I phoned her cell, I didn't even think to ask if she was still at the house...

Celina opened and peeked inside. A journal lay at the top, the brown leather cover faded with age. She opened it to the first page and scanned for the owner: Father Robert. A bookmark jutted from between the pages, and she flipped to it. Her breath caught inside her throat as she glimpsed a pair of sketches. Both were the items found at the scene of her parents' accident, the ones Marie had given to her in an envelope the day of Thomas' service. The text written next to the red stone sketch was so small she squinted to read it:

Developed by the original Lumen, the Aka stone was created to temporarily make a surrounding area impossible for a demon to stay in or approach once someone presses the button. The length and effects vary depending on the demon's strength. It is not a weapon, more of a defense mechanism for urgent situations.

Her eyes caught the next sketch, showing the pendant she'd worn as a child:

We only made one of these pendants because of the sacrifice it took to create. I gave it to a member of the church, Elizabeth Tayen, to give to her daughter, Celina. After explaining her circumstances when the child was born, Elizabeth visited the church often, hoping to keep her safe. When Celina turned nine, other members of our faith found out about her situation, and it forced me to tell her not to return. That was when the pendant was given to the child. It would, so long as Celina wore it, protect the whole family from demonic detection.

If her parents had any connection to Shiriki, she was willing to bet the necklace protected her from him. But Kai had been stalking her since childhood. Had they known? Was it him they'd been protecting her from?

She needed to get the box out of her sight, but even after she stashed it inside her bedroom, her mind remained fixed on her aunt's death and the mystery of these anti-demon charms.

Celina hurried to the mattress and lifted it to retrieve the stone and pendant. When she took the pendant off to lend to her mother, her parents died. Had that happened because her mother took it off at one point? Did that mean a demon killed them?

The journal said we were safe as long as I wore it. So why did mom borrow it?

Questions crowded out other thoughts. She shook her head, trying to disperse them, but all she did was make herself dizzy. Putting the two devices into her pockets, she closed her eyes for a few seconds, trying to think.

The papers Kai stole from the church lay on the nightstand, listing the names of the other potential Lumen suspects. She searched them and found David Corval's family tree. His was huge, with so many linking from one to another that they had folded the paper six times to write all the names. A few of the names belonged to the Giona Church, so none were in the vicinity of Ottawa. Whoever was doing the killings was from this region—Yonah Church.

"A sister?" Her head ached, and she rubbed her temple as she stared at the line that crossed over the link to her parents.

She grabbed the bank statements and flipped through them, trying to find the name *Alisson.* One Alisson, married to a Martin Kent. Was this David's sister with a married name, or just another member of the church?

Celina ignored the warning in the back of her head about disobeying Kai. Because of this new information about the pendant, she'd grown even leerier of demons.

She grabbed her purse, but with all the things she'd stuffed inside in the past few days, the thing seemed too heavy to bother with. Fishing inside, she grabbed a few pieces of identification. When she caught a piece of paper folded up small, she almost threw it aside before realizing what it was.

Unfolding it carefully, and flinching every time a tear ripped the paper, she gazed down at the playground sketch. She brought it to her chest and let out a breath. "I still love you, Thomas."

Even if I love Kai, too.

She slipped the paper into her jeans pocket, grabbed the bank statement with the address, and headed out the door, unwilling to wait for Kai. Besides, he'd fish inside her mind, and she wasn't ready to be denied explanations about how her family was connected to demons. Or talking about a love that shouldn't exist between them both.

She walked the streets, trying to come to terms with her aunt's death. Her parents' deaths were probably her fault, too.

I guess I really am going to Hell...or dark realm—whatever they want to call it, still sounds the same.

The address on the statement belonged to an apartment building in the slums. Most of the windows were shattered, cigarette butts and old food wrappings lay scattered on the sidewalk. She climbed the stairs, her head hanging as she entered the apartment building, the air scented with stale urine and vomit. Once she reached the fifth floor, she stopped in front of the five-fifteen and exhaled.

A woman answered the door, her bloodshot eyes partially hidden behind drooping eyelids.

"I'm sorry to bother you, but are you Alisson Kent?"

"I am." The woman moved away from the door, leaving it open.

Celina, surprised at her willingness to let a stranger in, trudged after Alisson into the living room.

Garbage and piles of clothes occupied every corner.

"Are you, by chance, David Corval's sister?"

Alisson rummaged under the cushion of the seat next to her until she found an open bag of chips and shoved a handful into her mouth. "Why do you ask?" She sprayed damp potato pieces as she spoke.

Maybe she got a lot of people searching for her brother.

Celina's heart beat faster. It was her. Emily Pierce hadn't mentioned her, yet Alisson's name had been in the Lumen family tree. "Do you have a way for me to reach him?"

"He'll be coming over in a few minutes with food for me." She glanced at the empty food packets around her. "Since my husband killed himself, I don't go out."

Her chest tightened. "He's coming here?" David Corval wasn't stupid. He'd suspect Celina was investigating him.

"Yes, do you want to wait?"

Celina forced a polite smile. "No, I can't, but if you could give me his number, I'll call him later to make an appointment."

Alisson smiled and stretched across the sofa to grab a piece of paper and a crayon. She wrote a phone number down and handed the greasy paper to Celina.

"Thanks for your help. Oh, and I'm sorry about your loss." Knowing the pain of losing a husband, Celina couldn't mask her sympathy.

The idea Martin Kent killed himself seemed off to her since the tenants of Yonah Church were anti-suicide.

"All three of my sons were killed a few months ago." Alisson let her head fall back and squinted at the ceiling. "Then, my husband killed himself not long afterward."

"What?" Why were they all murdered? The ritual didn't work like that, as Kai explained it.

"My husband was weak." Alisson shoved her hand under the cushions in a fresh search.

"People who are depressed sometimes do things that—"

"All he had to do was wait." She scowled. "David promised he'd try again, and after James found out that guy's secret, we had all the information we needed. Now, he has the other two boys. It should work this time."

Celina's stomach dropped. "What should work?"

"The ritual to become immortal!" Alisson's eyes widened, a crazed smile stretching her mouth. "It didn't work with my sons, but we'll keep trying until it works."

Celina edged to the door. "I'll go now." She yanked it open, but before she could step out, footsteps came from the end of the hallway.

David Corval talked on his smartphone, his strides eating the distance between them. "So, you followed her?" His smile widened. "Is that so?"

Her heart lodged into her throat. She backed away in quick, jerky steps and closed the door again.

Shit! Hide!

Celina avoided going near the living room so Alisson couldn't see her and ran into the bedroom. When the front door opened and closed, she dove under the bed.

26

BLACKMAIL

P lastic bags rustled as Celina watched David's feet from under the bed. He walked to the living room. "I brought you some groceries."

"Someone came asking about you—a woman," Alisson spoke in a quiet tone.

He chuckled. "Did you give her my number?"

"Yes, and she was sorry for the loss of Martin, but I told her he was a coward. When I said what happened to my kids, she seemed disgusted, but she didn't understand. The—"

"You told her what we did? Are you insane?" David shouted at his sister and then slapped her.

"But…" The woman's voice lowered, turning into mutters. Celina strained but couldn't make out the words.

"I know. It won't be long now." David replied, seeming amused. "Call James. Tell him I'll have his money before we leave."

His footsteps grew louder, and she froze. She breathed through her mouth as silently as she could. His shoes sauntered to the closet, and the door brushed against the carpet.

A few minutes passed, or maybe it was hours, but a knock on the door raised the hairs on the back of Celina's neck.

Who's here now? Kai?

More feet shuffled inside, and into the bedroom. "Looks like I've helped you twice now."

That voice…

"And I'm forever grateful, cuz." His pants shifted a little as he dug into his pockets. "Here. You deserve all of it."

Her mind flashed back to the lawyer's office. James C. Graull.

James Corval Graull? David called him cuz. Cousin? Fucking shit, his name must have been on the list for Giona Church—why was he here then? Maybe the Lumen hadn't updated for a while… my name was still on there.

James turned, but a sharp movement from behind threw him against David. Gasps and coughing rang through the room, and his body twitched a few times before he fell to the carpet.

The lawyer's dead eyes stared through Celina, and she clamped her hands against her mouth, muffling a whimper.

Alisson's feet came into view, and she spoke with a pleading tone. "We should go, David. The boy's body won't be fresh for much longer, even in that fridge."

He kicked his cousin's dead body. "All right, we'll leave now."

Celina shook. They were headed to wherever the ritual would be held, but she wanted Kai with her when she faced them.

"The other boy should be well on his way to madness by now." David moved to the bed.

He's still alive—good!

Alisson crouched and peeked under the bed right at Celina, a smile on her lips. "We're bringing her too, right?"

Someone grabbed Celina's ankle and yanked her from under the bed as she kicked and screamed.

"Of course." He glanced at Celina while still holding her ankle. "Her husband was the one who gave us the opportunity to correct our mistakes the first time. She'll be our guest of honor at our ceremony."

Celina yanked away from him and kicked him hard in the ribs, and he fell with a grunt. She crawled away, but he spun her around and smacked her face. Her lip split and Celina tasted blood as he stood and kicked her in the stomach. She couldn't breathe more than small gasps.

"Will you hurt her?" Alisson bent over Celina and stared down with a weak smile.

David crouched and traced his finger at the base of Celina's neck. The one good thing about having been with Kai for so long was that humans scared her much less now.

His lips curled into a malicious smile. "Oh, I think she'd be fun to…hurt. Yes."

Celina tried to sit up, but he pressed a hand down on her chest to keep her on the floor.

"I'll get the ropes." Alisson moved away.

"You won't get away with this." Celina gritted her teeth.

He gave her a hard stare. "Do I have to gag you?"

Alisson returned with a coarse rope and tied Celina's wrists behind her back. She tried to pull on her bonds, but David slapped her again, harder this time. Her vision spun as he checked the knots to make sure she couldn't squirm free. As his hand grazed her sweater, her pendant and the Aka stone met with a clink.

He reached inside and pulled them out, his eyebrows rising as he observed them. She hoped he didn't know what they were.

"Pretty little baubles." He pocketed them both.

More than anything in the world, she wanted to rip him apart, to watch him suffer and die.

Alisson surveyed their prisoner with a pout. "Our guest will be too bloody for the ceremony."

"Here's how this will work, Mrs. Leviet." David grabbed Celina's face to force her to meet his eyes. "You'll walk to the car and get into the back seat. We'll put a coat over your shoulders so no one can see I bound your hands."

"I won't."

"You will, or I'll hurt you." He glanced back at the lawyer who'd read over Thomas' will and even given her Marie's possessions.

That bastard deserved to die.

With her hands secured and no demon help, she couldn't escape. In a way, it was perfect. They were bringing her to where the boys were, and she'd be able to rescue at least the youngest once Kai found her. "Fine, I'll come quietly. Just don't hurt me."

I'm gonna hurt you, and that's a promise.

Celina tried to figure out where they were going, staring out of the car window for familiar markers. They reached a secluded area, and David stopped the car on the side of the road, pulled her from her seat, and shoved her into the trunk.

She lay in darkness, the smell of the gasoline and the movement of the car rolling her stomach and sending bile in the back of her throat every few minutes, but the darkness bothered her more. The idea of a corpse-like creature from Kai's realm lying beside her, its large, opened mouth wanting to swallow her whole, terrified her.

All the mysteries tied in together in one neat little bow. She figured Thomas was the one who translated the ritual for David and his sister, and once he became curious about it, they had him killed. That Lumen bastard used the Pierces' son against them to make them do all the dirty work. The desire for revenge that had wavered pulsed back with rage. Fucking bastard would experience a world of pain before she finished with David.

Before long, the car stopped again. David pulled her from

the trunk, but not before putting a bag over her head. The thick fabric pressed against her nose, and she opened her mouth to draw in more air.

After a flight of stairs that nearly broke her neck and a few more narrow doorways, David untied her wrists. He took the bag off and shoved her so hard she fell to the floor. She scrambled into a sitting position and cursed; they'd thrown her inside a large cage that stood in an underground room with cracked cement walls.

Why am I always in basements lately?

David came to the cage. "Sorry about—"

"Where the hell am I?" She stood and brushed grit from the thighs of her jeans.

"No formalities then? Have it your way." He shrugged and sauntered away.

She could just make out the small head of a child sticking out of an old bathtub in the center of the room. Her pulse raced, and every breath sent shooting pains into her lungs.

She rose on her tiptoes, clutching her chest. "What are you doing?"

Celina watched in terror as Alisson dragged a wheeled pallet loaded with bodies to the bathtub. The corpses appeared to be male and in early adolescence, all stacked one on top of each other like pieces of meat.

"I don't remember which one is the brother of the one in the bath." She scratched her head, the dirty, blonde hair matting further.

David considered them all, lifting various limbs to get a better view of the other ones. "This one here. He has dark-brown hair."

"You son of a bitch." Celina grabbed the bars and squeezed. "You caused my whole life to be eternally fucked, and how many others suffered because of you and your twisted mind?"

David grabbed the pale body and dragged it around the bathtub. He tied the ankles together with a thick rope.

"Many, I suppose." He checked that the knot held tight enough before moving away. He used a pulley to suspend the boy's body upside down over the bathtub. Then he secured the rope in position.

"Why did you have someone kidnap so many children? Why are so many dead?"

He shrugged. "The ritual didn't work the first few times, so we kept trying."

"You're sick." Her voice came out in a low tone.

"I guess you've already figured out I hired your husband to get this ritual translated."

"My husband's company might have been fake, but his translating skills weren't." She felt the need to defend him to this monster, despite his lies. "Who did you hire to kidnap those kids? I saw that video my husband had as evidence—"

David sneered at her through the cage. "You mean the one with no sound?"

"Yes." Her muscles tensed.

"It may interest you to know that through some connections, I looked up Mr. Leviet and his company. Imagine my surprise when I discovered the unit didn't exist." He grabbed the bars and leaned forward. "So, I offered him a deal to keep my mouth shut."

That's how the lawyer was connected to this.

She narrowed her eyes. "You mean, you blackmailed him."

"He'd have done anything to keep you from finding out. He wanted you to live a comfortable life. I told him he could do a few services for me, and not only would I tell no one about his little company sham, but I'd also pay him well for it."

"What were the services you asked of my husband?"

David grinned and strutted to a large table placed against the wall and then came back with a camcorder. "Take a look."

Celina took it, her hands shaking as she did. Her subconscious mind knew, but she pressed the play button and focused into the preview screen. It was the same video, but this time with sound.

This time, with Thomas' voice.

She stared in horror at the man she'd known, a gentleman, pointing the pistol at Wayne and Emily.

Oh, God…Thomas. What are you doing? No, this can't be. It isn't real. It's a trick. Someone recorded his voice and put it over the images.

The video continued. Thomas' amused tone churned her stomach as he pointed the gun at the parents.

"Are the three children I tied in the kitchen yours?" Thomas asked.

Wayne begged. "Please don't hurt them! We'll give you anything you want!"

I sold my life and soul for…this?

"Shut up!" Thomas took a step toward him, "Keep quiet while I fetch your eldest son. If you try anything, your children will suffer. Understand?"

No. Thomas, please stop.

He hit the eldest, Cedric, in the back of the head, and he fell unconscious.

"Don't take this personally." Thomas shrugged. "The person who hired me to do this paid good money."

It was like someone had ripped her heart out of her chest and stomped on it. The hole left in her chest ached, and she brought her hand to it and squeezed.

"You can keep your middle boy."

Tears blurred her vision, and her breath shortened with every second.

Thomas came back, dragging Simon's limp body.

The camcorder shook in her hands, and she grabbed one of the bars to steady herself, her knees wobbling.

I knew him. For nine years, I loved him. How could I have been in love with such a horrible person?

The screen went black, and as she was about to take her gaze away, it flickered back to life. Thomas stood in front of the camera, his hazel eyes staring at her through the screen. "Keep your end of the deal, David." Then it shut off for the last time.

The hairs on her arms prickled. She'd murdered for him.

The world spun. She was drowning in so many lies. He did this because of blackmail? No. That didn't make sense. There had to be another reason.

The reasons don't fucking matter.

She jumped when David took the camcorder and walked away.

The hate coursing through her veins belonged to Thomas, but David would do. Celina's vision blurred, and she dropped to the floor. The pain couldn't compete with betrayal. Had he known what David was doing to these children?

Of course, he did. He translated the text. Is this why he didn't want children? Because he knew he was a monster?

She pulled out the playground sketch and stared at it as her eyes burned. Something like a scream escaped her as she tore it apart in as many pieces as she could, desperate to mirror what her heart felt like.

"Why are you so surprised about your husband? You must have known. Or did you turn a blind eye to his strangeness?"

That's because I am strange. He'd said it right before his murder.

Fuck Thomas. Fuck everyone. I'll call the police instead, have David and Alisson arrested, break the deal and live. I don't want to avenge a monster. There must be a way…

She continued asking questions, craving answers she'd never have. "How did you know about this ritual?" Her own voice sounded far away as it echoed in the room.

"I'm next in line to becoming the Lumen leader after Father Christopher. Though the members thought I left temporarily—lost my way because of the temptation of money. I could've succeeded the priest sooner if I'd found the previous Father's journal, but Father Robert kept it well hidden. Damn, that thing was full of information."

David continued, but Celina focused on Father Robert's name, knowing his journal remained with her aunt's things. Then something from David's droning ripped her out of her thoughts. "Wait! What did you say?"

"I said," he pressed on, frowning as though annoyed that she hadn't hung on his every word, "that there was even information in there about how to make and break deals with demons."

She bit her tongue. Why hadn't she read the whole thing when she'd had the chance? She had to redeem herself, and she'd start by doing all she could to save Simon.

"It won't work, Corval. The ritual. Immortality can't be given to humans."

"We'll see about that."

The boy in the bathtub stirred, and her stomach clenched. He screamed and cried out for his parents, unable to move. The thought of what this poor boy was going through shook Celina to her core and only enraged her further.

Alisson read with a loud voice from a hefty black tome as her eyes sparkled. David approached the bathtub, still holding the knife in his hand. Shadows danced on the wall, joining with one another, and a female demon appeared from those same shadows with a cocky smile on her lips. Alisson bounced on the balls of her feet and closed the old book. "We did it!"

"The immortality ritual." The demon flung her long black

hair from her shoulder. "I have not been summoned for this one in some time."

"And we'll also throw in a little extra." David pointed toward the cage where Celina stood.

The smile on the demon's lips widened, but before she took a step, the room shook. Light flashed around them and when Celina could open her eyes again, hope pulsed through her heart.

Kai sat on the edge of the bathtub.

Trying to get out of a contract with him wouldn't end well. But maybe he'd understand.

Maybe he knew all along what my husband was.

He was in his true demonic form. The glow from a symbol on the floor illuminated the room as the only source of light, and Celina recognized it as the same brand burned into her abdomen. Kai surveyed the boy who'd stopped moving before he glanced up at the other demon in the room.

"Leave."

"They completed the ritual, Mekaisto. I am obligated," she said, holding her head high.

Kai prowled forward. "I will be obligated to rip you apart in the slowest and most agonizing way if you do not obey, Maili."

"Apologies." She bowed and disappeared into the shadows from which she came.

27

REVELATIONS

Alisson arched an eyebrow. "We summoned two demons? Where did the other one go?"

Kai examined the dead boy hanging by his ankles, silent.

David took a step toward his sister. "Are you here to grant us immortality?"

Kai ignored him and moved to the cage, his glare narrowing on Celina. "You only listen when you feel like it." He stopped in front of the locked door.

"I didn't want to waste time. I didn't know—"

"That is why I told you to wait!" He roared the words, and the whole room trembled as the darkness exploded around him.

Her eyes widened, and she backed away. In his true form, such a display of anger shook her soul. The darkness surrounding him squeezed against her chest, and she found herself unable to take a deep breath.

"I'm—"

"You are not sorry, but you will be." His lips retracted over pointed teeth as he spoke with a growl.

Imagine how he'll react when you tell him you've decided to end the contract.

Alisson approached them, her eyes wild. "Wait! What about our immortality?"

Kai's smile widened, and it sent shivers through Celina's body. He leered at her with the same cruel expression. "I know you are supposed to kill the ones who had anything to do with your attempted murder, but I wonder if you would allow me an indulgence."

"Indulgence?" Her voice shook.

"You will kill David Corval, but I will take his soul to my realm and hand him over to a group of Sanguis demons who will enjoy him for eternity."

"But, I—"

"As for Alisson Kent there…if you would allow, I will bring her to Shiriki. Alive. Though she will not remain that way for long."

"No. Please let me explain, I—"

"I do not care to kill her myself since she is not even a Lumen member; adopted children do not share the same bloodline even if they share the same faith."

That was why Emily Pierce hadn't named her as a remaining member. Alisson Kent wasn't a Lumen by blood.

She expected Kai to let her out of the cage and listen to her, but instead, he prowled toward the siblings. They tried to run, but Kai sealed the door. David pointed his knife at Kai, but the demon disappeared and materialized behind him. A horrible cracking noise sounded through the room, and David screamed in pain. Both his legs were broken, blood oozing from where a bone stuck out.

Alisson reached for her brother, but Kai grabbed her and held her back. She screamed as he squeezed her waist, blood soaking through her shirt as his fingers dug into her skin, and she went limp.

Celina pressed her lips together at the sound of their screams.

Kai dropped Alisson's unconscious body to the floor and

moved toward Celina again. He stood in front of the barred door. "I do enjoy the sight of you in a cage."

"Please, wait! I need you to—"

He materialized next to her, and she backed away until she hit the bars. "Though, the cages in my realm are a little more…exciting. The things I can do to the prey inside…" His wings folded against his back, allowing him to move within the confinement of the cage.

"The kidnapper was Thomas. David showed me the video with sound. I can't kill anymore. I've killed enough people, and it was all for nothing!" She tried to keep the fear out of her voice, but it didn't work.

They deserve to die for everything they've done, but it's not my choice anymore. Not when Thomas is just as guilty…

"You think stopping toward the end of our deal is allowed?" His tone turned so dark that she clutched the bars and squeezed.

She needed to stall. "Let me ask David more questions. I need to understand!"

He grinned, and the cage broke open on one side, setting her free.

Celina ran to David and crouched in front of him. Sweat made her clothes stick to her skin. "Because of you, I was forced to make a deal with that demon."

His face turned paler by the second. "Don't kill me, please!"

He'll bleed out before he can answer anything…

Kai appeared behind him and crouched, his hands glowing red. Her eyes widened as he grabbed the base of David's protruding bone, and she clamped her hand against her mouth when his burned flesh reached her nostrils.

I'll never get all those screams out of my mind.

He still looked pale, but at least he wouldn't bleed to death anymore.

She swallowed bile back a few times, and her eyes

watered at the burning sensation. "You came into a lot of money a few months ago, and that's how you started every-thing—paying my husband, the murders, the lawyer, every-thing. Where did you get that money?"

His breaths came out ragged. "Someone gave me the money, but I never knew who. I prayed in the church, begging for a way to live forever. I asked God every day, but he never answered my prayer until…"

She tightened her hands into fists to keep from grabbing him. "Until what?"

"I got a new bank card in the mail with an account number, but I've never opened one at that specific branch. I went to check, and the account held thousands and thou-sands of dollars."

"You expect me to believe an account with that much money was given to you, without ever knowing—"

Alisson regained consciousness and whimpered, her hands pressing on her wounds. Kai appeared above her, and she screamed again.

Celina lunged in his direction. "Kai, don't—"

The demon smirked and vanished along with Alisson.

David sobbed his sister's name.

Celina focused her attention back on him, grinding her teeth. "Who gave you that bank account?"

"God gave it to me." The pitch of his voice rose. "He answered my prayers. I deserved to be immortal, but I needed the money to do it right—get a translator, a room. The only message from the person who left the bank account for me was *just needed a little push.*"

"I'll report you to the police, and people will have justice for what you've done."

His lips curled into a weak smile. "You'll go to prison, too."

Kai appeared behind him and grabbed him by the hair. "You have a lot of courage to play with the fire you summoned." His hand plunged into David's lower back, and with one tug that brought forth the sickest scream she'd ever heard, he pulled out his spinal cord. David's scream gurgled off, and his eyes glazed over. "Well, he certainly had a backbone."

She stood and staggered away, her mouth opening and closing. "What...?"

"I will have to take care of a few matters here with the bodies." Kai dropped the spine on the mutilated body.

She brought her hands to her head, still backing away. "You didn't have to kill him! I was going to call the police!"

Kai smirked. "That is not how our contract works."

Celina stared at him. David deserved to die, but she didn't want more blood on her hands. "I need to bring the boy to the police station to be with his brother since—"

"No."

Her head jerked toward him. "No?"

He's going to kill him.

Celina's mind raced as she hugged herself and stared at David's body. The pendant and Aka stone peeked out of his pocket. Not taking time to think, grabbing those few precious seconds to have a chance at succeeding, she snatched them into her hand. Her eyes met Kai's as she pressed the button embedded inside.

A blinding red flash. He vanished, and she moved fast.

She ran to the boy and dragged him from the bathtub. He was heavier than he looked—all dead weight since he seemed to have passed out—but she ignored the strain and ran from the room. The place looked like the same kind of maze as The CrowBar's basement, and she cursed as she staggered blindly. The wooden floorboards creaked as she ran, her footing uneven as they lifted and warped. She hit one sticking out and spun herself to the side, protecting Simon from getting hurt. Her shoulder hit against the wall, and her hands clutched the child tighter as she watched the Aka stone roll away.

No, no, no.

She searched as long as she dared, but the stone had disappeared. One of the last defenses she had against demons.

She couldn't give up. What she needed was a safe place to hide the boy.

Bingo!

The door she opened was a closet filled with old blankets. She placed him on one of them and slipped the pendant around his neck before putting another of the blankets over the boy to hide him from view. Now she needed to get as far away as possible from the hiding place.

"I'll call the police as soon as I can," she whispered. Then she closed the door and ran down the hallway, trying to find a way out.

Haunting whispers echoing down the hallway froze her. Kai was nearby. She didn't have time to let fear take root since her priority was to lead him away from the closet.

"Come out, come out, dove."

The movement of her clothes brushing together sounded too loud to her, and she crouched. Her body shook so hard that her muscles tensed in her awkward position. She didn't want to get too comfortable, knowing she'd need to run again.

Footsteps grew closer, and she clutched her chest, her decision between fleeing and freezing. He'd catch her, but she wouldn't make it easy.

"I used to stand by your window and listen to the lovely little prayers you recited before going to sleep. Do you remember your favorite one?" His voice filled the air all around her. "I have a similar one."

Now I rise up to relive,
I pray the Devil my soul to give,

If I should fall before I wake,
I pray the Devil my soul to take.

Only Kai could turn an innocent childhood memory into something twisted. As she started into thoughtless running, she knew it was a stupid move, even if he had been human. She darted from her cover and their bodies collided, the shock of hitting the floor confusing her. Opening her eyes, her breath caught in her lungs as he crouched over her, his vertical pupils contrasting against his glowing irises.

"The last time a human attacked me," Kai pinned her underneath him, a sneer on his face. "I ripped his flesh off a few inches at a time and forced him to eat it."

She pressed her head against the floor hard, willing herself to disappear through it. The burning in his eyes that terrified her more than his words. Her flesh crawled; he didn't seem like her demon anymore.

"You didn't give me a choice!"

"I thought I had warned you never to threaten me again." His voice shook her so hard, even her heart felt like it skipped a few times.

She tried to calm herself, but his bared, pointed teeth and glaring blood-red eyes only accelerated her pulse, her vision filling with dark spots. Celina pressed her hands down on the floor and pushed herself back, all the while keeping her eyes on Kai. Once she got out from under him, she crawled away until her back hit the wall.

The splinters that pierced her skin kept her alert and unable to sink into despair.

"I don't want…" She took a breath. "I want to break the deal. Please."

Kai stayed in the same crouched position, watching her like a predator. She drew her legs against herself. This time, she was the prey, and her mind shut down at the horror. As she inched along the wall, his vertical pupils followed her every move. She darted to the side, but his claw-like fingernails dug into her ankle, and he yanked her toward him despite her kicking.

He pulled her to a stand with no effort. The runes on his horns glowed with the same strength as his irises, making his hair and wings darker than the pitch-black ink that swirled in his wake.

Before she could process her situation, they were inside their hotel room. She blinked to adjust to the light. When she still found Kai's face unreadable, she retreated as fast as possible.

The room shook. The white walls faded to black. Lights flickered and died. The shaking became so violent she lost her footing and fell. When she glanced up, Kai stood in front of her. She opened her mouth to say something but closed it when the sound of creaking echoed inside the room as if it would collapse on itself.

"That you no longer wish to take your revenge is problematic."

She stood and backed away, but he materialized close and snatched her wrist. "Let go!"

He dragged her across the room with no effort, the eerie darkness following wherever he moved. With all her strength, she scrambled for purchase, her free hand grabbing everything she passed. Once inside the bedroom, the door slammed on its own.

The light from the window disappeared, and the room darkened until her vision was useless. He released her wrist, and she stumbled away, fumbling behind her to find the wall. The strange creaking still rattled the room, but a new sound resonated—her own breathing. The lamp by the bed flickered, adding to the illumination of Kai's fire-red glare. She ran for the door, but he snagged her hair and hauled her back.

He leaned into her ear. "Even if you run, you will not escape me." Then he spun her around and fixed her with narrowed eyes, his jaw clenching.

She darted to the side, but he grabbed her wrist again. He pulled her to the bed and threw her on it. She struggled to get up, but then he was on top of her, and she couldn't move. His hand moved to her shirt and, when he lifted it, she panicked and tried pushing him away.

"Stop! Please, stop!"

He grabbed her wrists and held them above her head with one hand. He lifted her top, then traced his long fingernail along her brand, making her inhale sharply as it burned. "Trying to run from a demon is foolish." His smile widened. "Running from me is dangerous." His hand left her brand and climbed higher. When it passed between her breasts, tears formed in her eyes, but he didn't stop until his hand reached her neck.

"You knew Thomas was the kidnapper. You knew everything, didn't you?" Her eyes met his, and he let go of her wrists. She covered herself with her arms, her body still trembling.

"Of course, I knew. How could I not?" His eyes burned and his mouth opened, showing his pointed teeth.

"How could you?" She couldn't see clearly anymore as her tears blinded her. "You said you…" She stopped.

That's all those words were. Sweet traps to lure me in so I'd trust him. Now he's going to kill me, and it's my own damn fault. He lied…

Her eyes widened as he took hold of her face and turned it to one side. His mouth rested near the side of her neck, his breath warm against her skin. "I did not lie." He licked the crook of her neck, and she cried louder when his teeth grazed the same wet spot.

"You can't do this. Please don't."

He withdrew, his eyes piercing hers. "Cease your crying."

She shook her head side to side, more sobs escaping her. "I…can't."

"Why?"

His question took her aback, and she stared, her breaths coming in small gasps. "Because I'm terrified, and I'm hurting…" She narrowed her eyes, tears still spilling. "Why am I explaining something you obviously don't fucking understand?"

He leaned over her again. "Exactly."

She searched his eyes, confused. "I don't—"

"You cannot stop crying because of the emotions running through you. Just like I cannot stop my nature from turning dark when I am attacked." He slipped his arms under her and held her tight despite her squirming, trying to get away from him. Something like a growl vibrated through his chest, and she froze.

"You can't apologize for something like that—it won't work."

He withdrew, smiling hungrily. "I was not apologizing; I only explained." He stood, and his back tensed under his wings. "I am sorry about my instincts. However, you are not, despite the fact that you attacked me."

Tears rolled down her cheeks. "You're a fucking—" Her voice cracked.

"Monster?" Kai turned, the strange darkness disappearing as he did. Sunlight filled the room. "You seem to forget what I am."

She gritted her teeth. "I won't forget again. Especially now that you're about to finish the end of our deal with my life and soul." A thought crossed her mind, and she latched on to it like a lifeline. "I still have one person I have to kill for my revenge. The person who paid David Corval."

He smiled. "Of course."

She sat up, and he kneeled down in front of her, grabbing her knees so she couldn't get away. "Do not provoke me again. I do not wish to disturb the child growing inside you." He put his hand on her abdomen, a nasty smile on his lips.

Her skin tingled, and a heavy feeling settled in her stomach. That was impossible. It didn't make sense…until it did.

Coldness hit her core. "What?"

"You have been carrying a child inside you. I sensed its presence before we made our deal." His long black fingernails traced along her stomach, and she shook under his touch. "I have plans for him."

Celina backed up farther onto the bed, putting her hands over her stomach. "You're not going to hurt him!"

A child. She'd wanted one so much. Wanted a family with Thomas. Not now. Not after what she knew.

He's still my child. I can get out of this deal to save him.

Kai gave her a gentle smile. "I will not hurt him. But the child will die if you break our deal. I do not think you are foolish enough to try that." He stood.

Celina wrapped her arms tighter around herself, afraid he would rip her unborn baby from her. *Him. A son.* "He wasn't part of the deal."

"Remember when I explained about owning your body through your life?"

If he owns every inch of my body, as he'd said, then…

"You can't—"

"I will return when I have finished disposing of David, and the other corpses in that room." He vanished.

A long time passed before she could react to anything at all. The shock of discovering her pregnancy, Kai's violence, and Thomas being the kidnapper, left her terrified. She stood and cursed, kicking the bed with her foot. For all she knew, he'd lied about the pregnancy to keep her from breaking the deal.

She didn't want Kai to end Simon's life. He'd done nothing wrong, and, besides, he still had his middle brother. Her blood froze. Did Kai take him to the police station, or did he kill Henri as well?

It was time to save herself, and as the answer lay in Father

Robert's journal, it was possible. Her mind flashed back to her intimate moments with Kai, and she shook her head, tears filling her eyes again.

What the fuck is wrong with me?

The gentleness of his gaze, his reassuring words…would he hurt her unborn baby? Would he really kill her when the end came?

Celina grabbed the journal and flipped through it as fast as she could. She stopped skimming about halfway through and reread the last passage:

There are ways to break a deal with demons, but they can be tricky to carry out. The Exponentia Tome *is the only book left with the information and has been placed in the safekeeping of one of Yonah Church's most devoted members for protection.*

Underneath, someone had sketched the tome, its cover dark-green with golden swirls in the shape of a wreath. Her heart raced as fast as her mind. Marie had been the most devoted Lumen she'd seen, but that meant…

She rummaged inside the box again, desperate for any other hint. Most of the contents were her mother's possessions. Old pictures, knick-knacks, and even a picture of Celina when she was three, sitting next to her mother, who looked worn out…worried. A few papers caught her attention, but they were only old bills. She pushed a sealed envelope to one side, but when she shifted another bank statement, her eyes fell on the envelope again.

Her mother's handwriting.

To Celina.

28

LEAVING NOTHING BEHIND

The unknown feeling filled Kai like a boiling liquid, and he finally put a name to it.

Guilt.

Demons weren't supposed to feel that emotion. No remorse, no second guesses, and certainly, no love. Yet, the king of the dark realm felt all of them at that moment.

He paced inside the abandoned building, his steps echoing near all the dead bodies.

I scared her, and now she will never trust me again. She deserves better than the monster I am, but I have to...

He'd read Celina's train of thought as he left the hotel.

She thought I wanted to kill the boy, and that I did the same to Henri.

The room grew darker, but he stopped moving, using his senses to try locating Simon. The whole building shook and cracked under the darkness, but the boy wasn't anywhere to be found.

Did the little human run away?

He scanned one last time, to make sure, but the only humans he detected were dead.

Kai hadn't wanted to kill Simon. He never murdered children because their souls were the rare pure ones—they did not belong to him. He'd meant to erase the child's memories as he'd done with Henri before he'd dropped him off at the police station.

Waving his hand, the room engulfed in fire, but he sat on the edge of the bathtub, lost in thought.

A long time ago, he infiltrated the Lumen—well-known as the Venatores then—and wrote a few rituals. Most were fake, but a few of them called forth demons to bring him more souls. Over five hundred years later, he regretted the immortality ritual most of all. He'd done it to take the tainted souls of the humans who summoned demons, the ones who dared murder children. Knowing he was the one who created this... guilt filled Kai even more intensely.

The heat of the fire didn't bother him, but emergency vehicles would arrive soon, and having a demon standing in the middle of the flames would be counter to the point of burning all the evidence. He perched on a lamppost in his crow form and watched as the firefighters did all they could to subdue the fire, but they could do little against demon magic, and it would burn until he felt all the evidence was destroyed.

Will she ever forgive me even when she learns the truth?

The fire burned out, and he continued to watch as they pulled out dead bodies. He was responsible for the deaths of these children, but he'd always distanced himself by saying he wasn't the one killing.

She will not see it that way.

One of the bodies they pulled out wasn't as burned like the others.

Kai's blood pressed against every inch of his being, and his eyes focused on Simon—his skin had peeled and blistered, a section around his neck had melted as though metal had burned at a higher temperature.

Celina...the pendant.

Simon twitched, and the paramedics tended to the boy, injecting him with useless medication to help relieve the pain.

He won't survive.

His magic could work, but it would take time, and it was running out.

He stood ready when the paramedics left and followed them all the way to the hospital.

They tended the pitiful child in the burn ward and then placed him in bandages in a coma-induced state. Kai sat on the edge of the bed, invisible to humans. "How can creatures be this fragile?"

Simon's mind, despite the drugs, was clear and Kai had no trouble getting into it.

Though no place for a child, the demon brought him into the Silence; a sanctuary within his realm. Simon stood near a beautiful pond with ever-changing colors. His eyes widened when the demon approached him, but there was nowhere to run, and he seemed to understand that.

Kai crouched to be at eye-level with him. "Are you in pain?"

The boy shook his head. "Who are you?"

"That does not matter."

Simon's eyes reflected the red glowing ones.

"You will not survive this without my help…but it comes at a price."

"Why?"

Humans are always so curious…

"It is the way things work."

"Are you an angel?"

Kai tilted his head to the side, observing the child; he wasn't in his true form, and with the glowing red eyes and pointed teeth, it didn't make much sense for the boy to ask him that question. "Do I look like one?"

"You have black wings…I remember." Simon glanced at

the pond that stopped changing colors and instead, showed memories of the child.

His brother's body hung upside down over him. Kai appeared in his true form.

"Your mind is broken, Simon. You have seen things humans are not meant to."

The boy looked back up at the demon, and tears ran down his face as his tiny body shook. "I want my mom and dad."

Another pang of guilt surged forward. "Listen." He made to put his hand on the boy's shoulder, but Celina's fearful expression flashed back in his mind, and he let it drop to his side. "I can return you to Henri, but the price you will pay is with your soul."

"My soul?"

"It will not be now. We cannot take children's souls. But before you die, I will return to you and take it. Until that time, you will remember nothing that happened after they took you from your parents."

Simon nodded and wiped his nose with his sleeve. "Okay."

Kai stared at the watery eyes as he placed his hand on the boy's head. "I am sorry, but nothing is ever free."

29

BREAKING POINT

Dear Celina,

    I am writing this letter, unsure that I'll ever give it to you. You're nine years old now, and although you might not know it yet, your life will be filled with danger. Your father came to me after you were born, and though he didn't force me, he requested I hand you over to him. From that moment on, I was terrified he'd come back to steal you, so I took measures into my own hands. When you were three years old, you spoke of a man with white hair, and I knew he'd continued to visit you in secret, so I attended the Yonah Church every day, hoping it would keep you safe. But now, the members have found out about your parentage, and you are no longer safe with the Lumen. Father Robert gave me a pendant a few days ago that would keep not only you safe but me as well.

    I've blamed myself for some time now, and—I'll be honest with you—I thought of giving you to him. I was just so scared. But I couldn't, knowing who your father was, so I did what I could by attending church and taking you. It hurt me so much to see you hated it. When you drew yourself, you also put in a shadow with black wings, and I knew then we'd need more protection. I've been researching on my own, and I hope I'll be able to stop whatever is coming for you.

I hope, if you find out about everything, you'll be able to forgive me. I love you, and no matter who your father is, you are still who you are by your own decisions. You control who you are, not your blood. Though you may never believe what I wrote, it's important you know what your father is. Shiriki is a demon, and if you are ever to meet him, stay far away from him as I think he has sinister plans for you.

I'm so sorry for the pain caused by this,
Your mother,
Elizabeth

A crushing weight pressed onto Celina as her heart pulsed through her ears, and heat burned her insides. Her eyes focused on the name of the demon who frightened her more than words could describe.

It's a lie. It's a lie. It's not true.

Her stomach heaved, and she brought her hand to her mouth. She glanced around, as if the answers she needed were somewhere nearby, and pressed harder on her mouth as her nausea grew. Her flesh crawled, the hand still holding the letter shook even more. She crumpled the old lined page and let out a shrill scream as she pushed her forehead hard against the floor, trying to use physical pain to ease the emotional one.

She flipped the box upside down, searching for a tome until her mind snapped. If the lawyer was a Lumen, and he'd gone through her aunt's possessions, then he'd most likely kept the book.

She stood, staggering, with one instinct: escape. Beyond thought, she grabbed money Kai had left in a drawer for her to order takeout and stuffed it into her pockets. She didn't bother waiting for the elevator and ran down the flights of stairs, tuning out the searing pressure in her lungs and legs.

She waved down the first taxi and hopped inside so fast she almost hit her head against the side. "Graull's Law firm."

The cab driver couldn't push down on the gas pedal hard enough for her. The world blurred past, her hands gripped the seats, her feet digging into the car mat.

This was how Shiriki was connected to her parents. That was why he'd reacted the way he did when Celina told him her mother's name. She closed her eyes and inhaled for a count of seven seconds through her nose, trying to relax.

She should have died that night. A bullet wound would have been less painful than a pact with a demon and the wonderful hindsight it brought. Less traumatizing, too.

When the taxi driver told her the fare, she threw a stack of Kai's bills on the front seat.

Take the rest of the day off on me.

She dashed inside the building, her gaze darting to all the decorative mirrors on the side of the elevators. Her mind twisted her image into a demon, and she averted her eyes. Instead, she concentrated on finding the tome she needed to free herself from Kai. It was now or never.

The secretary smiled and then seemed to recognize Celina. "Mrs. Leviet, how are you?"

"Last time I was here, I left in a bit of a hurry." She glanced away, trying to look like she was embarrassed about it.

"It happens quite a lot, no need to worry," she said. "How may I help you?"

Celina glanced toward the lawyer's office door and then back at his secretary. "I left an important book here, and I was wondering if you'd found it?"

She frowned as she lifted a few binders and folders on the desk beside her. "I don't think so..."

"Would you mind checking in his office?" She pointed at the door. "It's important since I'm..." Taking a hollow breath, she blinked a few times. "Arranging for my aunt's funeral, and that was her favorite book."

Two funerals in one month.

She stood and offered a sympathetic smile. "I can go have a look since I'm not sure if Mr. Graull will be in today." Moving to the door, she unlocked it and glanced back at her. "What does it look like?"

"Dark-green cover with golden swirls that form a wreath pattern," she said.

Thank you, Father Robert, for such perfect sketches.

The secretary disappeared for a few minutes and then returned with the tome, but an uncomfortable smile touched her lips. "I'm afraid that I must speak to Mr. Graull before giving this to you, though. It's not that I don't believe you, Mrs. Leviet, I just can't go giving away things from my boss' office. You understand?"

Celina suppressed the urge to yell at her and forced a smile. "That makes sense."

With a nod, she went to her desk. While her back was turned, Celina grabbed the lawyer's business cards and pocketed them. The woman put the heavy book in front of her and picked up the phone, drumming her fingers next to it. Celina kept her gaze on her, knowing all too well the lawyer wouldn't pick up.

Lying dead on a floor had that effect.

After too many rings, she hung up and sighed. "I'm sorry, but he's not answering."

Celina's mind worked fast. "Does he have an email address so I could send him a message? Maybe he'd answer that faster than waiting to reach him."

"Of course," she said, smiling as though relieved Celina wouldn't insist on taking the tome with her. She reached toward the business cards and frowned at the empty cardholder. "I'll just get one of his cards, excuse me."

As soon as she disappeared inside the lawyer's room,

Celina grabbed the tome but leaned against the wall next to the door. If she left now, the secretary would call the police on her, and the last thing she wanted was to survive all this only to end up in prison.

But it should have been inside my aunt's things. I'm not stealing it; I'm taking it back.

The secretary returned with a business card and frowned. "What are you doing with that?"

"I just remembered I have proof this is mine." She fished inside her back pocket and pulled out the receipt for Marie's personal effects. "Mr. Graull brought me my aunt's belongings, and I signed for all these items, but the tome wasn't inside. And I know she wanted me to have this since she'd told me… before she died," she added the last part in a whisper, and her chest squeezed at the thought of her aunt burning to death.

The woman took the receipt and scanned down the list of items. "Ah yes, I remember when the police brought this to us." She frowned as though trying to remember, but then nodded. "I packed everything into a newer box, and it's true, I don't remember that tome being inside. I suppose Mr. Graull forgot."

That's because your boss fucking stole it.

"Can I still take the business card? In case I need to contact Mr. Graull again?" She had to suppress a smile since she had about a dozen stuffed into her other pocket.

"Of course," she said, handing over the card. Moving quickly to her desk, she grabbed another receipt. "Would you mind signing this? Just so we have it on record you received your missing item."

She signed, and the secretary handed her a cloth bag to put the heavy tome inside. After many thanks, Celina tried her best not to run out of the office toward the elevators. She pressed the button to go down and tapped her foot, wondering when Kai would return to their hotel.

Another of the nearby offices had their door wide open with a sign promoting a free diet consultation and people walking in and out. A TV blared away, and she half-listened to the news as she waited for the elevator. Her head jerked to the side when the name of the bank she visited with Kai came up:

Police are still investigating the mass murder at the downtown bank branch. They have cordoned off the area, but they have informed us all twenty-three employees were impaled on the free-standing flagpoles recently installed inside the bank to celebrate their new international affiliation with banks around the world. Police have no suspects, but they have described the crime as one of the most brutal…

She squeezed her head, hanging on the edge of insanity. That was why Kai told her to wait at the hotel. He hadn't wanted her to see what he'd do.

Oh, God. What the fuck have I done?

The elevator doors opened with a ding, and she rushed inside, holding her chest as if someone might rip her heart out. She edged by the doors, ready to run out as soon as they'd open, but a chill ran down her spine as a shadow moved behind her in their reflection.

A hand covered her mouth, forcing her lips against her teeth, and the elevator screeched to a halt. Slammed against the wall, her eyes widened, and she stared at Shiriki. He gave her a cold smile, and she tried screaming, but it came out muffled.

Dad.

"If I take my hand away, will you scream?" he asked with a smile.

She shook her head, but as soon as he released her, she ran for the emergency button, screaming at the top of her lungs. He grabbed her from behind and pressed his hand over her mouth again.

"Oh, dear, lying to your father is not very nice. Shall I correct that for you?" His voice was like ice.

She froze. Why would he admit to paternity now? Shiriki chuckled and spun her. He took his hand away again, this time slower.

"How—?"

"Mekaisto found your mother's letter in your hotel room. He came to see me, alerting me that you know of your heritage." He studied her with fresh interest. "I have come to inform you he is looking for you, and he is quite… furious."

"Why come tell me?"

Mekaisto was searching for her in a fury. She wouldn't escape him. Her hand gripped the cloth bag handle tighter, the weight of the tome inside reassuring.

"Call it paternal instinct, pet." Shiriki's lips curled over his teeth.

"You knew who I was, but…you kept torturing me." She spoke, and his cold smile widened again.

"Of course. What difference would it have made?" His eyes pierced through her. "The next time we meet, it will be under Mekaisto's orders."

He vanished, and Celina suppressed a yelp.

The elevator resumed its descent, and when the doors opened, she dashed out, taking deep breaths and trying to compose herself.

Nothing worked.

She walked aimlessly, trying to figure out a place where she'd be able to read through the tome without being ambushed by demons. A building caught her attention, and she darted inside the public library, hoping to find a quiet corner where she could read. At least here, she wouldn't stand out reading a thick book, no matter how ancient it looked.

She collapsed into a seat in the farthest corner of a reading area. Everywhere she looked, Celina felt like she could see Mekaisto.

How long before he finds me?

Pressing both palms against her forehead, she tried to push the revelation of her biological father out of her mind. Was this why she had such a strong desire for revenge? She didn't know what it meant for her to be the daughter of a demon, or if Mekaisto knew.

Of course, he knew. I was drawing a shadow with wings from a young age. Shiriki was visiting me until I was three. I don't remember that...

Mekaisto didn't make deals with humans...but she wasn't really human, was she?

Shaking her head to clear it, she opened the cover of the old tome. The pages looked so old she was sure, if touched, they'd disintegrate. Still, she turned each one until her eyes focused on one passage:

Demons have their charms and can manipulate humans to choose the wrong side. Some discover too late their mistakes; however, it is possible to break demonic contracts. It requires the power of the descendants of angels, also known as the original Lumen.

She frowned at the last part.

If I'm half-demon, am I still a Lumen?

The only one left for sure was Wayne Pierce, and she'd given him to the Sanguis demons. She turned to the next page, holding her breath for fear the page would crumble before she learned how to free herself. The instructions continued:

The blood of a Lumen still alive, if drunk at midnight in one of our churches, can clean a claimed soul and annul a deal made with a demon. Although many of our churches have been destroyed over time, the grounds stay sacred for all of eternity. Children cannot be victims of these deals as their souls are pure and cannot be harmed by any dark or light magic. Though some demons have tried, they cannot lure children who they believe are easy prey.

To rescue Wayne Pierce from the Sanguis demons' clutches with Mekaisto hunting her down could prove impossible. She cursed, which brought shushes from people reading nearby. Why weren't there more original Lumen left?

Because Mekaisto sends his demons to kill them.

That was why he'd made a point of pretending to be imprisoned by the Lumen. Her revenge was a perfect way to exterminate them all once and for all.

I'm such a fucking idiot.

Her hand traveled over her stomach, repeating the part where deals couldn't harm children. It was the last hope she could hold onto to save her baby, and herself.

Knowing what she had to do, she got to her feet and put the tome back into the cloth bag.

30

RITUALS

Celina planned how she would get the last Lumen member away from the Sanguis demons and hoped he wasn't already dead. This time, she'd make sure she had a better plan than when she'd gone to rescue Mekaisto. No spur of the moment. She'd ask to speak to Wayne, invent something about him holding back information, and get him out of there. The place was a maze, so remembering the way in for their escape was crucial.

She walked into the mall near the library and went into the pharmacy. Her stomach grumbled with lack of food, but she had the feeling the only thing she could digest would be one of those breakfast shakes. Her pregnancy came back to mind; was this why her appetite had been strange? She concentrated on little events that had meant nothing to her but now fell into place. When she'd tried drowning her anger with alcohol, Mekaisto stopped her. He'd also made sure she ate, even when she didn't feel like it. She remembered, after the massacre at Yonah Church…the next morning, she'd been sick, but assumed it was because of the guilt she felt.

Am I really pregnant?

She trudged to the aisle with the pregnancy tests. Recently, she'd hoped to take one and see a positive. But under these circumstances, more than anything, she hoped it wouldn't be it.

With her breakfast shake and the test in hand, she left the pharmacy, wanting to know, once and for all if Mekaisto had lied. The washroom was full, people walking in and out, and while waiting for the results, she continued to glance around her stall, worried a demon would appear.

She stared down at the two pink lines, informing her Mekaisto had spoken the truth. With proof in front of her, she couldn't deny it any longer. Her hand went to her stomach, and her whole body shook.

"I'm sorry," she whispered.

I'll do everything I can to save us.

What would happen if the demon appeared? Every shadow was a threat. He could manifest at any moment.

Before getting on with her plan, though, she needed a place to hide the tome so she could come back for it later. Remembering her frequent visits to this mall as a kid, she went to the lowest floor and picked a random public locker where she placed the book inside.

"Hope I don't need this again before it's all over," she muttered as she inserted a dollar, turned the key, and pocketed it.

Leaving the mall, she hurried through the streets as the sun set. Something deep down urged her forward, warning that when night would fall, Mekaisto would come after her.

The CrowBar building looked different somehow. A constant reminder of the murder she'd committed, all for a lying kidnapper who knew children were being murdered. Celina didn't care what it meant to have demon blood running inside her; it didn't change who she was, or her choices, as her mother's letter reminded her. Yes, she chose a dark path, but she'd also turned away from it. It was time to redeem herself.

She knocked on the back door, the sign above her head still buzzing as it had the first time. Linda opened the door. "What are you doing here?"

Celina hoped the demon didn't know she'd run away from Mekaisto, but, so far, it didn't seem like it. "I need to talk to Wayne Pierce again. Kai thinks he might have known something more about the Lumen who's having children killed."

She arched an eyebrow, giving Celina her signature sneer. "Why didn't he come with you?"

"He said something about hunting down someone else that might have information on who paid David Corval."

"This way then." Linda made her way down the steps, and Celina made a point to remember how many times they turned and in which directions.

Left, left, straight, right, left, straight, right.

The demon unlocked the door and pushed it open. Wayne Pierce stood against a wall, his ankle shackled by a large chain cemented into the floor, dried blood on his neck and arms.

"Do you mind if I talk to him in private? I have things I need to ask him about my husband, and...well, they're personal."

Linda narrowed her eyes and pushed her hair from her face. "Yeah, fine. I have to go back upstairs and take care of things."

Celina smothered the pleased grin that almost flickered across her face. "I won't be too long. When I'm done, I'll just wait outside the room here."

The door closed with a bang, and Celina remained silent, waiting as Linda's footsteps echoed away. She caught sight of keys hanging by the door and hoped one would fit the lock.

Wayne's eyes bulged as he stared at her. "What more do you want from me?"

"We don't have much time." She strode over to him. "I

need something from you, and in exchange, I'll do everything I can to get you out of here. Do we have a deal?"

His face tightened. "Why would—?"

"I don't have time to explain. Are you in or out?"

Wayne nodded.

She propped the door open and searched the other rooms along the hall, trying to find a weapon. The fourth room had a body hanging upside down, blood dripping from a gash in the man's neck into a bucket. After ensuring the door wouldn't latch behind her, Celina crossed the room, avoiding the body, and stopped in front of the tray of torture instruments. She focused on a familiar-looking pistol, the one she had used to shoot Emily.

Well, this time she'd be using it for good.

A few knick-knacks that might have belonged to the dead man hanging caught her attention, and she grabbed the wristwatch. Celina ran to Wayne's prison room and grabbed the keys. After unlocking his shackle, she motioned with the pistol for him to follow her and keep quiet. She recalled her path through the maze, this time, having to mirror the directions, which took time to organize in her mind.

Right, right, straight, left? Yes. Then right, straight, left…

"Let's go," she whispered.

So far, so good. Not gonna last with my luck though.

She came face-to-face with Linda, who looked surprised at first, then her eyes squinted. "Where the hell do you think you're going with him?"

"Kai asked me to bring him along to meet with the person who was paying David Corval, so that's what—"

Her hands went to her hips. "If Mekaisto wanted to take this guy, he would have done it himself in a flash. Don't—"

"Part of my deal with him is that I have to taint my soul, and to do that, I have to be the one to do the unpleasant things. Mekaisto's still in the room. Said something about a rift or something—go ask him yourself."

Linda arched one eyebrow and a smile curled one side of her mouth, but she nodded, and walked around them, heading to the room in question. Celina yanked the pistol from her sweater pocket and shot Linda point blank in the head. The sound echoed across the basement. Celina knew she wasn't dead, but it would give her time to get away with Wayne.

"Hurry!"

They ran as fast as they could up the stairs. The outside air hit her like a breath of freedom, but she kept running. They got on the first bus heading for Yonah Church and finally took the time to catch their breaths.

"Where...are we going? What is it...you want from me?" Wayne asked with ragged gasps.

"I'll tell you...when we get there." She glanced up at the front of the bus, staring at the time: eleven forty-nine. Ten minutes remained to free her soul.

The church looked eerie with only the outer walls remaining, the fire having burned all the wood and even cracked stone. They crunched over debris, and she stopped in what used to be the sanctuary. She could still picture Mekaisto pretending to be held there, her aunt trying to claw her way out of the burning room. Celina shook her head, trying to shake the memory out.

Her gaze landed back on Wayne, and she figured he didn't know she murdered his wife. He was too willing to trust her. She wanted to redeem herself, but she needed his help.

"Well?" His fingers tapped against his leg.

"I need some of your blood to break the deal I made with the demon."

"Where's my wife?"

Celina stared at him, debating what to tell him. "Here's the deal. I can take your blood by force," she took the pistol out and pointed it at him, "and bring you back to the demons afterward. Or you can give it willingly, and I give you your freedom." She slipped the pistol in her pants' waistband. "I hope you pick the second option."

He glared at her but nodded after a few seconds. He stuck out his arm and waited. "Do you have something sharp?"

She took the wristwatch out of her pocket and handed it to him as she glanced around. Kicking the debris aside, she searched for something to cut him with and something to hold the blood.

She picked up a jagged piece of metal with a sharp end. "What time is it?"

He glanced at the wristwatch. "It's eleven fifty-seven. Why did you give me a watch?"

"I need to drink it at midnight, and I can't keep track of the time while I'm searching."

I can't miss my chance!

"Here." Wayne handed her a varnished wooden piece with a curved bottom to use as a cup. He requested she cut his wrist, saying he could take the pain, but not inflict it himself. Celina didn't know how much blood the ritual required to work, but she figured any amount would suffice as long as she drank it at midnight on sacred grounds. She cut a small gash, collected a few precious drops, and waited.

Midnight.

Its coppery taste and thick texture affected her gag reflexes, but she put her hands over her mouth to stop herself from throwing up. A minute or two passed, and she put down her hands. "I never want to drink blood again."

Staring down at her hands, her eyes widened as a red glow sparked between her fingers and climbed her arms. Warmth tingled her nerves, and her skin crawled with goose bumps. The light dissipated, and nothing but the lampposts lit their surroundings.

"Did it work?"

"I don't know, but I'll assume so." She'd followed all the

steps to the letter. Glowing red sparks had gone through her. The deal was off.

She was free.

"I can go then?" He took a few steps forward as though testing her sincerity.

"Yes, and I suggest you run far from here. Don't come back, or they will find you."

His face tensed. "What about Henri? My son, you had him—"

"I sent him to a police station, but…" Her chest tightened. "I don't know if he ever got there." She didn't even bother telling him about Simon. With all her heart, she didn't want to believe Mekaisto would murder him or Henri.

He nodded with a frown creasing his forehead. "Well, I won't leave until I've found out."

"Do what you want but be quick about it or they'll find you." It was strange talking to the man who'd murdered Thomas in front of her. On the other hand, Celina murdered Wayne's wife, so they were even. "Thank you for—"

A hand ripped through Wayne's stomach, sending blood gushing to the ground as she screamed and backed away. His eyes widened with shock, and more red liquid dripped out of his mouth when he opened it as though wanting to scream.

The hand retracted, and Wayne's body fell to the ground. Celina's mind numbed as she stared at what was left of him, his death so familiar. The last movie she'd seen with Thomas almost identical to what Wayne had just suffered.

"I warned you." Shiriki sneered, and a shiver went down Celina's spine. "The next time we met, it would be under Mekaisto's orders."

She backed away, and before she could think things through, ran deeper into the ruins of the church. Diving behind one of the upturned pews, she clamped her hand over her mouth to stop from screaming.

Without her deal with Mekaisto, she was fair game to any demon.

"Are you playing hide and seek with me, pet? I like a game."

She crawled, desperate to get away from where his voice was coming from and stood behind pieces of wooden beams.

Through one of the small gaps, a pale silver eye stared back at her. No more showed, but she knew he wore a smile. She stayed still, her gaze not leaving the demon's line of sight. If she tried to run for it, he'd catch her...or she could stand still until he moved.

"You're here on Mekaisto's orders then? Why didn't he come to fetch me himself?" She stalled for time, trying to figure out a plan.

"I begged him to let me help. I thought you would prefer if I were to catch you and not Mekaisto, seeing as he is so furious at the moment."

She had to think of something, but every time the idea of running flashed through her mind, Shiriki raised his eyebrow as if expecting such a move.

"My mother's letter said you asked her to hand me over when I was a baby. And that you continued to visit me until I turned three." Shivers ran through her at the thought. "You could've taken me by force. Why didn't you?"

"Mekaisto had not given me the order to." The demon took a few steps closer so she could see his face. Her eyes stared back at her, the same gray irises she'd always found so bland were now filled with white fire in her father's eyes. "I came to fetch you by my own choice, but your mother refused. After that, I visited you from time to time. I thought it would be amusing to raise a child that was part human and demon."

"Raise?" Celina spat in disgust. "You mean torture and experiment on."

Shiriki's smile widened, but she didn't wait for his

response. She pushed her body against the beam with all her strength, and it toppled over him.

Dust rose all around as she ran toward the exit, but Shiriki blocked her path, and she froze. "You changed the game to tag without telling me." He was even more menacing when he'd been attacked and being cornered didn't help her keep calm.

She shuddered to think he was her father. He'd tortured her knowing she was his daughter, and it augmented her fear of him. "I really hate you."

"I am pleased to hear it. Hate is simple, while love only brings complication." He moved toward the exit and bent over Wayne's body, his white hair falling over his shoulders. "It is a shame I killed him. He would have made a nice souvenir."

"You're too late. I've already broken the deal with the Lumen ritual." To say it aloud was liberating.

He straightened with a smile. "Is that right? In any case, you will still face Mekaisto as my orders are absolute."

Her heart rate accelerated. "I'm not going—"

"Did I say you would go to him?" He took a step closer, and she inched away. "Mekaisto has given me permission to use force if you do not cooperate. While I believe he means something along the lines of holding you down to make sure you do not escape, in my mind, it means something a little more…physical."

His smile widened as she took another step back. "Don't touch me."

"Then are you staying put willingly, pet?"

"Don't call me that. It's disturbing enough to find out you're…who you are. Calling me pet isn't helping."

Shiriki crossed his arms, a teasing smile curling his lips. "Your mother enjoyed the nickname."

"You shut your mouth, you fucking—"

"Hearing you call me Daddy would make me much happier."

She opened her mouth to speak again but was afraid of what else he might say.

Celina was born for one purpose: to become Mekaisto's companion in the dark realm. She cursed her entire existence and hatred coursed inside her when she thought of Mekaisto, but even more for Shiriki.

Her mind went back to the demon she'd fallen in love with. Would he leave her alone once he discovered she broke the deal?

31

WHAT HE TRULY IS

The lampposts could no longer penetrate the dense darkness, and it surrounded Celina as though ready to consume her.

Something was wrong.

Someone stood in the road in front of the church, and her breath caught in her throat. Mekaisto raised his hand in front of him, and the building next to the ruins exploded. Celina staggered from the blast and squinted as the whole structure collapsed onto the building next to it. The fire caught from the debris, and her heart hammered as she stared at the rising smoke against the night sky.

That entire disaster was caused by a casual wave of Mekaisto's hand.

Shiriki's smile widened as he stared at the buildings. "I told you he was furious, pet."

But not enough to hurt me…

Her head jerked toward the road where he stood. She flexed her hands, trying to control their shaking as she backed away. She scanned the interior of the church for anything that could be used as a weapon and cursed herself for having lost the Aka stone.

The shriek of rending metal ripped from inside the ruins, spraying sparks as part of its structure tore away. Not waiting to find out what he planned, she ran to the other side of the church but froze when the bending metal warped in front of her.

She spun and watched as Mekaisto prowled toward her in the demon form she'd gotten used to. But for the first time, she could see him for what he was. Not her demon...not Kai.

The king of demons, enraged.

Power radiated from him, and that tiny part of her she'd pushed down all her life rose as though craving that darkness he emanated. His gaze landed on her, and a cruel smile appeared on his lips.

His visceral darkness poured into the church, pooling and writhing, twisting into every space. Screams and whispers accompanied black, slimy hands extending from the ripples of evil. Behind the hands, figures took shape, bodies with extra limbs and humanoid skulls. The lidless eye sockets wept blood around white orbs in constant, sightless motion.

One stepped in front of Celina and opened its mouth wide, dislocating its jaw until it could swallow her whole. She clambered through a small gap through the twisted metal, cutting herself on its sharp edges but determined to make a last-ditch run for it.

She stood inside the dim lighting of the church, trying to get a bearing, her gaze darting from side to side. Mekaisto towered in front of her, and she stiffened, her mind urging her to flee or fight.

Stall him, make him believe you didn't run away.

"I still need...to find out who...paid David Corval."

His head cocked to the side. "You found him."

"What?" She wrapped her arms around her waist.

"He *just needed a little push.*"

Mekaisto's words sent an icy shiver down her spine and

her throat constricted. "You're the one who paid him?" she whispered.

"He always had it in him, but humans rely on money for so many things." He took a step closer, his vertical pupils searching straight through her.

Her mind snapped, and she backed away until her back hit the metal. "I broke the deal! I performed the Lumen ritual—you can't take my life or my soul anymore!"

Mekaisto shook his head, but the glowing of his eyes surged in anger. "Yes, I heard from Linda what you did." His jaw clenched. "So willing to sacrifice the life growing inside of you to get away from me?"

"I did it to break the deal. The Lumen tome I read said it wouldn't harm my baby." Celina shook. "Besides, I'd have done it even without the guarantee if it meant making sure you never lay a hand on my son."

"It is too late to annul our contract; I will not let either of you go." His eyes held something more to the fury in his gaze—betrayal?

He grabbed her wrist, and once again, their surroundings changed. This time, she wrenched away and ran, her mind trying to make sense of her location. Her feet slipped in the soft mud, and skeletal branches caught in her hair.

I'm inside the woods near my house.

The wind grew stronger, following her into the woods, driving her forward. Every time she gained distance and hope flickered, she tripped and fell in the darkness, slowing her progress. Staggering against a tree trunk, she slid to the ground, unable to run anymore.

She glanced up into the glowing red eyes of Mekaisto, following his movements as he came close and crouched in front of her. He waved his hand, and a bright light appeared, shadowing everything around them in red.

"I am impressed you made it this far." A cruel smile showed his pointed teeth.

"Get the hell away from me." She gripped the tree and stood, her back pressed hard against the rough bark. Following her movements, a continued gleam of anger glowed in his red eyes. He stood as well and took a few steps forward, finishing inches away from her.

"You cannot escape your fate. You belong to me." His hand rested on her cheek, increasing the panic spiraling inside her. To think they shared a passionate night recently felt impossible. "I will not harm the child."

"I said get away from me, you—"

"You have always known there was a much deeper reason for me to make a deal with you, after millennia of never dealing with humans. I promised I would tell you in the end."

"You made the deal with me because you knew I was pregnant?" The world tilted as her breathing grew more rapid. "Stop! Just stop talking!"

His smile became dangerous. "Shall we talk about you being half-demon then?"

Memories of Shiriki's torture flooded her. "I don't want to talk about that."

"What is so terrible about having Shiriki as your father?" His hand slid from her face to her neck. "A regular human could not have endured everything you have. You should be proud of the demon blood that runs in your veins."

"*Shut up!*" She tried to pull his hand away from her neck, but he gripped tighter and cut the distance between them.

"You are upset?" He tilted his head to the side and drew his eyebrows together.

Tears welled in her eyes before rolling in big drops down her cheeks.

His eyes searched her, and for a second, it seemed like he was in as much pain as she was. A flutter of guilt filled her, but she pushed down against the emotion, unwilling to help him. He closed his eyes and pressed his forehead against hers. "Do you think the darkness inside you was a human trait?

That being defective drove you to revenge, made you shoot that Lumen member, murder Emily Pierce? Everything you did was the demon side of you."

"Stop talking! Just stop!" she begged. She couldn't hear any more of it, couldn't listen to him excuse her actions, dismissing her humanity.

He opened his eyes and gazed at her for a few seconds before leaning in closer, his lips brushing against hers until she turned her head away. He let out a sigh, and she glanced at him. "I assure you, I did not want to hurt you—not in any way."

Celina attempted to relax the knots in her stomach. "You knew Shiriki was my father?"

"Of course, I knew." His gentle smile brought a fresh urge to murder him. "I had been waiting for you for quite some time. But your mother protected you with a pendant that made it impossible for me to take you away."

"The day my parents died in that car accident. They were going to see Shiriki. Did he kill them, or was it you?"

"I did not kill Elizabeth Tayen or Dean Perry." He changed the subject, and she balled her hands into fists, knowing the answer to her question in his lack of explanation. "I ordered Shiriki to create a half-demon, half-human. There were many failed attempts before he had the idea to mate a demon and a human using a special…formula of sorts." The smile turned monstrous, and her chest tightened at the idea of her mother having ever been near Shiriki. "I needed company in my realm, but humans cannot live there unless they are dead and that rarely brings much entertainment. Shiriki was more than willing to obey my command. He has always wanted to be in my good graces…though I have no grace to speak of."

She turned away. "I don't want to hear this."

"I watched you grow up. You were kind and sweet, but I knew you held a demon's darkness somewhere inside you." His hand moved to her chest, and she shuddered. "However, instead of the demon blood tainting you as planned, it eradicated the Lumen part and left your human soul intact. Shiriki's bloodline was inside you, though. All I needed to do was let it out."

He let her go, and she ran off, only to fall on the ground after a few steps, her body collapsing in shock.

She felt him behind her, so she rolled to face him. "Stay away from me."

"In the end, I tainted the pure soul of my dove."

Tears sprang to her eyes, but she blinked fast, refusing to let them roll down. "You had a lot more to do with my husband's death than just paying David Corval, didn't you?"

"In a way, I am the one who started it, but I also went along."

She had no time to process that cryptic remark. He grabbed her wrists and pulled her up, holding them tightly to prevent her from running.

"You tricked—"

"I am a demon, Celina, and I reminded you often. But you never seemed to understand what it meant."

"You lied about everything."

"No." Fury flashed inside his red eyes, and the continued red light illuminated him in a horrifying way. "I just never revealed all the truth all at once. There were steps to follow."

"What are you waiting for then? My revenge is done, my soul is tainted. Kill me and my unborn baby, you sick son of a bitch!" Celina tried to pull her wrist away from him.

He drew her in and held her tight, but she didn't stop digging her fingers into his chest, desperate to claw away from him. "There is one last truth I want you—"

"I don't want any more of your fucking truth!"

"Then, your revenge will not be complete. Do you not want to know why your husband did what he did?" His voice was quiet, and she stopped fighting, exhausted from her futile attempts.

"He did it because David Corval blackmailed—"

He withdrew a little and stared at her. "Come now. You knew your husband better than that."

She gritted her teeth. "No, I didn't. Remember?"

"If you believe he would have done all those terrible acts because someone found out about his fake business, then I will not push further, and I will enact my end of the deal." He pulled her close again. "But deep down inside, you know your husband would not have done what he did because of simple blackmail."

Her shoulders slumped. "Why did he do it then?"

The question was more for herself than for Mekaisto. Celina had loved Thomas, and even after she saw the tape, heard what he'd done, she never believed David Corval's explanation of blackmail. It was too easy.

"Your house is close to here. Go sleep for the night. Tomorrow, meet me at our tree, and I will show you." Mekaisto let her go.

She took a few steps back. "Aren't you taking a chance I'll run away again?"

He chuckled, the sound dark, yet indulgent. "You will have until noon to come." He waved his hand, and the red light vanished, plunging them both into darkness and leaving his glowing eyes as the only source of light. "If you do not show, I will hunt you and enjoy what will happen when I catch you."

32

MY SOUL TO GIVE

Celina stood on the side of the road in front of her house. It looked the same except...in a way she couldn't explain, it didn't.

She watched a while longer before she headed toward it, broken inside, her identity shattered. Mekaisto said once he wanted to break her so he could fix her over and over; he hadn't lied about that.

She tried to guess what he wanted to show her before he'd make good on his end of their deal, but her mind drifted. Why hadn't the ritual worked?

One way or another, she wouldn't let Mekaisto take her son, despite a strange feeling that he told the truth about not wanting to hurt him.

Why do I still trust him? How is that even possible?

The sun filtered through her eyelids and Celina squinted as she sat up from the sofa where she'd slept. She hadn't thought she would have been able to fall asleep, but apparently, her body had desperately needed it. Still, she refused to sleep in her old bed, memories of Thomas' cruelty fresh in her mind.

She stood in the house she'd shared with her husband, but her dream home felt so far away. Her gaze landed on a photo of their wedding day. What would Mekaisto show her at that black tree? What *could* he show her to make what Thomas did acceptable?

There could be nothing. Whatever the reason, the memory of how indifferent he'd been while kidnapping those two boys, knowing what would happen to them, would stay with her no matter how long she lived or how long she took to die.

A sigh escaped her as she trudged onto her back porch. She jumped as her eyes met with Shiriki's, a grin on his lips.

She narrowed her eyes at him. "What?"

"I wanted to inform you the woman Mekaisto brought me, the one named Alisson, is dead. She is in the dark realm and will remain there as my toy for all of eternity."

"I didn't need to know that." Celina descended the steps.

"I am the sharing kind."

She didn't turn around. "Stop talking."

"If you ever want quality time with your father, feel free to visit." She glanced back, and he gave her a cold smile before he vanished.

Staring across her backyard, she focused on the forest she'd played in as a child, the place where she'd found the black tree. The sun rose higher, and she took a breath before walking amongst the trees. The birds sang, and the wind played through the leaves and grass. A beautiful morning announced the start of her new life. The atmosphere was so different from the night she should have died.

Her heartbeat pulsed in her ears as she approached the black tree. Celina froze, watching it with some amount of dread. The place she'd poured herself out and revealed so much of her feelings—all to Mekaisto in his animal form.

Leaves and sticks cracked behind her, and she spun, terrified. Thomas stood not too far from her, a gentle smile on his lips.

"Thomas?" The breath in her lungs disappeared.

He came a little closer. "I'm sorry about everything, Celina."

Was this what Mekaisto wanted her to see? Thomas' ghost, so she could ask him her questions? All his lies and deceits bombarded her, and Celina's heart squeezed as it did whenever she thought of his betrayals.

She took a few steps forward and grabbed his shirt. "Tell me why you did all those terrible things. Why you lied?"

He can't be a ghost…I can touch him.

Thomas rubbed the back of his light-brown hair as he always did when he was guilty of doing something wrong. She wanted to wrap her arms around him and never let him go…yet, she wanted to beat him to death.

He can't be alive. I saw him die. He's dead. I did all of this because he was murdered…

"David Corval found out my company was a sham and blackmailed me. I figured I'd play along, figured it could be my one chance to accomplish what I always strived for."

She narrowed her eyes as she backed away. "Play along? Strived for?"

"I felt bad this was the only way we could be together forever, but after we'd already been together for nine years, I realized it couldn't last that way."

"You're not making any sense, Thomas!" She didn't know whether to take steps forward or back away anymore.

"You'd eventually die, meaning I'd stop being with you. I always knew something had to be done, but when I realized you were pregnant, everything changed." He smiled. "And now, with our child growing inside you, he'll be able to join us."

Her heart hammered faster as her hand pressed on her stomach. Panic overwhelmed her, causing her to tremble.

"Join us? What are you talking about, Thomas? I don't understand!"

His smile chilled her. "I think you do, dove."

Thomas' features disappeared to be replaced by Mekaisto's true demonic form. She stood still, unable to utter a single word.

He took a step toward her. "Your kindness always intrigued me after you fixed my tree. It did not make sense you could be so kind with demon blood running through you. You came to talk to me every day for a long time, and the more you did, the more attached I grew." His eyes betrayed desperation for her understanding.

"No..."

All the memories of her life with Thomas flooded her mind, Mekaisto's face replacing his. Her entire life felt like a lie, something she'd fabricated inside her own head. As if everything surrounding her had always been pure and now, her protective shield burst when Thomas—Mekaisto—told the truth.

Heat filled her body from the inside out as the truth of her whole life lit a fire under her skin. Her heart would never heal, would never beat without hurting.

"I decided to be with you in one of my human forms. I told you I have two." He flashed his pointed teeth. "We met when you were sixteen, and we stayed together. You were happy, remember? But you had too much humanity, and I needed to bring out your demonic bloodline so that when you died, I could bring you to my realm. I wanted company, and I needed an heir." His gaze pierced her. "Most of all...I fell in love with you and could not let you go."

He materialized in front of her, and this time, she couldn't react at all. Celina's mind raced, trying to make sense of what she was feeling. A mixture of love for Thomas and for Mekaisto took root inside her heart, but hatred rallied and buried all other emotion. Then again, she'd been shattered so many times, it was impossible for her to feel any emotion for long.

She forced her mind blank as she concentrated on the material of his long black coat. Emotions would hurt too much if she started thinking.

"I needed to taint your soul so I could bring you with me into the dark realm, so we could be together forever. We will raise our son in my realm."

"But... I performed the ritual," she mumbled, random thoughts flashing into her numbed mind.

His features softened. "I infiltrated the Lumen a long time ago." His smile turned almost understanding. "Some of those rituals work...but most do not. Our contract is not annulled because I wrote that ritual. The spell was never real."

She couldn't breathe. "Did they know, when I was asking about...about Thomas? That it was...you?"

"You mean Adam and his children? No, I went to them in that human form, and they had no idea. I can mask my energy effectively. Which is also the reason the Lumen did not know I was in the human realm for so long."

Her head spun. "I saw him...*you* die. The body they cremated..."

"I put my...Thomas' features onto Alisson Kent's husband after he killed himself."

She scrambled for any loophole, trying to find a way for it to be untrue. "I saw a dark silhouette, on the night Thomas... you died—"

"As you may have realized by now, I can move rather quickly."

She stared back into his glowing eyes, tears blurring her vision before they rolled down her cheeks. "I got shot! Would you have let me die if I'd refused your deal that night?" She pounded her fists against his chest. "You let me believe the man I loved was dead, that he was a liar, a murderer. You let me love you and feel like I'd betrayed Thomas, but it was you…the whole time." She sobbed, her chest hurting so much she could barely breathe. "How could you do this, you fucking monster?"

His gaze lowered for a few seconds, but when he locked eyes with her again, his pupils thinned to tiny slits. "A demon's love is a dangerous thing, Celina."

She backed away, trembling. "I sold my soul to the devil the moment I was conceived. How is that fair?" She hugged herself as she collapsed on the ground, trying to control the shaking of her body, but nothing helped, and nothing ever would.

He crouched in front of her, his voice quiet. "I never wanted—"

She stared back at him. "You kidnapped those boys, knowing what would happen to them…you killed them, didn't you?"

He shook his head, his eyes filling with sadness. "I used to separate myself from the false ritual I created over five hundred years ago by telling myself I did not do the act of killing. But I regret having done it." He waved his hand and images hovered before her in mid-air, showing two separate locations. "I did not kill Henri and Simon Pierce. As you can see, the middle child is at the police station, and Simon is in the hospital recovering. They both had their memories erased, but they live."

A small smile appeared on her lips—it was bitter, but it was the only kind she could muster. "You can lie, though, can't you?"

"I said I did not lie, not that I could not. A lie within a lie."

She looked away. "Are you going to kill me now? Rip our son from me, and—"

He pushed a strand of her hair behind her ear. "You always assumed that giving me your life and your soul meant I would kill you. That was never my plan."

Her mind processed what he meant. "You always

intended to drag me there alive? None of this makes any sense! Why go through all this trouble? Why didn't you just take a demon bride or something?" The questions poured out of her. She wanted to scream, wanted to run.

"We are greedy beings, as you once pointed out." He grinned. "I needed to find an alternative."

Her hands curled into fists. She wanted to punch him so badly it almost hurt her muscles to stop herself. Instead, she stood. "When you realized I had too much humanity, why didn't you make a new half-breed? Why bother with me to this point?"

His eyes turned gentle, and his gaze shone with fondness as he stood. "Living with you for nine years created emotions —love, care, affection—things we are never supposed to feel. It turns into possession and violence instead." His hands went to her hips, his thumbs tracing along her clothes. "At first, all I wanted was a queen and an heir, but I also wanted to find out if a soul could survive in a half-demon, half-human. I have always been interested in Shiriki's experiments."

His eyes turned into tiny slits again, and her muscles stiffened.

"But as time went by, I struggled with myself, and not because I was fighting my true nature, but because more than anything, I wanted to be someone you could love, someone you deserved." He stared at her, his glowing red eyes becoming brighter with every emotion pouring out of him. "When I realized you were pregnant, about four months ago, I panicked." He placed his hand on her abdomen and stared as though able to see their son. "Having lost your Lumen blood, carrying a child that was three-quarters a demon is dangerous…giving birth could kill you, rip apart your soul."

He stared back at her, the pained look in his eyes hitting her with a realization. *He can love…*

"So, you did all this to make sure you didn't waste your

time for nine years." She was still angry. And she wanted to test his sincerity.

Her breath caught in her throat when he let himself fall on his knees in front of her, his eyes locking onto hers. "I did not want to lose you…" His wings drooped to the ground, and he glanced around, as though desperate for the right words to explain himself. "You and our son are poisoning each other. I had a time limit to taint your soul, to save you both."

"I—"

His voice was thick. "Do not ask me to watch you both die." He leaned his head against her abdomen. "Please."

She let herself drop to the ground in front of him. "Say it. I want to hear it."

His hand cupped her face, and the smile on his lips sent a shiver down her spine. "I have existed for millennia, never caring for anything but my own desires…until I met you. Because of you, I had a reason to exist, a chance to truly *live*. I love you, Celina."

She placed her hand over his and held it tight over her cheek as tears rolled down. "I love you, too, Mekaisto."

He pulled her into his arms and held her tight, his heart pulsing against her head. She cried against his chest, still sorting her emotions, but sure of one thing: what she last said to him was the truth.

Like me, he desperately fought for the ones he loves.

"You murdered everyone in that bank. All those innocent people," she muttered, gasping for air.

"Kill everyone that had anything to do with your husband's murder is what you asked for. The bank signed and approved the money David Corval received, making them part of everything." He rubbed her back as she shuddered. "You know what I am, Celina. And while I cannot promise never to kill again, I will try to fight my instincts if it means your happiness."

"But—"

His chest vibrated in silent laughter. "Although some deserved it, and I look forward to seeing their souls in my realm."

After a few minutes, she pushed him away and narrowed her eyes. "If you ever threaten me again like you did, we'll have a problem." She couldn't help smirk as his eyes widened for a second.

He chuckled. "Same goes for you, dove." He stood and held out his hand. "If you promise to help me work on it, then you have my word." She took his help this time, and with a smile.

He walked over to their tree and put his hand on the ground. A large black hole appeared, and the tree liquefied and poured in. Her gaze locked onto the swirling darkness, and she wrapped her arms around her abdomen. She walked forward and stopped in front of him.

A smile appeared on Kai's lips as he waved his hand and a folded piece of paper materialized in his palm. She arched an eyebrow as she took it, unfolding what looked like something that had been glued back together. Her hands shook as she stared at the playground sketch she'd ripped to pieces.

"It will be different from what you imagined, but we can still build it," he whispered.

Her vision blurred as she smiled at him. "Together."

He pulled her closer and kissed her as she wrapped her arms around his torso. The ground disappeared beneath her feet, and their lips parted as she gasped. Clutching him close, she stared into his glowing red eyes as they descended into the dark realm.

AUTHOR NOTES

If you liked the story, please leave a review!

There's around a month left before the preorder is available as I write this. While it may not be the first time this story is published, it feels like it is. This time, I can set up a preorder, promote ahead of time, set up ARC reviews; I have some control now and that is liberating. The manuscript has also gone through professional editing with Charlie Knight—an editor who knows their stuff and truly brings out the best in a story.

I also want to give a shout out to Wendy Vogel and Nikolas Everhart. They both started out as beta readers for me, but throughout years and years of knowing them online, they've become important friends to me. They've both read through many of my manuscripts, and not only have they helped me along my writing journey, they've also gotten to know me on a personal level as well. Thank you for everything.

To the people who've read my book: thank you. The idea that anyone read the words I put on paper is still amazing to me.

The dream of becoming an author began so long ago, and the publishing journey has been so long—it's surreal. But without readers, our stories vanish and end, so again, thank you so much for reading.

This book was written back in 2012 while I was in university. So much has changed since then, and yet, many have remained the same. One thing is for sure: the world of A Demon's Love series has grown bigger than I thought possible. Five series are planned with over twenty books, and I hope you stick around for each one! You can find out more about Monsters' Love universe by visiting my website authormaf.com

ABOUT THE AUTHOR

M. A. Fréchette writes the darker side of romance.

Being an extremist, she loves both the dark aspects of life and everything sweet. All her stories are either set in Canada where she lives or in alternate worlds she made up while living within her imagination. When not writing, she thinks of the next scene or plot while enjoying her work as a cover designer. Although she has a fascination for monsters, with a bachelor degree in criminology, she understands there's no need to create the paranormal; humans are capable of inflicting nightmares of their own.

Please feel free to reach out through any social media. I read everything I receive since I love hearing from readers!

ALSO BY M. A. FRÉCHETTE

A Demon's Love series

MY LIFE TO TAKE (book #2)

Unbroken series

A THOUSAND WORDS (book #1)